I0586799

MEMORIES OF MAGIC

THE FAY OF SKYE BOOK III

CARA MCKINNON

Stars and Stone Books

Memories of Magic

Editing by Literally Yours Editing
Cover Design by Stars and Stone Books
Images © Can Stock Photo Inc. / konradbak

Stars and Stone Books

starsandstonebooks.com

Printed in the United States of America

First Printing: May 2017
Second Printing: May 2018

DIGITAL 1.2

ISBN10: 0-9977081-6-6
ISBN13: 978-0-9977081-6-5

PRINT 0 1 2

ISBN10: 0-9977081-7-4
ISBN13: 978-0-9977081-7-2

❀ Created with Vellum

For Jamie.

I n the dream, the woman's intense, dark gaze met Olivia's. But no ephemeral figment created by Olivia's sleeping mind could hold such intelligence—such anger—in her eyes.

Whatever this was, it wasn't a dream.

Olivia's ghostlike perspective, floating around and through the people around her, changed abruptly. The woman pinned her into position, gave her substance in this not-quite-real place. When Olivia wrenched her gaze away from those piercing eyes, she observed the collar gripping the woman's neck, its copper surface worked with Greek letters and Devanāgarī script. Matching cuffs surrounded her wrists, and her hands curled into tight fists.

This was a sorceress, bound for trial. From her dress and that of the two mages beside her, Liv judged the period as late sixteenth or early seventeenth century, the same period as the remains she'd been cataloguing earlier in the day. Olivia had recently taken over supervision of a dig at the site of a mass witch burial in southwestern France, near the Atlantic coast. Most of the actual digging had stopped for the season, but she was attempting to organize the mess the previous foreman had left behind.

She recognized the pattern on the collar and cuffs. When she'd seen them this afternoon, fire had tarnished and warped the magical suppressants, fusing them to the woman's skeleton.

Olivia had noted the presence of the metal in a detached way before, wondering why they'd felt it necessary to restrain the woman until the moment of death. The magic in the pieces was still strong enough to buzz against even her weak talent. None of the other bodies had any evidence of wariness on the part of the magistrates.

But now she had no doubt why they'd feared to remove her bindings. Liv looked again into the woman's eyes, and three hundred years disappeared. The woman could see her, as though Olivia stood in the courtroom and was on the side of the accusers. The sorceress's dark eyes smoldered with hatred, but there was confusion, too. She couldn't speak—the collar would prevent that—but Liv understood.

I will tell your story, Olivia promised. The woman blinked, and Liv added, *You will not be forgotten.*

Some sort of link must have been forged between them, because a surge of magic came up from the woman. *My name is Izarra Balere.* The words weren't in English, but the meaning was clear anyway.

I see you Izarra Balere. I will remember you.

Memories poured into Olivia then: of the woman's life, her husband and children who had already been taken and put to death, her sister who had fled to the West Indies. The many people Izarra had put on boats, never joining them, always coming back for more, until she was captured and brought before the court.

And then there was pain. So much torture and suffering

that Liv started screaming, and though she tried, she could not wake.

Agony lasted an eternity, the way time in a dream can seem like a lifetime and yet be only a moment.

Then another presence entered the not-dream. He was warm, and solid, and somehow both calming and energizing, like a cup of milk mixed with spices.

He drew her out of the morass of misery and deposited her back into her unconscious body. As her other senses returned, she saw a luscious male form, strong and lean. She had no firsthand experience with spirit bodies, only a vague knowledge from magical studies courses, but if his was any reflection of his actual flesh, she would very much like to see him again when she was awake and aware.

Then he was gone, and she opened her eyes.

Her grandmother, the Dowager Marchioness of Hazelby, dropped her knitting needles and rushed to Olivia's side.

"Oh, love, you're awake!"

Liv tried to sit up, confused and disoriented. But her body wouldn't listen to her. Not because she'd lost feeling, but because her muscles were too weak. She finally forced her hand up to rest over Nan's. "What happened?" The words were half-whisper, half-croak.

"You went to bed and didn't appear at the dig the next morning. None of us could wake you."

The flesh around Nan's eyes crinkled with worry, and fear. She stroked an age-spotted hand over Liv's hair, and a strand fell forward, near her eyes.

The tress was silver-white.

When Olivia had gone to bed, her hair had been styled in an unusually short cut for a woman, but it had been reddish-brown, like everyone else in her family, including Nan before she went grey. But even Nan's grey didn't look like this. This looked like...

She gasped. From some hidden reserve of strength, she made herself sit up, lift her hands to her head, and pull what hair she could forward, into her face where she could see it.

Every lock gleamed in the gaslight, nearly sparkling with opalescence.

Olivia swayed back against the pillows, and her vision blurred. She had seen hair this color once a day during her early childhood, when her nanny and then her governess brought her to Mother's sitting room to be examined and recite her lessons. But Mother only had a streak of it, at her left temple.

Later, Malcolm and Viola got the streaks, too. And on the rare occasions when Olivia went with them to Scotland, her Fay cousins, aunts, and uncles had them, as well. But only ever in a streak.

Not even great-great-grandma Lilias—the powerful first Duchess of Fay—her hair gone naturally white after a century of life, had more than two thick patches at the time of her death, one on either temple. And that was from an equally long time working with magic. Olivia had never cultivated her extremely minor gift. And yet—she now had the Fay streak. On her whole head.

Nan frowned at her through the curtain of shimmering white. "It was like that the first day."

"The...*first* day?" Her voice still held a rasp, and Nan held out a glass of water. Liv managed to sip it without spilling—well, not more than a few drops, hardly more than a thimbleful—and handed it back. Her fingers shook as she wiped her chin.

"You've been unconscious for five days. I hired two girls to help me care for you, and we were able to get you to take a little broth and water, but it has been a trying time. There's been a mage-doctor in to see you, but he said he couldn't find anything wrong. We're in a hotel in Calais now, awaiting a boat back to England later today."

Liv shoved the hair away from her face, and then had to let her hands drop into her lap, limp. Great goddess she was weak. "We're what?"

"I didn't know what to do. When the doctor said he couldn't figure out what was wrong, I took some people off the dig and had them help me bring you here." Nan pulled her hands back into her lap and twisted the lace edging of her skirt. Liv tried not to think about the damage that being carted around like a blissed-out opium-eater would have done to her reputation on the dig. "With your hair like that, I knew I had to get you back to your mother."

Goddess preserve her. Not her mother. "Did you telegram her?" Nan must have been very, very worried to reach out to anyone from the Fay side of the family. When Olivia was a little girl, Nan and the first duchess had fought—over what, neither woman would ever say—and as a consequence Nan avoided the entire Fay clan, even her daughter-in-law.

Nan nodded. "She's to come down to London in two days. I wasn't sure how long it would take us to come up from Labourd and book passage, so I told her a week. But the boat leaves this afternoon. I'm glad you're awake and I don't have to hire porters to carry you on a pallet. We'll use a wheeled chair."

Damn, damn, damn! She didn't want to deal with Mother when she felt like a newborn kitten, blind and frail. And she was *not* going to be forced into an invalid chair. Not onto any damned boat, either. "Well, I'm not going, so you can just cancel our tickets and get us back to the dig."

"If you don't go, she may very well come here instead."

Liv tried to make her legs move to swing off the bed, but they just trembled when she clenched the muscles. "Telegram her again and tell her it wasn't serious."

"I don't think that will work." Nan went over to a satchel and pulled out two letters. She'd opened both.

"Nan, what are you doing reading my correspondence?"

"You were unconscious! They're from Cecily and Malcolm, and I thought they might say something that would help." She handed them over.

Olivia was furious. Nan always respected her privacy. If she didn't, they wouldn't have lasted so long as companions. But it did mean Nan had been very worried. And, from how weak Liv felt, perhaps Nan had cause.

She read the letter from Mal first. He shared the usual family news, most of which she'd had already from Perceval, their brother. Percy was the youngest boy, and off in Brandenburg on special assignment with the army. But Mal's letters were always welcome. Then she got to the part that must have twigged Nan's curiosity. Mal warned that their mother was going to ask Olivia to come home.

Apparently he and Etta were working on a big, secret clan problem and they needed a researcher to look into magical history—her specialty. But he also knew that her current work was important, and said that they would find someone else.

Mother, he cautioned, would not be so easily convinced.

For the first time in years, Olivia opened one of her mother's letters.

When she'd first come to the Continent, Mother had written once a month, and Olivia had written back, dutifully. But after the debacle of her return from boarding school and the scandals that followed, she'd started throwing the letters onto the fire, unread.

As Mal had warned, her mother had all but ordered her to come home. And this letter was dated more than five days ago. Now that she knew about Olivia's collapse, nothing would stop Mother from bringing her wayward child home.

If only Nan hadn't telegrammed.

Of course, Liv had already left the dig, and with Henri there looking for any excuse to discredit her and her work, it might already be too late to go back.

Damn and blast!

Her last chance, gone forever.

"Nan, what did Henri do when you left?"

Nan sighed and wouldn't meet her eyes, and that was answer enough.

If she could have, Olivia would have jumped out of bed and paced, fuming and furious. All her body managed instead was a violent tremor.

There had to be a way to turn this to her advantage.

Whatever the family needed to research might give her something else to write about. Something sensational enough to challenge the infuriating Dr. Reilly, *without* resorting to the wild speculations that had gotten his articles so much attention. Something that would bowl over the editors who had once loved her work and, thanks to Reilly, had started calling her articles dull and boring.

She'd hoped that witch hunts and mass-murder would fit the bill—something she need not embroider or embellish. The facts alone were staggering and would sell copies. Her publisher had agreed—on the condition that she work through the local university. And they, in turn, had insisted she share the project with their head of department, Henri. Who was a vicious, back-stabbing opportunist with no sense of respect for history or the items they uncovered.

She hated to leave her work in his hands, but if she knew him—and she did—he'd already blocked her from returning. He would have made up some story about her collapse, something that made it sound like her fault, and accused her of reckless and irresponsible behavior. The university would believe him, because he had a cock and bollocks between his legs and she didn't.

But if she knew anything about Clan Fay, it was that they tended to get themselves involved in exciting and important events. Perhaps, if she came home to help, she could manage to make Mother think she was doing them a favor *and* get some help with whatever had caused her vision.

Olivia ignored the voice in her head that said her publishers wanted university-backing and credibility. She'd make it work. Now she just had to get out of this bed.

First, she needed food. She was ravenous.

"I'm hungry. Is there anything to eat?"

Nan managed a smile. They had a long-running private joke that Liv's moods could be predicted by her appetite. When she was happy or starting a new project, she could consume massive quantities of food. When the work wasn't going well, or she'd just ended a relationship with a lover, she barely touched a plate.

At the moment, the hunger was a purely physical urge, but she'd let Nan assume the best.

"I'll ring for tea." Nan stood and yanked at the room's bellpull. A few moments later, a maid in the hotel's uniform arrived and took their orders.

Before the woman returned, Olivia had recovered enough to get out of bed and sit in a plush armchair by the fireplace. She devoured the food that appeared twenty minutes later, and made Nan tell her everything about the situation they'd left behind at the dig.

It was as she'd feared. That door was now closed forever.

Izarra's face and determined black eyes filled Olivia's memory. She'd made a promise to the woman, a promise she would not be able to keep. So many adepts murdered by the Magisterium, with only that ratbag Henri to shepherd their legacy. Appalling.

The vision descended, pushing through her consciousness like a ram through his flock of ewes. She floated, bodiless, above a mass grave. Some of the corpses still smoldered, wisps of acrid smoke rising into the chilled morning air. Several men wearing rough laborer's clothes shifted the burnt bodies from a cart into the pit. One corpse wore partially melted copper at throat and wrists. Izarra.

The lifeless form tumbled down, jostling with a horrifying crack against the piles of bones below. So much death, and all because the Magisterium and their patron god, Jeshuvah, wanted power and needed scapegoats to tear down their rivals.

Olivia shuddered, and the vision faded. Nan knelt in front of her chair, clutching her wrists in a painful grip. "I'm fine, Nan. I'm having visions. That one wasn't as bad as the first."

"You've been sitting there over ten minutes."

"I don't know what the usual length is for these things." Olivia didn't mention the darkness and pain of the first vision. No need to frighten Nan—Olivia was frightened enough for both of them. And yet, now that she'd had another one without the accompanying eternity of terror, Liv thought it was Izarra who'd managed to trap her in that awful space. Not on purpose, but as the consequence of a last, desperate attempt to free herself.

Even though this vision had been less intense, its existence cemented her fate. If the visions were going to keep coming, Olivia couldn't just turn around and go back to Labourd even if there was a place for her there. Neither could she seek another position here on the Continent. She would have to go to England, and seek advice from her maternal relatives.

"Since we're going back to London, I'll be able to see my cousin Sorcha. She's the Fay family expert on visions and she just moved down from Skye." She curled her hands feebly in her lap, annoyed at the frailty of her grip. She'd managed to make her tone positive and light, but inside she was fragile as a dry leaf in a windstorm.

When she was a little girl, she'd have given anything for visions—for something that would make her mother notice her.

Now? She just wanted Sorcha to tell her how to make them stop.

Nan's mouth was pinched in dislike.

"Oh, don't worry. Sorcha is one of the good ones."

"That still isn't saying much for *those* people." She turned her attention deliberately to the knitting in her lap. "Your mother at least is a healer."

"If she can help me, does it matter?"

"I suppose not." Nan still looked worried, but she stood and moved away. "We're booked on the next ferry. We leave in an hour."

Magic and visions aside, Olivia wouldn't mind seeing Sorcha, or even Mal. They were living in the big house in Kensington that Lilias had built nearly a century ago. Liv would go there instead of Hazelby House in Mayfair. From what Mal wrote about his new wife, Etta—the new Duchess of Fay and owner of Skye House—she would welcome another misfit under her roof.

Yes, Olivia would be pleased to spend time with her brother and cousin. But she had no interest whatsoever in seeing her mother. Liv contemplated ways to politely refuse a visit, and determined that there weren't any.

Damn it.

~

SAVIT PLACED THE BELL-SHAPED HANDSET BACK INTO THE cradle and marveled at the technology that allowed him to speak with the concierge at the desk downstairs and both call for a cab and send a telegram without needing to resort to spells, bells, or a porter to physically relay the messages.

He lifted the telegram that had instigated his telephone call and read it again. Telegraphy worked on similar principles as the telephone, but the subject of the telegram wasn't new inventions or innovations. What his friend and fellow member of the Irish Republicans asked about was the past.

Sav: have history quandary for you reply via Skye house Kensington -Ronan

What sort of quandary would prompt Ronan McCarrick to send for him? The last time Ronan had needed his help was a little over two years ago, when he'd played a small role in liberating an artifact stolen from a Scottish nature spirit and later acquired by Trinity College in Dublin. Fortunately, he'd been able to keep his part in the caper hidden, as he doubted his superiors in the history department there would take kindly to his assisting thieves, no matter the original provenance of the artifact nor his current popularity in academic circles.

Savit could attempt to assuage his curiosity via magical means, but he stifled the impulse. He would learn Ronan's purpose soon enough, and impatience was no excuse for flagrant wastes of magic. There was little enough here in London, compared to Dublin.

Instead, he leaned back in his chair and cleared his thoughts, relaxing his muscles and letting his conscious mind drift. A few minutes of meditation while he waited for the cab to arrive would leave him refreshed and open to possibilities when he reached Skye House.

As often happened, meditation became a chance to check

the astral plane for wanderers. He didn't find them often—and the fact that he'd helped a woman back to her body only recently meant he would not see anyone for some time—but he felt restless if he did not check at least once a day. His guru, Chaitan, performed this service for wanderers in North America, but no one else had this particular gift in the British Isles.

Across the room, his door banged open, and Savit snapped back into his body with the force of a whip curling back on its wielder. He flinched, and took a moment to center himself again inside his flesh.

"Alexander, are you sleeping at your desk again?"

Savit opened his eyes and took a deep, cleansing breath. Now was not the time to tell his grandfather that his name was not Alexander. That name belonged to a dead man.

But Brian Reilly still could not see past the pain of his loss, even more than twenty years after his son Alex perished. Savit missed his father, too, but to deny the name his mother Kashvi gave him—Savitendra—was to ignore half of himself. He refused to disgrace her memory that way.

The only time he'd broached the subject with Grandfather, they'd had a blazing row that ended with them not speaking to each other for months. When the tension had begun affecting Savit's magical studies, he'd resolved it by bending to his grandfather's wishes and never bringing up the subject again.

Now, he didn't bother to correct his grandfather on his assumption that meditation was the same as sleep. Much like his insistence in calling Savit by his father's name, Brian ignored anything Savit did that even hinted at the Sutra culture of his youth. It was one of Savit's greatest regrets that he'd allowed the chair of his academic department to convince him to publish under the name Alexander Reilly.

He hated the feeling that he would not have had any success as himself—as Savit.

"I am awake, Grandfather." He stood and came around the desk. "What brings you to visit today?"

Although Savit stayed in a hotel when in London, his grandfather had a townhouse in Chelsea. It was yet another point of contention between them that Savit did not join his grandfather during his visits from Dublin. Savit's claim that he wanted privacy was true, but his grandfather's assumption that he wanted that privacy to see a mistress was not. Rather, he didn't want to explain his daily rituals and practices, or to have his research and writing time interrupted.

The former was achieved by staying in a hotel. The latter was not. As evidenced by his grandfather's next words.

"I've set up an appointment this afternoon for you to meet with my solicitors and the owner of a shipping concern out of Bristol. I'm thinking of buying in, but you'll be running the business before long, and I'd like your input before I make the decision official."

Savit tensed, and took a full half-minute to respond. He controlled his emotions without effort around everyone but Grandfather. "We've spoken of this. I am not going to take over your company. I know nothing of shipping."

"You don't have the knowledge because you don't choose to learn about it. With all of the books you read, you could be an expert on international shipping by next week if you wanted to." The elder Reilly stalked to the corner of the room, where a decanter of port sat beside another of whiskey. As Savit might have expected, he went for the whiskey and poured himself two finger's-worth. Savit did not drink, and this was one area where his grandfather had learned not to offer. But then, teetotalers—while subject to mild scorn—were something Brian Reilly understood.

"I have a profession, Grandfather. Pass your company to someone else."

"And let Reilly Trading go out of the family? Not a chance." He sat in Savit's vacated chair, giving the impression that it was his space, and not Savit's.

"What makes you think I wouldn't sell it after your death?"

"You wouldn't. You're too sentimental. Once I'm gone, you'll learn what you need to know and keep things running. It's your way." He took a swallow of whiskey and sat back in his chair, satisfied that he'd scored a point.

The terrible thing was, as much as his grandfather liked to deliberately misunderstand Savit in most areas of his life, in this he was correct. Their relationship was far from peaceful, but Savit loved the old man and would not allow his precious company to be sold and likely dismantled without someone to take up the reins.

"I continue to hold out hope that you will find a similar amount of sentimentality within you, and allow me my own path." He stepped back, shifting his body so that there was a clear line of sight between his grandfather and the door. He wouldn't ask the old man to leave, but he wouldn't go out of his way to make him feel welcome, either. "In any case, I cannot accompany you as I have plans this afternoon."

"Plans more important than assisting your grandfather?" He knew exactly where to press to make Savit squirm and react, and before he could settle his emotions, Savit let his anger speak.

"If it was so important you should have told me sooner. I can't cancel my engagement now. It would be rude."

The elder Reilly growled and slapped the glass down on the desk. Golden liquid sloshed up to the rim, but didn't splash over. "Don't talk to me of rude! Your generation hasn't the manners of a tomcat fighting for the right to mount a queen in heat."

That was a picturesque description, and sometimes accurate of the boys—now men—Savit had gone to school with. But not him. He'd never fought with them over whores, dancing girls, or actresses. He'd had no interest in a woman who would take any man's cock for money, or, even worse, one who wanted him because she thought his dark skin exotic or barbaric.

He wasn't a savage, and he'd spent his entire adult life proving it.

"Have I ever given you the impression I am like other men of my age?"

His grandfather grumbled something under his breath and then said, "No. That you haven't."

"I don't wish to accompany you. If I go, it will only be proof to your investors that I'm not fit to succeed you."

"They know you aren't experienced. That's why they want to meet you, and why you need to be seen working with me."

"Grandfather—"

"I'll reschedule for tomorrow. We'll have a dinner meeting at Hatchetts."

With a good bit more gruff declaration on his grandfather's part and argument on Savit's, they finally came to an agreement that Savit would find out the nature of the work required of him by Ronan, and then give his grandfather a time when he could have dinner with his investors.

Savit's cab arrived and he left the hotel, headed for Kensington and Skye House, his emotions amok and his body tense from the argument.

Although the cab jostled him over the uneven streets, he let the physical fall away and focused on calming his mind and soul. Before the cab ride ended, he'd brought himself back into balance. That was, until they pulled up at Skye House and he tasted peppermint.

A memory attempted to stir at the flavor and scent of magic, but he suppressed it. He would contemplate the phantom sensation later, after he'd helped Ronan with his mysterious quandary.

2

Olivia hadn't returned to London or spoken in person with any member of her family save Percy in over three years, so it was with no small amount of trepidation that she hired a cab to Skye House from the train station where she and Nan had come up from the channel crossing at Dover. Nan, curse her soul, had made sure a porter helped her to the cab, then had turned around to get right back on a train headed south, to Brighton.

Not even for love of Olivia would Nan be forced to mingle with the Fays.

But that meant Liv had to face them alone, after years apart and a number of scandals in between.

Until this moment, she'd not minded the distance—much. Or perhaps it was more accurate to say that she understood. Her siblings had too many things going on in their lives for jaunts to the Continent to visit their baby sister, and she'd not been willing to make them a priority, either, except for Percy.

Percy was the closest to her in age, and like her, he had only a glimmer of magical ability. His general lack of magic had influenced his decision to join the army, and his posting in Prussia had given him the ability to see her whenever he was on leave or school holiday from the Prussian Staff School. She wondered what he would do, now that she'd suddenly developed a wild talent—one that had left her reeling from multiple visions since she woke in the bed in Calais.

As children, she and Percy each found solace in the existence of the other, both of them ignored by their parents in favor of more appealing offspring. Father had Giles, who was even more anti-magic than Father was, and Mother had Malcolm and Viola.

What would she say when she saw her siblings and parents again? She had no idea, and hoped to avoid most of them for as long as possible. Mal would be at Skye House with his wife, but she could handle him. He'd always liked her, even if he was too old to want to play with her and had gone off to school by the time she was out of the nursery.

She had no concrete news about Viola, but if Mother was in Scotland, then Viola was there, too. Olivia hoped Vi stayed there. It wasn't that she hated her magical siblings. She didn't. Neither of them had treated her badly, or teased her for her lack of magic. But she couldn't help feeling resentment when the approval she desperately sought from her parents was given solely to her siblings through no fault of theirs or hers.

Mal and Vi had both married in the time that she was away, Viola to their Scottish neighbor, Ian MacAlasdair, and Malcolm to an American woman, Etta Mae Cook. Etta had been named to the dormant title Duchess of Fay, once held by Olivia's great-grandmother Horatia. And, of course, by her great-great-grandmother, the imposing Lilias Fay.

Lilias had had even less time for her untalented great-granddaughter than Olivia's mother. If it weren't for the complete acceptance and love of her siblings and cousins, Liv might have come to hate everyone who was born with a gift for magic.

What would the new duchess think of her? Of the three previous duchesses, only Beatrice, Olivia's great-aunt, had ever been so much as kind to Liv as a child, and she'd died ten years ago. Olivia hadn't thought there'd ever be another duchess, much less that her older brother would end up married to the woman. Did that make him a duke?

She wasn't going to call him that, or 'your grace.' She never let anyone call her Lady Olivia, either. What pish. Just because her father was a marquess, she'd had to put up with that Lady nonsense at the Swiss boarding school where His Lordship sent her after Viola got herself expelled from the finishing school for ladies in London.

But as soon as she graduated, she set out on her own and she never let any of her digging crews or colleagues call her anything but Miss Seward, or Liv if they got to know her well. As some of them had.

She frowned at the memory of Natalya, whose kisses had been like honey and wine, pulling Liv into a deep ocean of passion. Until she finally surfaced and realized that her sweet lover was ruining her dig by not following proper grid and cataloguing procedures. Their arguments had burned as hot as their lovemaking had, and then Talya had stormed off the site and had never returned.

No more mixing archaeology and relationships. She'd nearly lost some very valuable pieces that had opened up a fascinating line of inquiry into an extinct Eastern European culture. Olivia would not make that mistake again.

That was, if she ever had the chance. She might never work another dig for the rest of her life.

The hired cab jostled to a halt, and Liv climbed down to the side of the street, pushing away the depressing thought.

She hadn't been to Skye House since she was very, very small, and had no memories of the place at all. The second two duchesses hadn't used the house, and it had been closed with only a small staff to keep it clean and in good repair for over ten years.

There was evidence of occupation now. Smoke curled up from several of the chimneys into the cold late-winter air, though she thought it was not coal smoke, but wood. Or, considering the eccentricities of the first duchess, perhaps even peat. Liv would not put it past the old termagant to have laid in a supply from the Highland moors just to have the familiar scents of home around her.

Olivia paid the driver, who had unloaded her valise and trunk onto the street. The door to the house opened as she approached, and an ancient Highlander in full great kilt and sporran descended, accompanied by two younger Scotsmen also in kilts. They nodded to her and picked up her trunk. The older man reached for her valise, but she snatched it up.

"I can manage this one, thank you." She pretended her arm wasn't shaking with fatigue, and lifted her chin. She wasn't entirely helpless, despite the lingering weakness from five days abed with no sustenance except what water and broth her grandmother had been able to spoon into her.

"Very well, lass," he said, and gestured for her to proceed him into the house. She made it five steps before her trembling hands could no longer support the weight of the valise. To his credit, the older man said nothing as he gently lifted it from the bottom step and offered her his arm. Her cheeks burned with shame as she gripped it.

"I'm Miss Olivia Seward," she said as they walked up the steps, deliberately omitting her courtesy title and pretending she wasn't leaning heavily on him. "The new duchess is my sister-in-law."

The butler's expression didn't change, but she caught the

slightest glimmer of amusement in his ancient eyes. "Her Grace is in the family parlor attached to the library. I will show you up."

Olivia hesitated, then finally asked, "Is my brother here?"

"His Lordship is with Her Grace."

Ah. Had marrying a duchess changed Mal's attitudes about titles, or was their butler simply being correct for her sake?

"Thank you..." Her voice trailed off.

"MacGroarty," he supplied.

"Indeed. Thank you, MacGroarty."

He kept them at a manageable pace as they moved through the richly appointed but tastefully decorated foyer and hallways, up the lovely but not ostentatious staircase to the second floor. Olivia had no more breath for conversation by the top step, and had to stop and gasp a minute until her lungs stopped screaming that she was going to suffocate. Once she'd recovered, he led her a few more steps to a cozy parlor.

One side of the parlor had sliding doors, currently open into a large library filled to the brim with packed bookcases. A man with long dark hair entered through the library just as she stepped in and said in an Irish accent, "The telegraph office is sending off the message. We should hear back soon."

The woman who answered had long, jet-black hair with a defined streak of opalescent silver over her left eye. How Olivia had envied that streak when it first appeared in Viola's hair. Now all of Olivia's hair had turned that tell-tale Fay color.

But this woman wasn't Viola. She had dusky skin, more reddish-brown than the olive tones Liv had seen in southern Europe. Her eyes were a warm golden-brown, and she wore a plain gown of good fabric and fine cut, but nothing close to fashion.

Could that possibly be the duchess?

"What sort of friend is this Alexander Reilly?" asked the woman, and the name pierced through Olivia's worries like a stiletto.

"Not Dr. Alexander Reilly?" Liv strode into the room, the question preceding her like a ship's prow. Every head in the room swiveled toward her, but Olivia's attention was fixed onto her brother Malcolm, who had leapt to his feet.

Mal swallowed her into a tight, crushing embrace. Citrus flavor and scent surrounded her, the essence of Mal's magic. She'd never been able to sense it so robustly before. The strength in his arms and the fervor of his concern was both shocking and so much what she needed that she felt a sob rising up from her chest. She shoved it back down and forced a casual grin when Mal demanded, "Liv! What in the hells happened to you?" and reached up to touch her hair.

She pulled away from Mal and tried to keep her gestures relaxed as she tapped at the pile of silver strands. She wore it short, shorter even than the man who'd spoken as she entered the parlor. But Mal had seen it since she cut it—on her last visit to London, just after she graduated from school in Switzerland. So he meant the color, not the boyish style. "Oh, this? It's been like this for a few days now, after I had a dream-that-wasn't-a-dream."

"What was it, if not a dream?" That was Sorcha, and something tense released inside of Olivia at her cousin's query. Liv hadn't seen her in the room and thought she wasn't there—Sorcha was short enough to have been hidden behind the high-backed chair she was sitting in. Olivia desperately required Sorcha's advice. Having visions wasn't such a dreadful idea in the abstract, but for a while they'd been coming nearly once an hour, and that was terrifying. She'd had one just before she disembarked on the ferry and expected another one any minute.

"Oh, thank the goddess. I was afraid you'd be in Scotland. You're the only one I know who has visions all of the time." Olivia stepped around her big brother to get closer to Sorcha. Mal gripped her hand and the unexpected support nearly undid all the work she'd done to control her features.

"So it was a vision, then?" Sorcha didn't look surprised.

"More than one! I keep having them." After that first terrible one with Izarra, they'd started coming faster, some about the dig, others random scenes from history. "I've had over two-dozen since I woke up this morning. I need you to help me make them stop."

Sorcha finally looked puzzled. "That many is unusual, but it may be a result of the delayed onset. It can be frightening to witness things and then have them come to pass. But don't worry. I can teach you techniques to deal with them, and to help interpret what you don't understand."

"No, that's not it." Liv's worry increased. Sorcha had assumed the visions were of the future. From everything Olivia had read, visions almost always were. Except for hers. Not that she wasn't grateful for the offer, but what if Sorcha couldn't tell her anything? "I mean, I'll take all the help I can, but it's not the future I'm seeing. It's the past."

The dark-haired, darker-skinned woman stepped up between Sorcha and Mal. "Can you control what you See?"

The question startled Liv, but more startling was how much this woman reminded her of great-great grandmother Lilias. There was almost no physical resemblance at all, yet the way she walked and even the way she spoke—not her accent, but the quality of her voice—was reminiscent of the first Duchess of Fay.

Mal released Olivia's hand and drew the woman closer. "Liv, this is Etta, my wife."

"Oh." Liv's cheeks heated, having been caught staring at the new duchess. She deliberately closed her hands over the dratted bloomer skirts that she'd put on in deference to social mores in London. If her palms were busy gripping fabric they wouldn't be covering her face. "I wasn't sure. You only said she was American in your letters." And now she was babbling. Just as she'd always done when she had to face Great-Great-Grandma Lilias. Apparently the intimidation passed along with the title.

But this was her sister-in-law, her brother's wife. She wasn't much older than Olivia. Liv refused to let old fears get in the way of becoming friends. She released her death grip on her skirt and held out her hand to Etta. The other woman took it without a moment's hesitation or any hint that young women of good family weren't supposed to shake hands. In fact, the duchess had a firm, decisive grip, and pine-and-soil scented magic that made Liv think of a quiet wood or a field tilled and ready for planting.

"I'm pleased to meet you," Olivia said, surprised at how much she meant it, "and I'm dying to talk with you about this clod here." She punched Mal's arm and he made a familiar face, half wince and half amused smile. "But to answer your question, I can only control them a little. I was able to move around sometimes, and the visions sometimes focused on segments that I recognized."

Liv didn't mention that the subject of one of her visions had seen her, too. Or that the promise she'd made to Izarra would now go unfulfilled.

"If you can control the visions at all, with practice you'll be able to control them at will." Sorcha pulled Olivia to a sofa and they both sat, Sorcha with grace and Olivia like her legs were about to collapse under her—which they had been.

Sorcha's magic was like moonlight, and tasted like mulberries and thyme. The combination of distant mystery and familiar comfort was quintessentially Sorcha. "Seeing through time is a rare gift, and very valuable."

The idea that Olivia might one day control the visions, and not be controlled by them, was very attractive. "That's why I came home. I knew you could help me." Or she'd hoped, anyway.

Mal plopped down beside her and wrapped his arm around her shoulders. It felt so good to let someone else share the burden for a little while that she sagged against him. His fingers squeezed her upper arm, and he dropped a kiss on her newly silver hair.

"I wish this had started years ago. I was always so jealous of you and Viola, getting all of Mother's attention." She startled and her gaze darted around the parlor and open library. "Is she here?" It didn't matter which 'she' he assumed Liv meant, Vi or Mother.

"No." Mal's touch was soothing, and she relaxed again, letting her eyes shut. "They're at home." Home could mean Hazelby House, or it could mean the Highlands. She would ask for clarification later, but for now it was enough that they weren't at Skye House.

"Why didn't you telegraph when this started?" Mal asked.

"Nan did, but she only told Mother. I assumed Mother would have told you."

"Why didn't you seek out your mother at Hazelby House?" Sorcha asked, and Liv opened her eyes again. "She's not there, but I'd think you'd want your mother's help." Sorcha's smile was kind, but she gestured to Olivia's too-thin arms and her face, which she knew from an angry perusal of the mirror in the hotel in Calais was sunken and wan.

"I knew you all were here, and honestly, I prefer Mal to Mother." She pressed her head back against his chest, and he held her close. She'd forgotten about this side of her big brother. He'd been too old to play with her, but he'd always been affectionate, and protective. He hadn't cared about her lack of magic. To Mal, family was family.

He dropped another kiss onto her hair and wrapped his other arm tight around her. "You'll not feel that way when you see her. She's thawed in the last two years. Having new magical grandbabies and an outspoken daughter-in-law has done wonders for her personality."

Olivia wasn't sure she could believe that. And even if it was true, that was with Mal and Viola and their loved-ones. Of course Mother would make a space in her heart for her favorite children's spouses and offspring.

Mal's spouse came and perched beside Mal on the arm of the sofa. Olivia barely registered the informal and unconventional action before Etta asked, "Why did you shout about this Dr. Reilly when you came in? Is there some reason why we shouldn't work with him? We're embarking on a sensitive project, and if you are familiar with him…" The duchess's voice managed to both rise in inquiry and fall off in volume, leaving Olivia to respond.

"Oh, him." Heat rose again in Liv's cheeks. She'd just had another article rejected in favor of the illustrious Dr. Reilly's work before the witch hunt project, and the refusal still stung. "He's a scandal-monger. Have you read any of his journal articles? Absolutely libelous, if the people in question weren't hundreds of years dead."

"Is he the one you wrote about last time?" Mal's voice rumbled from over her left ear. "The one who has been publishing the sensational articles?"

"Yes, that's him."

"I thought your new project was supposed to be your, um…" He trailed off.

She leaned her head back and forced a smile at him, like the loss of Izarra and the witch hunt digs didn't matter. At least he knew enough to care. She'd asked him a few times to come and visit her, especially after what happened with Viola and Ian, but he'd needed to assuage his guilt, and working an estate in the Highlands had been his choice of anodyne. She couldn't begrudge him that, although it would have been nice to have more of her siblings than Percy visit her digs. "Yes, well, *this* put a large damper in my work." She gestured at her hair.

"I see." Mal shifted her away from him so he could pin her with his narrowed gaze. "So how will that affect your chances for new publication?"

"I thought I might write about your new research project." She didn't mention that she had managed to get something in print recently—a scathing editorial she'd written about so-called 'sciences' that lacked a sufficient evidentiary basis. "But if you've invited that snake Reilly, I won't have a chance. He's already been submitting articles on similar topics to mine, and his are so melodramatic they always choose *his* to publish. I can't understand why. His methodology is specious at best. He's an *anthropologist*." She couldn't help the way her mouth tightened and the words spat out like acid. "That means he can concoct whatever he wants and pretend it's science. He's driving me mad!"

A shuffle in the doorway drew her attention away from Mal. One of the burly footmen in a kilt handed a piece of paper to the tall, dark-haired man who'd been the first to mention Reilly when she entered. He chuckled.

"Well, he'll be able to drive you mad in person, *colleen.* He's on his way here now."

3

Olivia nearly rose from the sofa, but Mal held her still —and she didn't have the strength to pull away, damn it.

"Relax. We need his help. There are many things you need to know." He proceeded to explain to her about a massive spell siphoning English magic, one that Lilias had first discovered. Thanks to Etta's efforts and many other witches and mages, including everyone in the room, they now knew that the spell had been around since 1688, which was the year of the Glorious Revolution when William and Mary invaded from the Netherlands and James II fled. Parliament was persuaded to accept his departure as an abdication, and his daughter Mary was installed as Queen, with William as co-regnant.

"But we have no idea if that has anything to do with the spell or not. It could be coincidence." Etta had joined in the telling of the tale, supplementing her husband's facts with her own.

"It could be coincidence, but I doubt it. A spell of the magnitude you're suggesting would have needed a very large group to cast, and would have required the monarch's approval if not assistance." Olivia's mind darted down corners of possibility, and she wished she could trigger a vision that might give them more insight into the problem. But she simply didn't know enough about the period. She could remember only vague details from a book on English history, as her studies had been far more varied and broad on the Continent.

She turned to Sorcha. "If I'm having visions of the past, is there some way to...scry for a specific time period?"

Sorcha frowned. "I know Seers who can seek visions of the future when they are worried about a particular turn of events, so that implies what you're asking is possible, but the future is mutable. The past is fixed. I don't know if that makes a difference in how to look."

"Can you help me try?"

Sorcha agreed, and Liv followed her to a more dimly-lit corner in the library, immediately plopping back down into a waiting chair. Amazing that only a week ago she would have eschewed the chairs and paced the room instead. Today her legs felt like aspic.

Sorcha took the chair opposite. "Sometimes it helps to work in the dark and quiet, so that other people don't distract your mind."

"So far, the visions have come willy-nilly, whenever they want."

"That's to be expected. I'll be honest with you, though. What I'm going to try to teach you to do is something I've never mastered."

"What? But I thought..." The expression on Sorcha's face stopped any other words Olivia might have been tempted to say. Obviously her lack of ability bothered Sorcha, and Liv wouldn't press at the wound. She abandoned the question and asked another. "What do I do first?"

Sorcha's visage cleared, and she led Olivia through a series of breathing and relaxation exercises. Perhaps it was the toll of days spent unconscious while being magically drained, followed by a full day of travel, but instead of having a vision, Liv nodded off. Sorcha nudged her and she could barely blink her eyelids open.

"Sorry." Liv rubbed her face and yawned. "Maybe we can try again tomorrow when I've had a good night's sleep." Although she was frankly shocked that she hadn't at least had a random vision. They'd been coming frequently in Calais and on the Channel crossing. But she hadn't had a single one since she stepped onto the shore in Dover.

"Will you stay here in Skye House, or go to Hazelby House instead?"

"If Etta agrees, I would prefer to stay here. Hazelby House is...cold."

Sorcha nodded in agreement. Neither of them meant the house had a chilly temperature. It was not a welcoming place, either for general visitors or for mages. The atmosphere inside its walls was formal, restrictive, and austere. Olivia had hated going to London as a child, and had made every excuse possible to stay at the Seward family estate in Wiltshire, where Nan lived most of the year in the Dower House. Their closeness had spurred Nan to leave Wiltshire behind when Olivia graduated, and now they traveled together with Nan as a putative chaperone. Not that Nan ever lived up to the role. She'd been the one to supply Olivia with her first contraceptive sheathes and teach her how to use them.

Unfortunately, her hatred for the Fay side of the family kept her from joining Olivia during this crisis. Liv couldn't help but feel the defection as a betrayal, even though she understood.

Voices intruded on the quiet conversation. The others

had been chatting softly so as not to disturb them, but Dr. Reilly must have arrived.

Olivia rose from her chair and walked back to the parlor. The little nap had helped transform her legs from quivering jelly back into functioning limbs, so the attempt hadn't been a total loss.

Everyone had clumped together around the new arrival, greeting him informally instead of following the more rigid rules of social introduction that her mother had always preferred. Olivia was glad to see Etta didn't stand on ceremony, even with outsiders.

Then someone shifted and there was Dr. Reilly. Heat rose from her core, sending waves of desire tingling along every nerve ending in her body.

Dr. Alexander Reilly was gorgeous.

Not gorgeous in the same way as the male lovers she'd taken in the past, many of whom had been student laborers from universities on the Continent and bulky with muscle from digging. In many ways, he reminded her more of her last female lover, who had been slender and had stunning, well-defined features. He was beautiful, compact and slim, and only a little taller than her brother, but with nearly-black hair that curled at the ends, eyes dark as a moonless night, and skin a shade darker than Etta's.

She had to suppress a very inconvenient desire to go and proposition him as she might a man met on her travels.

This was *Dr. Reilly*, the bane of her academic existence. She'd just skewered him in all but name in the last edition of *Walking the Past*, the premiere archaeological and historical journal in the United Kingdom.

So why was her pulse still racing, and why did her fingers itch to tangle themselves in his mass of black curls? She closed her hands into fists. She'd promised herself, no more mixing work and sex, and certainly no sleeping with the enemy.

～

SAVIT SHOOK RONAN'S HAND, THEN MALCOLM SEWARD'S, AND finally Etta Cook-Fay's. He was a little surprised to shake a woman's hand, and even more surprised when Ronan casually mentioned that she was married to Malcolm and was, by the way, the Duchess of Fay.

The woman looked nothing like his preconceived notions of a duchess. In fact, she looked more like his memories of his mother, with warm brown skin, brown eyes, and black hair. The only difference was a wide streak of opalescent silver that matched the one arching through her husband's red-brown hair, and eyes that appeared slightly slanted above high cheekbones.

Her magic felt nothing like his mother's, though. Hers was the deep pine of a forest, mixed with the scent of fresh-tilled earth and the taste of honeysuckle and salt. His mother's had been jungle-hot, a mix of lotus and lily.

He released her hand, and her expression changed, becoming more assessing. She'd been testing his magic even as he experienced hers. She said nothing, but he altered his first impression of her immediately. She'd been informal, almost casual, but she was not a woman to be underestimated or dismissed. She might not match his imagined picture of a duchess, but the title and the power it held rooted her like a banyan tree. What had she determined in her survey? Did she find him lacking?

Ronan drew Savit's attention away from the duchess. He had taken the hand of a very short, very voluptuous woman with pale blonde hair. He presented her as his wife, Sorcha

Fay. Apparently the Fay women did not take their husbands' names in marriage.

And then Savit saw the other woman, and such insignificant thoughts fled.

She was magnificent. From her tanned skin and heart-shaped face, to the toned body that spoke of an active lifestyle, to her tailored clothes that only barely edged over into femininity, he found her attractive, although a little thin and haggard, as though she'd recently been ill. But for that beauty to be crowned with such hair was a wonder and a delight.

Shorn shorter than he'd ever seen on a woman, her hair was no single color, caught somewhere between purest white, silver, and opal. Each individual strand would have been the crowning glory of a seashell, and put pearls to shame.

And even still, all of this only attracted him in a pleasant, aesthetic sort of way. There was something else underneath, an energy and a pulse of awareness, that roused his flesh, his mind, and his spirit all at once.

The flesh was easy to ignore; he'd not remained celibate for years now without learning to control his baser lusts. But the arousal of his mind and spirit was far more difficult to ignore.

Then Ronan said her name. Olivia Seward.

Olivia Seward? His shoulders shifted backward in a tiny, unconscious movement, pushing his chest out. He didn't believe in coincidences, and *Oliver* Seward had been running a campaign to have him discredited now for almost six months.

Savit held out his hand. With a tiny hint of a smile, she took it.

Magic flared between them. He experienced her gift with a befuddled sort of wonder. She was all dust, leather, and bone, a mix of old books and the storage rooms where his college kept antiques and specimens. But cutting through these familiar scents was a refreshing flavor of peppermint.

Up close, he could see her eyes were hazel: a mix of greens and golds and greys and browns. Her mouth was formed with generous lips, and her jaw had a stubborn, deliberate line. Beneath the severe tailoring of her coat, her breasts rose and fell, too quickly for her not to be experiencing the same desire as he did.

He wanted her. Again, his blood heated, his heart tripping into a faster rhythm. His cock stirred. Her lips parted, and she exhaled. Warmth settled in his chest as he pulled her breath into his lungs. As though he could make her part of himself.

He yanked his hand away and brought his body back under control. He could not do this. Must not give in to his physical desires. They clouded his thoughts, and his magic.

Once he'd calmed the raging beast within him, he recognized what else he had felt in her, mixed in with magic and desire.

Animosity.

She *was* Oliver Seward. Even if he was tempted to break his ascetic vows for the gorgeous woman—which he most definitely was not—he would never do so for the scathing author of "How Anthropology Fails to Uphold the Basic Tenets of the Scientific Method."

He deliberately turned his back on her and inclined his head to the duchess. "How may I help you?"

Etta invited him to sit, and a tray of delicacies and a variety of different teas and coffee appeared. Once everyone had gathered around the treats, she told him a tale of a long-standing drain on English magic, and its origins in the late seventeenth century. "We believe it may be related to James the Second's abdication and William and Mary's subsequent rule," she concluded. "Because that was the most significant thing that happened in England that year. Ronan says you study Magisterium and Academe conflicts, and since that conflict was precipitated by Anglican Academe sympathizers, we hoped you would be able to provide more insight."

Savit considered the question. His knowledge of the period was perhaps better than a layman's, but by no means exhaustive or even extensive. "Your assumption that the spell is linked to the abdication is likely correct, but I would like to consult with a few colleagues at the Society for the Exploration of the History of the Arcane and Mundane and find as many primary sources from the period as I can. This is the sort of thing that will not be explicitly stated in any established histories, or else everyone would know about it. I will need to look for journals, letters, and perhaps request access to the Mage Archive of the British Army."

He could feel Olivia Seward frowning at him, but he wouldn't acknowledge her. Yes, he did use actual data and sources in his research, and yes, he refrained from speculation and conjecture, despite her claims to the contrary. He would stand behind all of his writing, and had done so on numerous occasions. It was only that he gave his work a narrative—a human element—that Oliver Seward's writings lacked. Her essays were dry recitations of facts, lists of objects recovered at her digs, and detailed descriptions of everything from the terrain to the rock strata.

All of those things could be fascinating, if she understood how to turn them into a compelling story.

Or cared to do so.

He could only assume that she didn't.

But she did care about something, because she had shifted in her chair and leaned toward the duchess.

"I can handle this. We don't need to go to outsiders when there's a historian in the family."

Etta contemplated the other woman. It occurred to Savit

that Ronan had introduced the duchess's husband as Malcolm Seward. That likely meant that Olivia was the duchess's sister-in-law. Yet Etta's gaze was as measuring and calculating as it had been when she looked at him. He sensed an underlying warmth, but no true affection. Perhaps they had not known each other long.

"You've been working on the Continent," the duchess said. "How many people do you know in London?"

Olivia flushed. She was forced to admit that she didn't know many, and that she would have to write to friends abroad.

"So it would be wise to utilize Dr. Reilly's contacts here in England," Etta concluded.

"I suppose that *Dr.* Reilly will be heading up this inquiry then?" The extra emphasis Olivia had placed on 'doctor' left no doubt as to her meaning—she thought Etta was favoring him because of his degree. He had to admit that he'd seen the same thing happen often in academia. Skilled historians with vast practical experience were routinely overlooked in favor of men who had never left the classroom and library but had a piece of paper proclaiming their worth to the world.

The duchess glanced back and forth between them a few times. "Would it be so difficult for the two of you to work together as equals?"

"Not on my part," Savit hurried to say. Olivia agreed as well, with a glare in his direction. But she didn't object, either, so the duchess's declaration of equality must have mollified her.

"And what of my..." She trailed off, but shared a significant look with her sister-in-law.

"We'll utilize that if we can." Etta glanced at Savit and back to Olivia. "But I would prefer to proceed with this option, as the other is...unreliable as of yet."

"I understand." Olivia gave him one last, inscrutable

glance, then got up and walked away, leaving the parlor and disappearing through a set of sliding doors into a library. He sensed her move through the room and out again, then farther into the house. Sorcha followed her.

"I will make arrangements to visit a friend of mine at the historical society tomorrow," Savit told the duchess. "I will telegram to let you know the time Miss Seward should be ready to leave."

"Thank you, Dr. Reilly."

"Please, I am not so formal. You must call me Savit."

The duchess gaped for a moment before controlling her features. "My apologies. Ronan told us your name was Alexander."

Ronan lifted an eyebrow at Savit. The smuggler knew his true name because of their association with the Irish Republicans, but the last time they'd met, he'd still been using Alex even among his colleagues at the college. He'd come farther along his spiritual journey since then, and had attempted to reclaim some part of his work under his own name. Unfortunately, his publications—and his public persona—were still firmly mired under the anglicized pseudonym.

"I am known by that name in some academic circles, but my mother named me Savitendra."

For the first time since he'd entered the parlor, Etta gave him a true smile. When she spoke again, her accent shifted, becoming higher and slightly nasal. "That's lovely. And you must of course call me Etta. Back at home in the mountains of North Carolina, no one would even dream of calling me Miss Cook, much less 'your grace.' Formality's a little silly when you're living in a one-room log cabin. I only use the title when I need to impress someone."

"I am impressed, I assure you."

She laughed, and the severe façade disappeared, revealing a lovely woman. He was again reminded of his mother, with an almost painful stab of memory. He was seven, and had no idea that within a few months his entire world would be changed. It was Diwali, and he and his mother had lit every lamp in the house. She and his father danced in a circle formed by magelights that she had coaxed to life with her vibrant, lovely magic. He could smell lilies, could taste cooked lotus stems and feel the boundless energy of her. Kashvi had been so *alive*. How could anyone have guessed that, only a short while after the festival, she and her husband would be dead?

And his grandfather had taken Savit from India, from the heat and the light and the laughter and the *life* they'd had. In Ireland, he'd had only a shadow of a life, pale and incomplete.

He tasted peppermint on his tongue. Olivia's magic had carried this flavor, but it was not the first time he'd encountered it. There'd been a night, not too long ago, when he'd helped a restless traveler's spirit back to her body. Had that been Olivia? She couldn't be the only woman in the world whose magic tasted of peppermint.

"I'm sorry about Olivia." Hearing her brother say her name made Savit's head jerk unconsciously in Malcolm's direction.

"Why?"

"Before you got here, she had some…unkind things to say about your profession."

"I assure you, I've read the worst of it." But while it had bothered him before, he could now find the amusement in it. "I'll bring her around. Working together is the best way to show her that her assumptions about me and what I do are entirely incorrect."

"Better you than me, mate." Malcolm smirked.

"I must take my leave now. I have another appointment across town, but I will send word once I've made arrangements for tomorrow."

The others said their goodbyes, and Savit headed off to a small gathering of historians where he was to give a talk about how waves of invasions shaped the current culture of Ireland. As he jostled away from Skye House, he once again sought to realign and balance his mind, soul, and body. The act was harder than it should have been; his chakras were terribly out of balance, and he had to take extra time to center himself with spoken mantras.

Lingering on the edge of his consciousness, no matter how hard he tried to ignore it, was the elusive flavor of peppermint. Was his academic nemesis also the woman he'd saved—and now craved?

4

Olivia tried again to clear her thoughts and seek a vision. She and Sorcha had been sitting in Liv's dim, quiet room at the top of the house for over an hour, but nothing had happened. In fact, she was starting to question her sanity. Why had the visions suddenly stopped when she arrived in England?

She asked Sorcha.

"It could be that we're going about this backwards—that your visions are tied to things you're seeing, or feeling, or remembering. Maybe clearing your thoughts makes you unable to access them."

That was a very dispiriting idea.

"Or," Sorcha added, her brow furrowed with worry, "it could just be that the drain has pulled so much ambient magic from England that there isn't much here to work with. I know I haven't had as many visions since Ronan and I moved into Skye House."

Although even more dispiriting, Olivia liked that option better. It meant the fault wasn't hers, but rather the very thing they were trying to fight.

"Let's try it the other way and see if that helps. I'll try to summon a vision of something specific."

After another quarter of an hour, she gave up. Both of them sighed, and Sorcha summoned a trio of magelights to illuminate the room until Olivia could light the lamps. Skye House hadn't been modernized at all, with the exception of a handful of new bathing chambers and running water to the kitchens that Mal had talked Etta into installing a few weeks after they took up residence in the summer. But Liv was used to rough conditions in the field, and Sorcha's magelights were much better than the rushlights and single tallow candles she was often forced to work by.

"I'm sorry," Sorcha said. "If it helps, I've never been able to do this, either. The visions come when they want. And if it is the drain that has slowed things down, that might be a good thing. That first vision took too much out of you, physically and magically. You need time to recover. Just remember what I told you. If you have another one, try to concentrate on a specific person or object to make the vision show you what you want. Once you can do that, you should be able to dismiss them, or summon them, at will." Sorcha left, the magelights trailing after her like puppies.

Olivia still hadn't decided which of those options she would prefer. When the visions had been coming every hour, dismissing them had been at the forefront of her desires. But now that they'd stopped, and she had something she wanted to see, she wished she could summon one instead.

If she could learn to control the visions, would that make her a mage? She still couldn't do anything practical. Sorcha couldn't control her visions, but she could cast spells. Olivia still couldn't even open her Sight—something else Sorcha had tried to teach her tonight, and failed.

Not that she needed to be a mage, or wanted to be. That

was a childish desire, fostered by envy of Mal and Vi. She'd made her own life, her own career.

Which had now come crashing down around her.

Olivia closed and locked the door behind her cousin, then slumped onto the soft chair by the fire. She'd been right about Lilias and the peat—the old girl had, indeed, stocked her London residence with peat cut in the Highlands, then placed it in stasis spells so it would keep until needed. Etta thought burning it instead of wood or coal gave her an air of eccentricity and reminded those she wished to impress of her links to the first duchess.

Much of their dinner conversation that night had been frivolous tidbits like that as Etta, Mal, Sorcha, and Ronan shared clan gossip and subjects too delicate to have been entrusted to letters before.

Olivia chafed at the inanity of it. She wanted to be out there, digging into the mystery of the drain. She'd finished writing up her notes on the vision of Izarra and the data that had been available when Nan had packed her up to leave the site in Labourd. Not that she would ever be able to do anything with the notes. But she'd needed to do it, needed to fulfill at least that tiny portion of her promise, while the shattered remains of her hopes lay dashed around her.

And yet—now there was this new project, with its intriguing possibilities, even if she would have to share the credit with Reilly. Her assumption that Clan Fay would be involved in something sensational had been entirely accurate. She could just imagine the publisher she'd contacted about the witch trial book salivating over a secret of this magnitude.

Of course, they had to do the work first and uncover the secrets—and end the draining spell. She wouldn't be allowed to publish anything until English magic was safe again.

But where to start? Alexander Reilly had been correct.

She wasn't likely to find anything in the normal histories. This was too well hidden.

But might Lilias have acquired something and simply not understood the relevance? She had never known the origins of the siphoning spell, nor where it was going. Now Olivia knew where, or rather when, to start. Often, people wrote of commonplace things without bothering to provide definitions or explanations, and once the shared frame of reference was gone, later researchers might never fully comprehend what was meant.

Lilias might have had any number of books in her library with the answers she sought, if she'd known what to look for.

The hour was too late to begin anything tonight. As Sorcha noted, she hadn't fully recovered from the first vision, and the long trip from Calais hadn't helped. Most of the house would be going to sleep anyway.

She got up and paced to the window. There was a garden on this side of the house. Earlier today, she'd noticed the skeletal trees and winter-pale bushes and grass, but without lamps and under the smoggy sky, all Liv could see now was darkness. Somewhere out there, across London, was a frustrating man who had fit none of her preconceptions about him.

For one thing, she hadn't expected him to be so vital, so alive. She ought to have, from the verve he displayed in his writing, but she'd imagined him as oily and overbearing, smarmy and easily dismissed. The one thing she'd found hard to do was ignore him.

No, she'd barely stopped herself from staring at him. If she closed her eyes, she could still see him, could still feel the heat of his palm against hers, his fingers brushing her wrist, his thumb giving her an unbearably erotic caress for the eternity before he drew away.

And his magic! He'd never even hinted in his writings

that he was a mage, but she'd felt it, unmistakable and much, much stronger than hers. She had made a point, afterward, of touching everyone else in the family skin-to-skin to test whether all people with magic would make her feel so alive and unsettled. No one else, not even Ronan who was no blood relation to her, had the same effect. She could sense their magic: citrus for Mal, pine for Etta, mulberry for Sorcha, and apples for Ronan, but no one else woke that same sense of connection, of possibility and awareness.

She hadn't been able to place the scent and flavor of Alexander's magic, but it had woken something in her soul.

Not Alexander. Dr. Reilly. She mustn't use his first name, even in her thoughts. His magic had been spicy and both comforting and arousing at once. She'd had difficulty not stepping closer to him, and when she stared into his dark-night eyes, wetness and heat had bloomed between her legs.

Her fingers stole up to one tight nipple and stroked it.

What harm, to allow herself the fantasy of him? To pretend that he was someone utterly different than Dr. Reilly. Someone other than Alexander, who had deliberately goaded her with his reference to primary sources and research methodologies. Someone who looked and felt like him, but answered to another name.

It was that other, nameless man that she undressed in her mind, imagining the compact musculature that she would stroke and caress, the trim waist that she would grasp before delving lower to cup his arse in her eager hands. She'd pull him to her, pressing their hips together. Yes, she'd noticed that they were almost of a height, except that his longer torso made up for the few inches of difference so that, if she wrapped her legs around him, he'd be in the perfect position to slide into her welcoming depths.

Liv unbuttoned her blouse and unhooked the waistband

of the bloomers. She wore no corset, and never would, no matter how many social conventions she flaunted. Under her blouse and the voluminous fabric of the bloomers were a hip-length chemise and drawers, and these she stripped off quickly. She lay back on the bed and cupped her hands over her small breasts, teasing the tips with long strokes of her fingers. Her unnamed man, the one that only existed in her imagination, would do this, and then would take each into his mouth in turn, lapping and sucking and nibbling, until she writhed and begged him to fill her.

He would make her wait for that, teasing her slippery folds, pushing his fingers into her and finding all the spots on her internal walls that made her scream. Liv slid her own fingers into the wet heat at her core, brushing her thumb at the apex of her sex, across the engorged nub there. She teased at the hood as he would with his tongue, licking with firm pressure until...

Liv's hips bucked up against her thumb as pleasure swamped over her. She hadn't meant to climax so soon, had meant to draw out the experience more, but as it sometimes happened when she was with a lover, the orgasm had taken her by surprise. Shudders wracked her as waves of bliss and heat trembled through her body and limbs. Fluid flooded over her fingers.

Odd. She'd never managed to do that to herself before— to climax so hard she gushed. Sometimes her sex partners didn't satisfy her as well as she could on her own, but her most intense orgasms had always been with others. Natalya had been able to...

No. No thoughts of Talya, or not-Alexander, or anyone else. She'd had her release, and now she would sleep, and prepare for a day of research with Dr. Reilly. She would need to be rested and on guard. He hadn't said that he knew she was the Oliver Seward who'd been so vociferous against him in the journals, but he didn't need to. Among other things she'd noticed when they touched was a kind of sardonic gleam in those deep, dark eyes. He knew who she was, and he was going to make her regret every word she'd written.

Liv pulled the sheets over her naked body and burrowed under the thick woven blankets and quilts. She fell asleep thinking of ways to strike first.

∾

SAVIT WOKE WITH HIS COCK IN HIS HAND, SEMEN SPURTING over his fingers onto the sheets of the hotel bed. He hadn't taken himself in hand since his very first lesson with his guru, Chaitan, many years ago, so it was a bit of a shock to find he'd done so in his sleep.

The orgasm still resonated inside of him, his balls tight and hot, his body shuddering with intense pleasure. And the taste of peppermint flooded his mouth.

Olivia.

He rolled out of bed and almost stumbled to the fireplace. The hotel was old, and he'd requested a room that hadn't been converted for coal. He coaxed the banked embers back into flame and fed them with kindling and finally a log.

Then he folded his legs beneath him and sank into a trance.

Unbelievably, despite his lingering arousal and confusion, he wasn't out of balance. On the contrary, everything was simply…brighter. As though he'd become more alive, more aware, more himself as he dreamed of her, of touching her and tasting her, of burying his cock inside her.

How was that possible? Long ago, he'd learned to control his lusts because they clouded his mind and made it more difficult to embrace his magic and the world beyond. But tonight, even in a dream, it had been more than lust.

Something about Olivia Seward woke parts of himself that he had never known existed, parts that gave him an even greater awareness of the magical world and his place in it.

Fear spiked inside him as he tasted peppermint. Her spirit, her magic self, was roaming again—had come to him in his dreams. He needed to take her back, lest she lose her way.

He deepened the trance and let his subtle body take flight. In this form, the world was full of swirling energies. His mind interpreted them as colors and light, scent and taste, some familiar and easy to coax to his will, others reluctant or impossible to touch.

There she was, her astral form more like an amorphous cloud than a human body.

Again he remembered when he'd tasted peppermint before.

The last time he'd found her wandering, she'd been pulsing red, a sign that the soul was in danger. He'd found a thread of someone else's magic tangled around her, and had loosened the knots, setting her free and helping her find her physical body.

Tonight, the only magic touching her was his. And she wasn't projecting as fully as she had that night. Her form wasn't even as defined as a cloud; instead it was more like a shred of fog. She wasn't aware of what was happening, or if she was, it would be nebulous as a dream, gone in the morning when she woke.

Still, it was more of her soul than she could spare. He touched her spirit-form, and it lit with the brilliant blue-white of arousal, shot through with the darker blue of trust.

Olivia Seward was a fascinating study in contradictions,

and he couldn't deny the urge to study her and discover all of her secrets.

He shepherded her unconscious spirit back to her sleeping flesh, and returned to his own body. His eyes were still open, staring at the fire. She could be a flame, if he wasn't careful. But she needed his help, and he would offer it. He would simply have to guard against his own fascination with her, lest he find himself entirely forsworn.

5

That night, Olivia's dreams began with pleasant fantasies, and then changed, plunging into darkness, rage, pain, and despair. Memories from Izarra.

When she woke, she read through her notes on Izarra again, wishing there were something she could do to ease the guilt she felt for breaking her promise. Something to ease the suffering the woman still obviously felt, hundreds of years after her death.

Later, Liv sat in the downstairs parlor awaiting Dr. Reilly's arrival. She'd made herself repeat that name over and over again, lest she slip and call him something else. She could not let him know that she'd used thoughts of him to bring herself to one of the better orgasms of her life.

She was a little mortified even thinking about it. Not because of the pleasure, but because it was *him*. Her nemesis. The man responsible for her career's downward spiral. For the last six months of thankless and grueling work dealing with a crude lout who now got to reap the benefits of her labor. For her book proposal languishing in permanent limbo. He was not an eligible candidate for lust, or anything else. They would work together because Etta had asked, and because Olivia still hoped to turn this research into a new opportunity. Who wouldn't want to read about a secret spell?

MacGroarty entered the parlor and announced Dr. Reilly. Olivia stood when he entered, not because it was necessary for social conventions—she couldn't care less about those and she was nominally considered a lady who needn't rise when a gentleman enters—but because she would rather hurry him out the door and on to their appointment than dawdle about the downstairs parlor making polite conversation that would only partially veil their mutual disdain.

"Good morning, Dr. Reilly." She inclined her head in his direction. She looked ridiculous when she curtseyed in rational dress, since the point of a curtsey was to made long skirts sweep and drape a certain way, and her skirt ended at the knee with bloomers underneath. And anyway she didn't mind accepting the privilege of rank when it came to him. Ladies needn't curtsey to untitled gentlemen. And this lady was still having bouts of vertigo that made bending with fancy footwork unwise.

"Good morning, Miss Seward."

Did she imagine a tiny emphasis on 'miss'? One corner of her mouth twitched. She should not be so excited by the prospect of sparring with him, but she found that her pulse had already increased, her breath coming just that tiny touch faster.

"Oh, don't be coy, Dr. Reilly. We both know that you know I write as *Mister* Oliver Seward. And that, if I had my way, you'd never publish in a respectable journal again."

His eyes widened. She'd managed to surprise him. Good. What was the phrase the old duchess had used to say from the Napoleonic Wars? Oh, yes. Spike their guns. Well, she'd done that. Now to see what he came back at her with.

"I am very fortunate, then, that the editors of our

esteemed historical journals do not answer to you when making decisions about publication. I have not seen any of your articles lately." He had a very odd accent. Most of it was a variation on the familiar schoolboy pronunciation, learned at Eton or Harrow or Rugby. But sometimes he veered into an Irish accent, and sometimes an accent unlike anything she'd heard before, even on the Continent. But she mustn't allow that to distract her from her intentions. So he had the backing of the academic journals. *She* had facts on her side.

"Yes, you are fortunate to be beloved by the Seebach publications in our shared antiquarian circles. I was working on a project which would have spawned several new articles, but…circumstances forced me to abandon it." She hoped her smile didn't look too much like baring teeth. "But if you'd like my advice on how to revise your pieces to preserve even a modicum of historical accuracy, you need only ask."

Something glittered in his dark eyes. At first, she thought it was anger, but then she realized it was humor. He was enjoying this as much as she.

"I believe the peer-review panel found my research to be more than adequately rigorous."

A thrill chased along her nerves and settled again between her hips: a low, dark, hot sensation. Was it entirely wrong to find one's nemesis devastatingly attractive? And the attraction was not, surprisingly, because he was gorgeous. Although he was. It was the wit, and the intelligence, and the willingness to engage with her as an equal. Sometimes, when fellow academics found out that Oliver Seward didn't have a cock and bollocks hanging betwixt his legs, they dismissed everything published under that name. Dr. Reilly didn't agree, but he did not dismiss her.

"And," he added, "if you should like to learn how to turn your dry and dusty facts into stories that people might actually wish to read, I would be more than happy to give you advice."

The hairs on Liv's neck raised and she tensed. Oh, he knew how to strike. She ought to feel insulted, even hurt, at his words, since it was true that she'd not been able to sell a single legitimate article lately, and she'd just lost her best chance at future publication. Instead, the sally excited her, jolting through her like a charge through a copper wire.

"Perhaps we can continue this discussion in the carriage? I believe you said our appointment was for ten of the clock. We'll be late."

He bowed to her, far more elaborately than etiquette demanded, making a single curl fall forward into his face. Curiously, he folded his hands in front of him when he did it, palm-to-palm, and murmured something in a language she didn't recognize.

Then she swept out of the room ahead of him. Her breath puffed more quickly and raggedly than usual, and she told herself it was the fault of the tight bodice and not because she was still weak from the vision. The same with her legs that ached by the time she strode down to the waiting carriage. The vehicle was Etta's, and had both the Clan Fay badge and the duchy's arms painted on the sides. She'd never felt like a member of the clan without a usable gift, but things could change.

If she learned to control the visions, and not let them suck her dry.

If she ever had a vision again.

But she thought Sorcha might be right about the magic drain. Liv's hair hadn't gone back to a medium-brown, and she still had far more awareness of other people's magic than she ever had before.

Perhaps a trip up to Scotland was in order. Etta had said

the drain wasn't as noticeable up there. Not that she was going to leave Dr. Reilly alone to complete this project.

A footman appeared to help her into the carriage, but she waved him off. She didn't have on a corset or narrow skirts that would throw off her sense of balance and range of motion, and had never before needed assistance climbing up the few steps into a carriage's dim interior.

She swayed a bit with vertigo at the top, and had to grasp the doorframe for balance. Damn it. She would not let Reilly see her weakness!

Just to be contrary, she took the rear-facing seat normally occupied by males in deference to a woman's delicate constitution. It was a mistake, given the queasy lurch of her belly and the feeling of weightlessness in her head, but he must not think her someone who could be cowed by something as insignificant as a social rule. Nor as a woman given to fainting and vapors. She'd never fainted in her life until these stupid visions started.

He said nothing, merely sat opposite her and folded his hands in his lap.

Liv kept her expression neutral as she launched her next attack. "The editors of *Walking Through History* said that they asked you for a rebuttal to my letter, but you declined. Why? Can you not make a strong enough case for your methods?"

He looked straight into her eyes, and it didn't matter that the day was overcast and the interior dusky. Liv thought she could see straight into his soul. A whirlwind of need spiraled through her, down to the marrow of her bones.

"To respond to your letter would be to acknowledge that I feel the need to defend anthropology as a field of study. I do not feel that need. Far more brilliant men and women than I have already done so, and much more eloquently than I could ever do."

And that, of course, missed the point of her article

entirely. "I don't have a problem with anthropology in the abstract. It's a fascinating idea. I simply do not believe we will ever have enough data to make your field sufficiently scientific. You will always be crippled by your need to make assumptions about the missing pieces. You can only fill in that empty space with things you comprehend, and the truth of the culture you study may be so far removed from yours that you could never imagine those who lived it."

"I don't disagree with you." Although his tone said he did. "But what good is it to compile charts and lists without asking how the things you find were used? How they affected the lives of their owners? How can we learn from them, if we see only a catalogue of broken pieces?" He'd had perfect posture when they sat down in the carriage, but now he leaned toward her and she could feel the energy and passion inside of him like an electrical current. It struck sparks inside of her, too, washing away her fatigue.

"But if you manufacture the lost fragments, we see only what *you* wish us to learn. Only the connections that *you* think we ought to make. That isn't truth."

"What is truth?"

Every single particle of her being alit with energy. She hadn't felt this good since the last day on the dig. Maybe not even then. "You wish to debate philosophy now?"

"Why not? Isn't that what this is about?"

The carriage went over an obstruction and he jostled toward her, their knees brushing. The heat of the contact surged up between her legs, intellectual stimulation melding with sexual need.

"Not at all. This is about empirical data. About tangible objects that you can touch, and feel, and know. What you tell are lies. Beautiful lies, perhaps, but still lies."

"You don't know that. Not everything I have written about can be proven beyond a doubt, but I don't speculate wildly. There are reasons for my conjectures, as I explain in all of my articles. And you can't prove I'm wrong."

He braced himself on the edge of the seat, his legs now between hers. Thank the goddess for rational dress and bloomers that allowed her greater mobility than the narrow-skirted dresses of fashionable women. It would take only a little hop to straddle him and kiss those full, delicious lips currently daring her to prove him wrong.

"I could, if I found the right artifacts. But it doesn't matter. It's damaging to the archaeological field to have this nonsense in print. Almost as bad as all of the 'curse of the mummy' stories written by people whose ideas about Egypt are formed from bad reproductions and objects taken literally out of context."

Reilly laughed, and the sound of it thrilled inside her ears. She wanted to capture the laugh with her mouth, press it deep within her lungs, and make him part of her. "I doubt any of the authors of those works are claiming to be historians, or that their readers expect accuracy in the depictions of ancient curses."

"It's ridiculous anyway. What sort of spell could last that long without constant renewal?"

"None, but that's not the point. People can still learn from the stories, even if they don't believe them to be true."

"That is a frightening thought."

He frowned, and even that was adorably arousing. "Not as frightening as what you're doing at night."

Olivia froze, the happy tingle in her blood turning to ice. Every muscle in her body came to a complete, rigid stillness. Even her lungs stopped, and her pulse hung suspended between heartbeats.

He knew. Somehow, he knew what she had done. How she'd imagined him and made herself climax with the thought of him in her mind.

Then the carriage jolted to a halt and the door opened by a helpfully prompt footman.

"That came out perhaps a little more strongly than I intended." Reilly attempted a smile, and ended somewhere between sheepish and annoyed. "My apologies. I'll explain inside."

Inside where? She wanted to ask, since the building in front of them was not the Society headquarters, but a converted warehouse in one of the lower-middle-class areas closer to the river. On the whitewashed bricks, someone had painted the words, "Ayah Home."

What was an ayah? And how was it that Reilly knew anything about what had happened last night, or any night?

Reilly finished talking to the footman about the old warehouse stables where they could rest the horses for the next hour, and held out his hand to her in the polite manner of a man taking a woman into a park or a play. But this was no society meeting place. This area was only a few steps up from the slums.

She still had a little extra energy from their argument in the carriage, so she ignored the arm and strode toward the building. He went ahead of her and opened the door.

Walking inside was like stepping into another world. All of the questions she'd contemplated asking faltered and fell away.

The scent of cooking hung heavy in the air, but Olivia could not identify a single spice from the mélange that filtered through her nostrils. Whatever it was made her mouth water. She hadn't had a decent meal since leaving France. Etta's cook, while competent, was also very British.

Nothing about this place conformed to Olivia's idea of a poor house. In her mind it should be dim, sparsely furnished, and with very little decoration. Neither did the building look like the common Victorian house, with its densely patterned wallpapers and dark wood paneling. But she refused to betray her ignorance. Here, bright fabrics hung on the walls, and the big warehouse windows let in massive pools of winter light. To the left was a long wall with doors at regular intervals. To the right was a big room with long tables and benches that looked like the dining hall of her Swiss boarding school.

"Is this some sort of school?" The question came out before she remembered that she wasn't going to ask him questions that would reveal her inexperience.

"In a way. I'll let Rajani explain."

One of the doors in the far wall opened, and a woman entered. Three other women were with her, each carrying a large bowl or dish. Two of the women wore European-style clothing in dull colors. The other two wore brilliant silks in shades that must be impossible to achieve without magic.

All four had skin of varying shades of brown, black hair, and dark eyes. One woman had skin nearly as dark as her hair, and one was almost the same shade as Dr. Reilly. The women placed their burdens on a nearby table and swarmed around Reilly, speaking to him in one of the Indian dialects. Olivia could read some transliterated Sanskrit, and she'd read that the current languages were all derived from that, but she'd never heard it pronounced, and it was like trying to interpret a conversation in French when one has only read Latin.

Once the clamor had died down, one of the women came forward. She spoke with a distinct accent, although not nearly as thick as the other women when they used English. "Welcome to the Ayah Home, Miss Seward." She inclined her head and pressed her palms together in front of her heart. "I am Rajani. This one here was once my charge, many years ago."

Reilly smiled fondly at the woman, who was extremely

short, plump, and wrapped in a length of orange-and-turquoise silk embroidered in pink and green thread. "Rajani Massi was my ayah, what you would call a nanny, back in India. She insisted on coming with us on the steamer when I was a boy, but after we made it to England, Grandfather told her he was cutting all ties with India and to go back."

"But how could I leave my *beta* all alone in this cold country?" She swatted his arm. "I could not. So I stayed, and I found a room at a boarding house with other ayahs, and ten years later I founded this place with the funding of some Academe missionaries who want to teach us their magic and convert us to following Wothan and Frigga."

The women all laughed. "But they are good-natured souls, and all of the women who stay here are taught to read and write in English so they are harder to take advantage of by unscrupulous families who would abandon them far from their homes."

"That sounds awful. Does it happen often?"

"Often enough. This is not a popular season for traveling, since it is warm in India and cold here. But come the spring, they will return, to go sit in Parliament, look after estates, and go to parties for the Season. Then our home will be full to bursting with women. Most of them will only stay with us a few weeks or months and then return to India or China, but these ladies here stay with me all year."

Reilly had allowed himself to be maneuvered onto one of the benches, and was filling a plate from the selection of foods on the table. Olivia sat opposite and did the same, trying a portion of everything.

"I thought Rajani Massi had gone back to India after we arrived here. I didn't know she was still in England until ten years later. My grandfather thought it was safe to give her letters to me after I finished at Radley, but the first thing I did was go to London to find her. Where else can I find good food with the proper garam masala mixture?"

Rajani laughed. "You don't eat enough of it. You're thin as a swami."

"Massi, I keep telling you I'm not that different from a swami."

"I don't like it. You need fattening up." She turned her perceptive dark gaze on Olivia. "You, too, Miss Olivia."

Usually, having someone speculate on her weight or eating habits made Olivia angry. But this woman clearly saw it as her responsibility to feed the world—or at least the people she liked in it—and that instant acceptance and caring stripped away her defenses.

It helped that the food was amazing. Every single bite burst with flavor, igniting responses from every inch of her mouth and nose. When she took a bite of a soft, custard-like substance, she almost choked on a startled exclamation.

This was the flavor of Reilly's magic. Smooth and cooling, but with a strong, spicy, delicious flavor.

"What is this?"

"That's raita, with chaat masala for flavor. When we have more ayahs in residence, they sometimes bring fresh fruits and vegetables from home, and then we can mix those in, too."

"It's delectable just the way it is."

Rajani beamed, and prodded Dr. Reilly. "You see? Even the English know to eat good food."

He frowned at her, but with affection, not anger.

After they ate, Rajani and the other women cleared away the dishes. Olivia offered to help wash up and was firmly denied. Instead, she and Dr. Reilly sat with cups of hot tea and were left alone in the dining hall.

"I assumed we were going to the Society first. Rajani is lovely, but why did you bring me here?" None of this made any sense. She'd already accepted that he wasn't anything like the monster she'd imagined, but the new box she'd tried to fit him into had burst open, too.

He gestured at the room and the wall-hangings. "I wanted you to experience something of the culture of my childhood."

"It's fantastic. But why?"

"Because in my experience, the English tend to underestimate my people, or anyone who isn't English."

"Now wait a moment—"

"You must admit that it's true, even if that isn't how you feel. But I wasn't sure how you would react, and I needed to know."

The accusation curdled in her belly, turning the pleasant warmth of the meal into bitter heat. "I like to think that I accept all people as they are, or at least I make a conscious attempt to do so."

"Trust me when I say you are rare for an Englishwoman. But I have something to tell you that is going to require an… open mind, and I wanted to see how open you were to alternative explanations and possibility."

She set her jaw and glared at him. "I'm open to anything you can prove to me with supporting evidence."

"Even if it contradicts everything you've been taught?" His eyebrows lifted in disbelieving query, his head tilting toward her as though daring her to accept his challenge.

"As I said. I'll consider your evidence and decide for myself."

"Very well." He leaned back and folded his hands in front of him, palms together, fingers laced. "You're having visions, but no one in your family can help you control them."

Olivia simply stared at him, her body gone even more rigid than when she thought he'd witnessed her pleasuring herself with thoughts of him. She hadn't said anything to him about the visions. She hadn't planned on telling him about them, either, because even if she could summon up a vision that would help them achieve their goal, she wouldn't be able to prove her source of information to him.

But he already *knew*.

"Twice now, I have discovered some of the…essence of you, what you might term as your magic, or your spirit, far from your body." He demonstrated this with his hands. "The second time was last night, although I don't think you were conscious of the journey yesterday."

Her limbs came back to life. Her heart contracted again, pushing blood out into her body, and the breath rushed out of her lungs. So when he spoke of her nighttime activities, he was talking about magic, not masturbation.

Confusion followed relief. Her magic was doing what? She remembered the dark space after the first vision, and the sexy male form that had helped her. Was that what he meant?

"How is that possible?"

"It is not, for most who follow the Academe and Magisterium practices of magic. But many of those in your tradition who have visions are able to do this subconsciously." Did she detect the slightest bit of condescension in the phrase *your tradition*, or was that her own reaction to being labeled with the magic of her mother's clan? "They rarely travel far outside of themselves, however. In fact, I have most often observed that they do not leave their physical bodies at all, but instead enter a trance-state that allows them to access the visions while still firmly rooted in their flesh."

"So if everyone who has visions does this, where's the danger?"

"As I said, most of them remain near or within their physical spaces." He touched one palm to the other. "You do not. Your talents seem to align more with the Sutra of my people. It is dangerous to allow your magic to wander outside of your body, and I believe you are not even aware that you are doing it. I have only discovered you twice, but if you have been having frequent visions, I would assume you are doing it much more often than that."

"What sort of danger are you talking about? Will I lose the ability to see visions? Honestly, that doesn't sound like such a bad thing, in the long run. They've not exactly been a joy to experience thus far." If she could control them, they would come in very handy for research. But she'd rather not have them at all than have them take over her body and mind.

"The part of you that accesses magic is leaving your body, Miss Seward. If it does not come back, or the thread that binds it to your flesh is broken, you will cease being…you."

Her insides turned to ice, not just frozen but sharp and piercing.

That was much worse than simply losing time, or feeling physically weakened.

"I see." She looked for prevarication in his eyes, for any hint that he exaggerated or played a joke. There was none. "Then how do I stop doing it?"

"I'm not suggesting that you stop." Was that hope in his expression, or simply concern? "I'm suggesting that you learn to direct it consciously, so that you can return to your body safely."

"How do I do that, then?"

"I will teach you."

"You just said that people who follow the European traditions of magic can't learn to do what you do. The Fay Method is different from the Academe and Magisterium schools, but it's formed on the same basic principles. What makes you think you can teach me?"

"You weren't trained in the Fay Method. You have never been trained at all."

Olivia's face flushed with heat. He could tell? She had the

oddest sensation of being tossed into the ocean having lived all her life in a desert. Their earlier gibes and ripostes had been easy and familiar, even fun. That was a language she spoke, a world she knew intimately.

This? This was snow to a native of the tropics.

"Is that why you brought me here, then? To see if I can learn to do magic your way?"

"I don't believe you'll have much of a choice. You're going to have to learn to control this, and the Sutra is the only way that you can learn."

She'd made such strong statements before about evidence and proof, but now that the choice was in front of her, she feared that the proof he was right would be her death—or worse than death—and then what good would her principles be?

And nothing Sorcha had tried had helped. What would be the harm in trying something else?

"Then I suppose you'd better teach me."

6

Something passed between them, then, something that turned the ice in her belly directly to steam. If he'd been anyone else, if she'd not promised herself not to mix sex and work again, she'd have launched her body across the space between them, straddled his hips, and sank into his mouth.

Even with those reasons not to, she still might have done it, had Rajani not come back into the room. Instead, she sucked in a ragged breath and curled her hands into tight fists against the impulse.

"Have you frightened the girl with your warnings, *beta?*" Rajani sat beside Olivia and took her hand. "Don't let this one scare you. He is always so serious, trying to be like his guru. But I remember the silly little boy who snuck sweets from the kitchens and cried when his favorite rabbit was killed by a fox."

"My childhood exploits aside, what she is doing is dangerous without training."

"Yes, yes. But you will train her, and all will be well." She stood, pulling Olivia to her feet.

After sitting for so long, her legs had gone stiff and sore

and Liv had to hold on to the edge of the table to support herself. Rajani waited with smiling patience, and then led her across the hall to one of the doors. On the other side was a shrine, with statues of various humanoid shapes, some with extra limbs, some with the heads of animals. A pile of pillows sat before an altar with a single oil lamp in the center.

"Go and light the flame. Let it speak to you. My *beta* can talk himself hoarse, but it's much better to see and to experience than to hear."

Olivia needed Rajani's help to lower herself to the pillows. Dr. Reilly had come into the room after them and he sat beside her, folding his legs beneath him and resting his hands on his thighs, palm-up. She mimicked his posture.

There were several long lucifers—match sticks that could be struck against any abrasive surface—but Reilly merely inclined his head toward the lamp, and the wick sprouted flame.

"Watch the flame. See how it bends with the air in the room. Feel its heat on your skin. Smell the smoke rising from its heart." He kept up a soft, lilting series of instructions, moving on to feeling the breath moving inside of her, to relaxing each and every muscle. And then, she could see something else in the flame.

It wasn't quite the Sight, at least not the way her family members described it. But there was *something* there, and it responded to the gentle brush of her mind, twisting the flame into a golden spiral.

The shock of touching it broke her concentration, and she came back to herself to see Dr. Reilly beaming at her. "Well done."

Pride swelled inside of her, stronger than she'd felt in years. Stronger even than when she'd published her first essay as Oliver. She wanted to go and laugh in her mother's face. She wasn't a failure. She could do *magic*.

On the ride to the Society, she peppered Dr. Reilly with questions. He answered them readily, explaining the philosophies behind the Sutra, how there were many schools and teachings, and how she would try all of them until Olivia found what way worked best for her.

He spoke of the astral plane, and visiting dreams, and sharing pieces of one's soul-magic for specific purposes, like creating stronger magical effects or staying in constant contact. She wasn't sure she believed she would eventually have that sort of control, but he painted a lovely picture and she would give much to see it come true.

They arrived at their destination just as he started outlining their training regimen, which was perfect timing, as she wanted to stop talking about what they would do and actually *do* it. They alighted from the carriage and she stared up at the big brick edifice of the Society.

She'd not been to the Society for the Exploration of the History of the Arcane and Mundane in years. Percy had taken her to a lecture, once, when she was too young to go out alone. But they still held a strong stigma against women researchers, sadly perpetuated by the nation's queen. Despite being their monarch, Queen Victoria often said a woman's place was to defer to her husband and not appear in public positions. Olivia couldn't disagree more. She wanted all women to have the freedom to publish and teach, and she had no intention of ever having a husband.

At the door of the Society, a man in livery ushered them inside. His uniform was a garish red with the Society's emblem embroidered on the breast of his coat. Liv stifled a laugh.

In a big office on the first floor that was nonetheless dwarfed by the enormous desk its owner had managed to squeeze into the room, a portly man wearing a grey suit rose and shook hands with Reilly.

"It's so good to see you again, Dr. Reilly. Everyone is excited about your lecture."

"I will enjoy presenting, as always." Reilly turned to Liv. "Sir Archibald Flemens, this is Miss Olivia Seward. I believe you are familiar with her work under the name Oliver Seward."

Sir Archibald stared at her, frozen in the act of bowing. She could have laughed. He'd thought he knew how to greet her, even with her short hair and rational dress, until he found out her nom de plume. She wished Reilly had told her he was going to introduce her as Oliver, though. She wouldn't have bothered with the bloomers. In some places in France, there were people who never knew her as anything *other* than Oliver, the pretty man who dug stuff up. But Reilly had likely thought only to make Sir Archibald aware of her work, and not how the other man might react to being presented with someone who did not match the assumptions he'd already made about Oliver Seward.

Sir Archibald gathered his dignity and completed the bow. "It is lovely to make your acquaintance finally, Miss Seward."

Liv stuck out her hand. After only a moment, he took it and shook. "I'm pleased to meet you in person, too, Sir Archibald."

Olivia tried to drop into the seat on the right-hand side of the massive desk with something approaching dignity, rather than the relief she felt to finally be sitting down again, and Dr. Reilly took the other. Sir Archibald sank into his stuffed leather chair, puffing out a breath and dragging his attention back to Reilly. "I understand you need to have a look in the records room and archives, and would like a list of our members with specialties or private collections including documents from the late seventeenth-century."

"That's correct. Miss Seward and I are working on a joint

project in that period." She gazed at him in mild shock, and he shot back an unrepentant grin. He'd just effectively eviscerated any hope she had of continuing to critique his methods in the Society journal, as she would appear to be an enormous hypocrite. And perhaps she was. But by working together, she might have a chance at publishing her own material again, and she couldn't decide how she felt about that.

Sir Archibald looked shocked, too. His mouth hung open, his mustaches dangling over his upper lip limply. At least Olivia wasn't the only one. "Ah. Yes. Well." He fidgeted on the desk and picked up a sheet of paper. "I've written some names and addresses here. You may apply to any of these members with our blessing. And of course, many of them will be here for the lecture next week."

"Thank you, Sir Archibald. I appreciate it." Reilly took the sheet and folded it, then slipped it into his pocket. "We'll just go to the archives. I'm not certain how long we'll be." He rose, and Olivia followed him to her feet.

"Take your time, take your time." Sir Archibald smiled widely, obviously relieved that they would soon be out of his presence. "No need to rush. I've taken the liberty of leaving out several blank books for notes and put the archivist at your disposal."

"My thanks. Shall we visit again when we depart, or should we see ourselves out?"

"No need to trouble yourselves. Come and go as you please."

"Thank you again." Dr. Reilly bowed, and again made the curious gesture with his hands, and said the same word he had before. N-something.

The man in livery appeared at the door and showed them into the archives. The archivist pointed them in the right direction, told them where to find his office, then disappeared.

"You must be beloved here, for them to leave you alone in the archives." Liv tried to keep the bitterness out of her tone, but she failed. They approached a free-standing bookcase stuffed with books, and she scanned the spines and labels affixed to older volumes. She ran her fingertips over some, enjoying the feel of old leather and newer paperboard.

"Not beloved, but respected, yes. Begrudgingly at first, but it has gotten better the last few years."

"Begrudgingly?"

He didn't have a chance to answer her question. As she reached up to pull a volume from the top shelf, her body jostled the bookcase. The next thing she knew she was staggering sideways, pulled by Reilly's sharp grip on her arm. She stumbled and would have fallen, but he wrapped his arms around her to keep her steady.

A large bust of Ovid thunked to the carpet with a crack of wood splintering beneath. By yanking her out of the way, he'd saved her skull from the same fate.

Tremors of reaction wracked her body, and her pulse thundered like stampeding hoofbeats. His arms clasped her tight against a lean, sculpted chest, her ear pressed to his throat, his heartbeat curiously steady in contrast with her wild and erratic one.

He held her for a small eternity, and she remembered his calm voice showing her the flame, and the way her body had reacted to him in the carriage. For a moment she leaned into the touch. Warmth curled into her like creeping vines, and she tasted his magic again, spicy and sweet.

Liv pulled away. She'd promised herself. No more sex and work. Especially no sex and teachers, even if Reilly didn't have the same control over her as her instructors at boarding school.

She leaned to pick up the bust, but it was far too heavy. Even at her best, she wouldn't have been able to lift it, and with her weakness now, it was out of the question.

Reilly nudged it with his toe. "It's too heavy for me, too. I wonder how it fell?"

"I rocked the case a little. Maybe the room is out of level, and it's been slowly shifting toward the edge for years."

"Maybe." But he didn't sound convinced.

The archivist appeared, glowering at them as though they'd set out to disturb his peace as much as possible. He and Reilly together were able to lift the bust onto a table, and as he left, he glared and told them to take better care and not jostle the bookcases.

Olivia reached again for the book she'd seen before, giggling. In retrospect, the incident took on a more amusing tone. Yes, she could have been hurt or even killed. But it was just a freak accident. With another glance at the bust, Reilly turned to the stacks as well.

Neither of them spoke while they examined the volumes in the seventeenth century section. The surge of fear and pendulum swing to relief had left Olivia drained, and she didn't think she was up to her former banter. She'd rather avoid speaking than find herself swept away by him.

Because, damn it, the more she got to know Dr. Reilly, the better she liked him, invented historical narratives aside.

After a while, they both had an armload of books to take to the big table in the center of the archives area. They sat on opposite sides of the table and started scanning through their chosen volumes, making notes as necessary.

Liv covered several pages with lists of names of people who were likely to have been involved with such a major spellcasting and might have written about it in a journal or letters to a friend. Those types of documents would be their best option to discover what had happened two hundred years ago.

After a while, her hand cramped, and she stopped to massage the muscles at the base of her thumb and the webbing between thumb and forefinger. When she looked up from her ministrations, Dr. Reilly was staring at her.

He had an inquisitive expression on his face, something between curiosity and perplexity. Was he thinking about her strange magic? About how to teach her not to kill herself? She hoped so, even though he should be concentrating on their task at the moment. Or was she doing—whatever that was—right now?

Frightened, she blurted, "Why are you staring at me like that?"

He blinked, and his head jerked. His gaze found hers. "My apologies. I didn't mean to stare at you. I was taking a break, as you were, but I put myself into a light trance state. I will teach you to do this, too."

"Oh. I was afraid, from your expression, that I might be… doing it again. Sending my magic off, or whatever it is that I do."

"Not at this moment. You are all here, and whole."

"That's wonderful to hear." And it was. The relief swept through her like a warm breeze. "Have you found anything of note yet?"

"Nothing except possibilities for further inquiry. You?"

"The same." Liv's fingers tapped an irregular beat against the page where she'd been making notes. "But we knew there wasn't much chance that we'd find what we were looking for in easily-available volumes. We're going to have to hope that one of the people on that list Sir Archibald gave you has a collection that includes personal papers for someone who was indiscreet enough to write down what secret spells they were casting."

"What intrigues me is that this took so long for anyone to notice. Etta said that your first duchess noticed it in the late eighteenth century, when she was a young woman and first went to England. But it got worse throughout this century. If it had been going on for a hundred years before the first duchess discovered it, how did no one else notice?"

"I don't know, but that is an interesting question." Olivia's tapping fingers curled into a fist. "If only I could just have a vision about it. That would save us from what could turn out to be a fruitless search."

"Explain your visions to me, please. It may help me find the cause of your wanderings."

Olivia hesitated. She hated feeling on uneven ground with him, but she'd agreed to be his student in magic. She would have to get used to the sensation. And it would not help her to withhold information that might assist his instruction.

"I was born with a very small amount of natural magic. More than the tiny spark that everyone has, regardless of magic talent, but not enough to cast spells in the European fashion. Not even using the Fay method. I might have learned to do something very, very small if I studied diligently and practiced often. But it didn't seem worth the effort, and my mother…" No, he didn't need to know about that. "Anyway, I chose not to pursue it."

She picked up the wooden pen she'd been using and tapped it on the blank page. "Instead, I became an archaeologist. I specialize in arcane archaeology, since I have enough talent to sense magical artifacts and have spent my life around mages and witches. But until a little over a week ago, nothing particularly magical had ever happened to me."

"A week ago is the first time your magic left your body. You were caught in a spell. You must have been caught for days, as it was only a few days ago that I found you. I did not stay to discover how it happened, but brought you immediately back to yourself."

Liv's heart squeezed in her chest. He'd mentioned it before, but this time she was forced to face the truth that the gorgeous apparition after her first vision, the one that had made her feel warm and safe and cared for, had been Dr. Reilly.

She couldn't call him that anymore, not after he'd helped her out of the awful place her vision had left her.

No more formality, at least not in her mind. She would think of him as Alexander.

"That *was* you." She couldn't tear her gaze from his, even if she wanted to. "It was awful. The vision itself hadn't been too bad, but the witch in the vision saw me, too. She was about to be executed and I think she had just enough power left to try and reach me over the centuries. But whatever she did caught me up inside it and wouldn't let me go."

"Yes. I freed you."

"Thank you. I don't think I would have ever woken up, otherwise." She was sure of it, now, after he'd told her the dangers. Or, if she'd woken up, she wouldn't have been herself anymore. "When I did wake, my hair was like this." She tugged at one of the longer pieces that framed her face.

"It used to be the color of your eyebrows?"

"A little lighter. Medium brown with a little red in it. Now it's…whatever color this is."

"White opal," he said, certain. "Sometimes a little silver, or pearl, but there is a fire and a shimmer to it, like the inside of a seashell."

Her cheeks warmed at this very specific and flattering appraisal. When she'd tried to define the color, she hadn't been nearly so poetic. "Like I said, it's hard to call it one color. But it's the same as the streak in all of the magical members of Clan Fay's hair. Usually we just get a little bit over the left eye. Sometimes a particularly strong mage or witch will get a very wide streak. Lilias had two of them, one on each side."

"Lilias was the first duchess?"

"Yes. Anyway, after that I kept having the visions, but none of the rest of them ended like the first. They were just very vivid experiences of the past, mostly things from my most recent dig site in Labourd and a few from the history of Calais. Then some random things as we crossed the Channel. But I haven't had a single vision since we returned to England."

"That makes sense. With the drain pulling so much magic away, your gift doesn't have much to interact with. That might explain why it sought me out last night."

Olivia's entire face flamed with heat at the memory of last night. Did he know what she had done? Just how much could one see when wandering away from one's body in spirit form? She decided not to ask, since unlike the first time she'd wandered away from her body, she hadn't been aware of the second one. She did *not* want to know what he had seen.

"Do you think you might be able to help me trigger a vision?"

"With practice, yes."

"I want to try."

"Now? That's not wise."

"Why not now? We're both here. It's quiet. No one will interrupt us."

Alexander stared into her for a long, uneasy moment. Then he nodded. "Very well." He stood and came around the table to sit beside her. "Take my hands, and do everything I tell you to do."

7

Savit held back the shudder that threatened when his bare skin touched Olivia's. As before, her magic leapt toward him with unpracticed alacrity. He braced for the impact of it. He hadn't consciously sought to mingle his magic with another's since Chaitan, his guru and mentor, had gone to America.

With some effort, he managed to hold back the initial surge, and spoke to her using the same words Chaitan had the first time Savit had learned to go into a trance. He told her to breathe, to relax her body bit-by-bit, to open her mind to the universe and the divine. With every step, her magic sank deeper into him, like pebbles falling down into a still pool.

The ripples of her contact danced out along his body, and then he heard his voice say, "Why didn't you tell me you don't like to be called Alex?"

She was too far inside him, too aware of what she saw, too untrained to hold back her enthusiastic explorations. He built walls of ice between them, and her hands in his trembled. He gently pushed her back to a safe, public space in his mind, and took control of his voice again. "I didn't know that's how you thought of me."

Then she was out of his head, her hazel eyes blinking up at him. "What just happened there? I didn't mean to make *you* talk."

"Our gifts are reacting to each other and welcoming the other's presence. Your soul and mine recognize each other." Even now that they'd separated, the awareness of her throbbed within him, a resonance that his mind could not deny.

"How could that be? We've never met before yesterday."

"Not in this life, or these bodies, no. But in some other life, yes." He wouldn't say what he was coming to suspect: that they'd been lovers, most likely husband and wife. He didn't want to delve too deeply into that shared past. He did not believe he owed it to that past self to connect with a lost love.

"Another life?" Her confused expression was far too adorable, and he doubted she wore it often. He hadn't intended to discuss the afterlife and reincarnation for weeks yet, as they were not pertinent to her most pressing training needs, but it seemed that fate had forced his hand by bringing him together with his—he refused to call her a soul mate. Prior life mate, and that was all.

"Our souls are both tied to our flesh and transcendent beyond it. When our bodies die, our souls experience the karma they have gained while in the flesh, and then begin again in a new form."

"Is that true of everyone, or just mages who follow your type of magic?"

"Everyone. We are all born with the divine spark inside of us." He couldn't help a tiny smile. "But few people in the European traditions believe this truth."

"Maybe I'll be able to see something of that past life, someday. But not today." She rubbed at her head.

She shouldn't have been so drained from the few things they'd done today. He'd underestimated just how weak that initial vision had left her, physically.

"I think we'd better stop for now." He didn't want to stop. He wanted to try again to show her how to safely inhabit her spirit body. But he would need to think of a way to keep her from draining all of her physical resources before their next lesson, and in any case he didn't have time to try again now.

In order to call on the people on Sir Archibald's list, he'd need to leave, or risk missing calling hours. As it was, he would likely have to send around notes to many of them instead of going in person. He pulled the list out of his pocket.

"I will make arrangements for us to visit these people and see if they are willing to share their collections and knowledge. I'll send a message letting you know what appointments I'm able to make, and I will see you tomorrow for our next lesson, whether or not I can convince anyone to see us on such short notice."

Her lower lip peaked out in a sulky pout, but then thinned as she pressed her lips together. "Are you sure you don't need my help?"

"While your company would be welcome, I don't want you to overtax yourself. If you press your body too far in an attempt to do things quickly, you will collapse and then lose more time recovering."

Olivia's expression was still grim, but she sighed and gave him a nearly imperceptible nod in agreement.

She stood, a little shaky on her feet, and brushed down the peplum of her tightly-fitted jacket. The motion emphasized the curve of her waist and the flare of her hip. The muscles in his lower abdomen tightened, the only physical reaction he would allow to the desire that welled up within him.

She didn't turn in his direction, instead bracing herself against the table and contemplating the stacks. "I want to look around more here, and later I'll try the library at Skye House. Lilias hoarded books obsessively, and she might have something in her collection that will help. She didn't know when the drain started, so she wouldn't have known where to look. Now I have some ideas."

"Agreed. Would you like me to leave you the carriage? I can hire a cab."

"No, you have more places to go than I do. Etta won't mind if you keep using it. She has another one, and I can telegram her from here to send it over, or hire a cab. It's not far."

"Don't stay too long. I can see your head is aching." He could see it, and wanted to do something about it, but didn't think she would welcome his touch just now.

"I'm fine." She crossed to the bookcases and leaned against the end of one. "I'll reach out to the few people I know here in London who are interested in such recent history. And who knows? Maybe I'll finally have another vision."

"I wouldn't be so excited at the prospect if I were you. If that happens, send word to me immediately. My hotel isn't far from Skye House, and I can join you in spirit long before I can reach you in body." But even as he said it, he knew it would never be fast enough.

"I'll ask the staff and the family to keep an eye on me during the day. At night, though, I can't make any promises."

"Then we'll have to find another solution. Rajani teased, but I am not joking about how dangerous it is for your spirit to wander." So dangerous it chilled his blood to consider it.

"How can I stop it when I don't know I'm doing it?" Her

voice held just a trace of panic. He hadn't meant to frighten her that badly, but he did need to instill the proper respect for the perils of astral travel.

"I believe the only answer at this juncture is for me to be constantly vigilant, and watch for you to project again."

"But you won't be with me." Her confusion was palpable, as was her annoyance. He could already tell that she hated to be in the dark about anything, and always needed to understand.

"Not in flesh, but in spirit."

"Oh. Can you do that? I mean, you're going to be meeting people and going places. How can you do both things at once?"

"I won't be hovering over you in spirit form. I'll keep a small piece of my magic trained on you. It's similar to how you can worry over a problem, then go do something else. Your mind works on the issue while you're distracted, and then presents you with a solution later."

"So I'll be in the back of your head?"

"Something like that, yes."

"Well, if we're lucky, you won't have to bring me to the front."

He hoped he wouldn't, but in case he would, he sent a few tendrils of his consciousness into her, touching only lightly enough to be alerted if she went into another trance or had a vision.

He would keep this vigil over her, just in case.

OLIVIA SAGGED AGAINST A BOOKCASE ONCE REILLY LEFT. Damn it, what should she call him? In that muddle of connection, she'd sensed his dislike of the name Alexander, but then she'd been distracted by everything going on and had forgotten to ask what he *wanted* to be called. Which was vexing, because it meant she had to go back to Reilly until they spoke again.

More vexing was that connection. They'd blended so naturally, and if reincarnation was real as he claimed, she didn't doubt his assertion that their souls had once been close in another life. The familiarity had shocked her even during their first meeting yesterday. Discovering that his magic was a close reflection of hers had felt almost inevitable.

Being apart again was a relief. She needed time to work through these feelings and emotions, time to deal with the enormity of new magic, and new desire.

Because what she had felt, stronger than anything else when their magic merged, was a craving so fierce she'd flushed and grown wet.

Afterward, all the reasons why the connection between them was a mistake came rushing back. Especially when he so casually took over the next stages of the investigation, forcing her to remain behind and rest. The fact that he was right about her frailty was of no import. He shouldn't have just assumed that he could take the lead.

As much as she was coming to like him, and for all that her body was ready to take his in any number of inventive and carnal ways, he was still the overbearing Dr. Reilly of his articles, making assumptions and filling in information when he didn't understand the subtle nuances of his subject matter.

Just because some of his guesses were right didn't justify his actions.

Olivia pulled more books down and brought them over to the table. She'd found several mentions of the major witches and mages of the era in the general histories, but she wanted to narrow her search to the ones most likely to have cast a spell of this magnitude—the Sorcerers and Sorceresses attached to the monarchs.

She'd just opened a book called *King and Mage: A History of Magical Advisors to the Crown*, when a woman in a plain, dark-grey dress entered the archives. The woman had brown hair, a swarthy complexion that suggested either time spent in the sun or a non-English heritage like Dr. Reilly's, and cool blue eyes.

"Ach!" The woman stopped just past the doorframe, clutching a stack of books against her chest. "I didn't realize ze room was in use. I can return zis later." Her accent wasn't British, but it wasn't from anywhere that Olivia would have guessed, either. Oddly, she spoke as though German was her first language.

"No, no. You're fine. I shouldn't have stayed this long." Olivia pushed her chair back and moved to stand, but the woman waved her back.

"You are a guest. You may stay as long as you like." She put the books down at one end of the table. "It's my job to assist the archivist, and he's gone out. Is there something I can help you find?"

"Maybe. Do you know much about magical history?"

The woman nodded and pulled out the chair beside Olivia. "Ja. I'm a vitch myself."

"Oh. Academe?"

She nodded. "I'm Mina. Wilhelmina"—she said it Vilhemina—"Jones. From Potsdam, originally. My father is British, my mother Prussian. We lived there until I was fourteen, and now we are here in England." Her accent faded a bit as she spoke, and Olivia guessed that the earlier thickness had been a result of surprise.

"I'm Olivia Seward. I grew up here, but I've been living on the Continent since I was thirteen. So I know what it feels like to be pulled away from your home and sent somewhere else."

This bit of shared history brought a smile to Mina's lips, and Liv's body warmed as their gazes met. This was just what she needed to distract herself from the infuriating and too-attractive Dr. Reilly.

Olivia reached out a hand and covered the other woman's, leaning close enough that their mouths were only inches away. Mina wore gloves, so the contact wasn't skin-to-skin and no magic swirled between them, but it still made Liv's heart rate accelerate.

But then Mina turned her head away, staring intently at anything that wasn't Olivia, and a rush of disappointment whispered through Olivia. The woman was flustered, her lovely chest rising and falling in rapid exhalations, but was that from sexual interest or embarrassment? Over the years, Olivia had only had five female lovers, and nearly all of those were in boarding school. Most women of her acquaintance were only interested in men.

Mina looked enough like Talya—blue eyes, elfin face, voluptuous body—that a pang of longing and memory filled Olivia, then dissipated like smoke.

"What time period are you researching?" Mina asked, discreetly pulling away her hand.

Olivia explained their goal. She didn't divulge the theft of English magic—that, Etta had told her, was a state secret—but she did say that she'd learned of a large-scale spell cast around the time of the Glorious Revolution and hinted that she wanted to write an article on it.

Mina directed her to a different section of the archive, with texts written in languages other than English. "There are several histories here in Dutch and German that might give you a different perspective, since William was Dutch."

"If they're in German, I can read them, but I don't know

Dutch." She spoke English, Gaelic, German, French, and Latin, and could read Greek, Anglo-Saxon, and some Sanskrit as well, as long as it had been transliterated from Devanāgarī script into Roman letters. She'd picked up conversational Italian while working in Italy, but wouldn't call herself fluent. The same was true of Dutch. She'd been able to make herself understood in the Netherlands, and had been able to puzzle out some of what she heard, but reading was another matter.

"Ah. I would be happy to take a look and translate any relevant passages for you."

"Oh, would you? That would be most helpful."

They settled in with several books and notebooks and worked for another hour. A grandfather clock in the corner chimed, and Mina looked up and put down her pen. "Time for me to go home. Would you like to share a cab?"

Liv stretched her shoulders back and tilted her head side-to-side to ease the ache from leaning over the books. She shouldn't be so stiff after such a small amount of time. Before, she'd been able to spend hours digging or doing research without this much pain.

Another product of the visions.

But at least she'd have pleasant company on the ride home. "That would be lovely. Where do you live?"

"In Chelsea, near Belgrave Square."

"Oh. I'm in Kensington, off Holland Park." Skye House had been built on the edges of what had been the boundaries of London at the time. As a result, it had an unusually large piece of property attached. The space represented a luxury for most, but had been considered a necessity by Lilias Fay, who had grown up with the open vistas on Skye in Scotland. Chelsea was a bit more cramped, but made sense for a well-to-do diplomat's family.

Olivia gathered up her notes and accepted the pages from

Mina, who took a moment to shelve the books before leading the way out into the chilly late-afternoon. Olivia pretended that she'd simply allowed the woman to do her job, but the truth was she didn't think she would be able to carry the books across the room and reshelve them.

The walk out to the street felt interminable. The day's earlier freezing drizzle had cleared, leaving a smattering of grey clouds drifting overhead and a wan blue sky peeking through.

The stink of coal smoke and millions of bodies engaged in the activities of daily life assaulted Liv. She'd gotten used to the clean country air of the French coast, and this miasma wasn't helping lungs already weakened by her visions. She had to stop and take a few deep, gasping breaths while Mina continued to the cabstand on the corner.

There were two vehicles available. They chose the larger and both women gave their addresses to the cabman. Olivia complained of the air after she could no longer suppress a cough.

Mina patted her hand in a conciliatory gesture. "You'll get used to it eventually. I thought the same thing when we first moved here."

"I don't know that I want to get used to it. I imagine it's doing considerable damage to my insides."

"Perhaps. But it's worth it."

"Do you love the city that much?"

"Not the city for itself, no. But my work here, for the Society, yes."

"I can understand that. And maybe that's why I'm so keen to be gone. My work is elsewhere."

Mina asked about her work, and Olivia spent the rest of the ride pontificating on her new grid system and how she had perfected a process for logging soil samples with every discovery and subjecting them to both magical and scientific testing to learn more about the state of the world in the past as well as the artifacts unearthed.

"It all sounds so fascinating." Mina sat forward on the seat, her upper body twisted and leaning toward Olivia to take in her words.

Again, Olivia wished that even a smidgen of that interest was for her, physically. She decided to try again to see if Mina might respond to an advance, and she shifted so that their legs touched all down one side. Mina tensed, and moved discreetly away.

That answered that question. Her interest was entirely intellectual. Pity.

As the Society's headquarters were in Notting Hill, the driver called out Skye House's stop first. Mina asked the driver to wait and got out with Olivia.

They stood on the side of the street, Mina still asking questions. Eventually the cabman complained, and they laughed.

"I should go before he drives off," Mina said, and extended her hand. Olivia held out her free one to shake. But before they made contact, Mina shifted and pushed Olivia, hard.

Tyres squealed. Shouts, and the screams of horses rent the air. Liv landed beneath Mina and her head cracked against the curb. The world darkened, then returned to painful brilliance.

Mina leaned over her, asking something. A plaid-garbed footman was offering his arm. She took it, and he pulled her to her feet.

"I'm fine." Her insides felt like they'd been through a whirlwind, she'd likely have several bruises, and her head ached, but she'd sustained no major injuries.

"Ach, I'm so glad." Mina pulled her into an impulsive hug. The footman gathered up her papers where they'd been strewn across the footpath and handed them to her once Mina let go.

"What happened?"

Mina pulled away. "One of zose new autos! *Der dumme Fahrer* almost hit us."

"I saw everything," said the footman. He had a thick Scottish accent, as did most of the servants at Skye House. "He took the turn that end of the street too fast and swung too wide. It's icy and he skidded. He corrected just in time, but if you hadn't pushed out of the way, Miss, he'd've hit you both."

"It seems I owe you my life, or at least my lack of broken bones." Olivia took Mina's hands in hers and leaned forward to kiss Mina's cheeks, European-fashion. With their skin touching, she could sense Mina's magic, fire-bright and redolent of rosemary. "Thank you." The other woman looked flustered, but not displeased.

"Anyone vould have done ze same." She smiled shyly.

The cab driver shouted, "Oi! If you're wanting to go to Chelsea, get on before another of those rich idiots comes through."

Mina backed away. "I'll keep looking for information for you in my free time. Perhaps we can take tea later this week?"

"Absolutely. I'll send a note around to the Society."

"I look forward to it."

Mina disappeared into the cab, and the driver snapped the reins to urge the horses into motion. He clearly wanted out of the area, and fast.

"Do you need a hand into the house?" the footman asked Olivia.

"No. In fact, I think I'd like a bit of a walk to clear my head." Energy pulsed through her as a result of the accident, and she needed to *move*. "I'll just head over to the Royal Crescent, and then come back. But I'd appreciate it if you take my things inside and put them in my room."

He nodded and went into the house.

The Royal Crescent Garden was a little closer to the house than Holland Park, and was intended as a pedestrian park, with benches and a little wooded area where residents could relax and walk their dogs. By the time she got there, most of the burst of manic strength was gone, leaving her shuddering.

Liv dropped onto the first bench inside the screening row of trees and slumped back against the hard slats. Now that the initial reaction was gone, she ached everywhere. Her whole side would be bruised by tomorrow, and she suspected she had a cut on her cheek from the way it stung. Her hands were a mess of scrapes and bits of dirt and stone stuck in the cuts. She would have to clean them when she got back.

Fortunately, she had the park nearly to herself—despite the cessation of rain, it was too cold and damp for casual visitors today. That meant she could be alone with her thoughts—and her misery.

Why hadn't she recovered yet? All she'd done was sleep for five days. She ought to feel wonderful after getting that much rest. Yet her body was as weak as though she'd been running without sleep for the same amount of time, with no food or water.

She didn't want to think about the vision that had drained her—or the lingering memories of Izarra's torture at the hands of the Magisterium.

Instead, she huddled deeper into her cloak and contemplated the trees and grass, pretending that the tremors wracking her body were from the cold, and not delayed reaction to danger. Twice in one day. Maybe her new magical skills affected chance and probability?

No, she didn't believe that. But what reason would anyone have to want her dead? It must be coincidence.

Enough. Think about something else.

What had she learned today? Not much. She'd reacquainted herself with some facts, like the names of the major magical figures of the time: Eleanor Collins, sorceress to Anne; Leopold van der Bron, sorcerer to William and Mary; Richard Chauncy, Arch-Mage of Canterbury; and Daniel Gage, sorcerer to James II.

But those names, despite coming complete with biographical data such as date and place of birth, major accomplishments, education, and more, told her almost nothing about what was happening during the upheaval of 1688.

Why wasn't she able to have a vision? They'd come so easily in France, and on the boat here. She dug her boot heels into the muddy ground beneath the bench. Maybe if she connected herself literally to British soil that would help. Etta had said that the spell was draining the deep magic, but there had to be some left.

Maybe the connection aided her magic, or her contemplation of the major figures, because she blinked, and when her eyelids lifted, she was somewhere—and some*when*—else.

8

S avit's spirit-body slipped through the currents of magic
that tangled and rippled over London, following the
pulse of warning he'd gotten from the magic he'd left with
Olivia.

Thank the gods that the meeting he'd just left was on the
same side of the Thames as Skye House, because crossing
running water in this form was dangerous at close distances.
He could have gone high into the sky to avoid the shifting
currents, but that would put him too far away to do any good
to Olivia. Even without that danger, he was physically too far
away from her. Tomorrow he would see about finding lodgings closer to Skye House. If she had another vision and left
her body behind, he wanted to be near her in body as well as
spirit.

He found her not in the house, but in a nearby park,
blazing with light, her subtle body already hovering a few
inches beyond her flesh that was connected with the earth. It
was almost as though she'd projected it there. She was
already in the grip of another vision. He would never reach
her in time physically, so he let his subtle body drift to hers,

and put his arms around her to keep her spirit anchored in her flesh.

The vision opened like a flower.

Light flooded the colored windowpanes of an ornately decorated chamber. A long table, covered in a thick panel of embroidered satin and strewn with papers, candelabras, and serving dishes, filled the room. Many people sat around the table, dressed in rich fabrics studded with gold thread and polished cabochon gemstones. The man at the head of the table wore a thick filet-style crown.

Savit searched through the room and finally found Olivia. She was wispy—insubstantial—until he grasped her hand. Then she solidified, perhaps too much. Magical energy pulsed through her, and he held tight. He wouldn't allow her to be lost to the vision.

Focus, Olivia, he thought to her. *There is something here we need to see. Find it.*

She led him past the courtiers at the bottom of the table and up to the man wearing the filet. Two women sat on either side of him, both wearing their own thin crowns. *That's William, Mary, and Anne,* Olivia told him. *I think the woman to Anne's right is Eleanor Collins, who will become her Queen's Sorceress when she takes the throne. I know that the man to Anne's left is Leopold van der Bron, the King's Sorcerer. He looks the same as in his official portrait. Eleanor was older when hers was painted.*

Savit studied the group. They were talking animatedly, but he could hear nothing. *What are they saying?*

Olivia concentrated, the delicate fingers of her subtle body's hand squeezing his. Sounds drifted across his spirit-ears. Voices.

"I don't want to let him go," Queen Mary said. "Even to appease the Magisterium. He dropped the Great Seal into the Thames! All of that magic, lost forever!"

"We must, Mary," William insisted. "And if Leopold is correct, we won't need the Seal."

"The spell is ancient, but it will work." Leopold tapped a cylindrical case, presumably holding a scroll containing the spell in question.

"How can you be sure?" asked Eleanor. "It hasn't been used since Roman times, and we know how well that turned out for Hadrian."

"It wasn't Hadrian's fault his predecessor was a fool. Trajan should never have extended his reach so far onto this isle or into the newly conquered territories. He tried to force his subjects to become Roman. Yours are already determinately English. It will work." The sorcerer spoke with assurance, but here in the realm of memory, the truth of his doubt resonated.

He isn't as certain as he would like them to believe, Olivia said, echoing Savit's thoughts. *But history will prove him correct. Whatever spell they cast is still working now. Still, if they meant it to help consolidate power for William and Mary, why is it taking magic away from England two hundred years later?*

The conversation between the monarchs and their mages continued, once again silent as Olivia had stopped paying attention.

Seek out the answer to your question.

She tried, but she was tired, and he'd pushed her too far. *Never mind. You need to go back to your body and rest. Come with me.*

She resisted, of course, pulling free of his grasp and pushing herself across the vision-room. The magic pulsing through her weakened, the thread holding her to her body thin as a tendril of smoke from a dying flame.

Olivia!

He followed her and grabbed her around the middle, hauling her back from the group. The vision popped like a bubble, leaving them in the park again, her physical body slumped on a bench beside them.

Damn it! She squirmed in his hold. *We needed to hear more!*

*It was too dangerous. You **must** listen to me in the visions. Do you see that wisp, like a thread, connecting you to your body?*

Her spirit-form turned and looked, and he drew her attention again with a tug on her hand. *Now look at mine.*

She floated up a little, peeking over his shoulder. He didn't need to check to know that his cord was thick and strong, pulsing with energy.

When you push into the visions, you're draining every last drop of magical and life energy out of yourself, and that makes the cord thin out and destabilize. If it snaps or fades, you will be lost. You must not allow that to happen.

I understand. Sober and a little sullen, she moved out of his embrace. He explained that she had tapped into the earth magic, and must now recall her spirit body into her physical one. She grasped the concepts quickly and merged down into her flesh.

Her eyes opened, their startling multitude of colors now glassed-over with fatigue. She frowned and looked around her. She couldn't see him anymore. Eventually, he would teach her to see spirit forms while still inhabiting her body, but first she had to get these visions under control.

Olivia stood and staggered, gripping the bench so as not to fall. A moment later, she collected herself and limped off. If he were here in the flesh, he would help her, but he wasn't, and he would never make it here before she made the short trip home, even at her slow, halting pace. Spirit bodies didn't breathe or sigh, but if he could, he would have, as a surge of admiration, frustration, and resignation flowed through him.

She'd just reached the corner of the road that led to Skye House when a woman with pale blond hair came around the bend and wrapped an arm around her. It was Ronan's wife,

Sorcha. The two women walked slowly down the street. They ascended the steps and disappeared inside the house, and Savit left her to her family's care. With a touch of his magic still snagged on her, just in case.

OLIVIA'S HEAD STILL ACHED, AND SO DID EVERY MUSCLE AND joint in her body by the time she alighted on the gravel walk in front of Skye House. Sorcha hadn't said a word since she'd marched up and put her arm around Olivia's chest. Liv hadn't wanted to accept her help, and almost pulled away, but she was so tired and hurt so much that she reluctantly rested part of her weight on her diminutive cousin. It helped that Sorcha offered no pity or words of sympathy, just her arm and her body to lean against. Sorcha took them at a slow pace up the walk, and still said nothing about Liv's worsened state.

The lack of chatter left her mind free to worry over everything that had just happened. This vision had stripped her physical reserves in ways that only the first vision with Izarra had done. She would need to discuss her theories with Reilly later, but she thought that the earth magic had given her the extra kick she needed to have one—and then wasn't enough to sustain what she'd tried to do next.

Damn him for pulling her out, and for being right to do it. There were few things Olivia hated more in the world than both not being able to do something she'd set her mind to *and* being wrong at the same time.

They took the steps very slowly, resting both feet on a step before attempting the next. Sorcha still said nothing, and Olivia didn't need to ask how she'd known to come. Sorcha had explained that her intuition was much stronger than her visions. She knew when she was needed.

MacGroarty opened the door and ushered her and Sorcha inside, taking their heavy coats and murmuring that the family was in the second-floor parlor. He put extra emphasis on the word family, but she was too drained from the tumultuous events of the day and especially the magic, first with Reilly and now the vision, to do more than idly speculate about it. Sorcha tried to help her again, but she'd regained enough energy to move about under her own power now.

The footman from before must have mentioned her injuries, because MacGroarty had a basin of warm water ready and several cloths. Liv cleaned her hands and Sorcha dabbed at the cut on her cheek, which had already scabbed over.

After she looked more presentable, she mounted the steps, holding heavily onto the railing until she reached the second floor parlor. The footman from this afternoon reached to open the door. She stopped him with a wave. "What's your name?" she asked him. He glanced down. She was of more than average height for a woman, but all of the men in the employ of Skye House seemed to be strapping Highlanders, much taller than average, with nary an ounce of fat between them.

"Gillies, ma'am. Euan Gillies."

"Thank you for your assistance today, Gillies."

"You're welcome, ma'am."

"Oh, please, call me Liv. Or if you insist on formality, Miss Olivia."

That surprised a chuckle out of him, but he nodded and said, "Very well, Miss Olivia." Apparently he'd chosen formality. She'd bring him 'round eventually. Finally he opened the parlor door.

Inside was chaos.

Sorcha went inside, but Liv halted on the threshold, staring. The duchess was on the floor with a toddler, playing a game with a series of colored blocks that the toddler had stacked and now, apparently, was happily knocking over. Mal was on a settee with the other twin perched on his knees. The little boy clutched his hands and squealed with glee as he bounced his legs.

The parents of the children—her perfect older sister Viola and her husband Ian—sat across the room on a sofa, flanked by Ronan and Sorcha, who'd just settled into an armchair that matched her husband's. Lady Cecily Seward, Marchioness of Hazelby, sat on a straight-backed wooden chair and oversaw the scene. Pain flared in Olivia's head with roaring force.

Few things could have made this day worse, but to be presented with both her talented older sister and her disapproving mother was unsupportable.

Etta noticed Liv hesitating in the doorway and gestured her inside. The attention in the room turned to Olivia. She swallowed, straightened her spine, and strode in. She would stay upright, no matter the cost.

Mother stood. Her gaze traveled over Olivia with the usual judgment and disapproval. This was why Liv hadn't been home in years. But she kept her shoulders back and her head up, and when her mother's eyes finished their survey, Olivia met their look with a frosty one of her own.

And then Mother held out her arms. Liv couldn't help it. She backed away. Something broke in the cool demeanor, and for the first time that Olivia could remember, Mother showed an emotion on her face—regret.

But that didn't matter. She could regret all she wanted. That wouldn't change twenty-one years of neglect and disdain.

"Hello, Mother." Olivia kept her voice neutral, her features impassive. Movement drew her attention away from her mother's face. Etta had pushed up from the floor and was depositing her niece onto Viola's lap.

Mother's words pulled her attention back. "Hello, Olivia."

"I'm sorry you had to come down from Scotland. Nan's telegram was a bit precipitous." Olivia kept her back rigid, forcing her muscles to comply despite their attempts to give out and drop her to the floor.

"It does not appear so."

"I'm fine." What a useful word, 'fine.' It meant absolutely nothing, and yet could be employed in infinite situations. "Someone is helping me, a Dr. Reilly from Trinity College Dublin." In the background, she heard a muffled exclamation, probably at her sudden shift from rival historian to student, but Mother drew her attention back before she could address whoever had spoken.

"I've never heard of him." Mother's hazel eyes had gone extra green, a sign that she was not pleased. "Is he a Seer?"

"Not in the sense you mean, but he has already helped me control a vision and not be harmed by it." Drained and exhausted, yes, but he'd kept her from true harm.

"I want to meet him." The words were clipped, the tees pronounced with extra force. It wasn't a request, despite her phrasing it as a desire rather than an order.

"It's none of your business who trains me."

"Of course it is. I'm your mother!"

"Are you?" The words came out low, but the room around them was silent, even the toddlers staring at them in shock. Liv swayed, dizziness hitting her like a high gust of wind. She widened her stance so she wouldn't fall over.

A soft cough broke the silence. Mother flinched, and turned her head toward the sound. Etta stood just beyond them, one eyebrow raised in a 'you're going to do this now?' sort of expression. She took a step closer. "Now that you're here, Olivia, Mal and I have an announcement."

Mother whirled all the way around to look at Etta. Liv was both shocked by the uncharacteristically abrupt motion and pleased that Etta had drawn the attention of the room away from the awkward mother-daughter tableau.

Mal stood and handed his nephew to Ian. He put an arm around Etta's waist. Etta smiled, her gaze traveling over all of the family members in the room, but lingering for a moment on Olivia.

"In about six months, we'll be welcoming a new Fay to the family."

Everyone started talking at once. Congratulations and exclamations of surprise and happiness filled the room. Olivia took the chance to retreat. Etta would understand. When she'd held Liv's gaze for a few moments before she made her announcement, she'd then broken the gaze to glance deliberately toward the door. She knew that Liv needed to escape.

Etta was the perfect sister-in-law. Much better than Giles's sanctimonious wife, Caroline. Lady Abbinden was a prig of the highest order. Whenever Percy got around to marriage, which wouldn't be soon if his stories about his escapades in Brandenburg were true, Liv would recommend that he find a woman in Etta's mold.

Too bad Percy wasn't home now. He'd always stood with her against the rest of the family, and he was the one person she'd never minded needing for strength and support. Etta was lovely, and Mal wasn't too bad, but now that Viola and Mother were here, she wanted to find a way to get Percy reassigned back to England as soon as possible.

Upstairs, she stripped out of the jacket, blouse, and bloomers that she'd worn to go out. She ought to get into a nightrail and go to bed, but anger had given her another surge of energy, and she wanted to work until she fell asleep tonight. So she changed into the fitted knit trousers and button-down shirt that she'd had specially designed for use on her digs. They were both well-worn and scruffy, with patches and darning liberally sprinkled over the surface of the fabric. She didn't have a good excuse to don her work vest, with its special pockets for her excavating implements: tiny picks, hammers, spades, and brushes. Instead, she shrugged into a plain waistcoat that had been tailored to flatten her small breasts down to her chest.

She laced up her work boots, also special ordered from a cobbler in France, and pinned the long strands of hair in front tightly back from her face. She didn't have a dig to go to, but she felt more herself than she had since getting off the ferry in Dover.

Liv took the servant's stair down to the second floor and entered the library from the hidden baize door. The family still milled about in the parlor, but the folding doors were shut, their voices muffled by the paneled wood. Two lamps burned in the library, one on the big central table, and the other by the main door to the hall. Liv lifted the one from the table and carried it over to the shelves. She could have opened the drapes on the windows, but the late afternoon sky had turned overcast, the fog thickening to an impenetrable soup, and the meager light would make little difference. She set off to the first bookshelf to search.

9

Cecily stared into the empty doorway where her youngest had disappeared. Olivia was her last child, born after a decade of frequent pregnancies. She'd given Rand his heir and spare, and he'd agreed to keep trying until she got another daughter.

But Olivia had never been anything like she'd wanted.

She turned her head just enough to survey her oldest. Viola had not been what she wanted, either. How strange life was. The two girls she'd carried in her body had vehemently rejected the life she'd planned for them, while the daughter-in-law from America that she never would have chosen had taken up her cause with more verve, acuity, and success than Cecily could have dreamed.

When she'd made her choices as a young woman, she'd promised herself she would never look back and regret. But now, over thirty years removed from those choices, she did look back, and she did regret. Not those initial decisions, perhaps, but the ones that came after. The little, everyday choices, from leaving her non-magical daughter to be raised by nannies, governesses, and a foreign school, to keeping her magical daughter on such a tight leash that she felt trapped and stifled. Both extremes had reaped similar results: her daughters rebelled, choosing their own paths and their own futures.

At least Viola had found happiness. She'd been so adamant in not wishing to marry Baron Dromoss, but Ian and the twins had brought a new stillness to her rushing-river's soul. Not that she'd given up her dreams—far from it. In fact, Viola had made this trip for the purpose of moving permanently back to London to take up her position as Head Sorceress at the women's school she'd founded several years ago here in the capital.

Cecily could admit, to herself if no one else, that she was proud of what Viola had accomplished. Despite the magical accident that tore out part of her gift and lodged it permanently in her husband, Viola had proved herself to be a capable if not formidable witch. After weaning the twins, she and Ian had begun training again, and had astounded the teachers and students at the school in Glasgow. Even Muire-all, the chief of Clan Fay, had been impressed.

And of course her daughter-in-law proved Cecily's initial instincts wrong every day. When Etta had stepped off the train at Waterloo Station almost two years before, Cecily had seen a wild talent, and a wilder woman. She'd feared to place her clan—her family—into the care of such an untried and untested lass.

But Etta had proved her mettle, and her right to hold the title she now bore: Duchess of Fay.

Cecily had another daughter-in-law, Caroline, but she'd never felt like a daughter. Neither Caroline nor Cecily's oldest son, Giles, had a magical talent, and they preferred not to. So far, only their eldest had exhibited obvious signs of magic, but her talent was minor and Giles and Caroline had forbidden Cecily from revealing it to anyone. Their youngest…would be a different story. No, Caroline was her daughter-in-law, but not family. Not Fay.

So that left only Olivia. Olivia, whom she'd ignored. Olivia, whom she'd treated as a Seward instead of a Fay, but whose hair now shouted the lie at Cecily like a crowd in a Roman amphitheater, calling for blood.

Now that it was too late.

"Give her time."

Cecily didn't ask how her daughter-in-law had divined her thoughts. They were likely obvious, and even if they hadn't been, Etta had a talent for reading people.

"Time is what I've squandered with her. Her whole life, in fact."

"And you can't take those years back. Neither can she. But perhaps you can both move forward from where you are now."

Cecily scoffed. "If she'll allow it."

"Yes. It's good that you're thinking in those terms—her allowing it, I mean. As the injured party, she gets to decide whether or not to forgive and forget. You don't get a say, except to tell her you're sorry."

That rankled, especially coming from Etta. And yet, who else would put it so bluntly?

Viola called for Etta, who gave Cecily one last, direct look, then turned away. They started talking about plans to bring down Muireall's eldest daughter to Viola's school, giving her experience with the wider world of London while still keeping her under family supervision. Seonag was seventeen, a gifted instructor for all she was so young, and would make an excellent assistant for Viola and Ian.

Viola glanced up and gave Cecily an absent smile. They hadn't mended all of the rips in the fabric of their relationship, but they'd made a start, at least. She could only hope that Olivia would give her the same chance.

❧

A QUARTER HOUR AFTER PULLING THE FIRST BOOK OFF THE shelf, Olivia finally got her bearings with the organizational system the first duchess had implemented in her collection. The books were roughly grouped by subject, but the subjects weren't always obvious. One shelf held a book of botany, an engineering text, a guide to animal husbandry, and a discourse on astronomy, particularly theories of gravity and planetary motion. These, Olivia eventually discovered, were all written by scholars who had attended a particular college in Edinburgh.

Oh, Great-grandma. Have you never heard of enumerative classification? I know Dewey was past your time, but by the goddess!

Another hour later, Olivia finally stumbled on a section of the library dedicated to books on the Academie and Magisterium magic systems, and there she found two books that discussed the historical contexts for both systems in England. Beside those books was a blank volume that turned out to be a collection of correspondence, essays, and personal documents written by and to King James II.

This she pulled from the shelf and carried to the table.

She ignored the early papers, which dealt with his childhood in France and his first marriage. She skipped to the 1680s, after his older brother Charles II died and James took the throne. She read about plots and schemes, and learned that neither of his daughters cared much for him as adults, though he claimed they'd been devoted to him as children. Twice his daughter Mary and her husband gave tacit approval to invading forces, and twice he pushed them back with the help of his Academe-trained King's Sorcerer.

But then he publicly proclaimed a new Sorcerer, this one from the Magisterium, and began to pass laws in favor of Magisterium mages. James thought he was doing the right thing—he and his wife Mary had become staunch supporters of the Magisterium and did not like to see their fellow followers ostracized or defamed. But England had become a nation that cleaved to the Academe.

In one diary entry, James wrote that his old Sorcerer and his daughter Anne had betrayed him, joining forces with her older sister and brother-in-law. William no longer simply encouraged invasions—he was leading one himself.

The final entry was from James's flight to France and subsequent capture. He must have left the diary behind when he left England for good, because no further correspondence or daily accounts were collected. The entry claimed that he'd been informed that William was now officially King of England, but that the new king did not want to splinter the populace over James's death. James would be allowed to escape and take refuge on the Continent, but measures had been taken to preserve the succession and maintain Academe-approved rule for future generations.

That was the drain spell. Olivia was as certain of that fact as she could be of anything, even though nothing in the text explicitly mentioned magic. William could have meant the laws that would soon be passed prohibiting Magisterium-sworn candidates from the throne, or any number of mundane actions.

But she didn't think so. Now she just had to find unequivocal evidence to corroborate her theory.

A noise from behind drew Liv's attention away from the book.

Her mother stood by the door to the parlor. The room

beyond was empty, the family gone off somewhere or other. Olivia set her jaw and forced a smile. "Hello, Mother."

"You disappeared." It was both accusation and question. Mother had always been good at making every comment have multiple meanings, most of them derogatory toward Olivia.

"I'm working on something for Etta." Liv tapped the open book in front of her. "She understood. She nodded at me to go."

"Something more important than a new addition to the family?"

"She thought so, and so do I. It's not like my new niece or nephew's arrival is imminent. Etta has months of pregnancy ahead of her."

Mother took a few more steps into the room, oddly hesitant and mincing. "Sorcha told me the nature of your visions."

Ah, here it was. The probe about her abilities. Her mother had only ever been interested in the magical talents of her children, and despite what Mal said, despite the hints of warmth that Liv had witnessed breaking through the ice-queen's frost, she still had only one standard by which to measure her offspring.

"Yes. But of the past, not the future. Sorcha tried to teach me to control them, but whatever she does is not like my visions. That's why I've found someone else."

"There are other Seers in London. I can find you a tutor."

After what happened at the archives, when she'd made Reilly speak, and then again when the vision had drained her so badly, Olivia had been thinking along the same lines. If he couldn't control her, or help her learn control, she didn't want to risk his sanity or magic. Or hers. But she refused to accept her mother's help, for this or anything, and the danger of her spirit being severed from her body was real.

"My current instructor will do. He follows the Sutra school of magic, and is well-versed in mental and passive magics. He says he can help me."

Mother bristled. "You're a Fay. Why does he think his way of magic will work for you?"

"I still can't cast spells, Mother. The Fay method doesn't address passive magic, or at least not in any different way than the Academe and Magisterium methods. And everything Sorcha knows couldn't help me. It won't hurt to try."

The exhaustion headache afterward didn't count as hurting.

Olivia pushed away from the table, the legs of her chair scraping across the bare wood. Why wasn't there a carpet here? But her mother winced at the sound, too, so that was something.

"Will you come home to Hazelby House, at least?" Mother asked.

"No. I'm going to stay here. There's nothing for me there."

Mother flinched, and frowned when she saw the trousers and boots that had been previously hidden by the table, but Olivia didn't care. Or told herself she didn't.

"Very well. But I'm sure your father would be happy to put the family library at your disposal should you require it."

Olivia scoffed, and tried not to make it obvious that when she grasped the back of the chair it was because she needed it for support. "Father doesn't collect books about magic, and that's what I need."

"He doesn't, but I do."

Liv frowned. "Very well. Perhaps I'll stop by tomorrow and have a look. But I'm not moving in. Etta offered me a room here, and I'd much rather stay with her."

"I'm sure you'll be comfortable at Skye House. But if you need anything…"

"I'm fine, Mother. Please."

Her mother hesitated a moment, then reiterated her offer of books and walked away.

Olivia stared down at the open book on the table. She snapped it shut and carried it upstairs. Slowly. She needed to focus, regain her energy, and solve this problem. Her issues with her mother could wait.

S avit was not able to go to Olivia until much later that
evening.

He'd had another row with his grandfather. They'd
argued again about the business, and Savit's agreement to
help the duchess. Grandfather thought the woman was a
meddlesome troublemaker, stirring up forces in the Lords
that had been quieted only a few years prior when Gladstone
and Rosebery were ousted. Grandfather didn't have a seat in
Parliament, but he kept abreast of legislation that would
affect his business.

Only after Savit agreed to approach her on issues of taxa-
tion and trade did the old man subside, though he'd finagled
another meeting with Savit and some key player in the Lords
who was a heavy investor in Reilly Shipping. Savit would
attend the meeting, but he had no intention of pushing Etta
toward his grandfather's ways of thinking. He would
mention the issues, as promised, but he doubted the duchess
would agree to policies that were detrimental to the lower
classes and only lined the pockets of the wealthy. She'd

grown up in a cabin on a mountainside. She knew what it meant to be poor, as Savit's mother had.

The memory of Kashvi filled him with warmth. He missed her with an intensity he hadn't felt in years, not since he started down the path of magic. Was that Olivia's doing? Had the proximity of a woman he could learn to love inadvertently reminded him of the only other woman who had inspired that emotion in him?

Likely it had. But he could not deny the swift spark of pleasure, or the lightness in his heart that followed the longing. She had loved him, and that was a boon without price.

Olivia Seward was another matter. She was prickly, her thorns protecting a vulnerability that she would never willingly allow him to see, or touch. And so he watched over her in the only way she would allow.

As he approached Skye House in the cold darkness, he followed the deep pulse of connection that hadn't fully dissipated after their attempted practice at the museum records room. He still did not wish to examine that bond too closely. She needed his help, and he would not allow the weaknesses of his flesh to interfere with his sacred calling. He would be her teacher, her mentor, and nothing more.

But even her spirit form, with no flesh to be roused, no blood to pound or breath to catch, engaged his senses. Something about her awoke a response in him that went far beyond physical lust. She called to his mind, to his spirit.

That was a far more terrifying truth than a simple physical urge to mate. He could control lust, and passion. He had been doing so for years. But this was soul-deep desire, and he had no space for that in his life. He'd been trained that magic required a sacrifice, and for him, that sacrifice was the lower chakras, his animal instincts and physicality. Not that he neglected his body, as some swamis did. He ate, and slept, and kept himself fit. But he did not revel in the pleasures of the flesh, whether culinary, aesthetic, or sexual.

None of those things had the power to tempt him beyond his self-imposed limits, but Olivia Seward did.

OLIVIA DREAMED OF TALYA, OF THE SOFT, DELECTABLE SKIN OF her upper thighs, the strong, sultry scent between her legs. How Liv had loved to tease with her tongue, touching everywhere but the most sensitive part of her lover's flesh, until Talya broke and moaned and whimpered. Only then would she flick and suck and nip until Talya screamed and writhed, body trembling as she fell into ecstasy.

At some point in the dream, Talya became Mina, who begged her in a thick German accent to make her come.

A sharp rapping pierced the sensual haze of the dream.

Olivia woke in the chair by the fire, still dressed, with a book open in her lap. It was a habitual sleeping position, since she often worked late into the night or even the morning, especially when she wasn't on a dig.

The knock came again. "Come in!"

It was Sorcha. She entered the room, wearing an elegant-looking dress. From what Olivia knew of current fashions, it wouldn't make the ladies magazines, but it fit Sorcha perfectly and emphasized her lush curves. She must have just returned from an outing with her husband.

Olivia stretched and stood up. The rest had done her some good, although she was still weak and a little dizzy. "Can I help you with something?"

"Not me. Dr. Reilly is here to see you. He came in just after Ronan and I returned from the dinner party at the viscount's house."

Ronan's father was Viscount Ashtondell. Sorcha had explained earlier that the two had been estranged for years but recently renewed their relationship. Olivia wished her mother didn't hope for the same.

But her thoughts moved away from the problem of the marchioness to Dr. Reilly. "I bet he's going to scold me. I agreed to have him teach me the Sutra method of magic, and then I disobeyed him during my vision this afternoon."

"Not a good beginning."

"No, but it was necessary. I'll go and talk to him."

She pushed away from the chair, hoping the lightheaded-ness had passed. It had, mostly. Sorcha said nothing, but held her hand a little away from her body, so that Olivia could take it if she wanted to. One part of Liv wanted to ignore the subtle offer, but the other part said she needed all the help she could get so that she'd have all of her energy available when confronting Reilly.

He stood in the downstairs parlor by the fire, staring down into the flames. He pivoted when she entered, his expression neutral. She'd been inside his head, and knew he felt things like normal people, but her brief experience of him was that he rarely allowed those feelings to show. She'd managed to goad him into a passionate intellectual response in the carriage yesterday, and he'd shown real affection for Rajani, but otherwise he'd been very contained, even when he saved her from the falling bust. She wished she could tell if he was angry with her now.

"My apologies for coming to you so late. I worried that you would be having ill effects from the vision, but I had obligations this evening and you seemed somewhat recov-ered when Sorcha brought you to the house."

She wanted to laugh at his carefully chosen words, and his failure to mention her trousers and waistcoat. 'Ill effects,' indeed. When he'd joined her in the vision, she'd been excited. His touch on her spirit-hand had helped her focus, and they'd learned more from those few moments eaves-dropping than they had in hours at the archive. But then he'd pulled her back, and she'd surged ahead against his wishes.

"I was exhausted, but otherwise fine. How did you find me so quickly?"

"I placed a small piece of my magic into contact with yours. It alerted me when the vision began, and I was able to use it to find you."

He'd said he'd have a way to tell when she was having visions, but he hadn't said that would mean a permanent attachment of his magic to hers. "Will you have to keep it there forever?" She moved farther into the room so she could surreptitiously lean against a sofa.

"Only until you learn to control them. There's too much danger now."

"But this time was so much better! No pain, or fear, like that time with the witch. I think that must have been an anomaly."

He considered that for a moment, his head cocking a bit to the side as he thought. "Possibly. But the vision still drained you physically, and that shouldn't happen, even without interference."

"Maybe there won't be any more interference. Neither Eleanor nor Leopold sensed us watching them."

"No, but they were preoccupied with appeasing their rulers, not desperately seeking for any way out of a deadly situation." His mouth formed a rueful half-smile, his dusky skin gleaming a soft gold in the lamp and firelight. Olivia clamped down on a desire to leap onto him and taste those sardonic lips.

"True," she conceded. "But I also got the impression that

neither of them was as talented as she was. Or as in tune with their magic." She'd proved her ability to stand, and now it was necessary to sit. Immediately. The sofa was unusually soft for a show-parlor piece, which Olivia's bum appreciated. Reilly immediately sat next to her. He wasn't a large man, but his presence felt twice his size, heating her without touching.

"I did not see the witch from your first vision, but I am inclined to agree with you. Leopold in particular had a kind of reckless arrogance that I often see in Academe-trained mages. Even worse in some of the Magisterium, of course. But Eleanor seemed pleasant enough."

Olivia shifted to face him. Since she wore trousers, it was easy to pull one leg up underneath her, bringing it perilously close to his hip. "Yes. If she'd been trained in the Fay methods, or in your discipline, she might have made different choices. But I think she had Anne's best interests in mind. There was a loyalty there that didn't exist between Leopold and William."

"Do you think Leopold might have sabotaged the spell, and that is why it is taking power from the country rather than helping the monarch now?"

"No. What I sensed was not hostility or a desire to subvert the monarch, but rather that he would grab for whatever power he could at the same time." She pictured the room again, and the cluster of people making decisions that would affect the course of history. Something about calling up the vision must have pushed her too far back into that out-of-body space, because pain stabbed through her head. The ache spread through her body and down her limbs. She tried to ignore it, but stirred uncomfortably. "We should focus on him, and perhaps on Eleanor as well. Did any of your friends have documents from the monarchs, or any of the other policy-makers we identified earlier?"

Reilly moved on the sofa until his thigh brushed her knee.

He reached out and took her hand, and pulled her toward him. She went, not certain what he intended, but hoping he would gather her into his lap.

Instead, he clasped both of her hands and kneaded her palms, pressing with his thumbs into the base of each, where the wrists ended. He must have been using magic, too, because heat curled and tingled up her arms and into her chest.

"You shouldn't have pushed." His voice was very soft.

"We needed to know."

His face showed no sign of what he was feeling. He kept his features tightly controlled, and he'd blocked her from touching his emotions with her magic.

"Are you angry with me?"

"What purpose would anger serve? I am concerned for your wellbeing, but shouting at you or punishing you will not change your future actions. Only you can decide what to do. There will be other chances to seek the truth of this spell, but only if you don't kill yourself trying first."

She couldn't refute that logic, and anyway, his energy now glowed within her like a golden balm, soothing her aches and her frazzled nerves.

As he worked, he changed the subject, telling her of the few meetings he'd managed to schedule, and the promises to check collections and volumes. He'd learned nothing new until her vision. And now that he'd seen the results of that on her person, he wanted to talk with his former teacher and get advice.

Some of the tension in her mind released, and the soreness eased. She wanted to slump against his body in boneless relaxation, but again held back, uncertain. He seemed so... untouchable. And yet she craved the slightest caress, the simple pressure of skin meeting skin.

She edged closer. "You should have told me you don't like being called Alexander. I was calling you that in my head."

"I thought you would prefer to call me Dr. Reilly. You seemed to want to preserve the distance of titles."

"Not after you saved my life and offered to help teach me not to kill myself." She tentatively squeezed his hand. Magic sparked between them, hinting at the deep connection they'd felt earlier in the day, and she tasted—what was it called? Raita.

"Very well." His gaze met hers, dark and consuming, like a pool of water under a midnight sky. "My name is Savitendra. You may call me Savit."

Her lips stretched into a wide smile. Of course. It was no wonder he disliked being called Alexander, when he had such a beautiful name of his own.

"And you must call me Olivia."

"Shall I ease your weariness, Olivia?" He rubbed at the hand clasped in his, putting pressure at the base of her thumb. Her eyelids fluttered shut. The world was darkness, punctuated by little explosions of light. He pressed again, and a soft moan escaped her lips.

Savit's breathing hitched, and Liv felt his arousal like a brand on her skin. Magic flared again between them, bright and strong as a whirlwind, rushing like a torrent through her mind and soul. His emotions and thoughts opened to her, and she greedily clasped them, wanting to know everything about him.

She leaned toward him, drawn like a lodestone to her magnetic north. Their entwined hands clasped together with nearly crushing force, and she sought blindly for his mouth.

Before her lips touched his, he stiffened. He pulled away so abruptly that she yelped in surprise, her eyelids fluttering open. His face held no expression, the blankness a little frightening. Their magic took another moment to disentangle, but he did it with inexorable firmness, like an automaton.

"I must go." He leapt to his feet, his motions jerky and nothing like his usual fluid grace. He'd retreated somewhere far within, where she couldn't touch him.

"Must you?" Olivia asked, because it was the very last thing she wanted. How to make him stay?

"I must. I will send word tomorrow."

He stepped backward, not breaking eye contact but putting more and more distance between their bodies. She missed his heat, his gentle caress, his reassurance. She wanted to beg him to come back, to let her kiss him, but she would not beg any man. Especially not this one.

He strode into the hall and disappeared. She sat on the sofa, staring at the empty space, stewing. Although she burned with sexual frustration, her headache was gone and she felt more awake and aware than she had since the first vision. Damn him.

SAVIT RETREATED INTO A DARK IN-BETWEEN SPACE, NEITHER here nor there, a pocket of emptiness between the physical world and the landscape of pulsing magical energy. Olivia had almost kissed him, and he'd almost allowed her to.

She'd been halfway across his lap, her lips so close her breath stirred against his cheek, his nose, his mouth. Each sensation was more vivid than anything he'd ever felt, each gasp loud as thunder.

He'd brought that breath into his lungs, took her exhalation into himself, and ached to draw her closer.

He needed space. Needed to breathe and not feel her expanding in his lungs, pulsing through his veins, and shimmering under his skin. The spirit-world could not give him that grounding, but it did provide the blessed numbness of unreality.

He sought the oblivion of deep meditation, the mindfulness that was mindless, expecting to find his lower chakras, the ones governing sexuality and passion, to be in control. But it was the one at his solar plexus that pulsed with energy. The one that governed anxiety and fear. It was also the place where base instincts and emotions transitioned into higher thought.

So the problem was not external, or even physical. The problem was mental. He was stifling his body, forcing it not to respond to Olivia, and for the first time in his life that was not a wise choice. What he felt for her was not empty lust, or an animal's desire to rut and reproduce. No, this was the passion of minds and hearts and souls, and the all-too-human desire for connection and meaning.

Yet, he could not submit to that desire. If he did, what would happen to his magic? And if he lost his ability to do magic, what would happen to Olivia? One night, her subtle body could wander free and never find its way back to her sleeping flesh.

He must resist her, if he was to keep her safe. There was no other option. And to keep her safe, he needed Chaitan's help.

Savit took a moment to calm himself before seeking out his master. Although he would never be able to hide all of his arousal and discomfort from his guru, he would do his best to downplay his reactions to Olivia. Best to focus on the important matters at hand—namely, how to keep her safe when she insisted on pushing farther.

Chaitan was in America, which meant careful preparation and bolstering power. Distance wasn't equivalent in the spirit realm, but there were dangers the farther away something was physically. With the Atlantic Ocean between them,

Savit also had to be cautious and avoid the strong magical currents.

Although night had fallen on London, Chaitan sat in full sunlight with his afternoon meal laid out before him. The fare was sparse, consisting of a flatbread, cheese curds, and a flagon of water. A pang of shame shot through Savit. He kept to simple foods when he ate alone, but when with others, he politely ate whatever was provided. His grandfather's French chef had served a multi-course meal that evening, and Savit had at least sampled every dish, something his grandfather had insisted upon since he was a boy first allowed at table.

How many times must I tell you to not compare yourself with others, Savitendra?

Chaitan's physical body still sat beside the food, legs folded beneath him, hands resting, palm upright, on his knees. But his fully-formed spirit body now hovered in the aetheric plane, the cord connecting him with his flesh even thicker and stronger than Savit's.

At least one more time, Māṣṭara. Savit's spirit body folded forward in a gesture of respect, hands clasping at his heart. *Namaste.*

Namaste. Why do you seek me out such a dangerous distance away from your flesh?

Savit explained Olivia's situation, trying to keep his words neutral. He failed.

When he finished, Chaitan contemplated him for a moment that stretched into eternity. Early in Savit's training, they had done an exercise here in the astral that revealed no difference between the infinite and the singular. Savit had assumed that he must see everything as singular and yet connected, but now he began to see another meaning—that one thing—or, one person—could become everything. *She means much to you.*

More than she ought. He wasn't ready for the connection his new knowledge implied.

Chaitan, as always, saw too much. *Your soul knows hers.*

That shouldn't matter. You always tell me that I must strive to live in the moment, existing now, and not then.

True, but I did not instruct you to neglect the lessons of the past. That includes your own past.

The rebuke was gentle, but firm, and typical of Chaitan. *My apologies, Māsṭara. Her case has me struggling because I cannot control my physical reactions to her.*

Why do you seek to suppress that part of your connection with her? From your description, it sounds as though she draws too heavily on her own magic and flesh. If you were to meld your magic and flesh with hers, it would provide her the extra power she needs to experience the visions until she learns to control them on her own and draw energy from other sources than herself.

I will happily share my magic with her, but Chaitan... Even in an insubstantial subtle body, Savit could shudder with apprehension. Fear was never a good reason, on its own, to do—or not do—anything. But he did not think his worries unjustified. *I have always done magic this way—taking the path of the mind, and denying the body. Would it not be a danger to us both for me to try to learn a new way of working while in the midst of teaching her?*

You know your own limits. Only you can answer that question. But from what you say of Olivia, she is deeply rooted in her flesh. If you can connect her more powerfully to her body and help her define the limits of her magic within that space, I think you will both find fulfillment.

Savit flinched away from that word, and the implications of...what? Was he so terrified to be connected to another human that he could not even contemplate the physical act of joining without fear?

Apparently so.

I will teach her how to access her root chakra, and move from there.

Chaitan's spirit-body bowed to him in acknowledgment. But whether of his wisdom in choosing that course or his foolishness at ignoring his master's advice, Savit didn't know.

Cecily stared absently at the lurid green wallpaper in the townhouse of the Queen's Sorceress. A motif of vines and tiny pink flowers repeated in vertical stripes above the chair rail. Beneath, the reverse: overblown pink roses with a scattering of green leaves on a pale pink background. When Cecily was a child, visiting here with the first Duchess of Fay, the walls had been paneled in a dark wood. But then the owner of this house had been the Queen's Sorcerer, Amelia's predecessor, Ezekiel Pollard.

Usually monarchs were matched to a mage of the same sex, but Victoria had insisted on keeping her uncle's mage as her Sorcerer until his death, for reasons she never shared with anyone. Not that there was ever even a hint of impropriety. Not like with Melbourne or Brown, though Cecily had never been one to put credence in those rumors. Her Majesty was many things, but she'd only ever had one husband, and even if what she felt for the other two men was love, Prince Albert had always been the king of her heart.

After Pollard's death, Her Majesty had asked Cecily to

take his place. She had refused. Amelia was the queen's second choice. She accepted.

So few words to encompass the gaping chasm in her shared history with Amelia.

A maid had brought in the tea service a few minutes ago, but it would be the height of rudeness to serve herself without waiting for Amelia. Though Cecily was tempted to do so, just to see what Amelia's reaction would be. So far, Cecily had been made to wait long after the tea went cold on every visit, despite the peace-offering nature of these meetings. She supposed that Amelia wanted to goad her into saying something to Etta, and perhaps negating the terms of their agreement, but that would never happen.

Finally, the door opened and Amelia bustled in. She took in Cecily's presence, the untouched tea tray, and Cecily's folded hands in her lap with a raking glance, then seated herself with her usual cross between simpering correctness and secret flirtation.

Even after over thirty years, that hint of a smile on Amelia's rosebud mouth could set Cecily's blood to flame. And did.

Not that she would ever give Amelia the satisfaction of knowing that. She already prodded at Cecily's choices whenever she could, denigrating her husband, her position in society, and her children, none of whom had managed to follow in her footsteps despite careful grooming and attention.

What would Amelia do if she knew Cecily still dreamed of her? Of the taste of her skin, of the feel of that rosebud mouth closing over Cecily's taut nipple, of small, deft fingers stroking the wet, needy folds between Cecily's legs?

Amelia must never know that the torch they'd lit so long ago burned still.

"I am always surprised when you appear for these meetings. I assumed you would find an excuse to stop ages ago."

Amelia addressed the tea pot in her hands, which she'd just reheated via a warming spell. The casual use of magic shook Cecily, as it always did. She'd forced herself to hide her magic for so long, using it only in private, or in lessons with Malcolm and Viola.

What would her life have been like, if she'd become the Queen's Sorceress with Amelia at her side? Full of magic and laughter and desire?

This was why she'd avoided Amelia for the past thirty years. She hated feeling regret. It was also one of the reasons she'd insisted she be the emissary in these meetings. A reminder of choices made, and the consequences.

And anyway, she would not give up her children for the world, even when they vexed her, as Olivia did now. Or her grandchildren. She hadn't yet told Giles that his youngest had magic. What would happen when she did? Giles was too much like his father in some respects, and not like him enough in others. Rand had never wanted to hear about magic, but he hadn't hated it as their son did.

"If I did not come, you would have to deal with my daughter-in-law, and we both know how that would end."

Etta had bested Amelia several times since Etta's arrival from America two years ago. Amelia wasn't pleased, and didn't bother to hide her disdain for the American duchess.

"What do you have to tell me this week?" This time, Amelia looked her in the eye as she spoke.

Cecily stared at the cup of tea Amelia proffered rather than meet her gaze. She accepted the cup, taking it by the handle so their fingers wouldn't touch on the sides. "You were present for the casting of the spell that pinpointed the source of the magic drain, correct?" She took a sip. Very lightly sweetened, with a hint of cream. Amelia never had to ask how she liked it.

"Yes, I was there. Much good it did us." The pretty lips

pursed in frustration. "We needed to know who cast it, and why, and where the magic is going. Who cares that it began in the seventeenth century?"

"Indeed. To that end, the duchess has engaged an anthropologist, Dr. Alexander Reilly, as well as my daughter, Olivia, an accomplished archaeologist, to research the period and attempt to discover more about the origins of the spell. If they can trace it through history, they should be able to find out what is happening with it now."

Amelia eyed her over the raised rim of her teacup. "That sounds like an impossible task."

"Perhaps. My understanding is that a spell of this nature would have required a great deal of power and involvement from a number of mages. It is not common knowledge now, but at the time it might have been. And chances are at least one of those involved wrote about it, whether in letters or a commonplace book. Something will have survived."

"I wish them luck, then, but this is very little to bring to Her Majesty."

"When I have more, I will share it."

One corner of Amelia's mouth quirked up, as though she'd scored a hit. "You're prickly today."

Her tone had edged into exasperation, so she suppressed her annoyance now. "Is it prickly to speak the truth?"

Amelia placed her cup and saucer back on the tray and leaned forward. Cecily held her back rigidly against the urge to shrink away.

"You never show emotion anymore. What is wrong?"

"Nothing!"

"Does it have to do with your daughter?"

Cecily flinched. Obviously Amelia had heard about Olivia's return, and her startling change in appearance. With luck, the news of her visions had not yet gone beyond the family.

Years of holding back, of keeping silent, told her she should brush off Amelia's interest. After all, anything Cecily said could find its way to the ears of the queen. And yet... Amelia had never revealed anything Cecily told her in confidence, all those years ago, not even when their tempers were at their fiercest flame.

"Olivia's return is a concern. She has changed. Or perhaps I've never known her at all. She's..." Cecily hesitated. Amelia waited in silence, her features unreadable. Cecily forced out the words. "She's like me. Like...us."

There was no need to elaborate.

Cecily's mother had taught her, first as a girl and then as a young woman, that her desires were not something to be ashamed of. But they *were* something to keep private. The one time anyone had even guessed at the closer relationship between Amelia and Cecily had been a disaster.

Olivia's affairs were very public. She courted much more stringent censure, and worse: disgust and disdain.

"And this worries you, because you don't wish her to be hurt, as we were?"

"Yes. But she won't listen to me about anything."

"Perhaps if you had kept her closer to you, had allowed her to *know* you, she would listen to you now. I know how it feels to be denied your affection. You haven't allowed anyone to get close to you in years."

Waves of heat and cold splashed inside of Cecily. Shame brought bright warmth to her cheeks, but left her hands icy. Then anger surged in shame's wake, roaring like a bonfire in her chest.

"Whereas you will allow anyone close if you've something to gain from it."

Amelia blinked, her pretty mouth opening in a surprised and hurt O. They'd had this argument before, but not in years. Amelia had chosen a rich, affluent, older, and titled husband not long after Cecily accepted Rand's proposal. Amelia had wed herself to a man she didn't want and didn't respect, all for the benefits of being his countess. Then she'd accepted the post of Queen's Sorceress, a position that required her to dance to Victoria's tune, but which brought with it immense political and magical power.

Cecily knew that Amelia would have made different choices, if she'd been given different opportunities. It was unfair to blame her for making the most of what she had available to her after Cecily left. And yet, Amelia's words had stung.

So had Cecily's, because Amelia's expression shifted from shock to an ugly, vivid rage. "What did I ever get from allowing you to get close?"

Their gazes met over the tea set, its simple domesticity a stark contrast to the violence just beneath the surface of both women. Porcelain rattled as Cecily put down her tea cup. The taste in her mouth was now bitter, all sweetness forgotten.

"Nothing," she murmured. "And neither did I."

Cecily fled.

"WHILE THE CONFERENCE YOU AND SAVIT SAW WASN'T precisely confirmation of the spell's origins, I'm convinced that you're correct, and this is the moment when they decided to cast it. Do you know much about the reference they made to Trajan and Hadrian?"

Olivia and Etta sat in the family parlor of Skye House, lounging comfortably before a roaring fire with a loaded tea tray between them as Olivia explained her vision. Whatever Savit had done last night before he bolted had allowed her to sleep deeply, without dreams—at least none that she remembered. Today she felt almost like her old self again.

"Emperor Trajan expanded the Roman Empire well beyond anything that had been attempted before. I've never read about Trajan trying to use magic to maintain the new borders, but they may have been referencing the Aegis, a spell from ancient times that acted as both protection for a certain geographical area and a magical focus for its ruler." She'd found numerous references to that spell during her time in Italy.

"Is it possible Trajan tried to cast this Aegis spell over the entire empire?" Etta gestured to the tray with its array of delicious offerings, as though sandwiches and cream cakes were the far-flung Roman colonies. Either Etta wasn't prone to morning sickness, or she'd already started in on the maxim 'eating for two,' because she'd polished off a fair number of pastries. But there were plenty left to stand in for ancient Europe.

"It's possible, although it's difficult to be sure about anything at that period in history. There was a practice at the time that no one was allowed to document the activities of a ruler until after his death. If records do exist that refer to the spell, I've never seen them. Van der Bron must have had access to a unique manuscript." She would give up a limb to have access to that work.

"I imagine the Aegis would have failed spectacularly for Trajan, though. His rule was contentious, and there was constant revolt and uprising on the borders. It might have worked at the heart of the empire, but what I know about the spell requires cooperation from magical practitioners who are native to the area, and as van der Bron mentioned, a certain sense of nationalism. Or in the Roman case, imperialism. Trajan would have had difficulty finding enough of mages to participate and he wouldn't have had enough people in the colonies who considered themselves Roman." She picked up a cream cake from a position that would have been in the Balkans.

"So that would be why Hadrian had to build the wall to keep out the Picts later. Trajan overreached, and there was a backlash." Etta pushed a set of cheese and pickle sandwiches away from the others. Olivia wondered whether the Scots would appreciate being represented by pickle.

"Yes. But I'm guessing that van der Bron and Collins were much savvier. They would have kept their spell to the borders of England, and used English mages." She gestured to the watercress and cucumber pile.

"I agree. If they'd failed, it would have caused more unrest. There was some, of course, but there always is during that kind of political upheaval. All things considered, their conquest was relatively bloodless." Etta popped one of the cucumber sandwiches in her mouth.

"Yes, hence the moniker 'The Glorious Revolution.' That's why I think they succeeded."

"But somewhere along the way things must have gone terribly wrong."

"Yes." Not that a pile of sandwiches and cakes was going to help them find out what had happened, or when.

The door to the family parlor opened and MacGroarty handed over a pile of letters, telegrams, and hand-delivered notes. Two were for Olivia.

She ripped open the one from Percy. He'd gotten her telegram from Calais and reported that he was on his way home from Brandenburg, by way of a number of military postings. He'd asked for leave, and was informed that he'd been reassigned. But as usual with a bureaucracy, it could take months for him to set foot in England again.

The second telegram was from Savit. She opened it and scanned the brief message. He would collect her at noon, and they would spend the afternoon making calls on various contacts that had collections including magical doings in the late seventeenth and early eighteenth centuries.

He said nothing of his visit, of their aborted embrace, or his abrupt departure from the house. She hadn't expected him to, and yet it rankled that he didn't even offer her an apology.

"What's wrong?" Mal slid onto the settee beside her.

Liv almost crumpled the telegram. "Dr. Reilly is...frustrating."

"Frustrating how?" Etta sat on the table in front of her. Liv managed not to guffaw in shock at a duchess sitting on a table meant to never hold anything more substantial than a tea set or books.

"There's a connection between us, and he refuses to acknowledge it."

"A magical connection?" Etta asked.

"Yes, but a physical one, too, and that's the problem. He's shy enough of the magical one, but if he's going to help me learn to control the visions he can't exactly ignore it. What makes me angry is that he flat-out ran from me when I tried to kiss him."

"The bounder." Mal's words were half-sarcastic, and half-in earnest. "What made him run?"

"I don't know. It isn't lack of interest. He was practically humming with desire. We both were. It must be something else, but he took the coward's way out and ran."

"Not everyone attacks their problems with as much zest as you do, my dear sister."

"They should. The world would be a better place if people would just talk to each other honestly."

"Would you like me to go rough him up? Er, honestly?" The lopsided smile on Mal's face told her his offer was mostly in jest, but she knew if Savit had harmed her, her brother would have moved the earth to protect her. If she asked. That was something she could count on from Mal—he respected her ability to fight her own battles.

"No. I'm rather fond of his pretty face."

Etta laughed. "He'll be a captive audience while you drive around town today. Once you're in the carriage, wallop him with your honesty until he has no choice but to be honest in return."

"That's a good idea. I just need to figure out what I want to say."

Mal's hand covered hers. "You look a little better this morning, but you're still pale. Are you sure you're up to an afternoon gallivanting around London?"

Respecting her abilities did not, apparently, equate to trusting her to know her own limits. On that score, however, he was correct to worry. Although she would never admit it to him, it made her feel warm and safe that he cared enough to say something. And that he would go rough up a fellow if she asked.

"I'll spend most of the day sitting down. I'll be fine, I promise."

"We'll have a nice big supper here tonight, just us and Sorcha and Ronan. Using my highly honed powers of observation, I noted you weren't best pleased to see Viola and Mother, so we'll leave them to their own tables tonight."

She ought to be annoyed at this high-handedness—and she was, a little—but since his plans perfectly aligned with her desires, she let that pass.

"Depending on how your conversation goes, perhaps you can invite Dr. Reilly," Etta suggested.

"Depending on how our conversation goes, I might slaughter him and serve him up as the meal."

Olivia fumed in the front parlor while she waited for Savit. How dare he run away from her like a frightened rabbit? What kind of man bolts instead of facing a problem head on? She hated dancing around issues, or using pretense to obscure intentions. Was it such a terrible thing to feel desire for each other? Or to act on it?

She couldn't think so, and had never restricted her desires when it came to choosing lovers. From her very first experience with Elsa, her roommate in the Swiss boarding school, to Jean, a strapping lad from the village near her excavation in Labourd, she'd never once felt shame or regrets. And with few exceptions, she hadn't felt a deep connection, or any connection at all except the physical. Why should she? A few hours of mutual pleasure was its own reward.

But obviously Dr. Savitendra Reilly didn't agree. He wanted her. She'd felt that, both as a pulse of awareness through their magic and in the brief brush of her body against his. He'd been tense, his muscles taut with the effort to hold back, to not explode into a furious passion.

What was wrong with him?

MacGroarty announced His Fastidiousness, and Olivia swept out of the room and into the hallway. She had no intention of hanging about the morning room with him, pretending that last night hadn't happened and she didn't still want to leap on him and rip off all of his clothes.

Damn him for making her finally feel fit enough to do that, and then deny her the opportunity.

He swiveled to follow her, almost stumbling as she passed. She'd worn her excavation outfit today, and anyone who objected could go straight to the seven hells. He hadn't said a word about the garments last night, and she needed to feel confident and strong today. She stopped by the outer door and turned back to MacGroarty. He handed her a tailored men's-style coat and a pageboy hat. She donned the proffered items and stepped out into the cold February morning.

Etta's carriage awaited, the horses standing with a groom at their noses, munching from feedbags attached to their tack. Once she and Savit were seated, the bags would be taken away and the coachman would flick each horse with the tiniest of touches to stir them into motion.

Olivia wished she could entice Savit to her as easily. Didn't all men want sex? And all women, too? At least, all women who'd been allowed to experience it and not subjugate their physical pleasure to a domineering husband who would always think of her as a possession rather than a person.

Savit settled beside her and the carriage moved away from the house with a jolt.

"We need to talk about last night," she blurted into the silence.

"What is there to say? You had another vision, and I

helped you recover from the physical effects. We will take what we learned and apply it to our search. That is all."

"That is not all! You wanted me to kiss you as much as I wanted to do it. Why did you stop me and run off?"

He went very still, then heaved a breath and put his hands on his thighs, palms upright and fingers curled, as though he were a supplicant or expected something to be placed into them. He shifted so that one hand rested on the other, still palms up, thumbs touching. He moved deliberately, as though the gesture and the contact helped to clear his thoughts.

"You do not yet grasp how magic such as mine works, so you cannot comprehend that the price paid for it does not come as exhaustion or hunger, the way your clan's gifts do. For me, I must concentrate until my body is no longer a fleshy weight holding back my mind. Only when I transcend the physical can my spirit and my magic fly free."

"So what does that mean, exactly? You obviously pay some attention to your body, or you'd be emaciated and starving. Not to mention dirty and smelly."

That surprised a smile from him. She decided not to make another joke, even if she'd meant that one sarcastically. His smiles were potent and she didn't want to find herself agreeing with something he said—or doing something else out of character—just to make him grin.

"That means I do not indulge in empty pleasures. I bathe and eat, but I do not scent my bath with expensive oils or perfumes and I do not order rich foods."

"Food is not an empty pleasure! It is precisely the opposite. It fills your body as it lifts your spirit."

"Some food does. Others expand within you at an alarming rate, until you feel sick."

"So that's a bad analogy." But he couldn't mean *all* pleasures. "Are you saying that you don't…"

"Yes. I am celibate."

Liv sat back involuntarily, her shoulders meeting the cushioned back of the carriage seat with a soft thud. "But...why?"

"I told you. The desires of the flesh cloud my magic." He said that with such a straight face, as though pleasure was a nuisance, instead of her favorite pursuit.

"Are you saying that I have to give up sex in order to control my visions?"

Savit frowned, but so slightly she almost didn't notice. "Probably not. There are, of course, many who practice magic in India who are married and have families. My mother was one such. But she died when I was too young to be taught, and I don't know her way." His expression suddenly shuttered, even the frown of intellectual curiosity replaced by a blank mask. But she knew, now, that he used the mask to hide deep emotion. He missed his mother.

A moment later, he forced a bland smile. "I have already sent word around to other mages in the Sutra community to find books that we can use, but the problem is getting them in English for you. Until then, I know only the way I was taught."

"And that way requires you to give up anything that makes you feel good?"

"In so many words, yes."

"I'm sorry, but that's rubbish. You've already helped me through several visions, and I haven't given up anything."

"Exactly. You needed me to help you through it. You couldn't control it yourself."

"I refuse to believe that I need to stop eating good food or taking lovers unless you prove to me that I need to do it. Like you said, your mother didn't give up sex. She had to have done it at least once to have you."

He flinched, and shame clenched in her belly. "I'm sorry.

That was rude. But what you're asking is foreign to my nature."

"I know." He surprised her by taking her hand. The full force of his magic seeped into her, instead of her into him, as it had in the archives. "I don't deny that there are other paths. I spend most of my time researching human interactions and relationships, which are driven by emotion and passion."

He embraced her. Not physically, of course, except for her fingers grasped in his palm. But mentally and emotionally, he surrounded her and filled her. *So much of you is dust and bone, dry facts and absolutes.* The words were inside of her, resonating inside her mind, in the marrow of her bones, and within the chambers of her heart. *But then there's the peppermint, the vibrant bite of sweetness, that gives the lie to your wish for black and white. You are a creature of color and brilliance. For you, I think, the way will not be to deny this truth, but to embrace it.*

Her soul woke and sang for him, and her body heated, her quim dripping moisture into her drawers. In another moment, she would roll over onto his lap, straddling him and rubbing her aching clit against his cock. But before she moved, before she could do more than wish for his touch, ecstasy swept through her.

Liv convulsed and cried out, pleasure singing through her flesh, awareness rising from the base of her spine through her body and up into her brain.

Savit dropped her fingers.

Olivia's gaze cleared, the haze of lust and need and wanting lifting with his magic.

"That was…" She swallowed. She didn't have words for what she'd just experienced. But he was right. In the wake of her orgasm, she saw not only the interior of the carriage, but the pulsing lights, colors, and scents of magic. He'd helped her open her Sight deliberately, for the first time.

"Why can't it work like this for you?" She tried to pose the question in a detached way, but he had to know that she asked because she wanted him. Now that her Sight was open, she could see the magic pulsing between them, brilliant and beautiful and so *right* that she almost trembled again.

"My mentor taught that attachment to an individual distracts from my ability to serve all mankind."

"Bullshit." Olivia shifted until their thighs pressed together, twisting to face him and take his hand back in hers. "With the right partner, you work together to achieve great things. You help each other. Your weaknesses with their strengths, and their weaknesses with your strengths."

"I hope you find such a partnership one day, Olivia." He held her hand so tight it hurt. "But I dare not attempt it. You need me to be at my best, not fumbling through new ways of magic. I could not forgive myself if something happened to you that I could have prevented."

His body radiated tension, and she could See it, a ball that pulsed with dark colors and flashes of sickly green and yellow. There were other little balls, each of them tainted by the darkness, but most of it clustered at the base of his throat. She reached out and stroked a finger down the mass of energy, and he cried out, his body going rigid.

Olivia flinched back, squeezing her eyes shut. When she opened them again, she'd lost the Sight. Savit looked like himself again, just a man of flesh and blood, his expression inscrutable.

The carriage came to a halt.

Olivia stared at him until the door opened. "We need to talk, after."

He said nothing, but gave her a curt, affirmative nod.

She climbed down in front of an elegant townhouse and waited for Savit to join her. She would make him show her how to open her Sight again, and next time she wasn't going to stop until all of that dark tension was gone. Whatever he wanted to believe, she knew exactly what he needed to do to relieve it.

1 3

Control nearly eluded Savit as he followed Olivia into the building. He'd spoken nearly by rote in the carriage, parroting the tenets he'd been taught in near-desperation. Because in truth, his instincts and his emotions no longer harmonized with those teachings, and that was more frightening than anything he'd ever experienced, including his first day at an English boarding school.

This way of life had served him well for years. It had saved him when he didn't know who he was or his place in the world. He could not abandon it now because he was attracted to a woman, not even Olivia.

Yet what more could he do to stifle the wanting? He'd tried meditation, grounding, suppression. The only other thing he knew would work was separation. That was why he'd torn himself from her last night. His choices had been violent removal or passionate capitulation.

But he couldn't avoid her forever—she needed his help.

Savit handed over his card, and Olivia did the same. The glimpse he got of hers was of a plain cream card with block letters. He had the wild thought that it might say "Oliver Seward" on it, but then changed his mind.

Did she see Oliver as he did Alexander? A sop to the egos of their colleagues? Or was Oliver something more to her—a representation of the desires that Society would not allow her to express?

He could hide behind the name Alex in person if he wished, whereas she could only be herself, even if that self was radically different from any other woman Savit had ever known. She'd dressed today in what looked like a casual suit of men's clothing, but with extra pockets on her waistcoat and thicker boots than any fashionable gent would be caught dead wearing. But despite the clothes and the weight she'd lost after her visions, her face was far too feminine, her hips round and her breasts obvious. She couldn't hide her femininity—and he didn't think she wanted to.

They were shown to a small sitting room, and a few minutes later the master of the house arrived. Gregory Carston, second son of the Earl of Olcestair, entered the room looking disheveled and distracted. His cravat was loose and askew, his hair a mess as though he'd been worrying at it with his hands.

Savit rose from his position on a stuffed chair. Olivia didn't stand, but did come to the edge of her seat, alert. Carston stopped just inside the door, staring at Olivia. Then he found his composure again and continued into the room.

"I'm sorry to keep you waiting, Dr. Reilly, Miss Seward," their host said, hurrying over and shaking Savit's hand. They'd met a few times before at lectures and academic events, and were friendly but not friends. Carston waved him back to his seat and plopped down on a chaise longue. "We've had a burglary overnight, and I'm afraid the papers you wanted to see were destroyed."

Cold clenched in Savit's belly. "A burglary?"

"Yes. The library is on the first floor, and someone came in through the windows. I have several valuable editions bound in leather with gold and even jeweled accents, and those are gone, but a good portion of my collection was ransacked in the process."

"Did no one hear the thieves?" Olivia asked.

Carston shook his head, his eyes tight with anger. "No. Scotland Yard has been here, and their mage found residue of a mild ward that would have prevented us hearing anything. I wish to the god and goddess that I'd listened to my mother when she told me to hire a mage to lay protective wards around the place, but I haven't heard of a magical burglary like this in years."

"They're more common in Dublin." Dublin, where the magic hadn't been drained away for an indeterminate number of years. There was a reason why magic was not the immediate solution for English thieves.

Savit caught Olivia's worried expression. He imagined she didn't believe this was a coincidence, either. "I know someone who might be able to help you with recovery. Shall I send him to call on you this afternoon?"

Carston's countenance lit with renewed hope, but then shuttered again. "To be honest, I'm not sure I can pay anyone. The house and the collection are an inheritance, but I don't have much income of my own beyond what I pay out for maintenance, staff, and taxes."

"Perhaps you can offer him something from the collection, provided he recovers it."

That sank in, and Carston's face turned positively gleeful. "That is an excellent suggestion, and will give him a perfect incentive to do his best. Thank you, Dr. Reilly."

"It's no problem. But tell me, how familiar are you with the documents we came to see?"

"Oh, quite familiar. I can still answer your questions if you like."

Savit asked him to first summarize the writings. Carston explained that he'd had about two dozen pieces of correspondence from Queen Anne, who was only a princess at the time, and an ancestress, the then Countess of Olcestair, who was a great friend of Anne's and later one of her ladies in waiting. Carston didn't mention if the relationship was any closer than friendship, but Savit had learned in his research the day before that Anne's confidantes were often also her lovers. The letters detailed Anne's worries over the spell being cast, and how she was afraid to have to bear it one day.

Her sorceress had explained how it would be transferred to her after King William's death, and how she would then become both a focus for the strength of English magic and a channel for that magic to return into the land and the people. The spell would tie her to the hearts, minds, and souls of her people, and just by being their Queen she would intensify their magic.

Savit watched as some of the tension Olivia had been holding around her shoulders and neck relaxed. Savit continued to pepper Carston with queries, skillfully drawing out details the man didn't realize he knew.

At the end of the interview, Carston apologized for not having more to say. "Unfortunately, I don't know if such a spell was ever cast on Anne. Once my many times great-grandmother became a lady-in-waiting, they had no further need to correspond. And then they had a falling out some years later, so we're lucky the letters survived as long as they did."

"Lucky indeed," Savit agreed.

But the rest of the day was not so lucky. The not-coincidental-at-all burglars had visited all of the houses where Savit had paid brief calls or sent messages the day before.

Some of the owners recalled useful information about the writings, but most were only hobbyist collectors and were more interested in owning a thing rather than reading it. They were also not best pleased to answer questions posed by Olivia, whom most viewed as a kind of odd secretary. And at least one man's butler had shut the door in their faces once he got a good look at Savit.

The prejudice was alarming, but unfortunately commonplace. The thefts and destruction, however, were clearly targeted at stymieing their search.

Back in the carriage after their final interview, Olivia swore and banged a fist against the squabs. "How did they know about us?"

"Someone may have followed me yesterday. Or we could easily have been overheard chatting in the archives at the Society."

"I suppose we should have guessed that there would be people protecting the spell."

"By now, Ronan will have met with Carston and possibly some of the others. He'll have information for us at Skye House."

They'd sent word to Ronan immediately after their first visit, and he'd met them between two later visits to find out more information before heading over to check out the scene for himself. He lamented that Evie Finn—his former partner in crime and one of the best magical trackers alive— had gone back to Scotland, and he said he would telegram her to come back to London straightaway.

The sun was sinking through the haze of smoke and fog, turning the sky to crimson flame by the time they reached Skye House. As Savit had predicted, Ronan was already there. The family had held the meal for them, and as they ate, Ronan explained what he'd found at the few burglary sites that had accepted his services.

"Without Evie, I can't tell you much. None of the owners used magic to secure their items, so there were no spell-traces to track. And the spells used in the thefts were all token-based, with the tokens left behind at the scene. None of the items were much-handled or of particular emotional resonance with the possessor, so I couldn't track them that way, either."

"So the thefts are a dead end?" Etta asked.

"Only in the sense that they won't lead us directly to the ones protecting the spell," Olivia said. "But it's definite proof that we have an adversary. Yesterday I had two near-misses where I could have been seriously injured or killed."

"Two?" Savit exclaimed. What had happened to her while he wasn't paying attention?

"Yes, two," she repeated irritably, and turned her face back toward Etta. "The first was in the archives at the society. A bust nearly brained me. The second was just outside the house here. An auto took the turn at the end of the lane too fast, swerved, and would have hit me if the person I had shared the cab with didn't pull me out of the way."

She'd nearly been hit by an automobile and didn't think to tell him about it?

"When was this?" he demanded.

Her bottom lip pushed out the tiniest bit, in a mulish expression, as she faced him. "Just before the vision, when you found me in the park. I went there to calm myself before entering the house."

"You should have told me. I would never have allowed the vision to go on so long had I known."

"And then we wouldn't have learned the little bit we now know about the Aegis spell. I'm not sorry for that."

"Neither am I, but Dr. Reilly has a point," Malcolm said. Olivia glared down the table at her brother, who shrugged. "You're pushing yourself very hard. Perhaps past your limits."

"I'm fine. Yesterday was too much, I'll admit that. But I am not nearly so weary or weak today. I can do this." Instead of seeking out any of the males at the table, Olivia beseeched first Sorcha, and then Etta with her gaze. Both women nodded. "I would like to try for another vision."

Savit didn't allow the worried protest to pass his lips. She'd just said she was ready, and he would have to accept her judgment. He would provide as much of his energy as he could during the vision, and help her draw on local sources, weak and pitiful as they were.

"We'll try after dinner," he agreed. "Someplace private and quiet."

"You can use the Casting Chamber," Etta said. "It's the best place for spellcasting in the house. And I wouldn't be surprised if the old girl hadn't included various other magic systems in her plans for the room, in addition to things that enhance our way."

The conversation turned, then, to more benign topics. Malcolm suggested that his sister look through the collection at Hazelby House for hints about Queen Anne or her successor, George I. Olivia's expression soured, but she agreed. Clearly she did not want to go anywhere her mother might be.

Savit couldn't imagine *choosing* not to be with his mother. But then, their relationship had been strong, warm, and vibrant. He'd loved her, and she'd loved him. He would give almost anything to have her back again, even for a few moments.

Not everyone had the privilege and joy to have such a mother.

After the meal, Etta showed them to the Casting Chamber, and then left them alone. She had to pull her husband away, and he grumbled as he went. Savit wasn't sure if Malcolm was more worried about his sister or more interested in viewing a different system of magic. Probably a mix of both. But the duchess correctly interpreted Savit's pointed look as a plea for privacy, and hooked her arm around Mal's.

Olivia wandered around the room, touching the symbols on the walls. Once the door shut behind Mal and Etta, she said, in a soft voice, "I was never allowed in here as a child. I only came to Skye House a few times, and Lilias had no use for a child with such a miniscule magical talent."

"It is unfortunate that your family places such a high value on magic. All living things are the same, equally worthy of respect and honor, no matter the concentration of the divine within them."

"If only Clan Fay agreed with you. At least Mal isn't so bad. And Etta is wonderful. I can't believe he had the good sense to pick someone like her."

"The duchess is, indeed, a rare woman. But then, so are you."

She pivoted away from her examination of the wall, one hand still raised from running her fingertips over an inlay of pearl in a swirling triple-spiral design. Her face flushed with appealing color, and the memory of her, rapt with pleasure as his magic brought her to ecstasy, slammed into him with breathtaking force.

Her mouth had opened a little in shock, and he wanted it. Wanted to seal his lips against hers, taste her tongue, drink her essence until he was sated—no—glutted, beyond excess, bursting with her vital spirit, suffused by her breath and her soul.

He pushed the need down deep, locking it away. He couldn't ignore it, but he must control it. She wanted to try a vision, and he would need every measure of control.

"Thank you for saying that. I don't get many compliments as a woman. Mostly I hear about my work. Others have been fond of my body, but not *me*, if that distinction makes sense."

It did. He was fond of her body, too—more than fond. But it was the whirlwind spirit inside that had him roused and craving.

"Come, let's sit here. The first duchess had the foresight to place a few symbols of my faith and magical practice into her room, and they are here in this little alcove." He gestured at a small, half-circular opening in the wall. Inside was a wooden table holding a box with hinged doors on the front. He opened it to reveal tiny figures of various gods and goddesses, and a single-wicked lamp in a bowl of oil. On the walls of the alcove were symbols of the chakras, picked out in colorful gemstones, and a number of mantras written in Sanskrit. Beneath the table sat a pile of colorful mats, pillows, and cushions, neatly stacked.

Obviously someone had tended this area along with the rest of the chamber, because the linens weren't musty, there wasn't a speck of dust on anything, and the lamp oil was full.

Savit pulled out a mat for himself and a cushion for Olivia and placed them in front of the altar. "Sit with your legs crossed, like this." He demonstrated, and then rested his arms on his thighs, hands palm-up, thumb and forefinger touching. "Eventually, you won't need to use the hand gestures, but in the beginning they're useful as a focus."

Olivia mirrored his pose, including her fingers, but she sat stiffly, her back rigid.

"Now I want you to close your eyes and relax. Start with your toes, and your feet. Consciously release the tension in your muscles, moving up your legs, your torso, your arms, your shoulders, your neck. Pay attention to your breath. On every exhalation, release more tension." Gradually, Olivia's posture loosened, although the way her eyelids creased shut in concentration meant she was still over-thinking. That would come next.

"What your people call magic is merely energy, produced

by every object in the universe. It is the presence of the divine in our world, a manifestation of Brahmahnn as are all things."

"If that's the case, why isn't everyone a mage?" She asked the question with her eyes still screwed shut.

"Why isn't everyone an artist? A musician? A scholar? A mathematician?" He smiled at the way her mouth opened, about to interject. "I know. Many of those skills can be trained. But some people will never be able to sing a true tone, and some are born with an innate ear for pitch. To keep this analogy going, you were born with a good voice, but not one suited for opera or a music hall. I am going to show you how to find your pitch."

She made an inarticulate noise, but subsided, eyes still firmly shut.

He explained the concepts of atman, or the true self, and the multiple "bodies" that make up a human being. The one that was causing her trouble was called the subtle body, made up of mental and vital energies.

"So is the idea to use the subtle body to reach through to the divine and do magic?"

"In a way, yes. But also, not at all." She made a noise of frustration, and he suppressed a smile. She would learn, as he had, that this philosophy was full of what could seem like contradictions, but were simply alternate paths toward enlightenment. He would take her down as many paths as necessary for her to find her own way.

"First, we will focus on the magic of your eight-fold subtle body. This body animates your flesh. You are already well-attuned to your gross body, but you draw too heavily on your own flesh, and I want you to learn how to access other sources around you, including me."

Olivia proved to be a good student, chanting "Lam" with him and accessing her root chakra, grounding her energies and reaching the first stage of meditation. From there, he explained the other chakras, and how hers were out of balance, with too much energy pulling from the lower chakras and not enough from the higher ones.

He didn't expect her to be able to balance things on her own, so it was no surprise when, after opening her sacral chakra, she started to tremble with magical energy. This was one of her stronger affinities: her sexual drive and emotions. She pulled magic from the chamber into the chakra but it was too much for her to channel on to the next.

Savit took her hands in his, redirecting the flow up and out, feeling the opening of each of her chakras like a blossoming flower, happening both inside of her and within himself. His sacral chakra pulsed in unison with hers, and yet he was still in perfect balance. He'd feared this, feared he would be overwhelmed by her passion and his, and yet...he wasn't. Instead, he felt alive, aware of the universe in ways he had never experienced before.

He remembered the way she'd touched his throat chakra in the carriage, how the blockage there had been pulling his magic and his awareness out of balance. He'd been suppressing his own intuitions, forcing the desire and emotional intimacy down, where they could not affect his mind and crown chakras. Even as a novice, Olivia could see what he'd done, and had instinctively reached for the knot of tangled energy.

What would happen if, instead of suppressing those feelings, he gave in to them?

He pressed his thumbs into Olivia's palms, rubbing firmly on the base of her hand, and trickles of magic seeped from his skin to hers. He'd never done this before, never initiated intimacy.

The only time he'd even touched a woman had been the dancing girl in the tavern. When his untrained magic latched onto her thoughts, he discovered she only wanted his coin and the experience of having an exotically dark man in her bed. He'd pushed her away, repulsed.

But that was years ago, and not Olivia. Olivia saw *him*, Savitendra, sometimes more than he would have liked. Before he could doubt and question himself out of the action, he leaned forward, and pressed his mouth to hers.

14

_____

Olivia hadn't anticipated a lesson. She'd thought he would reach into her with his magic as he'd done in the carriage, bringing her pleasure so she could open her Sight. But after a while, she grasped that he was teaching her what she had done, instinctively, after her orgasm. If she knew the steps, she could take them on her own.

Except that something went wrong on what he called the sacral chakra. She'd felt a steady stream of warmth coming up through her body, but when she accessed that point, deep in her pelvis, power surged up like a gaslight with the gas opened all the way.

Her eyelids fluttered, but Savit grasped her hands and she shut her eyes again, letting him take control of the wild power. Whatever he did brought every nerve and sensation in her body alive and awake. Her spine lengthened and straightened of its own accord, the rise and fall of her lungs and even her heartbeat falling into perfect sync with Savit's.

Something else pulsed between them—an awareness that made her skin tingle and heat pool between her legs. The brush of her outstretched arms against the sides of her breasts made her shudder, and Savit's thumbs on her palms were a point of molten pleasure.

And then, he did the very last thing she would have expected.

His lips were tentative, almost wary. He pressed and shifted against her awkwardly, his mouth closed, and she suddenly knew that he'd never done this before. He'd never kissed anyone. He'd proudly stated his celibacy, but now she understood. He was a virgin. And yet his unpracticed kiss made her burn hotter than any lover she'd ever taken.

Liv angled her head and opened her mouth, teasing her tongue along the seam of his lips. They parted for her with surprised alacrity, and she took her prize with relish. His tongue was hesitant, but after she stroked it tenderly twice, he reciprocated, and shocks of pleasure burst through her from the contact. She groaned into his mouth, and yanked her hands from his to caress his chest, his back, down to his waist, then up his stiff arms to his shoulders and neck.

She giggled, and his tongue froze. She broke the kiss and murmured, "Relax. Touch me back."

Her heart pounded hard against her ribs as his finger traced her arm from shoulder to wrist. The touch was light, only a hint of a caress, and she craved more. Her nipples had hardened to tight peaks beneath the soft fabric of her blouse. She grabbed his other hand and placed it over one breast.

He cupped it gently, almost reverently, and she couldn't help arching a little to rub the pebbled flesh against his palm. He slid his fingers down, grazing the taut nipple, and stroked it with his thumb.

Olivia gasped in pleasure and he jerked his hand away. Laughter burbled up in uncontrollable delight. "It doesn't hurt. It feels good. You can do it harder, even pinch it a little. I'm not made of glass."

He reached out again, still tentative, and closed thumb

and forefinger over the other nipple. Pleasure coursed through her, along with a jolt of magic, and then the world dissolved.

This time, Savit was right beside her in the vision, still grasping her breast. He dropped his hand and grabbed both of hers instead. *Don't let go of me. I will keep us both grounded. Remember to keep some part of your awareness always with your material form, and to pull energy from the Casting Chamber. I will help you, but you must learn to do this for yourself.*

Olivia nodded, and squeezed his hand. She could still feel the cushion beneath her legs, back in Skye House, but also cold marble. She turned away from Savit to survey the room.

They sat in another Casting Chamber, much larger and grander than the one Lilias had constructed. Olivia had never been to Fay House on Skye, but she thought that even the great chamber there would be no match for this one. Although she'd never seen it in person, Olivia guessed this was the great Chamber of Westminster, built on the site of the Thames Nexus, one of the most powerful magical confluences in England.

Over a hundred mages stood in the room, their bodies positioned along key points in the symbols laid out on the floor. In the vision, she could see the vast quantity of magical energy they'd raised in swirling colors and lights. In the center of the maelstrom of power was a cot, on which lay William III. Beside him, in a chair, sat Anne. Tendrils of magic lifted out of him, twisted, and then burrowed into her.

They're transferring the Aegis Spell into Anne. William must be near death. According to official records, he died suddenly in Kensington Palace after an injury, so they must have transported him here, maybe even under a stasis spell.

It's a very complex spell.

Yes. I wish I'd had a vision of them casting it for the first time.

This will do. His fingers closed around hers in a reassuring squeeze, along with a surge of additional energy. *Concentrate. Things are going fuzzy around the edges, and I can't hear them.*

So she did, taking the power he offered and the magic from the Skye House casting chamber to ground them in the vision. Everything brightened, becoming more vivid. They could now hear the vocalizations of the spell and see the precise shape of the transference matrix.

I've never seen a spell being cast, Olivia admitted. *I had no idea it looked like this.*

Try to commit the various shapes to memory, as well as any of the words you can make out. It means very little to me, but should be instructive to your family.

Everything seems to be contained in this room, Liv noted. *I don't see any magic escaping. There's massive power coming in, but it's all being channeled into Anne through William.*

As she spoke, the spell reached a crescendo of power and the lines and sigils in the web surrounding the two monarchs flared to painful brightness, then contracted, whirling deocil, into Anne.

Now the magic flowed into her alone, and for a moment, she absorbed it in a hushed silence. Then, it began to seep out of her, some of the power dissipating into the air, some of it cascading back into the ground.

That's how it's supposed to work, based on what I've read about the Aegis Spell. The magical energy of the land and the people is concentrated into the monarch, and then refracted or enhanced and released back into the country.

Savit's hand squeezed hers, hard. *Your connection is weakening rapidly. I think part of your energy got caught up in that last burst—you're English, and the spell is meant to concentrate English magic. All that is sustaining you now is my magic and what you're drawing from Skye House. It's time to go.*

Now that he'd drawn her attention to it, she could see a thick stream of power running from her breastbone into the

Chamber. It was different from the cord that tied her to her flesh—it pulsed white rather than the shifting multi-hued tones of the other. But that, too, was fading, going grey and wispy at the edges.

Yet, when she tried to pull away, she couldn't. The thread of magic tethered her like a rope. *I can't break free. Savit, help me!*

He reached around with his other arm to sever the thread, but his hand passed through it like smoke. *I'm not substantial enough, here. Too much of my energy is vested in keeping you tied back to your body. You have to do it.*

Olivia trembled, her spirit-form wavering. She could see the Chamber floor through her outstretched fingertips. In fact, it had gotten more distinct, more vibrant, and she had begun to fade.

Panic surged through her, fear overpowering every other emotion, white hot in her chest. Across the room, Anne's head jerked in Olivia's direction. Her dark eyes widened. Could she see them, as Izarra had in Olivia's first vision?

Olivia had no heartbeat here, and yet her subtle body pulsed with a rapid tattoo as Anne's gaze locked onto her. Anne was a witch—not incredibly powerful on her own, but she had all the magic of England flowing through her now.

Olivia! You must break free. Now!

Liv flailed at the thread of magic, willing it to break, using her fear and her desperation to hone her will to razor sharpness. Across the chamber, Anne lifted her arm and pointed towards Olivia. The other mages shifted and began to turn her way. If they bound her spirit to this place, her flesh would die—or become an empty shell.

She had to do this, had to get back to her own time —and Savit.

Olivia grasped the thread with one of her not-hands, imagined the other as a heated blade, and slashed.

The thread broke, and she stumbled backward.

A blink, and she was on the floor of the Skye House Chamber, Savit hovering over her, one of his hands still clasped tightly over hers.

"Olivia!"

She sucked in breath after breath, heaving each out as quickly as the last, the pounding of her heart in her ears a physical sensation, like a drum mallet striking her skull.

"Please, Olivia." Savit ran his hands over her, deftly manipulating her energy, and pushing her hands flat to the stone floor. The cool smoothness against her palms felt good. Here was something she could grasp with both mind and fingers. Stone, shaped by human hands, polished and protected by skills both mundane and magical.

Her heart slowed its rapid rhythm, and her lungs ceased demanding such a frantic pace.

Eventually, she sat up. Savit took her hands again. The world was a blur except for his face.

"I can't decide if that was a success or a failure."

Savit laughed, but it was a hysterical laugh, born of the sudden cessation of fear more than true mirth. He drew her against his chest, and she mourned the loss of their earlier arousal. But the comforting warmth of him calmed the last frazzled edges of her soul, and she relaxed.

"Both, I think," he said once his chortles died away. "Next time, let's stick to theory until we're sure you can get your-self out of the vision. But we did learn something important. The spell is meant to be passed on to the next monarch. And, unless the queen is being deliberately coy, I doubt she ever received it."

"So we need to speak with her."

"Indeed. But not tonight. You need to rest."

It was a measure of just how much the vision had drained her that her spurt of indignation lasted only a moment, overwhelmed by the truth of what he'd said. "Very well. But we'll talk to Etta in the morning."

Across town that evening at a gentleman's club that had almost refused him entrance, Savit tried to pay attention to the incomprehensible discussion of taxes, subsidies, and trade routes that so enamored his grandfather and the other men around the table of a private dining room. He couldn't think of anywhere he wanted less to be.

He checked, again, on the piece of his magic tied to Olivia. Of course she was fine—still sleeping, as she had been every other time he'd checked. But after he'd been unable to pull her free of the vision today, the last vestiges of his attempt to keep his distance from her had disappeared. He could no longer deny that she meant something to him, more than the disinterested concern he might feel for another person in trouble. More, even, than the affection of a teacher for a student. She'd blown into his life on the winds of history, and now he could no longer imagine a future without her.

"Alex!" His grandfather's voice held a tone that suggested he'd called several times. Savit almost corrected him—but now was not the time, in front of his grandfather's friends and investors, to explain that he preferred the name his mother had given him.

"My apologies, Grandfather. My mind was wandering."

"I could see that. This is the Marquess of Hazelby." Grandfather gestured at a man that had just joined them. He was younger than Grandfather, but at least twenty or thirty years older than Savit. He looked familiar, but Savit couldn't place why.

The marquess held out his hand and Savit shook it. No

magic tingled along the connection, but Savit's sense of recognition deepened. "I'm pleased to meet you, my lord."

"Old Brian's grandson can call me Hazelby," the marquess said, smiling first at Grandfather and then at Savit. "Your grandfather has made me a great deal of money over the last thirty years."

"Always a pleasure, Hazelby."

Hazelby pulled up a chair and sat beside Savit. "I'm told you're a professor?"

"Yes, at Trinity College in Dublin. I'm on sabbatical now to do a lecture tour and some research here in London." Of course, the nature of that research had altered from what he'd originally intended, but he couldn't complain, since the change had brought him to Olivia.

"Ah, excellent. You study history?"

"Primarily."

"I will have to introduce you to my daughter. She is also a devotee of the past."

Savit wondered what the daughter was like. If her father would stoop to looking at him as a marriage prospect, it must mean she hadn't 'taken' in society. No one used the term 'bluestocking' anymore, but a woman who had more interest in books than young men was still something of an anomaly.

He gave a noncommittal agreement, and asked how Hazelby had come to meet his grandfather. That got the two of them reminiscing, and Savit was able to safely turn his attention back to the problem of Olivia.

Despite his worries, it was a good sign that she'd been able to free herself. They would have to figure out a way to shield her from mages encountered in the past. With the nature of their inquiry, the chances were high that most if not all of the visions she would have about the Aegis Spell would include sorcerers and sorceresses, all of them more powerful than he and Olivia together.

Something Grandfather said caught his attention.

"I'm not getting any younger, and it's time to pass on the reins." He beamed at Savit.

"Will you be giving up your teaching, then?" Hazelby asked Savit.

"I haven't decided," he hedged, wishing he could glare at the old man and didn't have to keep up the polite veneer. He spent most of his life perfectly in balance, with no extraneous feelings or desires, but being around his grandfather—and now Olivia—had made him subject to a wildly escalating range of emotions. It was like being a young man again, going through puberty without any friends or anyone to guide him through the Samskārā rituals. He hadn't met Chaitan until university, and it had been such a relief to learn a way to suppress and balance those unruly passions.

But now, he found he could no longer find the balanced center of his being—something inside him had shifted.

"Oh, you'll come around." Grandfather smirked, and everyone at the table chortled, as though Savit's acquiescence were a foregone conclusion.

But while he loved his grandfather, he could not be what the old man wanted. He wasn't a businessman, and he hated politics. Dealing with the infighting in his college was bad enough. Having to navigate these treacherous waters would drive him mad.

He paid lip service to the rest of the conversation, saying as little as possible. He knew his actions were making his grandfather unhappy, and he'd gotten a few curious glances from the other men for his clear lack of enthusiasm about their business, but he didn't care. He longed to be somewhere else—beside a woman who exasperated but accepted him.

15

O livia woke at her usual early hour, not long after daybreak, feeling tired and shaky but unable to sleep more. Savit arrived not long after she'd mulishly accepted the help of a maid to dress and Gillies's arm to come down to the breakfast room. He had Rajani and a basket of Indian delicacies in tow.

Last night, he'd helped Olivia up to her room after the vision, and she'd had to shoo him away at the door, assuring him that she could make it to her bed in one piece. Part of her had wanted to invite him to join her, but she rarely chose to be humiliated by propositioning a lover she knew would say no. So she'd shut the door in his face and stumbled off to her bed.

Where she fell, still fully clothed, and slept until she heard the soft scuttling of a maid rebuilding her fire and her body told her it was time to get up.

Now she faced a breakfast table full of far-too-awake and cheerful people. Mal and Etta sat side-by-side, not bothering with the social convention that required them to take up posts at opposite ends of the table. Savit, looking far too alert

158

—not to mention handsome—sat at the foot of the table. Rajani sat across from Etta, happily describing the mix of spices in whatever Etta was eating.

Ronan and Sorcha, Mal explained, had gone off to the train station to collect Evie, who would be arriving from Glasgow on the sleeper.

Once Olivia blundered to her seat, Savit started telling Etta and Mal about the vision and everything they'd learned, including pulling out some sketches he'd made of the Aegis Spell structure. As though she'd sensed that Olivia was not yet fully lucid, Etta then took Savit on a tangent, asking him about how he did magic. She was curious to know if she could try any of his methods, since many of the more advanced European spells were dangerous to cast while pregnant. He explained about chakras, and magical energy, and the divine in the world, and offered to instruct her whenever she wished.

Rajani chimed in that the Sutra wasn't just for mages, but for everyone, and even if Etta's magic didn't work using their methods, she could still use them for other purposes. "I start every day by meditating. I feel scattered and unsettled if I have to skip it."

"I would love to learn. That sounds like how my mother worked. She never created spell nets like we do, and she rarely used spoken magic, except for chants. And I always thought the chant wasn't magic—just her way of accessing magic."

"That's correct," Savit said. "When I speak a mantra, I'm not performing a spell. The mantra opens me to the possibilities of the magic, and then it is my will that interacts with the world energy to make things happen."

"For me," Rajani added, "the mantras also open my mind to possibilities. Just not magical ones!"

They philosophized a while longer, and then Mal left to

meet with his estate agent and took Rajani back to the ayah home. Liv had almost forgotten about his Scottish property, all the way on the northern coast. He'd bought it from a desperate clansman who couldn't afford the taxes and the upkeep but didn't want to sell to a rich Englishman who would turf out the tenants in favor of sheep.

The last she'd heard, Mal had sunk his entire personal fortune into the place, and it was recovering slowly. But the tenants were still there, and thriving.

Her attention wandered back to Etta and Savit, who were comparing stories of their treatment in Society. Etta finished telling a story about a particular set of ladies who continued to snub her despite her title, and how she'd never been sure if it was her skin color, her magic, or her American upbringing that they used to justify giving her the cut direct.

"Likely all three," Savit suggested. "I've been in this country since I was seven years old. While some of my former countrymen and women are here as well, most of them are middle or lower class, or servants like Rajani was. For many, it doesn't matter that the Reillys are gentry and have owned land in Ireland and England for generations. They see that I am Indian, and thus I am lesser. My grandfather had to fight for me to go to public school, and even now no gentleman's club will have me as a member. I am accepted by the historians because we're an odd bunch, but even there I have my detractors."

Olivia wanted to say something, anything, to tell both Etta and Savit that she cared about them, that they were two of the best people she'd ever met. But what could she say that would matter, weighed against the opinions of the rest of the world? Yes, she was different, too. She had a profession, and until recently had earned her own money, although not enough to finance her digs without the allowance her father gave her. She preferred to dress in clothes society deemed masculine, and keep her hair cropped short. That was how she felt most comfortable, most *Olivia*. She had never fit into the mold society proscribed for women—corseted and restrained and good only for making an advantageous match and bearing children. But she didn't see herself entirely as a man, either. She inhabited a space somewhere between.

If she needed to, however, she could grow out her hair. She could wear gowns and go to balls. She had the funds and the lineage and the right color skin. She would hate it, would feel like she lived a lie, but she could fold herself into that world and be accepted. Etta and Savit never could.

Their conversation must have shifted back to the topic of the Aegis Spell, because Etta said something about the queen taking weeks to grant audiences, what with her Diamond Jubilee approaching and the plans consuming her attention.

"We're lucky she agrees to see me at all, after the way we met. She was afraid I would be a threat to her. But the last time we spoke, she told me I'd become just like all of the other members of the House of Lords—annoying, persistent, and outspoken—but contained. I'm pretty sure she meant it as an insult."

Savit laughed. "In any case, a delay may be a good thing. Olivia needs time to practice. She's far weaker this morning than I'd like."

Liv glared at him. She hated that she still felt groggy and listless, despite consuming a full cup of coffee and polishing off a plate piled with everything on the sideboard, including Rajani's offerings. Olivia had been an early riser since childhood, a habit that served her well on digs when fieldwork could only be done during the sunlit hours. Now she felt like a spoiled debutante, sleeping in and lounging about, and the last thing she needed was Savit calling attention to her laziness.

"I'm perfectly well, thank you very much." She took a

defiant sip of her second cup of coffee. "But you're right that I need more practice. I want to become proficient enough that I don't need your help to control the visions."

"Don't push too far too fast." Etta leaned toward her, breaking several social etiquette rules by putting her elbows up on the table and propping her head in her cupped hands. "This is important, but not more than your safety. Considering how poorly the academic side of your search is going, your visions may be our only option to solving this mystery. So take it slow, and make sure you can continue to help us when we need it."

"I will, I promise."

Etta's gaze shifted back to Savit. "I think it would be best if you moved into Skye House while you're training Olivia. We've plenty of room, and you won't have to worry about going back to your hotel every night. Plus, it means you'll be right here if she has another vision out of the blue."

For a moment, Olivia thought Savit would refuse. It was obvious he feared proximity would lead to greater intimacy, and she felt his hesitation like a blow. But he wasn't a fool or a coward. Staying nearby until she learned to control her visions simply made sense. He acquiesced with a nod.

"I'll bring my things over later today. We shouldn't practice until later tonight, though, or possibly tomorrow. Last night's vision drained me almost as much as Olivia. I need to meditate for a while."

"The Casting Chamber is at your disposal."

Savit inclined his head in thanks.

"Perhaps today would be a good time to check out your parents' library," Etta said to Liv. "You already found something here that Lilias didn't know she had. Your father collects all sorts of things that he could care less about, but are worth money, including rare books. He may have something in that overstuffed library that will help us."

"Are you offering to join in the search?"

Etta laughed. "Under other circumstances, I would, but I'm meeting with some of my fellow parliamentarians today to discuss a workmen's compensation act that we're going to introduce this year." She lifted her elbows off the table and sat back, adopting a more socially-appropriate pose. "Stopping the Aegis Spell from draining English magic is always my priority, but there are other causes that need champions in our Empire."

"Agreed. Although I'll miss having you as a buffer between me and the rest of the family. Will Mal be back soon?"

"I'll go with you."

Liv's attention jerked to Savit. His lips were in a firm, straight line. Why was he offering? Because he wanted to help or because he thought she couldn't do this on her own?

"As Etta says, it's best that we stay together as much as possible." He spoke carefully, choosing his words with precision. "And I am very interested to meet the rest of your family."

"You won't think that after spending an afternoon with them, but it's your choice. The work will go faster with two sets of eyes on the books."

"Good, that's settled." Etta stood. "Oh, and Olivia. When you see your mother, ask her to set up the meeting with the queen. She's been our liaison with Amelia, the Queen's Sorceress, for the last six months on the matter of the draining spell. Amelia might be able to get us an audience more quickly."

Olivia tensed, her insides clenching like a fist, her stomach roiling. She didn't want to ask her mother for anything. But the request came from Etta, so it wasn't the same as Olivia asking for help. "I will."

16

Olivia rode with Savit to his hotel, then debated going up with him to help him pack. Eventually she decided against it. She wore a different set of work clothes today, but they were much the same as all of her other outfits. Tailored for comfort and movement rather than fashion, they were almost indistinguishable from menswear despite the need to accommodate her hips and small breasts. She might pass for a boy, or a servant, but she would prefer not use her small store of energy on engaging with an outraged public if anyone noticed she was, instead, a woman.

So she lounged in the Fay carriage, holding her hands over the small coal heater placed between the seats and trying to stay warm.

Savit returned quickly. She watched him out of the window. He had a trunk—likely full of his books—a satchel, and a duffel. Two of the hotel bellmen hoisted the trunk onto the luggage rack of the carriage and tied it down. The driver covered it with an oilcloth to keep out the sleet and snow.

Olivia settled back against the squabs cushioning the carriage seat as Savit climbed back inside, and they set off for

Mayfair and Hazelby House. Neither of them spoke for a while, and Olivia studied him as he stared absently through the window. When he spoke, his words seemed to blossom out of the silence, growing naturally from the rapport between them.

"I never saw snow until I was seven years old. Nearly eight. My grandfather told me stories about it, but I couldn't believe him. My life was hot and humid, and full of lush, growing things. We had the dry season, and the wet season. The concept of your temperate seasons was never real to me. But when we landed in Ireland, it was during a bitterly cold winter, and instead of frost and freezing rain, they had a rare deep snow."

He turned his face away from the window, and she looked directly into his dark, depthless eyes. "I thought it was the earth, mourning the loss of my parents. That all of the warmth and hope and light had gone, if only for a short while."

"Perhaps it did mourn."

"Perhaps. More likely it was what I needed to believe. But ever since then, snow has made me feel melancholy. Grandfather doesn't understand." He waved a hand at the window. "Not about the snow, but about what it meant for me to leave Gujarat, and to lose even Rajani once we reached England. What it means for me to be here, now. I arranged this speaking tour because he begged me to visit, but I put it off for months because I know what he wants is for me to learn more about his business. When I'm with him, he asks me to hide so much of myself."

That was not unlike the way her mother had always expected her to hide—to wear dresses, to grow out her hair, to pretend to be *normal*. Or at least to be what society deemed acceptable.

"Is he the reason you publish as Alexander Reilly?"

"Yes. He's called me Alex since my parents died. He doesn't realize—how could he?—that by denying the name my mother gave me, he took her away from me more permanently than death ever could."

Liv rose, stepped over the coal heater, and nudged Savit over in the carriage seat. He slid sideways to accommodate her, and she wrapped her arms around him. After a moment of stiff uncertainty, he relaxed and embraced her in return.

"She would be proud of you." Olivia said against his shoulder. "I'm sure your grandfather is, too. Why did he pick Alexander?"

"It was my father's name."

"Ah." She pulled away a little so her eyes could focus on his face. "So in his grief, he clung too tightly to what remained—you, and the memory of his son. Have you told him you prefer Savit?"

"Only once in so many words, and it was long ago. But he's aware of how I feel, and that my colleagues at Trinity College call me Savit." His fingers moved in soft strokes up and down her spine. She wondered if he was conscious of the movement.

"Perhaps it's time to tell him again. It's not like me publishing as Oliver. I chose that, fully aware of what I gained and lost by the choice. And Oliver is a part of me." She shifted, pressing a hand to her chest. "In here, I'm not entirely Olivia *or* Oliver. I'm both. For me, it isn't a betrayal of self to publish under that name. I would love to have the world accept my work universally as Olivia, because that would mean that any woman could be accepted." And it might mean that her mother would accept her, too. Although, if she were honest with herself, she knew that her mother's worries came from the same place as Savit's grandfather's—love, and fear. And neither Cecily nor Brian was entirely wrong. "Sadly, it's only good sense to choose the name that will open more doors."

She put her hand on his chest, over his heart. "But for you, Alexander is a mask. You know that, and it's pulling you out of balance."

His hands pressed into her back muscles in a jolt of surprise. "How do you know that?"

"I could see it, last night. Before the vision, but after you helped me open my Sight. You've got so much going on up here." She ran her hand over his thick mass of black curls, then trailed a finger down his forehead between his eyebrows, over his nose and lips, and stopped under his chin at the bump in his throat that covered his vocal cords. "And you're using that to deny everything going on down here." She slid her finger down over his chest to his waist and a little below, stopping just before she would have encountered his cock. He wasn't ready for that yet.

"I can't let that take precedence right now. You needed me during the vision last night. If we'd...done more, I'm afraid I wouldn't have been of much use to you, magically."

Olivia disagreed with that, but there was no point in saying it, so she changed the subject. "It's so strange to me, seeing these events that I could only speculate about before."

"And chose not to speculate about due to lack of evidence."

Liv laughed and poked her finger into the taut flesh of his lower abdomen. "I don't publish my speculations because that's misleading to my audience. But I do make them, and I try to find the evidence to prove them. If that happens, I write about it."

He'd squirmed at her touch, and when she'd thought he would pull away, he surprised her and brought her closer, until their noses touched. "And now you're seeing the evidence, but can't prove it."

"Yes!" She laughed.

A smile lit up his eyes, their corners crinkling. "You've accessed the narrative." She didn't miss the reference to their pleasurable argument from the first day they'd spent together.

"I suppose I have. I did promise Izarra that I would tell her story, even if it's a promise I can't keep. But it is incredibly frustrating. If I ever tried to write about all of this, all I would hear is, 'can this evidence be examined or duplicated?' and of course the answer will be no." She growled, and was shocked again when Savit leaned over and kissed her. He didn't linger. It was a playful, almost chaste kiss. A friendly kiss.

But it *was* a kiss.

The carriage jolted to a stop, and despite her worries about seeing her mother, a smile lingered on her lips as she led Savit into her own personal hell.

THE HOUSE WAS COLD. SAVIT HAD NO OTHER WORDS FOR IT. IT was adequately heated in a mundane sense, but in a magical one, it was sterile, almost a void. Etta had mentioned that the marchioness and her husband disagreed on the practice of magic, and from what he could tell, the lady had diverted all of the natural magical energy around and through the house into a few specific points—one upstairs, one in the garden beyond the house, and one below, perhaps in the servants' quarters.

Olivia shuddered as they crossed the threshold, accompanied by a butler who had deliberately *not* looked at Olivia's clothing when she shed her overcoat and hat and handed them over. "I've always hated this house." She frowned at the elegant tables in the foyer, topped by arrangements of hothouse blooms that would have cost a great deal in the middle of winter.

"It is not...welcoming," he agreed. "From a magical perspective."

"It isn't?" She shot an inquiring glance at him before following the butler up the large central staircase to the second level. Her movements were a little ungainly. She was already tiring. He would make sure she rested and read while he searched the shelves of her parents' library.

The chandelier over the stairwell had been intended for either candles or gas, but now sported clusters of glass bulbs with glowing metal filaments. Electric light. It was warm, orangish, and curiously flat. It cast precise, defined shadows, unlike light from a flame that flickered and danced no matter how one shielded it from draughts.

"No, it isn't. Although I suppose you wouldn't have sensed that before. Or, I should say that you might not have understood what you were sensing."

"That's probably it. I never bothered to train my tiny gift, but I could sense strong magic when the clan cast the bigger yearly spells or for weddings, deaths, and births."

"Then you can also sense the absence of magic, which is what is happening in this house."

"How is that possible?"

"I'm not certain. You'll have to ask your mother."

Olivia might have said something else, but they'd arrived at a particular closed door, and the butler had stopped. Rapping twice, he opened the door and announced them: Lady Olivia and guest. Savit had handed over a card, but it had apparently not been read. No matter.

Inside the room, two gentlemen stood at their entrance. There were two ladies present as well who remained seated, and all four people were dressed impeccably for visitors. It must be time for afternoon callers.

Olivia, with her usual disregard for etiquette, strode into the room and nodded at the older man. Savit froze. It was the Marquess of Hazelby. Apparently Olivia was the daughter devoted to history.

He could have laughed, except that the carefully constructed façade he'd created for his grandfather was now colliding with his true self.

"Everyone, this is Dr. Savitendra Reilly. He's assisting me with an enquiry for Etta. Savit, this is my father Roland Seward, Lord Hazelby," she gestured at him with a casual wave. "Over there is my brother Giles, Lord Abbinden and his wife Caroline, Lady Abbinden." Again, a negligent flick of her fingers in their direction. He looked back at the marquess, who was eyeing him with surprise and confusion. But then she paused, and took a breath that caught in her throat. Olivia's distress drew his attention away from the assessing eyes of the marquess.

"And this is my mother Cecily, Lady Hazelby."

The lady in question rose, and her gaze passed over her daughter quickly, with only a hint of pain or perhaps distress. Did she not approve of Olivia's clothes? The marchioness wore a splendid day gown with lavish puffed sleeves and a lot of colorful ruffles and ruching. Her waist was tiny by comparison, clearly held in by a tight corset that also kept her posture rigid and severe as she stood.

She held out a hand to Olivia. Liv went, her steps reluctant, and took it. Everyone else watched the pair with something between amusement and disdain. Amusement from her father, disdain from her brother and his wife. Was it her clothes? Her hair? Her mannerisms? All of the above?

Lord Hazelby strode over and held out his hand. Savit took it and they shook. The marquess had a firm, decisive grip. "So. Savit. I'm glad to make your acquaintance."

Savit shifted backward a tiny step in surprise. "Ah…yes."

Did the marquess truly not know who he was? He'd experienced other Englishmen's inability to distinguish the difference between any two people with brown skin, but he'd thought Hazelby had recognized him when he entered.

"I see you've already met my daughter." Of course he'd recognized him. The man had clear, intelligent blue eyes, sharp as glacier ice. "I assume there's a reason Brian introduces you as 'Alex?'"

"He...prefers the English name."

"And you prefer something else. Does that extend to your feelings on taking over his company?"

The man didn't pull his punches. He couldn't have been more obvious in his sally for information.

"I'm proud of his achievements." Savit hesitated, but then admitted the truth. "But no, I have no interest in being his successor."

"Then the rumors are true. He told me they were groundless, but I thought it might be a blind spot. I see I was correct." The marquess did not betray even a hint of what action that information might cause him to take.

"He insists that I'll do the right thing, but I'll admit that his idea of the right thing and mine are incompatible." Had Savit just cost his grandfather an investor? "Does that affect your willingness to continue using his services?"

"Not at the moment. He's hale and healthy, and there's time to groom a different man to take his place. But I'll admit, when the time comes for him to give up the helm, I will likely sell my shares."

The pained breath left Savit's lungs in a rush. Not immediate doom, but an acknowledgment that Reilly Shipping would not be the same without Reilly. "That's what he's trying to avoid by asking me to join him. But I would be a disaster. I'm trying to convince him to do what you said and groom one of his underlings to take over. Someone he can teach the right way to do things."

"Wise of you to know your limits. What is it that you're doing with my daughter?"

And now they came to an altogether different matter, but obviously the topic the marquess had aimed for the whole time. "Investigating a spell cast in the seventeenth century."

"Ah. Magic history. Olivia's pet topic."

"It's more than a pet topic, Father." Olivia had pulled away from her mother and now stood beside the marquess. The resemblance between them was striking, and explained why he kept thinking he recognized Hazelby last night. Her eyes were the same shape if not the same color, she had the same wide mouth, and she even had his nose. The only difference other than her hazel irises was in the shape of the face—his was lean and strong-boned, and hers was more subtly rounded, with a pointed chin.

"If it were more than a pet topic, you would have found a publisher for your book proposal."

She was planning a book? He knew about the articles for the historical society journal, but she'd yet to mention a book.

"I have a publisher interested. They are only waiting to see how my next few articles are received."

Except she didn't have any articles lined up, and wouldn't, since she'd had to abandon her dig in France. He knew that— it had been the basis of their first argument, that day he'd taken her to meet Rajani. And if she didn't wow the historical field in the journal soon, he suspected no book she wrote would ever see a printing press.

But the mulish line of her mouth said she would never, even gasping out her last breath, admit her failure to her parents.

"The next few articles?" The harsh voice came from

across the room. Her brother, Giles. "You haven't published in months, and if anyone who matters sees you dressed like that, you never will. Don't kid yourself. I think it's time that Father stopped your funding. It's one thing to support scholarly research and discovery. It's another to stroke your over-inflated ego."

"Of the two of us, I'm not the one who thinks he's superior to everyone else just because he's got a cock and a title," Olivia flung back. "And if you want to cut off my funding, fine. I'll raise my own. But right now I'm here at the duchess's request." She whirled to face her mother. "Etta needs you to set up a meeting with the queen. We found out more about the spell and Her Majesty may have answers we need. In the meantime, I'm going to look through the library and see if there's anything you all weren't aware you had lurking in the mess of Father's collection."

She stalked out of the room without waiting for a reply, her gorgeous opalescent hair swaying with the motion. Anger, stronger and hotter than he'd ever felt before, rose up within him like a tidal wave.

He skewered her brother with his gaze, then turned his fury on both of her parents in turn. "You do not understand her at all. She is a brilliant archaeologist. She has made more discoveries than any man in her field and is far more rigorous and exacting in her methods, which means her discoveries have weight. I have respected her for years, even when she was less than flattering to my own work. You are her family, and you should be ashamed that you cannot see her worth. She brings honor to your name."

The marchioness had the grace to blanch, and the marquess's expression turned stony. Her brother looked like he might try to argue, so Savit pivoted and followed Olivia out of the room before he could speak.

He did not slam the door behind him, but only because there was a footman there closing it for him.

He had no idea where he was going, but the tiny piece of his magic he still had attached to Olivia guided him down the hall to a set of steps made of pretty dark wood. Although more utilitarian than the grand sweep of the central stair, this one had a warmer feel, as though it was actually used by the family.

The library was back down on the first floor, in the public areas of the house. It held one of the few pockets of magical energy in the building. Perhaps it was used as a spell-casting area as well as a place to study and read. He felt more comfortable the moment he stepped across the threshold.

Inside, Olivia pulled down books and slammed them onto the surface of a long wooden table. Her fury was nearly palpable—and it was giving her temporary energy he didn't think she could spare.

He considered taking her by the hand and having her sit, calming her mind and releasing the tension of her anger. But calming and release was what he would have done. Olivia thrived on her wild emotions, and he had a feeling they were the key to controlling her magic.

May the gods help him control his emotions while he unleashed hers. He strode to her and opened up his arms in invitation.

She threw herself against him, her mouth latching onto his with hungry aggression. He absorbed the force of her embrace into his body, her passion and need a monsoon wind inside him. This was nothing like the practiced kisses of the barmaid who'd so disgusted him ages ago. This was honest, and raw, an earthquake of need, stirring him past endurance.

He wanted to do something, to touch her and make her

body come alive the way his had, but he didn't know what to do—how to give her pleasure.

She ripped her mouth away and dropped to her knees, her hands reaching for the buttons of his fly. She paused, waiting for him to give her permission. He stared down at her, unable to move, or speak. Incapable of telling her to stop, or begging her to continue.

"Please," she said, and licked her lips. "I've wanted to taste you since the first day we met. Let me. Please."

His shaft had already become semi-hard, but as her fingers stroked lightly over it, it filled and lengthened against her hand. His head fell forward and his chin bobbed twice, both nod of acquiescence and admission of his need.

She opened the buttons rapidly, her hands practiced at the task, as well they might be—she wore similar trousers. She pressed aside the fabric of his drawers and drew out his cock, stroking the length of him with a firm grip.

The pleasure was lightning-hot, stabbing through him until he gasped and shuddered. She stared up at him, the greens and blues and golds of her eyes vivid under a messy curtain of opalescent hair. He ought to tell her not to do this, that it was she who responded to pleasure, and he who must remain above it. But he wanted. By all that was divine, how he wanted.

Then, ecstasy.

He had no other words for it. Hot, yes. Wet, deliciously. Pressure and suction, the soft stroking of her tongue. Simple actions, and yet his reaction was like nothing he'd ever experienced before. He'd used his hand on himself as a young man, but that was long ago. He hadn't deliberately given himself pleasure since he first learned how to do magic. He'd never regretted his choice, or his path, had never even felt much desire for another woman. Brief hints of lust, perhaps, but never this all-consuming wash of bliss.

Sounds rose up out of his throat and mingled with the soft gasps and moans she made around his cock. He stared at her, unable to look anywhere else but at her lips, pink-red and plump like the inside of a *jamphal* fruit, sliding over his cock, leaving it glistening and aching. One hand cupped his balls, stroking back to the sensitive skin underneath, and she hummed with pleasure when his hips jerked involuntarily, shoving his cock farther into her mouth. Her voice vibrated around him and through him, and then her magic was there, too, sliding over him and into him. Her pleasure, her arousal, beat inside him like a second pulse, exquisite in its purity.

She wanted him, wanted *Savitendra*. Not because she was angry with her parents and her brother, although she was. The fury was still there, a spicy tang that filled his mouth with peppermint flavor. But stronger than that was her need for him, her affection and desire. This woman who embraced him when he shared his troubles with her, who gave him her own to bear in return, was twisting him into knots of delight tangled with a joy that suffused him down to the bone.

Her other hand grasped his arse, fingers digging into the muscle, and he responded with another thrust toward her that filled her with so much need that he knew it was what she wanted. She wanted him to move, to take his pleasure and not just receive it.

Savit wasn't sure if he could. It would push him past a line in his mind, a line that he'd never even known was there much less considered crossing before.

She made a little frustrated sound and wrapped one hand around the parts of his cock she couldn't fit in her mouth, cupped her tongue along the hyper-sensitive spot just under the tip, and sucked, hard. Raw fire burst from his balls, shot up his spine, and exploded in his brain.

He came into her mouth in hard spurts, his body shuddering and jolting, and the force of his orgasm pushed her into bliss as well, her body spasming in an erotic echo.

His cock, still hard and twitching, slipped out of her mouth, and he dropped to his knees beside her. They leaned together, and she kissed him, the taste of his seed on her tongue as it tangled languidly with his.

Then she jerked away, her eyes gone blank and staring. Another vision.

Her magic was still tangled up inside of him, and he moved to control the flow, to ground her and steady her. But she was already doing it, just as he'd taught her, touching the pocket of magical power that had been concentrated into this room to give her additional strength. He made sure every link was strong and steady, took a moment to button up his fly in case anyone else came into the library, and then altered his consciousness to join her in the vision.

This was someplace different than in any of the visions Olivia had experienced so far. She recognized a few of the mages from the transfer to Anne, all of them older now. Gone was the Dutch Sorcerer. Instead, the figure at the center of the room was Eleanor, now Queen's Sorceress. Beside her was Ludwig Schürholz, Sorcerer of the Electorate of Hanover. Liv recognized him only because she'd gone looking for portraits of all the mages attached to the monarchs of England from James II onward. She wanted to recognize them when she saw them in the visions.

Ludwig would become King's Sorcerer when the crown passed to George I.

Savit appeared beside her, and smiled. *Well done. Your control is much improved.*

She didn't answer, but smiled back, then shifted her attention to the group of mages.

They were arguing about the spell.

"We're going to have to expand it," Eleanor said, talking over an elderly mage who grumbled but subsided as she continued. "Ireland rose up for James, and the Scottish Highlands have never been happy that their lowland countrymen signed the Acts of Union. Half of the Highlanders are Magisterium-sworn, and will not be pleased to put a German Academe on the throne, especially since there's a clear line of succession without the Act of Settlement."

"Will the spell remain stable if we expand to include the whole island? Remember what happened to Rome." Olivia didn't recognize the speaker, a middle-aged woman with fading red-blonde hair. She may not have been of enough historical import to include in the major accounts of the period.

"I agree that the whole of the island is likely too ambitious, and that Ireland, while tempting, is not feasible at all. It will be difficult enough to include Hanover—"

"His Most Serene Highness has indicated his desire to move freely between his domains," Ludwig interjected. "The spell must accommodate that wish. The people of Hanover are equally his to rule."

"No one is objecting to that necessity, Meister Zauberer." Eleanor looked weary, as though this was something she'd already repeated a number of times. "But it does create some logistical quandaries that this coalition must address. We cannot expand over water in two directions. We cannot expand to cover the entire isle." She tapped a paper in front of her. Olivia focused on it, and found that the vision shifted so that she could see it more closely. It was a map of the British Isles, including Ireland, the Isle of Wight, and even the Orkneys. An additional small blob sat off to the east, labeled "Hanover." Parts of the map had been shaded purple, others green, and others red. "The purple area marks the boundaries of the current spell. The green is the proposed expansion. The red are areas I do not feel comfortable encompassing."

The size of the original spell was impressive, but it was

clear why they did not wish to push too much farther. They'd cast it as an ellipse, with one of the focal points over London. To shift the boundaries was to shift the focus of the spell. Perhaps that was why later monarchs had chosen to reside outside of London? And now there would be an odd spur on one side, making the whole thing unstable. Olivia would never have considered stretching the Aegis to the Continent, but Eleanor likely had little choice in the matter. And while William and Mary had needed the spell to supplement their power, George I would need it much, much more.

The map moved down the table, each mage assessing it and passing it on. Some made notations on it or drew in a new angle, but most simply took in the information and handed it on in silence.

Eleanor accepted the piece of parchment after it had made a full circuit of the table. She studied the notes and suggestions. "I will attempt to implement as many of these changes as I can, but I can make no promises. This is going to be dangerous and delicate work, and we must be cautious and prepared."

The others nodded and the meeting broke up. The vision tried to, as well, everything going fuzzy and indistinct. Olivia held on, willing clarity. She didn't want to see just the planning this time. It sounded very likely that the spell had gone wrong, and that might be why it now drained off English magic without giving any back to the land and people.

The room and the people blurred, shifting to smoke-like wraiths, then disappearing into a flat grey like fog. It was like holding sand on the beach, each grain slippery and impossible to grasp with blunt force. So instead of squeezing, she relaxed. She let the vision fill a space in her mind, as though she held the sand in cupped, outstretched hands.

Color and sound burst around them. Once again they

stood in the Chamber at Westminster. Anne had had her stroke, and was near death. The spell was being drawn out of her and reshaped, reformed, and stored, awaiting George's arrival some seven weeks later. Although the room nearly vibrated with tension, nothing went wrong. Olivia frowned, and let things shift around her again. Now George was in the room, being invested by the spell.

Nothing went wrong, at least nothing that Olivia could see.

If not at this point in history, then when?

THE VISION FADED, LEAVING THE COMFORTABLE VIEW OF BOOKS all around them. This room had been her refuge in the house when she'd been too old for the nursery or to stay behind in Wiltshire, and too young to be sent away to school. She loved the smell of slowly decaying leather, dusty paper, and ink. Loved the warm golden tones of the wood bookcases and tables. Even the electric lighting didn't bother her here, as it protected the books from open flames.

Mal had enjoyed this room, too, which was likely why Mother had pulled magic into a pocket of power here. And lucky for Olivia that she'd been here when the vision started, as there'd been enough energy in the room to keep the spell from draining her.

Or was it the other way around? Maybe she'd only had the vision here *because* there was enough energy in this room. She'd been having visions what felt like constantly back in France and on the Channel crossing. If she left England, would that be her new reality?

But no, Savit had said that once she learned to control them and with much more training, she would be able to either dismiss them immediately or be almost co-conscious with them—able to pay attention to what was happening to her body in the physical world while exploring the vision in her mind.

And, with enough practice, she would be able to call them up on command, say, at a dig. The secrets of history would be open to her in a way she'd never dreamed before. She would be able to scout a site through the lens of the past, would know exactly where to find precious artifacts and proof of the theories she'd only been able to guess at before.

But that was all for later, when they'd learned the truth of the Aegis Spell and given Etta and the others the means to dismantle it.

"It worked. And I feel fine. Tired, but it's the normal kind, like after a long day on a dig."

"Yes, it did work." Savit looked flabbergasted, and for a moment she took offense. But he wasn't surprised by *her* abilities. He was surprised at himself. He'd done magic with her only moments after having an earth-shattering orgasm. One piece of evidence to disprove his theory that intimacy would ruin him as a mage.

"I think, as long as I practice in spaces where magic is stronger, like here and the Casting Chamber at Skye House, and we work together, I won't have any more repeats of those first, terrible drains on my magic and body."

"I hope so. And you didn't even leave your physical self behind this time. Well done, Olivia."

Warmth flooded her cheeks, but he leaned over and kissed her and nothing else in the world mattered.

He was still awkward, touching her only hesitantly, as though she were a spun-sugar decoration on a dessert.

She let him set the pace this time, and he kept things light, breaking away when she would have just been getting started. But she had the memory of him crying out and spilling into her mouth to sustain her.

They moved to the bookshelves and pulled down likely titles, then sat side-by-side and skimmed through. They didn't find anything, but if she could control the visions, that wouldn't matter. They'd be able to discover everything they needed to know using her magic.

She half-expected her mother to arrive, or someone else, but other than a maid who popped in and asked if they wanted tea, no one did. On the ride back home, she asked, "What are you going to do when this is over? Go back to Trinity?"

They sat side-by-side, despite the impropriety, fingers interlaced. "I don't think so."

"Why not?"

Savit reached up with his free hand and brushed a stray lock of hair away from her face, tucking it behind her ear. "Because you're right about my grandfather, and about trying to be Alexander. If I stay at Trinity, if I keep teaching and doing all of my research out of books and publishing as Alex Reilly, I won't be living as I should. I'm thinking of going back to India. There's a new dig starting on the Indus River. I would like to know more about the history of my country, and perhaps find a place for myself there, with my mother's people."

"That sounds wonderful. Have you been on many digs before?"

"Nothing so grand as you have. A few smaller excavations in Ireland." His fingers tightened on hers and he shifted, cupping the back of her head and turning her to face him. "According to the stories that survive, the Indus River culture knew much more about visions than we do. If the tales are true, they could move freely along the threads of their lives: past, present, and future. Perhaps there would be something for you there. That is, if you would like to come with me and show me how it's done."

Her heart thudded against her ribs. She didn't mix pleasure and work anymore. She'd promised herself.

And yet, she and Savit had muddled along well on this project. Of course there'd been difficulties and arguments and likely would be more. Right now, he was the teacher, she the learner. On the dig, she would instruct him. But maybe it was possible, as long as they talked to each other like this.

"I think…maybe, I would like that. When this is over."

Cecily sat again in the formal parlor of the Queen's Sorceress. Amelia had left her waiting for over an hour. She would not be pleased at how their last meeting had ended, or at Cecily's return earlier than scheduled.

Once again the tea tray sat on the small table, the water cold. She would not take anything off the tray until Amelia arrived, and had prepared for this eventuality by eating before she left Hazelby House.

Thoughts of the house brought back memories of the previous day, of Giles spewing hatred at his sister. How had her children come to that? She'd left the raising of Giles to Rand, and that had been a mistake. He was a good businessman and provider, but had no idea how to be a good father. His own had been distant and cold. His mother, the dowager marchioness, had balanced the indifference with warmth and acceptance, but that experience taught him that only mothers are supposed to nurture.

At that task, Cecily had failed. She loved all of her children, but she'd spent her entire adult life as a slave to the causes Lilias had given her.

Keep Fay magic alive in England. Seek out the cause of the drain. Prepare to pass on the torch when the time came.

As it had. How had Lilias known? Cecily always assumed that Viola would be her successor. Neither of them could hold the title, of course, having come from the male line, but Cecily was here, in London, working for the clan's cause. Perhaps she would have been easier on Viola—on all of her children—if she'd had the foreknowledge that the new leader of the clan would be a wild, American offshoot. If she'd been able to see that her own efforts, while laudable, were almost entirely meaningless.

She could have spent more time with the children, especially Giles, Perceval, and Olivia. She could have been open with them about her goals, her hopes, and her promises. But she hadn't.

And now Olivia paid the heaviest price. Giles was an ass, but he was a socially-acceptable one. He was not well-liked, but he commanded a certain respect among his peers. He had a wife and children. Viola and Ian had found in each other a true mate and were happy now, pursuing Viola's dreams of a school despite the problem of their permanently melded magic. Percy had his military career; he'd graduated last spring from the Prussian Staff School and had just finished a tour on the continent as an advisor and aide to diplomats at the embassy in Potsdam. Mal had found Etta, and Etta had changed everything.

But Olivia had none of the advantages of the others. She was different, eschewing femininity, choosing her career and independence over everything else. The words of Dr. Reilly had lashed Cecily like a whip. She was proud of her daughter, and what she'd accomplished. But she feared for her, too. Olivia had taken lovers of both genders on the Continent openly, with no care for how her reputation would fare back at home. She insisted on dressing in men's clothing. There were no laws—yet—forbidding women to take other women to bed, but a man could be jailed or forced to hard labor that usually resulted in death. How long before someone decided that love between two women was unnatural, too? Even though it was the most natural thing she'd ever experienced?

The pang of long-dead love clutched at her heart. She'd found happiness with Rand, and pleasure in his bed. Her discreet friendship with Diana Westin, Viscountess Rosminster, had provided her with an outlet for her other cravings, and Rand with two women who enjoyed him as much as they did each other.

And yet. Her memories of Amelia were of pure, open, honest love. No hiding from each other, as she must hide her magic from Rand. No secrets or games, as Diana liked to play. Cecily and Amelia's love for each other had been the one truth underpinning her life since she was a young woman.

It hurt, to be forced to hide that love. And she was so afraid for her daughter, who refused to hide.

Amelia entered the room in a whirl of energy. Cecily couldn't tell if she was pretending to be 'too-too busy' and that's why she'd kept Cecily waiting, or if it was simply residual anger, covered over by false civility.

Today, Cecily didn't want anything false. She didn't want games, or aversions, or masks. She stood, startling Amelia into stillness. "I have news."

Olivia had been too angry to share the details of her visions in person, but Etta had sent over a document listing the relevant points. Cecily condensed the account still further.

"So as of George the First, the Aegis Spell was in place, and set in roughly the same geographic area that it currently draws from. We have not yet discovered what happened to draw magic out of England instead of distributing it back to the country. The duchess wishes an audience with Her Majesty to discuss anything she might know about her family's history with the spell."

Amelia had taken a seat at some point during her recitation and request, so Cecily now felt like a schoolgirl reading her lesson for her teacher. She sat, and Amelia reached for the teapot.

"Her Majesty is very busy with preparations for her Diamond Jubilee." Amelia prepared the tea without looking at Cecily.

"I am aware."

"Who would the audience be with?"

"Myself, the duchess, my daughter Olivia, and the historian Dr. Reilly."

Amelia handed over a cup. Once again, Cecily was careful not to let their fingers touch when she accepted it.

"Olivia will have to wear a dress. The queen will not speak to her if she isn't properly attired."

"She will hate that, but I understand." She took a sip. Perfect, as always. Amelia could have shown her displeasure by making it too bitter, or to sweet, or too cold. But she never did.

"Very well. I will speak to Her Majesty. But only because I feel it is in her best interest to do so. Not because you asked." Amelia took a sip of her own tea.

Cecily put down her cup and saucer. "I am not asking. I am merely the mouthpiece for the duchess."

"She's your daughter-in-law. Have you no control over what she does?" Amelia watched her over the rim of the teacup.

"I won't honor that ridiculous question with a reply. But I will say this. You are the Queen's Sorceress. Have you no control over what a noble mage does in your kingdom?"

"Empire. We're an empire now."

"Yes, yes. I suppose you already know that Dr. Reilly is a child of that empire?"

Amelia's lips quirked. "Indeed. I also know that he is a practitioner of Indian magic, although my source, the Queen's Munshi, was not entirely certain what that meant as he is an adherent of Allhah. Can you enlighten me?"

Cecily lifted her cup again and used the few moments gained by sipping and swallowing to prepare her answer. "The practical effects seem similar to ours. He simply goes about it in a different way. Beyond that, it requires a very rigorous mental discipline and perhaps allows the mage to have access to other ways of seeing and existence than we do."

"Interesting. Are there any ways that might benefit Her Majesty? She'll be more apt to schedule your meeting in a timely fashion if I can give her a carrot to go with the duchess's stick."

"I have no idea. You're free to call on him and inquire. He's staying at Skye House."

"Yes, that was noted." Amelia's smile turned sly. "And that your daughter is there, as well."

Cecily's cup clattered back against the saucer. "Just what are you implying?"

"Nothing. But I hardly need imply something that she makes no effort to conceal. At least he's a *he*, even if he is half-savage."

Cecily shoved the cup and saucer back onto the tray with a crash of porcelain. "Amelia Du Vayne, that is unworthy of you." The rebuke, and the use of Amelia's maiden name, had flown out without Cecily's conscious control. Incandescent anger filled her. How dare she disparage a good man just because he did not look like her?

But Amelia flinched, and lowered her head rather than

bite back. She took a long gulp of tea. "You're correct. That was unjust and unkind. I apologize."

"Apology accepted." Cecily rose, and Amelia waved her back down.

"Don't go yet. I'm sorry. I'm still angry with you, but neither your daughter nor Dr. Reilly deserves my insults."

Cecily sat, warily. "That's true, but I'll admit that Olivia is...open about her affections. That was not an unfounded accusation."

"The world is changing. Perhaps in a few years, women will have the vote and go around dressed in trousers all of the time. Perhaps those whose love takes...other forms won't need to conceal their feelings anymore."

"Perhaps. But perhaps not. People fear anything that is different. And men are terrified of anyone who asks for the same rights they have, because they fear losing power."

"Petticoat Rule, you mean?"

"I suppose. Your queen doesn't help. If it were up to her, we'd all go back to being chattel."

"She's your queen, too."

"But I didn't choose to serve her directly. I couldn't."

"I can, and do. Don't forget that just because..." her voice trailed off.

Cecily reminded herself it was not a day for hiding. "Just because we used to mean something to each other. Just because we used to be in love."

Their gazes met. It was nothing like the last time they'd sat here, angry and hurting. The pain was still there, but it was the deep ache of a wound that had never properly healed. A bone never set, that had grown back together but had never worked as it ought again.

"Used to be?" Amelia asked, her voice very, very soft.

Cecily couldn't answer. Instead, she got up and went

around the small table. She knelt beside the woman who would always, damn her, hold her heart. She picked up Amelia's left hand. It was encased in a thin, gauzy glove. Cecily stripped it off, and touched her finger to the curving crease of her heart line. Then she lifted the palm to her mouth and kissed it.

Placing Amelia's hand back onto her lap, Cecily rose and walked away.

O livia had almost forgotten that she'd arranged a meeting the next day with Mina to search the archives again, but a note came to Skye House in the morning, after another bad night of dreams of Izarra, asking to change the time to later in the day.

Liv found herself back at the historical society on a frigid afternoon with a list of questions that a girl who grew up in the German-speaking part of the Continent might be able to answer.

Savit had been unhappy about her decision to go on her own, but after their success with the last vision, she felt confident that she could take control and push away any that came when he wasn't around. He'd made her swear that she would do so, and she had.

Mina met her in the foyer, wearing another sober dress appropriate for a woman at work: a drab brown with only a little grey piping for contrast, barely present gathering on the top of the sleeves, and a tiny bustle that was probably just extra fabric gathered together. No ruffles or flounces anywhere, not even at the collar. Liv wondered what the woman wore when she went out. She seemed the type to adore soft, billowy gowns with lots of lace and petticoats. Yet would she be so daring as to allow the low neckline with abundant cleavage currently in fashion? Or would she opt for a safer style, cut in a shallow oval around her neck?

Best not to imagine either. Mina had given her a look of surprise and almost horror when she arrived dressed in her trousers and waistcoat. She'd barely blinked at the bloomers Liv wore the first time they'd met, but those were common among working-class women who rode velocipedes to their jobs. Very few women wore trousers.

Mina contained her shock, however, and they went to her office—more of a closet than an office—for tea. They chatted a while about Mina's projects, and Olivia mentioned the robberies that had stymied them so far. "Fortunately, enough of the collectors were familiar with the missing material that they could summarize relevant information for us. We've pushed our line of inquiry forward to the early eighteenth century, and the reign of George the First."

"I thought you said you were interested in a spell cast in 1688. Why would it still be in place nearly thirty years later?"

"That's part of what we're hoping to find out." That was partially true, anyway. What they wanted to know was not why in 1714, but why *now*, in 1897.

"If there's any way I can help, please give me a task."

"Well, the spell I'm researching is linked to the royal family." That ought to be obscure enough. There were lots of spells on the monarchs, and plenty of them were public knowledge as they had to be cast or renewed at major events such as births, coronations, and weddings. Let Mina assume she was talking about one of those. "George spent most of his life in Hanover, and even returned there for nearly a fifth of his reign as King of England. It is likely that there is something relevant there still, or perhaps in the possession of one of his descendants on the Continent. I'm hoping you will know of any extant letters, commonplace books, or journals that might be of use to me. Or, if you don't, that you'll be able to ask someone who might."

"Of course. My father has friends back in Prussia, and I went to university there for a year. I will telegram one of my professors who lives in Potsdam."

"Excellent. I'm so glad to have your help on this project."

Mina's smile was shy, but warm and pleased. She must not receive much praise in her job. It was such a shame that Mina wasn't interested in women. Not that Olivia would be able to pursue the attraction at the moment, anyway. She didn't have the patience for more than one serious lover at once, and Mina needed lots of attention and affection.

But perhaps someone else could. Taking a lover would be just the thing to bring Mina out of her timid shell. It would have to be the right lover, of course. A gentle man—and not necessarily a *gentleman*—who would compliment her and give her pleasure. Who amongst her acquaintance here in London would fit that description? Perhaps Percy, once he arrived. He was handsome, gallant, and kind. He spoke fluent German, too. Yes. Percy would be perfect.

"Do you like to go out in the evenings?"

"Oh, sometimes. When I have the funds. My parents don't believe in amusements. They are very strict Reformists, you know." Reformists were an off-shoot of the Academe that eschewed frivolity and any sort of excess. They would have hated Olivia's siblings, who spent most of their early adulthood providing massive magical illusions for the edification of the Prince of Wales and his Marlborough House set.

"Then you must allow me to take you somewhere. There's the theatre, or opera, or a music hall, or there are a number of gorgeous panoramas, and I've read that there are several fine kinetoscope shows as well."

Mina flushed and hid behind her teacup. "I'm sure I would enjoy any of those activities."

"Of course you will. And I'll bully my brother into coming along to escort us. He'll be back in England soon. He's been in Brandenburg, so he'll be able to give you all the news and gossip from the court."

"Your…brother?"

"Yes. He's very handsome, too, so you needn't think I'm selling you a pig in a poke."

"Perhaps you ought not sell me anything. I don't think my parents would approve of me being escorted by a man." She'd drawn inward, her shoulders rounding as she turned her face away in embarrassment.

"Whyever not? He's reputable in all the ways your parents could wish, I assure you. Son of a marquess, decorated military man, and all of that. And he's disreputable in the ways that *you* would want."

Mina stared down at her hands clutching her teacup. "My parents wouldn't want me to be seen with any man not of their choosing."

"How mediaeval of them. I can bring him round and they'll fall in love with him, I promise."

"Lad—I mean, Olivia." Mina put her cup down and laid a hand over Olivia's. The gesture bordered on inappropriate, so Liv knew Mina was very rattled. "My parents are already upset that I took this job, although we need the money and it's what I love to do. Father's charitable endeavors far outweigh his stipend, I'm afraid. They would be devastated if I started walking out with a man. They would disown me."

"If that happens, you can come to me. My family will take you in. The duchess already has a houseful of misfits."

"I don't want to be a misfit." Mina's fingers squeezed over Olivia's, her expression apologetic and miserable. "I can't be like you, Olivia. You're so bold, going so far outside the bounds of propriety. I'm not like that. I need...I need to feel safe. I want to be normal."

Liv shifted away, her fingers sliding out from under Mina's to rest in her lap. She knew she wasn't like other women, but she'd thought most would be more than happy to break free of their chains, if freedom were offered. Yet Mina chose the cage.

What did that say about Olivia?

They adjourned to the archives, but Liv had only half of her mind on researching eighteenth century mages. She recalled the looks of disdain and hauteur, the day she and Savit had gone calling on his contacts. Even his friend had stared at her openly before recalling his manners. Some of them had been shocked by his dark skin, but he was a man and a respected historian. After a few minutes, he'd had them all talking openly and sharing whatever he wanted to know.

They'd ignored Olivia, treating her like a secretary or an aide. Not a researcher in her own right. Not even as a person —as a position.

She frowned down at a passage she'd now read over three times. She wasn't accomplishing anything today.

"I have appointments later this afternoon, so I'll be off," she told Mina, who looked worried but said nothing.

On the way back to Skye House, she hugged her arms around her middle and slouched into the seat of the carriage. She could only do that because of the way she dressed. Her mother's spine was fused into a perfect line after years of wearing a corset. Olivia had chosen comfort, first out of necessity to work, and later because this was how she felt most herself.

But who was that, exactly? Giles's words had hurt more than she'd wanted to admit. Yes, she'd been angry, but at herself more than him. He only spoke the truth. She hadn't published an article in months. Henri had taken over her dig, and would get all of the credit for months of work collating data and cataloguing artifacts, something she was better at than he.

Or was she? Was her whole life built on presumptions of competence and delusions of grandeur?

At dinner that evening, she still couldn't settle. Mal kept trying to engage her in conversation, then frowning at her mightily when she responded with absent, one-word answers. Savit just watched her, puzzled. Etta left her alone. Sorcha, Ronan, and Evie were out, taking Evie to investigate the burglaries again.

The tiny red-headed girl had looked envious of Olivia's clothes when they'd met earlier, and had asked her where she'd gotten her waistcoat. So there was at least one other woman in the world who wanted to be different. Who wouldn't choose the chains of 'normal' if given a chance.

But they were only two, against millions.

19

Savit took his place at the lectern in the big meeting hall of the Society for the Exploration of the History of the Arcane and Mundane. The Society's walls reverberated with the clamor of their conversations. They quieted as Sir Archibald introduced him. He'd considered having Archie introduce him as Savit, but at the last minute changed his mind. Almost everyone here knew him only through his writing, and in print he was Alexander. No need to confuse the issue until—unless—he decided to start publishing under his true name.

Olivia sat in the back of the hall with the other ladies, and he had to scan the room to find her, as he'd removed the piece of his magic tied to her after her successful attempt to control the vision at Hazelby House. She'd agreed to turn away any visions that came when he wasn't around to help.

She wore a dress—well, bloomers—for the event. He'd been surprised to see her don them again, but she'd offered no explanation to his awkwardly-worded query.

After they'd finished dinner, he'd suggested that they not practice so she could rest, and she'd surprised him again by not objecting. She'd gone up to her room and did not appear again until it was time to leave for the lecture.

There was something seriously wrong, and once he finished here he was going to devote all of his attention to finding out what.

He began the lecture with a brief overview of the history of the schism between the Magisterium and the Academe. Part of his lecture tonight would touch on events he'd now witnessed with Olivia—the investiture of George I as king of England over the would-be James III. Not that he could say that in the lecture. The problem with visions was that they weren't proof. He was comfortable making informed guesses about the past as long as his audience understood they were guesses, but with those conjectures he could point to all of his sources and documentation to explain how he'd come to his conclusion. No one else would ever see Olivia's visions.

He moved on from George I's crowning and the Rising of 1715 and to the main topic of tonight's lecture—the second Rising of 1745 and the successful campaign of Charles III of Scotland.

His audience listened with mostly rapt attention as he brought them through the shifting politics of the time, including the clashes between Magisterium, Academe, and Reform-Academe, in Scotland in the mid-eighteenth century.

But Savit wasn't thinking about the gods who'd given the various sects their patronage or the new Acts that had ensured Scottish independence as something more than a suzerainty—able to self-govern and with its own leadership —but less than a sovereign nation.

He spoke of the way they'd modeled the system on the High Kings of Ireland, but thought about how Olivia balked under the yoke of feminine expectations in British society, just like the eighteenth-century Scots under the rule of a foreigner they didn't respect.

In many ways Charles had been just as foreign, and had argued with his followers on many issues they felt were important. If not for a few persuasive clan leaders and an illness that had left Charles bedridden for several weeks, he might have continued his push south into England as he'd wanted, and then all might have been lost. But fate had intervened, and England had accepted him as ruler of Scotland, with his father named King James VII in absentia.

Still, that wasn't the lesson he wanted Olivia to learn. He didn't want her to cave to external pressures, no matter what she might gain from doing so. He wanted her to live, work, and love as herself, not following some fashionable template decided by society.

He finished the talk to thunderous applause, but as gratifying as it was to share knowledge with others, he was unsettled within. People mobbed the podium, asking questions and thanking him for an excellent lecture.

He allowed himself to be swept into the tumult of excitement and congratulations. There would be time to ponder the question of Olivia later.

LIV SLIPPED OUT THE BACK OF THE LECTURE HALL AND HEADED for the archive. She'd been useless the day she was here with Mina, and she was certain she'd overlooked something. Or many things. Not that she felt much better now.

She would never be allowed to give a lecture like that, except to an audience of women, who usually couldn't afford to pay as well as the bigger, male, societies could. And if her father did cut off her allowance, she'd never be able to support herself by writing. She could try to teach at one of the new female colleges, but it wouldn't be the same. She would no longer have control over her life. She'd be answerable to a dean, and a board of governors. She would have to dress "properly" and provide a "good example" by not being seen with men. The repression would destroy her.

Etta would help, perhaps, if Olivia could bring herself to ask for it. But there was a difference between taking her father's money and taking the duchess's. Perhaps because she felt her father owed it to her for her terrible childhood, and for sending her away to Switzerland for school, a punishment for a crime she hadn't even committed—Viola had, by starting a riot at her finishing school.

Though that hadn't turned out as he'd intended. She'd had several romances at school, but it was when Talya arrived that Liv fully embraced who she was. Talya taught her to rebel and awakened possibilities that forced Olivia to look at the world differently. Everything between them had been passionate and wild, from their first kiss, to the first time they made love, to Talya cutting off Olivia's hair, to their final, tumultuous parting.

Talya had given her the courage to embrace a different way of being. Yet she was gone, now, and some of Liv's fire and verve had gone with her.

Who was she, now? Olivia? Oliver? Liv? Savit's lover, begrudging though that last might be? She didn't know. The visions didn't help. In some ways, they were amazing, giving her more information and insight into the past, igniting her passion for history. In others, they were terrifying. She wasn't a mage, and had never wanted to be one. Yet magic now shaped her life in ways she would need years to fully discover and comprehend.

Across the room, the door clicked shut. Olivia looked up to see Mina, arms crossed over her chest, dressed for the evening in a still-sober grey gown, neckline cut high and with gloves that reached far above her elbow, leaving only the tiniest patch of bare skin before her puffed sleeve.

"I saw you slip out," she said, and came forward. "Did you not enjoy the lecture?"

"Oh, no. It was wonderful." And that was the problem, because even if she was allowed to speak for an audience like that, she didn't think she *could*. Savit had a way with words, and was a natural storyteller. Olivia would have just gone up and started reading off lists of data.

"Yes, I was surprised, given his…background."

Olivia stiffened. "What do you mean by that?"

Mina's expression of puzzled pondering shuttered, leaving her face an empty mask. "Nothing. Just that one doesn't expect a man who grew up in the wilds of India to be able to speak so authoritatively on matters of European politics and religion."

"He's been here since he was seven, and his father's family is Irish. But that shouldn't matter. I speak authoritatively about my discoveries, and I didn't live in ancient Rome or mediaeval France."

"But that's different." Mina held up her hands as if to demonstrate the difference by the width she held them apart.

"How? Savit's parents and his personal history do not define him. He is a remarkable person, and someone I respect very much."

"I didn't mean to offend you. I've just never met anyone like him."

"Neither have I, although not in the way you mean."

"I'm sorry." The apology sounded more like appeasement than sincerity.

Olivia was tempted to walk away and not accept the apology, but Mina's opinions weren't unusual or even uncommon. "We're all human. Try not to forget that."

"I will." Again, the words lacked conviction, but Olivia

was tired of fighting tonight, so she didn't press. Mina came over and gestured at the bookcases. "Is there something I can help you find?"

"I wanted to look over some of the books I had the other day. I wasn't feeling well and I'm sure I skimmed right over important information." She picked up the book she'd pulled off the shelf before Mina entered. It was a collection of papers from the mid-eighteenth century, and the subtitle purported that some of them were letters written by George III. She pointed at the claim. "I wonder if that's true."

"It might be. But even if it is, it won't do you any good. He was quite mad. His ramblings are enough to give me a headache."

"I'll risk it," Olivia said, and sat with the book. Mina placed a different one by her elbow.

"This one has writings from the same period by the Prince Regent. They might offer a more sane opinion."

"Thanks. I'll check that next." She flipped open the book and started reading, giving more of her attention to the words on the page than she had yesterday. Although Mina was right—deciphering the Mad King's parlance was enough to bring on a migraine.

Then she found a reference to Hanover that made her breath catch. He was the first Hanoverian king born in England who spoke English as his first language. He wrote that he wanted to distance himself from the German-speaking Electorate while still providing for the citizens there. In the mess of tangled words, Olivia sought—and found—meaning. He wanted to send one of his sons to rule in his stead, and either pass part of the spell on to him, or withdraw it from the Continent entirely.

The vision came as a shock.

At first, she thought to dismiss it. After all, Savit wasn't here to help, and Mina was in the room. But Savit wasn't far away, and to Mina it would just look like she was lost in thought or concentrating on the book, so she went through the steps he'd taught her to ground herself and power the vision. There was very little ambient energy in the room, but beneath the building she felt a strong channel of magical power. A leyline.

She'd never tapped into something that powerful before, even if this one felt relatively weak compared to others she'd sensed in her lifetime. Still, with the part of her mind that was already engaged with the vision, she could see and hear an argument about how to honor the king's request. She needed to know this, and couldn't pass up the opportunity. She reached for the leyline, and let the power flow up and through.

The vision overwhelmed her.

She could almost have been in the room. All of her other visions had been misty, dream-like. If she concentrated she could make things sharpen into focus, but otherwise there was always a tiny blur as though she was very far away. But now it felt real. She could smell sweat, and perfume, and the unique scent of very old buildings made of stone—a musty tang, mixed with the sweet aroma of wood smoke and the almost meaty reek of tallow.

The sound of the mages' argument echoed off the chamber walls. Again, she recognized only the major figures —Francis Mayes, the King's Sorcerer, and Richard Clifton, the Arch-Mage of Canterbury. There was also a man who spoke in a thick German accent she did not recognize— possibly whoever represented Hanover in the coalition.

"No one has ever attempted to alter the Aegis while it is invested in the monarch. I told you all this would not end well." That was the King's Sorcerer.

"His bout of madness has passed." The Arch-Mage. "And it was what he asked of us."

"Yes, but we should not have done it." That was the Hanoverian. "Now, I fear, we may have caused him irreparable harm."

"Nonsense." Mayes. "He has recovered. We put everything back the way it was."

"Not everything." Olivia didn't recognize this woman, but she also spoke with a thick German accent. "His Majesty was unable to retain the entirety of the spell."

"A tiny fraction—"

The woman interrupted Clifton. "His mind was not the same. The Aegis will give him a semblance of sanity for a time, but it will not last."

"You have no proof of that." Mayes again.

"No," the woman agreed. "And yet I know. Wait and see if you do not believe me."

Olivia already knew the woman was correct. If this was the first bout of madness, there would be another in a few years, and then more and more until the king finally agreed to a regency.

With the thought, the scene blurred and sharpened again to a different room, but many of the same people. The German woman spoke again, and she sat much closer to the head of the table this time—right beside the Electorate Mage, in fact. "We must begin the process of removing the spell. He is too unstable, and he will cause the spell to become unstable as well."

"But removing the spell now could cause him to go into a permanent decline." The King's Sorcerer looked older, and much more haggard. The Arch-Mage of Canterbury was not in attendance. But if she remembered her history, there would have been a new one by now. Perhaps he had not been admitted into the coalition.

"Yes, it will." The woman spoke with the same certainty. "And so we will remove it slowly, making sure to leave the spell and as much of His Majesty's sanity intact as we can. But we must remove it. If he can tap into it again—the next time he might not simply injure someone."

Everyone at the table sat in silence as her words sank in.

Olivia appreciated having a moment to come to grips with this new information. George III had managed to channel the Aegis spell? All of the Hanoverians had very mild magical abilities, but he shouldn't have been able to injure someone with it. If he had done so, the German woman must be correct. And they were justified in taking the Aegis away from him.

"What happens to the spell once it's removed?" A different mage, with an English schoolboy accent asked, after the silence had stretched past the point of discomfort.

"Prinny is the heir, and he'll be named regent when his father's mind goes. We ought to give it to him." Yet another mage, a woman this time, and Scottish.

"But we don't know what effect that would have, giving him only pieces at a time. If we're going to remove it slowly, we ought to wait until it is entirely gone from His Majesty before transferring it to the Prince of Wales." That was the Electorate Mage. Olivia had an odd feeling, like he'd planned to say that. Something was wrong.

"So where does the power from the spell go, until we're ready to transfer it to the prince?" asked the Scottish mage. "Westminster Chamber can hold it for a few days, but not for the months or years it will take to safely remove it from the king."

"We prepare a simulacrum of His Majesty, and use it as a new focus for the spell." That was from the German woman. Olivia's instincts tingled with apprehension.

"Then, do we remove the spell from Hanover at the same time, as he once asked us to do?" asked the English mage.

"War is looming in Europe. Hanover could use the extra magical protection," said the Electorate Mage.

"His Majesty was expressly against keeping additional power on the Continent," argued Mayes. "That's what started this whole mess to begin with."

"Circumstances have changed since he made that request. His people in Hanover are at risk now. And we can no longer ask him what he wishes." The Electorate Mage folded his hands. "I, for one, feel it is the best option at this juncture. We can, of course, revisit the issue once the spell has been successfully withdrawn from His Majesty."

"Let's put it to a vote," the German woman said.

The King's Sorcerer and several other mages voted against, but the coalition must act by simple majority, because a single extra vote was cast in favor and they agreed to remove the spell.

The room melted away around Olivia. She found herself back in the archives, but no longer in her body. Whatever she'd done with the leyline, she hadn't been able to hold her subtle body within her flesh.

She followed the shimmering cord still attached to her body, but her body was no longer sitting at the table. Panic spurted through her. She tried to push it down. Mina had been there. Perhaps she thought Olivia had fainted and they'd simply carried her off to an office with a sofa. Or maybe she'd called for Olivia's carriage to take her home. But then why hadn't Savit found her in the vision? He would have looked for her as soon as he realized what had happened.

The world of magic looked different from the world of flesh. Bright colors of potential energy swirled around her, peppered with dark spots where magic did not flow as easily —around the bookshelves, table, and walls. She drifted through the door, following the cord from her navel.

Her body was draped over the shoulder of a big man in an overcoat. She didn't recognize him as her carriage driver or any of the footmen from Skye House. And in his free hand, he carried a pistol.

In a blink, Olivia was out of the corridor and streaking toward the lecture hall. Savit was still surrounded by a small knot of people, but his head snapped in her direction the instant she entered the hall. He made his excuses and strode away from his admirers. He reached out a hand and latched onto her with his magic.

What do you think you're doing? This is dangerous, Olivia! Your cord is wire-thin!

I didn't do it on purpose! I'll explain later, but someone is kidnapping my body. You have to go, quickly!

Savit ran, but he wasn't fast enough. A plain hansom cab pulled away just as he leapt out of the back entrance to the Society headquarters. He scanned the alleyway, but there were no other vehicles around.

Damn. You have to go with them. You must return to your body. You don't yet have enough experience to be drawn so far away, and already your thread is weakening. But I will find you, Olivia. I swear it.

His magic surged inside of her. He was cool and spicy, soothing and arousing, and so very dear to her. *I know you will. I'll give them hell when I wake.*

He let her go, and she sped down the cord, following the cab and merging with her flesh. But instead of opening her eyes and thrashing the men like she planned, she fell into a deep pool of darkness.

20

Savit's heart thundered in his chest like runaway horses' hooves. He'd gone as fast as he could back to Skye House and collected Etta, Mal, Sorcha, Ronan, and most importantly Evie Finn. He'd met the red-headed Irish girl on several occasions back when she and Ronan ran a gang in Dublin, and there was no one he would rather have tracking down someone he cared about.

He'd foolishly withdrawn the piece of his magic he'd placed in Olivia after she successfully controlled the last vision and he moved into Skye House. He'd assumed they would remain in close enough proximity that he wouldn't need a warning via magic. Obviously he'd been wrong, and he had a strong urge to flog himself for putting her in danger. He *knew* that someone in the society was set to thwart them. That bust falling had not been an accident, and neither had the out-of-control automobile that must have followed her home. And someone had followed him around and found out all of the people he and Olivia meant to visit to investigate their collections. Their enemies were well-organized, had excellent resources, and good funding, since they could afford an auto.

To Savit's everlasting relief, Evie picked up the trail immediately. It seemed they'd placed a sleeping spell on her body to keep her from coming out of the trance-state, and the spell left enough of a residue for her to track.

"They didn't take her far," Evie said, "and not across the river, thank the goddess, because otherwise I might have lost the spell." She directed them northwest to the edge of the city, where a shabby-looking set of terrace houses stood near the city gas works and the carriage shed for the Great Western Railway.

The end-unit looked like it had been abandoned for some time. Most of the windows were boarded up and part of the roof sagged and probably leaked. But a thin curl of smoke rose out of the central chimney, and there were other minute signs of current habitation.

Their little group huddled in an alley across the street, sticking to the shadows. The weather had cleared and there was very little fog to obscure their quarry. But it also meant no cover for whatever action they would take next.

"How do we find out what's going on in there without alerting them to our presence?" Etta asked. "I can't do anything substantial, magically, without risking my child."

"There are a few spells I could cast," Ronan said, his gaze moving over the building as though he could see through the walls, "but if any of them are mages, they'll be able to sense the magic."

"I'll do it." Savit sank into the lotus position right there in the alley. "Unless any of them are practitioners of my kind of magic, they'll never see me." He entered a light trance and drifted away from his body, letting the thread that tethered him play out like line from a fishing reel. In this form, walls meant nothing. He passed through them and into the house.

The first floor was deserted, and nearly empty of anything but grime and old animal nests and droppings. Upstairs, he sensed life.

Three men sat in what might have been an upstairs parlor or bedroom prior to the house's abandonment, eating meat pies and passing around a bottle. Two of them were burly, one with the swollen nose and cauliflower ears of a long-time boxer and the other with a ragged scar along his jaw. The third man was thinner, and would have been handsome if he had a bath and a shave.

Olivia's body had been laid on the floor. She wasn't awake, and her subtle body was safely within her flesh—but he couldn't contact her, either. When she attempted to rejoin her body, the sleep spell must have trapped her spirit form as well.

He touched her lightly on the forehead to assure himself that everything was present and she was safe. For now, at least.

The problem would be getting her out. It would be simplicity itself to get inside, but the room had only the one door and the window was too high up with no safe way down. These men had not had the foresight to plan an escape route—but it wouldn't be easy to get in, either. They were all in the room with her, and one of them or all of them could easily harm or kill her before Savit and the others could incapacitate them.

They could attempt casting a spell, but someone must have put Olivia to sleep. He didn't see any spell tokens, so one of them was the sorcerer. Savit slipped around each man in turn, testing their auras, looking for signs of power. But there were none. Perhaps whoever had done the casting had gone? Evie had tracked the spell, not the caster. That person might not even have come here.

That was an issue for another time, because the mage must be the leader, and these men only guards. Considering everything, it was even possible that all of this was set up just to see how he and the others would react. Why else leave the daughter of a powerful magic clan alone in an abandoned house on the edge of Town with three non-mages as guards, when they must know that her family and friends would come for her?

Could it be a trap, with powerful adversaries waiting just beyond his awareness?

Perhaps, but Savit didn't think so. It was more likely that there were spells here that he couldn't interpret or perhaps even see with his magic, meant to record the events about to take place in the building. Or maybe the mage was nearby, watching. An itchy feeling washed over him, but his subtle body had no skin to scratch. He would find the mage soon. But for now, he must spring the trap. Without a mage in the building, these men could be overwhelmed with a few simple spells.

He drifted back down to the group waiting in the alley and slipped back inside his body. "They're on the second floor. Three men and Olivia. None of the men are mages, but she's still in a spelled sleep so there must have been one around at some point. Something is wrong, but I can't decide what. It's known that Olivia is a member of Clan Fay, and anyone with even a touch of intellect would know that the family will come for her. And though the Society was open to the public for my lecture tonight, it's unlikely that someone randomly discovered her and carried her off. This was a targeted attack. A test to see what we will do in response."

Sorcha nodded. "Yes, I agree. And, unless my intuition has suddenly become unreliable, this was planned by the same person who orchestrated the other attempts and the robberies. Someone doesn't want us finding out the truth about the Aegis Spell."

"Too bad for him," Etta said. "We're getting Olivia back, and we're going to keep looking."

Savit's insides twisted. He wanted to tell her that Olivia wasn't going to be doing anything for them anymore. She'd already been put too much at risk. But now was not the time for argument.

"How do we do this?" Mal asked, directing the question at Ronan and Evie. They looked at each other and had an entire conversation without words. Finally, Evie shrugged, and Ronan nodded.

"Right," Ronan said. "A spell-cocktail, if you will. A glamour on us for silence and stealth, a dazzler for interference with other active spells in the vicinity, and then something to incapacitate the guards. I'd suggest sleep under normal circumstances, but that takes forever to wear off and I assume we'll want to question them. So perhaps binding instead."

Etta stepped forward. "Agreed. Sorcha, you're best with glamours. Evie, you dazzle our absent mage. Mal, you and Ronan will take out the guards. Savit, you will retrieve Olivia. I'll be the rear guard." She patted her belly, and the occupant that made her unable to cast complicated or powerful spells.

It was a sound plan, but everything went wrong when they entered the house.

Sorcha's glamour died after the first steps over the threshold. "Damn!" she muttered, quietly, but with heat. "There's some kind of suppression or revelation field in place. It's not blocking all magic, but I can't keep up the concealment."

"The field is fighting back against my attempts to overwhelm it," Evie said, just as quietly. "I think the mage must be nearby. Close enough to adapt to our attacks."

Etta cursed. "Right. No point in hiding, then. We'll still attempt to detain without resorting to harm or lack of consciousness, but getting Olivia out is the top priority. Let's move."

She leapt up the stairs like a warrior goddess. She was dressed not very differently from Olivia's daily garb: trousers, blouse, and boots, with her dark hair secured in a tight braided knot, but in his mind he saw flowing robes and hair and glowing spells ready to strike—even though he knew she wasn't planning to do magic because of her pregnancy.

Mal cursed, and ran after her. Savit and the others followed.

The men had been alerted to their presence and had barred the door. A shout from inside the room told the attackers not to try anything, or they'd hurt the lady. Savit's blood heated with rage. His hands curled into fists and raised as though he could batter down the door himself.

Sorcha touched his shoulder and he flinched. "Relax. She needs you to be calm, and to keep your head. You can fall to pieces when it's done."

That shocked him out of his fury. He took the brief second to realign his chakras, and grasped deeply of the magic around him. He could feel the spells he hadn't been able to sense in the spirit-realm. They had fought back against attack, but he didn't try to interfere with their workings. He simply stole the magic that made them function.

Little sparks of magic exploded everywhere, revealing a pervasive net that had covered the space. They dimmed and floated into nothing, like dust motes falling through a beam of light and disappearing into darkness on the other side.

"The spell net is down," confirmed Ronan. "I'm going to hit the door."

"Good," Etta said, standing just behind him with her hands outstretched. "Everyone be ready to take out a guard."

The others took up similar poses, even Sorcha, who Savit would not have thought was a battle mage. He had no magic that would be useful here, but his priority was Olivia.

The door wrenched itself apart, splinters flying out in a V that intentionally missed their party. Inside the room, one of the guards knelt with a blade at Olivia's exposed throat. The other two stood with pistols raised and aiming at the door.

They both got off a single shot, and then the pistols flew out of their hands and crashed against the walls out of sight. Sorcha gasped beside him, and clutched at her arm. Ronan's gaze flicked to her, hardened, and then turned back to the men. Evie and Mal had cast some kind of net around the kidnappers, keeping them from moving, and Ronan walked right up and slugged one in the face. He slumped into his bonds, dazed.

The third man growled and pressed his knife harder against Olivia's neck. It was the skinny one, and his eyes were dark with malevolent intelligence. He knew they couldn't wrench the knife away without risk of harming Olivia. He'd wrapped his arm around her head to make sure they couldn't push him away with brute force, either.

"If you kill her, this will end very badly for you," Etta said. "Whoever paid you to be here has abandoned you. No one is coming to help, and there is no escape. Let her go, and I will let you live." That was a bluff, of course. They were very aware that the mage who ensorcelled the house was still nearby, and still paying attention.

"I don't trust ya. If I let her go, you'll be on me faster than a whaler on a whore after a three-year-voyage."

"Do you know who I am?"

"Nah. You don't look like much, though."

"I'm the Duchess of Fay. The woman you hold is my sister. You have no choices left except my mercy. Kill her, and you swing. Make us fight you, and you swing. Let her go, and I allow you to live."

The man blanched under the smears of dirt on his face. He'd dismissed her as a woman in men's clothes, some kind of odd foreigner with her dark skin and flat, elongated accent. But Etta could command lesser mortals to her will, and this one had no chance. He trembled.

"You'll let me go?"

"No. You will be imprisoned. But I will see that they spare you the noose for attacking a noble lady."

He stared at her, his eyes wide, and then looked down at Olivia. "I didn't know, lady, honest. I was told this gel had done wrong to a friend of my boss. We was hired to take her out of some posh building and bring her here, but I didn't know she was a lady, ma'am. I swear it."

"Then let her go."

The knife clattered to the floor beside Olivia's head. It lifted of its own accord and flew across the room, burying itself into the wall with a thunk. The man flinched, scuttling away from Olivia's body. Her head fell back against the dirty floorboards with a muffled thump.

Savit darted forward, between the immobilized guards. The third man stopped in mid-scuttle, caught by bonds from one of the mages behind Savit. He didn't know which, and didn't much care. He slid his arms beneath Olivia's body and lifted her against his chest. He stood and carried her out of the room. Mal and Evie had their hands outstretched, maintaining the spells that trapped the guards. Ronan had a wad of fabric pressed against Sorcha's arm.

"Sorcha, you two go back to the carriage and return to

Skye House with Olivia." Ronan helped his wife to her feet. "We'll stay here and interrogate these bastards."

"Don't kill the one that shot me, Ronan." Sorcha lifted her uninjured hand to his face. "He's not worth the stain on your soul, my love."

"I won't kill him, *a solas,* but when I'm through with him he'll wish he'd never been born."

She smiled wanly. "That's all right, then." He leaned over and kissed her, then nudged her toward the stairs. She followed Savit down and out.

21

"Well," Sorcha said once they'd made it to one of the two carriages and set off back to Kensington. "I haven't had that much excitement since we stopped a gang of radicals from destroying London last summer."

Savit raised a questioning eyebrow, and she spent the ride filling him in on the long version of the story of how she and Ronan had met and fallen in love.

At Skye House they were met by the rest of the Fays, including Olivia's mother. She took one look at Olivia in his arms and went pale as snow, but after she used her magic to examine both women, she proclaimed Olivia stable, but in need of more extensive healing than she could manage in the house. She cast a quick mending spell on Sorcha's arm and directed Savit to carry Olivia outside.

In the back garden was a very large glasshouse, and every natural flow of energy in the vicinity had been redirected into it. It nearly rivaled the Casting Chamber for power, but seemed disused. There were a few plants around, but not the profusion he would have expected. Lady Hazelby showed him to a small curtained alcove containing a cot. He placed Olivia on it gently.

"Lilias built this place for me when I first started learning to use my magic for herbs and healing. I work best out-of-doors, where I can sense the soil. I don't know if our magic is compatible, but I believe your connection to my daughter will help with what must come next. The sleep spell is an amateur one. It only has enough imbued power to initiate the spell, and then after that it draws energy from the sleeper. She was already weak when it started, and the life force inside of her is nearly depleted."

Savit shifted his consciousness to look for what she'd described, and cursed. She was correct. He'd been so preoccupied by the fact that her subtle body was safely inside her gross body that he hadn't noticed how insubstantial the subtle body had become.

"What can we do?"

"Feed her energy, and place a spell on her that will pull ambient energy into her for a while. It's a temporary measure, because the only way to regain her life force is through rest and time, but time is something we may not have the luxury for."

"I agree. We have an enemy, and their actions are escalating."

"So I'll do what I can to get her back on her feet, but she'll have to be careful, and even under the best of circumstances the effects will only last for a few days, or a week if she's unusually indolent."

"Which she won't be."

Lady Hazelby smiled, a wan thing, but still a smile. "I think you know my daughter better than I do."

He didn't want to respond to that, as anything he said could sound like an accusation.

"If you could, please use your gift to embrace hers. I will seek out the connection and use that to cast my spells."

The entire experience was foreign and strange. Being wrapped in European magic was like his first year in Ireland, surrounded by people speaking English, a language he'd only spoken infrequently at home before.

The marchioness worked with confidence and a deftness that impressed him, despite the oddity of the different style of magic. She kept her emotions tightly controlled during the casting, not allowing her worries and fears to influence the timbre of the spell.

At the end, she closed her eyes and slumped a little, leaning on the cot for support. Savit rose and put his arms around her. She put her face into his shoulder and wept.

A week ago, his first reaction would not have been to comfort someone with touch. He'd have offered words, explanations. But Lady Hazelby—perhaps he ought to call her Cecily—did not need his intellectual skills. She needed to be held, and reassured that her youngest child was well, and safe.

He stroked her back, soothing, and murmured nonsense that neither of them paid any attention to. It was the tone, and not the words, that mattered.

A long while later, Cecily pulled away and swiped at her eyes with her sleeve. Savit offered her a handkerchief. "My apologies, Dr. Reilly. It has been an...emotional few days."

"No need to apologize. And please call me Savit."

She nodded, but in a distracted way, her attention returning to Olivia.

"I'll carry her up to her room."

Cecily followed as far as the second floor, and then said she needed to check on Sorcha. Savit found the right room and placed Olivia on the bed. Would it be monstrously improper to undress her? She wore the odd dress with voluminous trousers beneath called bloomers, so the prospect was not as easy as it would have been if she'd worn her usual garb. But the door to her room opened and his problem was solved by the entrance of a young woman he had not yet met.

She was the image of Lady Hazelby, however, so he could guess that this was Olivia's older sister, Viola.

"You must be Savit," she said, and held out her hand. He shook it, which made her smile. "I'm Viola. I was sitting with Sorcha when Mother came in. She told me what happened, and said we just need to get her comfortable until the last of the sleeping spell wears off and her new spell can gather enough energy."

She bustled over to the bed, and he helped her shift Olivia's limbs and torso around until they'd gotten her down to her shift and then covered her with her blanket.

"Much better. She'll be asleep for at least an hour. Would you like some tea while you wait for her to wake up?"

He wanted to say no, wanted to curl up beside Olivia in the bed and hold her until she woke. But Viola watched him with a too-knowing look, so he nodded as though tea were an excellent idea and followed her out of the room.

The next hour was extremely awkward.

Sorcha sat with Viola and Cecily, her arm now bandaged. The bullet had gone through the skin and muscle on the outer part of her upper arm, but hadn't hit bone or any major arteries. Savit could sense magic overlaying the wound, but as with many European spells, he couldn't decipher the shape or significance of the weaving. Something to promote healing, obviously, but how it worked, he couldn't say.

Viola attempted to include him in their conversation several times, and while he appreciated her warmth and friendliness, he had no patience for polite chatter. His attention kept slipping back to the piece of his magic he'd firmly re-attached to Olivia. He refused to let her wake alone, and he would sense the moment she stirred.

"She'll be fine," Viola said, this time addressing the issue head-on. "If I know my sister at all, she'll wake up angry and ready to go out and get some of her own back. I just hope there's something left of the men after the others get through with them."

"There will be." Sorcha shifted to face them. She frowned as the movement jostled her arm, but that faded after she settled into the new position. "Ronan will want to beat the one who shot me to a pulp, but Etta will restrain him. I already telephoned Lucien, and he'll take over the questioning and interrogation in an official capacity."

"Who is Lucien?" Savit asked.

"He has one of those hard-to-describe jobs, doing whatever the government needs him to do. But he's a friend who helped us with the difficulties last summer."

"Caused them, you mean," Viola said. "None of that would have happened if he hadn't stolen the Wells from Fay House." Now Savit put together the name with the story he'd only half-paid-attention to back in the carriage.

"Agreed, but he was acting under orders. He thought we'd stolen them." Sorcha grinned wryly at the memory. "But he gave them back when he learned the truth, and he helped me save Evie and defeat Donn. And now Etta is using the Wells to help prop up some failing infrastructure spells around London, so it all worked out for the best."

Viola said something back to that, but Savit had stopped paying attention. Olivia was waking up.

He stood, and the conversation faltered. "I'm going to see to Olivia." The others made to follow him, but he waved them back. "I think it's best if we talk alone first. I need to check that she's recovered from what happened *before* the abduction, and that's best done with just the two of us."

Viola and Sorcha both looked to Lady Hazelby for the final decision. She stared at him, and he clenched and unclenched his fists, chafing to leave. But he needed Cecily to agree to stay behind—having her mother descend on her when she woke was not what Olivia needed right now.

"Very well. But I will see her after."

He gave a curt nod of agreement and strode out of the room.

Olivia was still groggy with sleep when he entered, her body arched in mid-stretch. The room was dark, but the light from the hall cast a beam of illumination over her. He wanted to go to her and wrap his arms around that lithe, graceful form and never let her go.

Instead, he sat beside her. There was a bedside lamp, and he whispered to it through the currents of magical energy in the room, reminding it of what it felt like to burn. It burst into flame, and he could make out the lovely curve of Olivia's cheek, the dark purple smudges of exhaustion under her eyes. No matter what Lady Hazelby had said about the sleeping spell, it shouldn't have done so much damage, and neither should a few minutes of moving around outside of her body.

She must have had another vision, before the abduction. Damn it! Why hadn't she dismissed it, as they'd discussed? She'd promised him she wouldn't take any risks.

The fear and anger twisted up inside of him. This was what it meant to care for one person, to form attachments of the flesh. But he'd come too far along this path to turn back easily. He had no choice but to feel something now—the fear, or a deep, tearing pain of loss if he tried to break free of her.

"I went back to my body, but then I was trapped in sleep. What happened after that?" she asked, her voice rough as though sandpaper covered her vocal cords.

"Evie tracked you to a house on the edge of the city. The

men guarding you were not mages, but a mage had prepared the house with spells so it was not easy to get you back. The duchess, your brother, Evie, and Ronan remained behind once we'd subdued the guards. Sorcha and I returned here to Skye House with you. Sorcha was wounded."

She gasped, and he clutched her hand in assurance.

"Don't worry. It's not bad. Your mother is here and already has done something to help heal the wound."

Olivia sagged against him, and something inside him broke. All of the tension and panic and horror of the last few hours spilled out and he squeezed her harder than he'd intended. "By the gods, Olivia, how did this happen?"

She spoke against his shoulder, her words partially muffled by the fabric of his coat. "I went to the archives to look up more information about the Hanoverian dynasty. I'm getting out of my depth the closer we come to the modern era, and I wanted to read up on the Georges and their sorcerers."

She curled tighter against him, as though she could burrow inside him. He wished that she could, that he could keep her safe that way. And he was terrified that she needed his touch and reassurance so badly.

"I started reading a book of letters by George the Third, and I realized that what the person who'd collected and printed the letters thought was mad ramblings was actually him referring to the Aegis Spell. Not long after that, the vision started."

A tremor ran through him, and he wanted to shout at her, wanted to demand to know why she hadn't pushed it away as she'd promised she would.

He kept his temper, barely, and she continued, explaining about the leyline and how she'd thought everything would be fine. He was nearby, and she had a power source. "I learned so much from the vision, I can't regret having it, no matter the outcome."

"You mean, the outcome where you were abducted and had to be rescued, injuring your cousin and leaving you once again drained and exhausted, so much that your mother had to stuff you full of magic just so you can be sitting upright?"

She pulled away from him, her eyes glittering gold and green with dangerous effrontery, even though she'd paled at the mention of her mother. "Yes, that's the outcome I mean. I'm sorry about Sorcha and about all of you putting yourselves at risk for me, and I wouldn't have asked for my mother's help, but what I discovered is important, Savit!"

She blurted out that they'd changed the spell while it was inside of George III, and that had caused his madness. As a consequence, they'd slowly withdrawn the spell over the next several years, forcing him farther and farther into oblivion.

"And his son wasn't crowned for years, so it would have made sense for them not to transfer it to him while he was Prince Regent. He might even have predeceased his father—he was a heavy drinker and womanizer, and his hard living might have killed him before his father wasted away."

"But it didn't." The new information diverted him—at least for the moment—from the dangerous risk she'd taken. He was too much of a historian to ignore valid data.

"No, and I think that the members of the coalition changed while the spell was being held in abeyance." She tentatively touched his chest. "I want to seek another vision to confirm my suspicions, but the German members seemed to be working together in an attempt to keep the spell in Hanover. I don't know why, but if they had enough support, they may have been able to convince the rest of the members to keep it there, and maybe it has never come back. That would also explain why nobody knows about it now. I imagine it was common knowledge among the mages of the seventeenth and early eighteenth centuries, but magic users don't like entrusting big, powerful spells to paper, especially spells that are integral to the workings of the throne, so they would have referred to it only generally. What was originally intended as secrecy to protect against the Jacobites would have worked in the coalition's favor in hiding what they'd done."

That was quite an accusation, and, if true, would change the entire nature of their investigation. He put his arms back around her.

Someone knocked on the doorframe and they both startled. Etta stood in the open doorway. "I heard the tail end of that, but I'd like to hear the rest. Will you come down to the parlor? We're all down there."

Olivia struggled to extricate herself from his arms, and he let her go. She stood, bracing herself against the bedside table. She still wore only her shift, and he was very distracted by its thinness and the way the light from the lamp shone through, turning her into the most erotic silhouette he'd ever seen.

"I'll be down as soon as I've dressed."

Etta inclined her head toward Olivia and closed the door.

Olivia stumbled across to a clothespress, and Savit followed her. "I don't need your help." She yanked on a drawer pull and ripped out a white shirt. "I can dress myself."

"I don't doubt it. But before you go down there, I need to check your aura and your subtle body, and make sure there are no lasting difficulties from the vision and your experience outside your gross body."

Her eyes flashed with anger, but she stood still while he examined her.

"You are far too weak."

"I used the leyline. I don't understand why it didn't work."

"It did work, but leylines are different from other sources

of magic. The energy there wants to keep going in the same direction, and depending on how strong it is, if you pull some out and do not use it up or keep telling it what to do, it will pull back into the line. And leylines are collections of ambient energy, which means they draw on your magic, too. If you don't take precautions, your energy can be sucked into it. And that is exactly what happened. You got a lot of power out, and gave too much back."

She blanched a little. "I'm sorry. I didn't know that would happen."

"I know!" His voice had a dagger-sharp edge and sounded loud as a whip-crack. "That is why I told you to divert any visions that came when I was not there to help you. You are not ready to do this on your own."

Olivia flinched away from the vehemence in his voice, and through the touch of magic he sensed her mingled shame, fear, and anger. "I said I was sorry. But what if that particular vision never came to me again? We haven't been able to conjure one yet. I didn't think I should let any opportunity pass if I could help it."

"What good would it do us if you try for a vision and it kills you? We'd never know what you discovered, and you'd be dead." She was trembling now, and so was he. "I need you to be safe, Olivia. Your family needs you, too. Swear to me you won't do that again."

Her body was weak, her limbs shaking, but her spirit blazed within her. "I can't. I'll take better precautions next time, but I can't swear that. I shouldn't have promised it in the first place. I...I *need* to do this, Savit. I don't know who I am anymore. What's the point in digging things up if no one will listen to what I have to say? But this is something I can do—that Etta *needs* me to do. Do you understand that?"

He did, but for the first time in his adult life, the understanding of his mind and the comprehension of his heart refused to come together as one. His mind could accept what she said, but his heart could not.

He stared at her, at this woman who had torn his soul apart, and could say nothing. The conflict within him was too great. He turned away. If he kept looking at her, he might say something he could never take back. Something like: *I love you, and I can't live without you.*

He wrenched the door open and fled.

22

Olivia struggled to dress. Her fingers trembled with fatigue, shock, and a terrible mix of anger, shame, regret, and despair. How Savit must hate her.

He'd looked at her with such loathing: a broken thing, who couldn't even manage to get through a vision without someone holding her hand and her *mother* fixing her up afterward. He would never understand how it felt to have everything that mattered about him stripped away—his career, his self-respect, his confidence—by some stupid vestige of magic passed down in his blood. His magic had been his secret joy, buoying him through whatever happened to him in his life.

Hers was poison and salvation all at once. She hadn't wanted to see the cracks in her life abroad, but now she was forced to gaze at them in minute detail. Mina had been so very right about her—she'd rebelled because she needed someone to look at her, to notice her. She'd thumbed her nose at both sides of her family and alienated anyone who ever deigned to criticize her actions.

But it was all a lie. Her career had been stalling for

months. Years. She'd blamed Savit—*Dr. Reilly*—because she didn't want to admit that there was something wrong with her, with her methods and her work. How ironic that she, who had always felt everything deeply and never flinched from her own desires, had failed because she kept that exuberance deliberately separate from her work. And Savit, who denied every passion he ever experienced, succeeded because he gave his work emotional depth.

And now all she had to cling to was this stupid magic that she'd never wanted, but that made her, for once, indispensable.

So no, she would not promise to avoid the visions. She would learn what she must so she could control them, but she would not turn them away. Etta needed her. England needed her. She didn't even care anymore if she was ever able to publish the story.

She managed to get her clothes on and buttoned, despite the tremors in her hands and fingers. She got out of her room by propping her hand against the wall and letting it hold up part of her weight. Halfway down the hall, a footman —Gillies again—detached himself from his station at the wall and held out his arm to her. Savit's doing, or Etta's? It didn't matter, and she wanted to tell the man to go to the devil, but the fact was she needed his help, and he was only doing his job. So she leaned on his arm and let him take her downstairs.

Her entire family waited in the parlor, with the exception of Giles and Caroline—and Percy, of course, who wasn't yet back on British soil. Even her father was there. He gave her an awkward hug, kissed her cheek, and said that she needn't go to such lengths to get his attention. He would not withhold her allowance, no matter what her brother thought.

She hid her pleasure at seeing him deep inside, where he wouldn't notice. Where her relationship with her mother had been built on disapproval and neglect, her father had always been aloof, but jovial and indulgent—right up to the moment when he sent her off to Switzerland.

Since then, he'd quietly given her whatever funds she requested and kept up a distant but light-hearted correspondence. The fact that he'd come today, into a building as teeming with magic as Skye House, told her more than any words ever could that he loved her and cared about her.

Then he took himself off, claiming an urgent appointment. It was obvious to everyone that he was just uncomfortable to be in a room with so many mages, but they all allowed him the fiction. She envied him his ability to escape.

Mal got to her next, holding her tightly and then maneuvering her into an overstuffed armchair near the fire.

For a few minutes, Etta kept the conversation going, giving Olivia time to relax and adjust. How her sister-in-law always knew exactly what she needed, and managed to provide it without making her feel weak and worthless, was almost a magical talent.

And with that same keen sense of awareness, Etta brought up the topic of the Aegis spell the moment Olivia felt steady enough to address the assembled company. Etta skirted the events that had followed, saying only that they'd gotten very little out of the guards and that Lucien and his team would continue to try. At this point, all they knew was that a well-connected mage had hired them, and that all three of them had a strong memory spell in place over the identity of that mage. Breaking it without permanently damaging their minds would take time, and a skill that no one in this room possessed, not even Liv's mother.

"But one good thing has come out of this night," Etta said. "Before the abduction, Olivia had another vision. Will you tell us what you saw?"

Olivia sat forward in the chair, but did not stand. She

would never have been able to tell the whole story on her feet.

She started with the Mad King's letters and then moved into the visions, explaining how they'd first tried to alter the spell while it was still attached to the king, and how doing so had caused the first bouts of madness. Then her second vision—the one where she sensed that the German faction had deliberately maneuvered the group into voting to remove the spell and store the excess power in Hanover.

"What makes you think it was deliberate?" Etta asked when she was done.

"A feeling that I got. Their arguments were too well-timed and perfectly rehearsed. They fed off of each other and managed to sway a majority of the mages to vote with them."

"That's when the spell was lost," Sorcha said, with a certainty that rang through the room. "It never returned to a British monarch after that."

"That was my guess, too," Olivia said.

"Then it is even more urgent that we speak with the queen," Mother said, looking off into a middle-distance and not making eye contact with anyone. She looked...sad. What did she have to be sad about?

"If we don't hear from Amelia tomorrow, perhaps you can call on her again." Etta made the suggestion gently, but Mother still flinched as though the words had been a pinch.

"Yes, yes. Of course."

Who was this nervous, melancholy woman? Her mother had always hidden every emotion behind a thick wall of ice, appearing serene as a frozen lake, untouched by anything so mundane as the elements—or human feeling.

"Has anyone heard from Percy?" Viola asked. "If he's still over in Potsdam, he may be able to look into things for us."

"He's headed home," Mal said. "Not directly, but in stages. He ought to be in Belgium by now, though, and then he'll be in France for a week or so, and then across the Channel to us."

"Too bad," Ronan said. "It's always nice to have an operative already in place."

"I could go," Evie suggested. "My mother was German...sort of."

"Sort of?" Viola asked, and Evie's extremely pale skin flushed.

"It's a very, very long story," Ronan said. Evie, who was sitting near enough to be in striking distance, walloped him on the leg.

"I can tell my own stories, Ronan McCarrick." She faced Viola again. "I'm part-fey. My mum's father is one of the Elf-King's court, and her mother was a German peasant born, as far as my mother could tell, during the eleventh or twelfth century. Mum grew up in Faery with the Erlkoenig until she was traded to the Tuatha De Danann as a teenager. She escaped into our world in 1878, had me, and then disappeared again when I was eight. We spoke German, Irish, and English until my father stole her back into Faery, but she taught me how to call on the German fairy courts."

Olivia stared at the petite woman. She had only met Evie the day before, and had been too caught up in her own problems to notice the ethereally beautiful features, the hair that was just-slightly too red to be natural, and the eyes that were too vivid and jewel-bright green to be entirely human.

If she didn't know the truth, she might have assumed that Evie had cast a glamour over her features. Some mages did that—male and female alike. But now that she knew, the proof was all there, easy to see.

"In any case," Evie added, "I still speak the language and I've been itching to run another con. This saves me from doing something illegal just for kicks." She grinned and everyone laughed.

Liv allowed her shoulders to relax back into the chair. The attention of the room had shifted away from her now and she could let the weariness take hold for a moment. She was so very tired.

She blinked and the room was nearly empty, save Mal and Savit, who were talking quietly by the door. She must have fallen asleep, damn it.

She struggled up from the soft cushions of the chair and Mal crossed to her with swift strides. He helped her to her feet, and she rewarded him with an elbow to his side. He let her go and rubbed at the place she'd prodded. "What was that for?"

"Did you clear the room so I could nap?"

His sheepish smile answered the question for her.

She groaned. "I'm fine."

"You're not fine," Savit contradicted. "You need more rest. Your mother said her spell would take a while to infuse you with enough magic to keep you on your feet for a few days, and then you'd need total bed rest for some time to recover. In fact, it may be better if you don't go back out for a while except when absolutely necessary. Obviously you have been made a target, and we need you to be safe."

"So I'm to be a prisoner?"

"So melodramatic," Mal said. "Of course you're not a prisoner, Liv. But you have to admit that someone is after you. Why make it easy for them?"

"Maybe we can use their interest in me to lure them to a place of our choosing," she suggested.

"What, use yourself as bait?" Mal seemed to honestly consider the idea, but Savit grabbed her arm.

"No. I will not permit it."

"You don't get to permit anything, *Dr. Reilly*. You don't own me. You don't control me. Just because I sucked your cock—"

Mal choked, and it was easy to turn her anger on him, too. "Yes, your sister has sex. With lots of people. Including women. Accustom yourself to the idea."

Mal had the same pale complexion as all of her siblings, and he'd gone red as a ripe tomato. But he was angry now, too. "I know who you are, Olivia, and I know about your lovers. I was never bothered before, because I assumed you were mature enough to make your own choices and live your own life. But what you just said was crude and unworthy of you."

Shame whipped through her like a gale, lashing at her soul. He was right. What she'd done for Savit had been a gift, freely given. He hadn't asked for it, hadn't encouraged it. Had refused to fuck her mouth as she'd tried to entice him to do. He'd accepted the pleasure, but had taken nothing from her.

She whirled away from them both, unable to face them. But her balance was off, and she stumbled over the edge of a carpet, catching herself on the armchair. Savit put his arms around her.

Great Goddess, how could he still be so solicitous to her, so gentle? She'd been a complete ass and he had every right to be upset with her. Yes, his protection was overbearing and they would need to find some sort of compromise there. But it came from his genuine fear for her safety, and that was something she didn't think he'd ever experienced before. He didn't know how to handle what was between them any more than she did.

She'd just made up her mind to apologize when Etta's voice came from near the door.

"I've just had a telephone call from Amelia's secretary. We have an audience with the Queen tomorrow, scheduled for the morning. Her Majesty is at Windsor, and the secretary warned me to be prepared to stay over in case it takes all day for her to see us."

Liv pulled out of Savit's embrace. Etta strode over and handed her an envelope. "This was delivered earlier but was forgotten in all the ruckus."

It was a note from Mina. Apparently she'd rushed off for help when Olivia collapsed, but came back to find her gone from the Archives. She hoped Olivia had recovered and was resting peacefully at home, and would like to visit and check on her whenever she was free.

"Who is Mina?" Savit asked, after glancing at the discarded envelope.

"A woman who works for the Society. She has helped me in the Archives a few times. She was with me when the vision started, but must not have found someone to help until after you'd chased my body out the back door."

Olivia crossed to a desk in the corner and drew out some foolscap. She dashed off a reply that she was feeling better, but would be out of town for a few days and would send a note once she'd returned.

She felt a little guilty excluding Mina, but despite her willingness to help, Mina's prejudices and rigid, linear way of thinking made her a poor research assistant. And right now, Olivia didn't have time to maintain their fragile friendship. Perhaps when all of this was over, they'd have time to catch up, but not now.

Liv folded the note and addressed it to Mina, then carried it out of the room to Gillies, waiting outside the door. "Can you see that this is delivered tomorrow?"

"If it's urgent, one of the lads can take it over tonight."

Olivia considered. Mina might be worried. "Yes, that's better, but only if someone doesn't mind the trip."

He smiled. "One of the underfootmen is courting a lass that works in a house near there. He'll not mind."

That errand seen to, Olivia bid everyone good night. She contemplated the stairs and was just about to ask Gillies for assistance when Savit came into the hall and offered his arm. In any other house, it would be monstrously improper for him to escort her to her room, but Etta didn't follow any social rules.

Olivia waited until they'd closed the door to her room to apologize. "I was angry, and I should never have said what I did. But it's hard to define what's happening between us. Are we friends? Lovers? Teacher and student? Protector and protectee?"

"We're all of those things, I think, and none." He placed his hands on her upper arms and rubbed gently. A few days ago, he wouldn't have touched her—would have eschewed the physical contact that she craved. Either he was doing it because he understood her needs, or because touching gave him comfort, too. Maybe both. She hoped both.

"I don't want to fight with you, but I need my independence. I'll accept reasonable restrictions and precautions, but I can't be made a prisoner in this house."

"I understand. I'm…" His voice trailed off, and he pulled away, settling onto the chair beside her dressing table. "I am having some difficulty regulating my emotions where you are involved. This is a new problem for me. I have not… cared for many people since I was a small boy, except my grandfather, Rajani, and Chaitan. And they are all authority figures. I love them, but it is not my place to worry about them." His hands moved in his lap, making a series of complicated gestures, almost as though he carried on a second conversation with his fingers. "I have avoided attachments because focusing on the individual takes away from the collective. If I allow a single person's need, even my own, to overrule what is best for many, I go against my most basic principles."

"That theory is nice in the abstract, but it also means you can never experience the full range of human emotion. You cannot love without attachment. And you also cannot love without risk."

"This is why I have avoided love."

"Avoided?" She emphasized the past tense, and he raised his head, finally, to look at her. His eyes were dark, depthless, and yet brimming with desire. He wanted her.

"Some force in the universe has put us together, as we have been many times before. Even if I were to walk away this moment, I could not stop loving you. And this truth terrifies me."

Olivia pulled him over to sit beside her on the bed and took his still-moving hand in hers. His fingers stilled as she laced hers between them. "I don't know what it is that I'm feeling, except that it is strong. You make me so angry, and so aroused, and so full of joy that I sometimes think I will burst with sensation." She rubbed her thumb over the base of his palm. "I don't know if that's love, but if it isn't yet, it could become love, given time."

"Is that something you want? Time?"

"With you?" She squeezed his hand and lifted her other hand to his face. "Yes. I want to discover all of the secrets of your body. What your skin tastes like just here," she slid her fingers under his jaw to his throat. "All of the sounds you make when you're aroused and pleasured and when I make you come." She leaned in close enough for their breath to mingle. "And how our magic will entwine when your body enters mine."

His breath came shallow, almost panting, his dark skin flushed to a dusky hue, his barely-discernible pupils dilating with arousal. She brushed her mouth over his. Against his mouth, she said, "But I also love to argue history and philosophy with you." She pulled back, and his eyes crinkled at the corners with a sudden smile that stole inside her and filled her with light and heat. "And I think that if we listen to each other, we can both improve our scientific work." Which was a first for her. She'd always been so certain that her way was the best. And to be fair, it usually had been. But Savit took his work as seriously as she did, and she had to admit that one of the things she'd hated most about *Dr. Reilly's* articles was how engaging she found them. Not that different from the man himself.

"And what of the Aegis Spell research?" He'd twisted toward her, his free hand reaching up to clasp hers where it rested on his collarbone.

"That comes first, of course. But we'll be working together. And maybe you can learn to do magic the way I do."

"I don't know if I can, and I don't want to find out I can't when you're in the grip of a vision and need my help. Or if our enemy tries to take you again."

"Then we'll wait for that until after this is over. When we're on the ship to India to search for the Indus River civilization."

He smiled again, and she needed to taste the amusement on his lips. She surged forward, and after the barest hint of surprise, he opened his mouth and welcomed her in.

THIS WOMAN WOULD DRIVE HIM TO MADNESS AND BEYOND, BUT what bliss he would find there. She did everything with her whole body, from arguing to kissing. What started as a meeting of lips and tongues and teeth exploded into more as she crawled into his lap, straddled his hips, and pressed him backwards onto the mattress.

She made a very pleasant weight on top of him, and the heat at the apex of her thighs seeped through her trousers to rouse him to near-painful stiffness. Her body undulated over him, her hips pressing down and then dragging up, and sparks of pleasure burst inside him from his groin, to his chest, to his brain.

But he didn't want to be the receiver of pleasure this time. He needed to learn how to please her. He could touch the pleasure center in her mind, but for Olivia, that would only ever be an empty delight. Much more gratifying for them both if he learned to make her writhe beneath him with his hands and mouth, as she had for him.

The skin of her cheek and jaw tasted of salt and Olivia's own, potent flavor. He slid his tongue over her chin and down the long column of her throat, and freed his hands to unbutton her collar and discover more. She moaned as he dipped his tongue into the little hollow he'd uncovered. She tried to speed things along, reaching for her buttons, but he gently pushed her hands away.

"Let me set the pace this time. You need to learn to savor."

She groaned, arching her back and pressing her breasts forward for his attention. The motion also ground her bottom delectably against his aching erection.

He ignored his own arousal, his own pleasure, putting it into a tightly sealed box within his mind. Instead, he saturated his senses with Olivia's desire.

Each button undone became an individual world of stimulation, each new expanse of skin a landscape for his fingers and tongue. She'd told him she wasn't made of glass, and wouldn't break, so he dragged his teeth lightly down the slope of her breast and took her nipple into his mouth, thrilling at her gasps when he teased the pale bud.

She groaned when he abandoned her breasts after ages of gratifying torment and continued his journey south, past her delectable navel, to her quim. He had to strip off her trousers and combinations first, and so he took a pleasurable detour through the soft fur of dark hair on her calves and up to the smooth skin of her inner thighs.

At this point, he balked, only because her flesh was so unfamiliar. What would she like? And so he asked.

Olivia gurgled a laugh, but with surprised satisfaction, not mocking or disdain. "Do you know, you're only the second person ever to ask me what I wanted? Usually I let things go as long as we're both having a good time, and offer little hints of encouragement or outright demands, depending on what style of direction my lover likes best." Her eyes had gone a dark sapphire, glassy with desire, and he wanted to drown in them. "But it means so much more that you ask, and do not assume or guess." She sat up and took his hands. She placed them on the outer folds of her quim, and told him how she liked to be teased and stroked, sometimes outside, and sometimes on the sensitive flesh within. She pressed one finger deep inside of her, and he groaned at the slick, hot clutch of her passage.

"I want you there," she told him. "Your hands, your tongue, your cock."

He wanted that too, so much it made his body shake with suppressed craving. If he could see his own aura now, he would be pulsing blue, or even white from his sacral and root chakras. But as much as they both wanted it, he could not do it. The line inside of him shone brightly—the line between accepting and giving a gift, and taking his own pleasure inside her body. He could not cross it.

But he could give her some of what she wanted, could satiate one small craving in his bones. He bent and licked across her folds, from the base of her opening to the tiny, hooded bud at its peak. He teased that impudent crimson nub with his tongue, pressing two of his fingers deep inside her and stroking a tiny hollow he found there that made her cry out, begging him not to stop.

In another time and place, he would stop, just to make her writhe for him and prolong the rapture. But tonight, he needed the feel of her muscles clutching at his fingers, her tangy-sweet flavor gushing over his tongue, and her desperate, keening moans. He had tried to keep his magic safely tucked inside, but her peppermint-flavored gift reached for his as she scaled the peak of bliss, dragging him up with her and over the edge into the wild, infinite plane of ecstasy.

Savit came back to himself with his head pillowed on Olivia's hip and upper thigh, his hand resting on her mons, his fingers nested in the dark, wiry hairs there. Strange that only the hair on her head had shifted to pearl. Her eyebrows and other body hair was a reddish-brown, similar to her mother and siblings.

Her fingers were tangled in his black hair, several shades darker even than that under his hand, and she tugged at him lightly. It took a monumental effort to rise and settle back down beside her. He was still fully clothed, but that was for the best. He hadn't ejaculated, but he'd nevertheless had an intense orgasmic experience, and his body was weak in its wake, his cock still erect. He ignored its faint urgings to strip and bury himself into the slick, tight channel waiting for him between her thighs.

Olivia curled into him, wrapping arms and legs around him as though he were a pillow. She went limp, satiated, and his cock finally gave up and subsided to quiescence against his thigh.

"Why won't you join with me?"

He didn't pretend to misunderstand her, though he'd have expected her to use more direct language. Perhaps she was trying to meet what she guessed were his scruples. He didn't mind the crude or specific terms, though. Down in the parlor, when she'd spoken of sucking his cock, far from being offended, the traitorous member had stiffened with inconvenient interest.

Still, it took him a moment to wrangle his thoughts into words that might make sense to another person, even one who knew him as well as Olivia did.

"I have felt pleasure in what we've done together, but to this point I have not sought that pleasure. It has been either a gift from you, freely given, or a pleasant side-effect of giving you pleasure. But if I were to put my cock in your cunny, I could no longer separate my wants and needs from yours. I would be taking my pleasure in you."

"And giving me pleasure, too." She placed her palm on his chest, right above his heart. Why did it have to feel as though it now beat at her request? As though his very pulse existed to please her? He must not allow his mind to be so wrapt in her.

"Yes, but I can give you pleasure by other means. The only reason to do so with my cock is to take my own pleasure as well. And I cannot do that. I can sense a balance within me, and if we take each other as you suggest, that balance will permanently shift. I will be changed. The consequences to my magic could be catastrophic."

"There are other ways of doing magic, as you are teaching me right now." Her hand pressed against his heart chakra, then lower, to the solar plexus chakra, and then lower still, to his sacral chakra. Finally, she slipped her hand over his hip and touched the chakra at the base of his spine, her finger pressing lightly into the crevice between the globes of his arse. She'd deliberately moved backward from the path of enlightenment. He'd explained to her the four goals of human life, and she'd been particularly interested in kama, something that he typically eschewed, or only touched on lightly in his own life. The pursuit of sensual activities and pleasures as a focus for magic and power was the opposite of the way he'd learned, and he might get lost along the new path.

"Yes, but I am not familiar with them, and it will take me years to relearn how to do everything. We have an enemy who could have killed you several times. The first few attempts were only meant to scare us off, but that didn't work. This last one was meant to discover our abilities. They don't know how we're finding our information. No one outside of the family knows about your visions, or else they'd have taken one of these numerous opportunities to kill you."

She propped herself up on her elbows to look down at him. "By that logic, I should still be safe. They aren't going to find out about the visions because we aren't going to tell them."

"No, but we have an audience with the queen in the morning, and we will have to tell her. It is probable that she will then seek guidance from advisors or ministers, perhaps even the Arch-Mage of Canterbury. Any one of those people could be among the group maintaining the Aegis spell."

Olivia sighed and flopped back down, pillowing her head on his chest. "You're right. These people are well-connected, and there's every reason to believe they have agents placed in the highest of the queen's councils. But I wish you were wrong."

"So do I. We'll work out something that keeps you out of danger without confining you too much. I promise."

"You'd better." She kissed him on the sternum and fell almost immediately into a deep slumber, her breath evening out and her body going entirely limp. Savit wondered if she always fell asleep this way, and prayed that he would have many more chances to find out.

He fell asleep worrying over the problem of how to keep the feisty, opinionated, volatile, and precious woman in his arms safe.

WINDSOR CASTLE HAD BEEN IN A STATE OF RESTORATION OR renovation of one kind or another for most of the last hundred and fifty years, and there was still work going on when the Fay party arrived the next morning, this time to add electricity to some of the rooms used for state visits and gatherings. A group of laborers had taken the morning train in with them, and they headed off around the side of the building to whatever portion of the castle was to receive the new wiring.

Olivia fretted with her skirts as she followed Mother to the magnificent main entrance. She'd wanted to wear bloomers, but even Etta had told her that was not a wise decision. The queen expected a certain level of formality, and rational dress was not on her approved list of appropriate garb. Etta had offered to have one of her plainer court dresses altered for Olivia's slightly greater height and more slender build, and the thing fit well enough, but she wasn't used to yards of heavy fabric changing her stride.

At least they'd allowed her to go with a boned bodice rather than a corset, and only a suggestion of a bustle instead of setting a full-blown horsehair monstrosity on her bum.

Still, she hated that she had to pay attention to not tripping over the lace that had been used to lengthen the hem instead of admiring the architecture, art, and curiosities on display inside the castle.

She also had the promised energy this morning—either a

result of her mother's spell, or good sex, or both. That meant she could spare the attention needed for not tripping, because otherwise she'd have been focused entirely on not collapsing into an exhausted heap.

Their party was shown to a sitting room and offered refreshments. Mother accepted on everyone's behalf. When the servant bowed and left, she explained, "We're likely to be here a while, and once we do see the queen, even if it's tea time, she'll have only plain fare. Best to fill up now."

The trays that arrived held tea and an assortment of sandwiches, cakes, and biscuits. Olivia ate, but her usual healthy appetite had deserted her. Something about this place made her feel distinctly uneasy.

When she mentioned the sensation to Etta, she said, "You mean, apart from the damp chill?" That made everyone laugh and eased some of the tension. But the crawly feeling remained, and Etta explained, "Joking aside, it's the convergence. There's an unusual multiple leyline convergence beneath the property, which is why William the Conqueror built a castle here and Henry the First claimed it for a home. Magic is both stronger and more unpredictable here."

Savit, who sat beside her, made a sound of interest. Olivia looked up just in time to see his eyes go unfocused. He was probably examining the convergence. She wished she could enter the trance state that easily. When he came back to himself, he smiled at her attention. "Yes, that is odd," he said. "But interesting. I should like to study it, if given time."

"Unless I miss my guess, we will be in this room for several hours," Mother said.

"Good. Then please do not be alarmed if I cease participating in the conversation for a while."

Everyone gave their assurance that they wouldn't disturb him, and his spirit wandered off again.

"When we speak to Her Majesty, let me lead," Etta said. "I

know you're the one who has seen the evidence, Olivia, and of course if the queen asks you questions you should answer. But over the last two years I've learned some ways to get around her in conversation, and I'd prefer to keep charge of the interview if possible. She's a wily and canny bird, and although I have every respect for your intelligence, I don't want her to poke at you, and possibly Savit, as unknown quantities and get one or the other of you to accidentally reveal something. I'll do my best to divert her."

"I can manage. I'll treat her as I did my old headmistress. With respect, but demanding respect in return."

"That should work, although do not mention the headmistress to her."

Olivia laughed. "I won't."

After she'd discovered the source of her disquiet, it was easier to ignore the slight roiling in her stomach and eat. The queen's cooks were too talented to waste their offerings. Etta had tucked in, as well, demolishing a significant portion of the treats. Baby Fay must be hungry.

Mother's estimate proved to be inadequate. Halfway through their fifth hour, they were summoned to the queen.

They were received in a large receiving room. There were two people in the room aside from the queen, although the only one Olivia recognized was the Queen's Sorceress.

Her Majesty sat on a sturdy cushioned chair, wearing her habitual black. Her husband, Prince Albert, had been dead for fifty years, but still she mourned. Olivia snuck a glance at Savit. What would she do, if she lost him? Everything between them was new, untested, and much had still been left unspoken. But last night had been transcendent, and she wanted more. Maybe even...

The queen spoke, acknowledging Cecily and Etta by their titles. Lady Falcestershire introduced Olivia and Savit to Her Majesty. Olivia would have thought that Etta's title made her responsible for the introductions, but perhaps the role of Queen's Sorceress edged a dowager countess to the top of the social hierarchy.

Olivia curtseyed. Her motion was stiff and jerky, as she'd started off with a bow and had to change in the middle. The heavy weight around her ankles didn't help. When she was able to divert her attention from not falling over, she found the queen looking at her with open curiosity. Perhaps because of her hair? The dress could make her look presentable from the neck down, but she'd refused to wear a wig, and there was no disguising silver-and-opalescent hair that only reached chin-length in front and barely brushed her neck in back.

All of the other women in the room, including the queen, had very long hair, pinned up on their heads. Only the queen wore a cap, as was the fashion for married ladies and widows when she was a girl. Today, women wore fashionable hats instead, although not indoors. Olivia had never owned anything more fashionable than a straw boater with an unusually wide brim that she wore while digging to protect the skin on her face and neck from burning in the summer sun.

She doubted the queen would have approved of the hat any more than the hair—or the woman—beneath it.

Next, Lady Falcestershire introduced a man standing off to the queen's side. His skin was even darker than Savit's. He had a full beard and a turban covered his head. He wore traditional Indian garb with a high collar and sash around his waist and incongruous patent leather Oxford brogues. This must be the Queen's Munshi. Lady Falcestershire gave his name as Mr. Karim and said he was there to translate for the queen if necessary. He and Savit regarded each other coolly, and Olivia wondered why. Surely meeting a fellow coun-tryman would be a cause for happiness, if not joy?

Savit bowed again to the queen, and said, in a perfect upper-crust accent, "That will not be necessary, ma'am."

The queen didn't seem to notice her secretary's staring contest with her guest, or if she did, intentionally ignored it. She flicked her fingers at the Munshi and he bowed to her and left. Once he was gone, she said, "We have been informed that you have news regarding your inquiries."

Etta nodded and stepped forward. She explained what they'd learned, glossing over the mechanics of Olivia's visions and stating only that magic had been used, as well as traditional research methods.

"From what we can determine, ma'am, the Aegis Spell was stripped from King George the Third and held in abeyance using a simulacrum of His Majesty. Said simulacrum was most likely taken to Hanover to protect the state from Napoleon, with the intention of passing it on to his successor when the danger of the Sicilian had passed. But from the tenor of the last exchange witnessed, it seems there were elements among this coalition of mages who did not desire either of your crowned uncles to have the spell. We believe neither spell nor simulacrum came to George the Fourth at the conclusion of the regency, nor to your predecessor. And of course, if the spell had come to you, ma'am, we would not be having this conversation now."

The queen sat in silence for several long minutes, considering the information. She eventually signaled to Lady Falcestershire, who stepped forward. "What do you know of this?"

The lady frowned. "Nothing, ma'am. When Sorcerer Pollard passed, he said nothing of this spell, and his predecessor died before I was born. My best guess is that they did not know, or I would have been informed."

"My uncle Clarence rarely spoke of his father's madness in my presence, but during the scandal when the Earl of

Caulper lost a particularly valuable magical artifact in a burglary, he quipped about the old king having lost magic, too." The queen's face at rest was imposing and stern. But the expression on her face now was disbelief and anger. "What proof do you have of this spell and its theft, beyond some magic you say you cannot recreate?"

Etta gestured to Savit and Olivia. "My sister-in-law and Dr. Reilly are gathering as much written proof as they can. We were hoping to examine the royal archives to assist in the search."

"I will want more than lines in a book to prove your story, Duchess. And none of what you've told me so far indicates where the magic is going—the Kingdom of Hanover doesn't even exist anymore."

"No, and we've already scryed for a destination with that in mind, to no avail."

That was a surprise to Olivia, but then Etta wasn't required to tell her everything. And knowing that they'd failed to trace the spell to her only lead would have made her more discouraged, so it was for the best that she hadn't known.

"Then until you can provide me with tangible proof, I must assume that the magic is simply draining away naturally."

"Ma'am, with all due respect, many of the finest mages in the land helped us cast the origin spell, and we've proven that the drain is not natural."

"Then bring me proof of where it's going and who is stealing it, and we shall dedicate all our resources to getting it back." She waved a hand at Lady Falcestershire, who inclined her head toward the queen and gestured them out of the room. They each curtseyed (or bowed, in Savit's case) and left.

The Queen's Sorceress led them into an adjacent wing of

the castle, where rooms had been prepared for them. Savit was told his quarters would be in a different location, but he would be allowed to stay with them until it was time to sleep.

Etta strode past the sitting room and into one of the sleeping chambers to change from her elaborate gown into something simpler. Savit took a seat by the fire and resumed his study of the leyline convergence. Liv wanted to ask him about the Munshi, but he obviously didn't want to talk right now, so she moved to follow Etta and help her out of the dress, but paused in the doorway of the chamber when she heard her mother's voice.

She and Lady Falcestershire had gone into the adjoining room, and although the door had been swung behind them, it hadn't latched and stood partially open. Olivia wouldn't have eavesdropped, except that Mother said something so unexpected.

"Amelia, please forgive me for my behavior the last few times we've met. The last three or four years have been full of upheavals for both of us, and neither of us reacted well to the changes. But that does not excuse my actions. All I have ever wanted is what is best for Britain and my family."

Olivia stood, staring helplessly through the gap between door and frame, as her mother took the other woman's hand and brought it to her mouth.

The dowager countess stepped closer to Mother and put her free hand on Mother's cheek. "I regret that those desires placed us on opposite sides of this undeclared war." The gentle touch turned into a caress, and Mother's eyes closed in pleasure.

Olivia staggered away from the door and sat down hard on an armchair. Mother...and Lady Falcestershire.

Viola had told her once that she'd seen a woman in their parents' rooms late at night, but Olivia had always assumed that their father was simply brazen enough to bring a lover into his house. She had never suspected that her perfect mother was the one who'd invited her. Or perhaps they both had.

Liv shuddered. No one liked thinking of one's parents having intimate relations, despite the knowledge that one would not exist without such activities. But this—how could she never have suspected that her mother was attracted to women, too? Perhaps because they'd only met formally when Olivia was a child, with Olivia reciting lessons and trying to be a good girl, and Mother performing the role of the Marchioness of Hazelby. A marchioness was not a sexual deviant, although Olivia thought calling a natural attraction deviance was balderdash.

Why, there were many examples in the natural world of creatures forming relationships with members of the same sex. Why should humans not follow that example? The Magisterium and Academe had much to answer for in that regard—their patron gods and goddesses were too rigid, and too interested in their followers upholding their examples of marriage. Other gods and goddesses didn't force their people to take such unnatural stances.

But like it or not, most of British society found relationships between two women or two men distasteful, and Mother would do anything to avoid being censured by Society. If she had kept such a secret for so long from everyone, including her children, what else did she hide beneath that oh-so-polished exterior?

What a shock to find out that her mother was a warm living being beneath the veneer of ice.

The door opened, and both ladies emerged. Their cheeks were a little flushed, and Olivia suspected that touching had progressed quickly to other things. She stopped her thoughts there.

Etta strode out of her chamber, now dressed in a shirtwaist and skirt that might have been bought ready-made at any shop in the city. She caught sight of the two older women still standing too-close together, and a single dark eyebrow rose in surprised query. Then her lips quirked into a grin.

"It took you two long enough."

Mother turned bright crimson, but Lady Falcestershire—or perhaps Liv ought to start thinking of her as Amelia—smiled in a very satisfied fashion.

"While you're here at Windsor, you ought to take a tour of the place," Amelia said. "I will have one of the upper maids show you around. But make sure not to go to the south wing on the second floor. The Royal Magic Archives are there and you don't want to upset Her Majesty by doing more 'intangible' research without permission." She winked. "And I believe I may have forgotten to renew the protective ward spells today." Then her face transformed as she smiled—a true, beautiful smile—at Mother. And Mother, despite her blush, smiled back.

Amelia left them then, and Savit stood. He must have come out of his trance at some point, and Olivia had been too distracted by her seemingly transformed parent to notice.

"That was a fairly obvious bit of instructions." There was a thread of laughter in his voice, and in a world that had just tumbled upside-down and inside-out, Olivia wanted to go wrap herself in its comforting stability.

Etta looked a little dumbfounded, and turned a gimlet eye on Mother. "If I'd known that all it would take to get her to come 'round to our side was for you two to kiss and make up, I'd have suggested it two years ago."

Mother went stiff, and Liv thought Etta had gone too far. But then something happened that Olivia had never seen in her entire life. Mother laughed. Actually *laughed*, loud and from her belly. Peals and ripples of laughter.

Savit touched Liv's arm and she blinked. Then she closed her mouth. She'd been staring, slack-jawed, at the incomprehensible sight of her mother displaying a sense of humor. She wanted to go find Amelia and bring her back. If this version of her mother had been around during Liv's childhood, so much would be different.

Suddenly, resentment and anger curdled in her belly. Why had her mother chosen to hide behind the ice for so long? Why had she destroyed her relationships with her lover and her children? What had she gained by making herself a slave to Lilias Fay's ambitions?

Savit's fingers wrapped around her hand and squeezed. "She has much to answer for, but not today. Today, we need to follow her lover's directions and find answers."

His words pierced through the haze of fury and disappointment. A hot flush filled her cheeks at the thought that she'd allowed her problems with her mother to overcome her sense of duty and her commitment to her work. This was why she'd stopped working with lovers—when her emotions were engaged, she lost all sense of objectivity. Apparently the same thing applied to family.

Liv pulled her shoulders back and lifted her chin. She had work to do.

24

Windsor Castle, for all its grandeur, was cold, damp, and draughty. Most of it had been lavishly restored in terms of décor by previous monarchs, but modern comforts and conveniences were few. The Royal Magic Archive had been maintained, for the most part, but the area of the castle that housed it had not yet been updated, and indeed, had been passed over by the decorators and designers brought in by George III and George IV. Olivia frowned at a large patch of mold on the plaster wall outside the library door. Mold and books were not a good combination.

Their guide had led them on a tour, and had conspicuously noted the directions to the library as they passed the branching. The duchess and marchioness had followed the guide, and she and Savit had taken the other passage.

"Those workers from earlier ought to come to the aid of this section." They'd peeked into the room and found it empty, but had hesitated on the threshold for Savit to check that the wards were down. He said he believed that Amelia was trustworthy, but she did have assistants, and if someone had noticed that the spell hadn't been renewed today, they might have taken on the duty themselves.

But the room was clear, aside from the mold and mildew.

"I'm afraid not everyone finds as much value in the written word as you and I do." Savit crossed the threshold, and nothing happened. She hadn't expected anything to, but still experienced a wave of relief as they went the room.

Unlike the Skye House library, which was organized according to the whims of a madwoman as far as Olivia could tell, this collection had been carefully catalogued and shelved. Helpful index tomes sat on a table near the entrance where a searcher could quickly locate a desired reference.

Savit flipped open the first index and scanned through, but Olivia moved past him, straight down an aisle created by two bookcases.

At the end of the aisles a small reading nook had been created. On a square table between two overstuffed armchairs sat a pile of books and folios, and two large blank copybooks.

"Well," Savit said, coming out of the aisle behind her. "This is a lovely welcome."

Olivia sat, pulled a folio and a copybook toward her, and settled in to read. But she couldn't concentrate with Savit still moving around the empty room. She could guess why he was worried. Either Amelia or one of her underlings had done this, against the wishes of the queen. Although, thinking back on the interview, Her Majesty had not precisely forbidden them from accessing the archive. What she'd said was that she did not accept printed word as fact. Which was fair enough, but what she and Savit sought here wasn't the whole story, but rather clues that might trigger a new set of visions.

Of course, they might not trigger anything. She'd learned to control the visions once they started, but other than sexual activity with Savit, she had no consistent causes. And even sex didn't always work—she hadn't had a vision last night after he'd brought her with his mouth.

Her body tingled in memory. He'd taken her direction perfectly, building from what she showed and asked and discovering new ways to pleasure her. And then his *tongue*. Great goddess, but she'd thought only women were that good at cunnilingus.

Not that his technique had been perfect, but more that he'd responded to her and listened, and seemed to be enjoying himself. In fact, she was pretty sure he'd climaxed, although she'd been too drained and sleepy to notice. Next time, she would make sure he had an orgasm, too.

Or would there be a next time? He'd been gone when she woke up this morning, and explained that he'd used the casting chamber to meditate before breakfast. And all day he'd treated her like an acquaintance rather than a lover. Was that for her family's benefit? The queen's?

Whatever the case was, she didn't like it. Either they were lovers, in which case she refused to hide or feel ashamed, or they weren't.

"Now that we're alone," she said, to make him come and sit beside her, "explain to me what was happening earlier with the Munshi."

He came, as she'd hoped, and sat in the other chair with an uncharacteristic thump. "It's nothing. I should be pleased that the queen keeps him around. I've heard that the staff here hate him and try to exclude him from everything because he is different. But I've also heard—from sources that I trust—that he sometimes misleads Her Majesty about my people."

"What do you mean?"

"He doesn't follow the Sutra. Not everyone in India does, of course, and as I've told you before, the Sutra teaches that all ways of worship and magic are worthwhile. But that doesn't mean everyone agrees with us. Members of his faction have caused trouble in the past."

The door to the archives shut with a loud click and both Olivia and Savit startled. Olivia dropped her pen. Amelia strode down the aisle and nodded at them. She carried two impressive-looking tomes. "Good, I see you made a start. I'd already asked one of my assistants to gather materials for you, and the queen didn't precisely bar you from the premises, so I thought it best that you have the access."

"We appreciate that," Savit said while Olivia dealt with a rush of confused feelings that tied her tongue. This woman had been her mother's lover in some distant past before Olivia was born. And judging from the level of hostility that Etta reported had existed between them as recently as a few months ago, they had not parted well. Just like Olivia and Natalya. The memory of her last argument with Talya—and last, frantic lovemaking—was stark and sharp in her mind.

Had something similar happened to her mother and Amelia? Had they been deeply in love until they found a place where neither could compromise and neither could give in?

Liv's gaze flicked to Savit, and for a moment she soaked in the sight of him, his face so handsome with its defined chin and jaw, and straight, somewhat thick nose, bracketed by dark eyes and topped with curly black hair.

What would be the hill on which their relationship died?

Or maybe it would never die at all—if Savit could get over his fears and embrace their love.

Love? Yes. Not just lover, but love. Olivia's heart cracked a little at the thought. She hadn't been in love since Talya, and even Talya hadn't understood her, challenged her, and aroused her as Savit did.

She suspected that no matter what the outcome of their

time together, a large portion of her heart would be his forever.

Amelia dropped the two heavy tomes on the table and the bang knocked Olivia out of her reverie. "These are the secret histories of the Royal Sorcerers. I am bound by oath not to reveal their contents, but the oath is written in such a way that it allows me to share details if it's for the good of the Realm."

She pulled a third chair closer to them with magic, a display of kinesthetic power that was both nonchalant and intimidating. Moving objects like that took some people years to master, and even then they would require a focus or a more elaborate spell. Amelia simply gestured and the chair moved. She sank into it gracefully. "In truth, the 'secrets' are mostly boring accounts of daily life at court and the petty intrigues of the time period, but they do also record important spells involving the Royal Family. By the time my predecessor, Ezekiel Pollard, got around to keeping the journals, someone had tabbed the relevant spells so future sorcerers wouldn't be forced to read through everything."

Amelia ran a finger down the cut edge of the pages, where wooden tabs had been pasted in place. "I'll admit to not being incredibly curious about the doings of the mages of the past, so aside from keeping my own daily record and occasionally referencing rarely-used spells, like marriage bindings and funeral rites for the Royal Family, I'd never actually read the rest. I did check through the marked spells when the issue first came up, and I thought since it wasn't marked it must not have happened, because a spell of that magnitude would fall under the purview of the monarch's mage."

She opened the top book to a page that had been marked with a piece of scarlet ribbon. "But I placed too much faith in my predecessors. Either someone made a mistake, or these books have been tampered with." She pointed at a particular entry. "Fortunately, the words themselves are spelled in place and can't be changed, so the information is still here. This is when it was cast." She flipped forward to a spot marked with a green ribbon. "This is when they expanded the territory." A blue ribbon marked the mad king's first bout with insanity following the attempt to remove the spell, and a cream one sat at the spot where the shift in the council had begun. Amelia explained that, as Olivia had surmised, the King's Sorcerer was not happy about being maneuvered by the Germans.

Then she opened to a purple ribbon. "This is what happened next."

The Mad King's sorcerer, Francis Mayes, wrote of continued argument among the Coalition, and of the machinations of Dieter Seebach, the Electorate Mage, who had managed to take over the group in the wake of the French Revolution and the rise of Napoleon, and more and more power had been diverted into the simulacrum, now held by Seebach on the Continent to protect Hanover from the encroachment of foreign powers.

But the entry she read for them was the day in 1804 that Mayes was barred from the Coalition for demanding that the spell be returned and used to defend their borders against invasion. He raged in the journal about his own short-sightedness and how he'd allowed things to go so wrong. But in his guilt he abetted them further—he said nothing to the Prince of Wales, not even when the king's madness became complete and Prinny became Prince Regent.

"I'm afraid Mayes's entries end soon after that. His successor, Henry Wraight, writes that Mayes died foiling an attempt on the Regent's life, but he suspected there were other forces at work. Unfortunately he was very busy dealing with a war and couldn't find the proof he needed to convince the Regent, who believed that his father's Sorcerer was just as mad as he was. And of course Wraight was never invited to join the Coalition, and Mayes was often vague in the journals about the names of members. Dieter Seebach was named, but he went to Hanover to help maintain stability under a succession of conquering powers, and so Wraight assumed another Head had been named, but he never discovered who."

"And Prinny never pushed the issue because he didn't believe in it," Savit said.

"Correct. Wraight also died suddenly, but as far as I can tell, no one was suspicious about the manner of his death—it's recorded as an apoplexy. Then came my predecessor, Pollard. He told me himself he never read the old histories, except the parts for keeping up spells. I can't imagine that no one ever bothered to mark the Aegis Spell, so I have to believe that the tab was removed during the end of Mayes's tenure, or perhaps Wraight's."

"I suppose, since the histories were not enough proof for the Prince Regent, that means Her Majesty doesn't see them as proof, either?" Olivia asked.

Amelia hunched inward as far as her corset would allow. "To be honest, I don't know what she'll accept as proof. I'll bring these histories to her attention, but even though I believe that the two independent sources of information are convincing, I think she would rather ignore this and hope it goes away."

"Why?" Olivia's voice came out harsher than she'd intended, and Amelia reached out and touched her hand. It was a curiously maternal gesture, meant to soothe. Which was odd, because while Mother had chosen to have children, Amelia had not. Or perhaps it hadn't been a choice. She turned her hand around and clasped Amelia's fingers in hers.

"Her Majesty is old, and she is tired. Her Diamond Jubilee is taking up all of her attention, and she's cranky because of the change in government last year and the defeat of the Irish Home Rule bill, which she supported. She is terrified to die and leave the country to her son, whom she views as a wastrel and a sot, not to mention a womanizer and a spendthrift."

"So you're saying she has other priorities, and this is too big a problem for her to solve."

"Yes. And she always wanted to be a mage. Did you know that? Her mother's family has magic in it, and she has a small gift, but not enough for practical work."

"Rather like mine," Olivia said wryly.

Amelia flushed, but smiled when she realized that Olivia wasn't upset. "Yes, I suppose so. But she's always considered the slow waning of English magic to be linked to her own lack of talent. As though she is the embodiment of the empire's power. Which she is, in some respects. Moreover, to admit that this is happening is to acknowledge that she allowed someone to steal our magic for years just because she was miffed at not having much herself. And she isn't disposed to believe information coming from you, Dr. Reilly. I'm afraid she has some…incorrect notions about you."

"I wondered. So our task is nigh impossible," Savit said.

Amelia reached out and took his hand with her free one, and drew their two hands together. "I have faith in you both, and in that termagant of a duchess. If anyone can convince Her Majesty, it is Clan Fay."

25

Back in their quarters, Olivia paced the sitting area while Etta and Mother strategized. Savit had been sent off to a different suite of rooms. The queen's sense of propriety would not allow an unmarried man to share a suite with three ladies, even if two of them were married.

She missed him more than she wanted to admit. Once Mother and Etta went to bed, she planned to sneak out and join him. And her intentions were only slightly prurient. Yes, she wanted to sleep beside him and touch him in any way that he'd allow. But more, she wanted to try for a vision. They needed to know exactly what had happened to Sorcerer Mayes and who had taken over the Coalition after he was forced out.

The other two ladies took another hour to retire, and then Liv changed into a set of her usual clothes that she'd smuggled in with her nightgown. She hoped, in the dark, she would pass for a man. Her chest was flat enough, and her hair was short. If no one looked closely enough, she ought to get away with it.

She passed a few servants in the halls going about their

end-of-day tasks, but no one stopped her or asked where she was going. Either they were familiar with guests wandering about and didn't bother asking them their destinations, or they knew who she was in particular and had been told to avoid her, possibly by Amelia.

No matter, because it meant she got to Savit's door unaccosted.

He opened the door wearing a set of pyjamas and a banyan gown. He didn't look surprised to see her, although he kept his expression neutral and so she couldn't tell if he was upset or happy.

He did let her come in, after a moment's hesitation. She darted in as soon as he stepped back and gave her room, and he closed the door.

This was a much smaller suite than the one she and the other women had been assigned. It had a tiny sitting room and a bedroom. In the bedroom was a privacy screen and a washstand with a basin and pitcher and chamber pot.

"Goodness! We at least have a watercloset nearby. Is someone going to have to collect that for you in the morning?"

Savit did not smile, or respond to the jest.

"Oh, very well. I was only trying to lighten the mood."

"I know what you're going to ask, and I don't think it's a good idea."

"Why not? The convergence is here. We'll have plenty of energy. And the queen is here. She's a blood relative of the last person who held the spell—that we know of, anyway."

"Exactly. Someone else may have it now, meaning her blood connection could be worthless. And I don't trust the convergence. It's...odd. You aren't experienced enough yet to handle the energy it would produce."

"But you are, and you'll be with me. This is important,

Savit. You promised me you wouldn't try to shield me from necessary risks."

He stiffened, but set his jaw and didn't flinch away. Good. She liked it when he argued back. "I don't agree that the risk is necessary."

"Of course it is. But since you disagree, I'll go back to my room and masturbate. Orgasms often trigger the visions." She turned and got all the way through the sitting room before he grabbed her arm. She allowed him to swing her around, and poked him in the belly. "Unless you'd rather assist me with that *onerous* task?"

One corner of his mouth twitched. Not quite a smile. But his eyes had gone all dark and hot and it wouldn't take much to entice him into bed. "You are the most exasperating woman."

She ran her free hand down his breastbone and over his flat belly. The banyan gaped in the center, revealing the pyjamas. She slipped a few buttons free and a soft sound erupted from her throat when skin met skin. How could just touching him feel like paradise?

Her fingertips danced along his chest, over the patches of dark curly hair that dusted his pectoral muscles and made a trail down his abdomen to the waistband of his pyjama bottoms. He didn't stop her from untying the drawstring, or make a move to hold up the suddenly loose garment. It slipped down, and snagged on the impressive length of his erection.

Olivia giggled, and shifted the fabric away, letting her fingers dance over his cock.

She placed her other hand flat on his chest and stared into his dark, depthless gaze. "Tell me you want this. Tell me you want me."

He bent forward like a marionette with its string cut,

sudden and yet somehow graceful. His forehead came to rest against hers. "You know the answer to that, Olivia."

"I need to hear you say it."

His eyes closed for a long moment. She felt his heart thudding under her palm, and the echoing throb of blood filling his cock. If he said no, they could still do other things —he could bring her to ecstasy with his mouth again as he had last night—but it wouldn't be entirely...complete. Something would be missing.

He opened his eyes again, and the shift within him was visible. Magic welled up inside of him, and a sharp but sweet smell, like a strongly spiced stew, flooded her nostrils. He took a deep breath, then spoke. "I don't want you to stop."

It wasn't the answer she'd hoped for, but it wasn't a no, either. She tightened her grip on his cock and thrilled at his hissed intake of breath. Then his magic wrapped around her and burrowed inside, and it was like that time in the carriage when he'd pleasured her entirely with his gift.

Her skin tingled and flushed with heat. Moisture dripped from the folds of her swollen cunny, and her nipples tightened to aching, needy points. It was as though Savit had a thousand hands and tongues, and each one had found a point of arousal and stroked.

She nudged him toward the bedroom and he went, gliding backward gracefully even though she still had her fist around his cock. She stripped him beside the bed and then let him take off her clothes. He kept up the assault on her senses as his real mouth and hands traveled her body; she was an instrument built for pleasure and he was quickly learning how to make her sing.

He let her push him back onto the bed and he eased back on his magical touch, allowing her the mental capacity to consider how best to tease him. She decided to use her hands and mouth, but to take things slow this time. In the library at

Hazelby House they'd both been on edge, and if she hadn't moved fast he might have had second thoughts.

But that time had long past. He might believe in some imaginary line within himself, but if such a thing existed for Olivia, she'd already crossed and had no desire to look back. She silenced the little voice that reminded her of how dangerous this path could be to her career and her self-esteem. Savit was not Talya, and she was older and wiser now.

She wet her lips and slid them over the head of his cock, licking the sensitive frenulum with firm, measured strokes. He shuddered beneath her, moaning her name. She pulled back, licked her palms and settled back to surround him from balls to tip with her hands and lips and tongue.

At some point he started teasing her with his magic again, thrusting power inside of her and pulsing against her clit, keeping in perfect sync with each dip of his cock into her mouth.

She lost the rhythm as pleasure bubbled up from her clitoris, building to a fiery whirlwind inside her quim that lit her entire body like a piece of flash paper. She convulsed with ecstasy as hot seed filled her mouth.

And that was when the vision started.

Savit didn't allow her to anchor herself this time. He took charge of the conduits of power, and she was grateful because even her subtle body was quivering with aftershocks of pleasure.

They were not in any of the locations they'd been to before. The room was a plain, if spacious, office. There was a desk and several chairs, shelves on one wall stuffed with books, and a wall of square cubbies filled with papers.

The door of the office opened and three people came in. One wore an army uniform from the Napoleonic War era. One was dressed in civilian finery from the same period, and she recognized him as the Electorate Mage from her earlier vision—Dieter Seebach. The third person was Lilias bloody Fay.

Olivia froze. She'd gotten complacent around the other practitioners, who never seemed to notice her in the visions. Queen Anne had been the only one to see her since Izarra that very first time. But if anyone was going to sense a visiting presence from the future, especially a visitor who shared her blood, it was the matriarch of Clan Fay.

Beside her, Savit finished securing their power anchors, and must have noticed Olivia's rigid posture. *What's wrong?*

That woman is my great-great grandmother. The first Duchess of Fay. Shite.

Truly? How old is she here?

I dunno. Late twenties? Thirty? I'm not sure what year it is.

Will she see us?

Probably.

Then we should stop.

No! This meeting is important, or we wouldn't be here. We need to know what they're talking about.

For the three figures were speaking. Olivia hadn't engaged fully with the vision yet, fearing Lilias's notice, so they couldn't hear what was said, but all three people were excited and upset. Savit tried to hold her back, but she plunged herself into the vision. Lilias might notice her, but that was a risk she needed to take.

"It was reckless to come here, Herr Seebach," the army officer was saying. "We appreciate your offer of assistance, but we need your eyes and ears on the Continent more than the possibility of magical power."

"I disagree, with all due respect, sir," Lilias said. "If there's a source of power anywhere near Napoleon's troops I want to know about it."

"You have your own...sources. They ought to have had

time to fill up again after the last use." Olivia wasn't certain what he was talking about, but it made Lilias go rigid with anger.

"Absolutely not. I told you I would never utilize those again in war, and I meant it. They are locked away in a place only I have access to, and you know there is nothing you can do to me that would incite me to bring them out."

The army man went pale and a little greenish. Lilias in a fury was not someone to be crossed, and Olivia suspected he knew it. The German spoke up.

"We want Napoleon back out of Europe as much as you do. He's advancing quickly, and this power might make all the difference at turning him back before he can muster his forces again."

If this was Napoleon's return, then it was 1815, and the Hundred Days that would end with Waterloo and the Restoration of the French monarchy.

Savit touched her arm. He looked furious, but he kept it contained. He didn't want to draw attention to them. *Is he offering your ancestor the power that she will spend the rest of her life seeking?*

It seems that way. I wonder if she was suspicious about it later. At this point, she seems too desperate to be thinking clearly. Otherwise she'd have noticed us.

Lilias was talking again, telling Seebach that she would be happy to accept his offer and that her battalion was ready to deploy. She had gotten permission from the Prince Regent to cast a gateway spell that would take them directly to Wellington's cantonment outside Brussels.

When Lilias Fay wanted something, she got it. The army man's objections were overridden, and Lilias shook hands with Dieter Seebach. Then Lilias looked up, and directly into Olivia's eyes. She smiled.

Olivia—

Savit's mental tone was a warning, and yet when Lilias beckoned with a tiny nod of her head, Olivia followed.

The scene shifted, to a huge room full of opulently-dressed courtiers. Lilias stood before the Prince Regent and he named her Duchess of Fay.

But Olivia was off to the side, where Dieter Seebach stood arguing with the Scotswoman who had been present at the Coalition meeting that determined to remove the Aegis Spell from George III.

"The war is over, Seebach. It's time to bring the spell back to England."

"That corpulent fool isn't worthy of it," Seebach said, gesturing curtly at the Prince Regent. "He sent his little brother as viceroy to Hanover, and can't be bothered to meet with me except at his convenience."

"That's true, but the magic belongs here. At least bring the statue back."

"What does that matter? Prinny won't live long anyway. Either his heart will give out, or someone will kill him."

"So you propose to wait?"

"The next two royal dukes are tolerable. We will decide based on which of them succeeds to the throne."

Something was dragging at Olivia, pulling her away from the muttered conversation. Other than the two speakers, everything else had gone muted and blurry. She looked down at her subtle body and it, too, was nearly transparent. Savit was shouting inside her head, but his words made no sense, and she couldn't see him anywhere.

A tearing sensation, and then a snap, and everything went black.

THE VISION WAS GONE, AND IN ITS PLACE A VOID. THERE WAS

nothing here, no light or breath or magic. And yet, there was *possibility* here, for all of those things and infinitely more.

With the thought, came a long thread, shining and golden. The thread was everywhere and everything, and yet singular and unique. It was everything that could be, and everything that could not, creation and entropy, at the same time. At all times.

Within the thread was Olivia—the gathering of matter that now answered to that name, and all of the previous and future incarnations of the divine essence that was her spark of life.

Twisted along her thread was another, never far apart, and often so close the two nearly merged. Her soul's eternal mate.

The knowledge of him—of *Savit*—pushed the essence that was Olivia away and into the golden thread. Here, she was not with him. Here, she was alone. And he needed her.

So she returned from the place where everything happened—and nothing—and fell down into darkness and light.

SAVIT HELD OLIVIA'S UNCONSCIOUS BODY AND WANTED TO scream at her. He'd almost lost her. Even now, he wasn't entirely sure that he hadn't. She was much thinner than when the vision began, as though the magic had stripped away her flesh. Her cheeks were sunken and her bones were clearly visible.

They should have dismissed the vision the moment she saw her ancestress. He didn't know what the woman had done, but it had gotten mixed up in the anchors of power and then there'd been a flux from the convergence, shifting the balance of energies.

Instead of pushing power into the vision, power had been stripped away. He'd tried to pull Olivia out, but she'd kept wading deeper in, feeding the magic with her own meager resources, until her thread had broken, unraveling under his spirit-fingers.

He'd grasped both ends and pulled them together, his subtle body the only conduit between her soul and the flesh she'd left behind. But the force dragging her away was strong, and her thread was slippery as silk. Sometimes the twisting threads disappeared in his hands like smoke, forcing him to clutch again, farther up the cord.

And then the tension had reversed, and her subtle body was there, falling into his arms. He'd shoved the cord from her gross body into the solar plexus of her spirit form and dragged her back into her flesh.

He couldn't stop trembling, now, shock and anger and fear rippling over his muscles and into his bones. He could have lost her, and then *he* would have been lost.

Outside his window, the sun was coming up. Eventually Etta or Liv's mother would send someone to find out where Olivia was. And he was going to have to wait for that, because he couldn't move. He'd exhausted his own reserves bringing her back, and it was all he could do to hold on to her until the reckoning came.

LADY HAZELBY WAS NOT PLEASED. EVEN ETTA, WHO TENDED toward pragmatism, cast him an accusatory glare. But he had no defense. He'd agreed to try for the vision. He'd allowed her to strip him and he'd given and received pleasure from their mutual acts on his bed. And if he was honest with himself, he'd agreed not for any noble reason such as finding out more about the Aegis Spell, but because he wanted that intimacy with her. Because he craved her touch, her mouth. And he'd underestimated the consequences.

The ladies managed to get Olivia dressed and bundled discreetly into a carriage. They drove back to the city rather than taking the return train, and once in town, Lady Hazelby insisted on keeping her daughter in her care, at Hazelby House.

"She wouldn't like that," Savit objected.

"She needs me to look after her."

"Cecily is an amazing healer, Savit," Etta said, her voice gentle. He knew that already—that wasn't why he'd objected. "She won't let anything happen to her daughter. And anyway, I think it will help Olivia to be away from magic while she recovers, and Hazelby House is one of the coldest magical places in town."

He glared at the two women, but he knew when he had no chance to win an argument. They'd already made up their minds, and the truth was, he had no right whatsoever to gainsay them. Lady Hazelby was Olivia's mother and Etta was her sister-in-law. He was...

The right words refused to come to him. Was he her lover? Not truly. He was her mentor in magic, but it wasn't as though he was her teacher in a school and had any power over her. The only thing he could latch on to, and it was unsatisfactorily meager, was that he was her friend.

And that was all he could allow himself to be from now on. She'd nearly died, and still might. All because his lust had gotten in the way of his good sense.

No, it was time to do the job he'd been hired to accomplish, and return to research. He had a pretty good idea of where to look, now—after he'd gotten over his shock and horror and reexamined what they'd seen, the final vision had given him some strong clues about what had happened after Napoleon's defeat.

Dieter Seebach had gotten a taste of power, and he didn't want to give it up. He also had no respect for the Prince Regent—to be fair, few people did—and would likely have been even less a proponent of William IV. Victoria's predecessor had left his little brother as viceroy in Hanover and generally went about passing reforms that gave commoners rights, including protecting their right to practice magic, something that, if Savit's memory served him, was a stance the Hanoverian Mage had been against.

On the other hand, Ernest Augustus, the Duke of Cumberland—who took the throne of Hanover under Salic Law—was an absolutist and cruel. And he'd been implicated —though never outright accused—of plotting against his niece for the British throne. Several times. Including at least one attempted assassination.

What were the chances that Dieter Seebach had passed the Aegis Spell to Cumberland, in the hopes that the assassination would succeed?

Yes, he had a very good idea of where to look, and that meant Olivia wouldn't have to risk herself again.

With luck, he'd be able to convince her not to try.

26

A week later, Savit's optimism had fled. He'd found plenty of information in newspaper records accusing Cumberland of all manner of atrocities, and other pieces praising him for his later work in Hanover, when he seemed to have reversed course and become moderate, if not outright liberal, in his policies.

There was nothing here to find, not even the slightest hint of magic, much less something of the magnitude of the Aegis Spell. He found vague references in sources at the Society and books provided by Amelia, but nothing that gave a concrete lead. What made the least sense was, if the Aegis Spell had transferred to King Ernest, why had his son George V almost immediately lost the country to the German Empire? Or perhaps the power did not work correctly to maintain a ruler outside the shores of Britain.

He had too many questions and not enough answers.

He'd gone back to the Society and updated his requirements, and in despair had even gone to speak to his grandfather, who had been a boy during the early days of Victoria's reign and might remember something of interest.

But Savit had found nothing. Without Olivia's visions, the investigation had stymied.

Her mother was keeping her at Hazelby House in a magically-induced slumber. They woke her at intervals to feed her and take her to the washroom, but she was never fully alert during those brief periods. It would be another day, perhaps two, before Olivia had regained enough of her physical and magical energy to be brought out of the coma. Even then, she would need several more days of rest and quiet before she would be able to function normally.

Beyond his frustration at his inability to search without her, he simply missed her. She'd been in his life for so little time, and yet her soul belonged with his, and always had. He needed her back, beside him, driving him mad with laughter and desire.

When she awoke, he was going to keep her safe, and never let her go.

OLIVIA WOKE IN HER OWN BED. SHE BLINKED AT THE DIMLY-LIT room, disorientation making her dizzy. For a moment, she was a teenager again, forced to London to the house that she hated, choking on the foul miasma of fog, coal smoke, excrement, refuse, the stinking river, and millions of unwashed bodies packed together like tinned kippers.

Then reality rushed back in, and she tried to sit up but failed, her body not responding to the desperate urges of her brain. Panic gripped her and she screamed.

Except, she didn't. Her voice wouldn't work. All she could do was push air through her mouth and suck it back in, which she did, rapidly, for what seemed an eternity before blackness rushed back over her.

SHE WOKE AGAIN TO MORNING LIGHT, PALE AND insubstantial. She could remember, vaguely, many wakings. But the memories twisted away and vanished as she tried to grasp them, like the shreds of dreams in the light of dawn.

She still couldn't move.

But this time, she could scream.

The door to the hall opened and Savit rushed in, mashing the button that sent electricity to the bulbs overhead. She blinked and squinted against the sudden glare.

What was he doing here?

He sat beside her on the bed, nearly crushing her hand. He must have felt it under him because he shifted and pulled her arm out from under the covers, draping it across her chest. She managed to make her mouth move, though her words were slurred and she didn't know if he'd understand her.

"Wha…ha'en'?"

He leaned over and stroked the side of her face. "Don't try to talk yet. You almost lost everything for that last vision, and you're in no shape to do anything yet but rest."

She growled, which had the pleasing nature of not requiring her mouth to move.

"I know. And I'm sorry we're here in this house. Your mother insisted, and I didn't have the right to say her nay."

This time, the sound she made was more like a whimper. If he didn't have the right, who did?

"She's had you under a spell for the last sennight that has kept you asleep while your body and soul recovered from your ordeal. She started to strip away parts of it this morning, but she said it would keep you roughly immobilized for about twelve more hours. It's supposed to also rebuild your strength and restore some of your flesh."

Her eyes widened, and something cold and sharp clutched low in her belly. She couldn't see her body, but when he'd lifted her arm it had seemed oddly—thin.

His expression was grim. "You've lost almost two stone in weight and you look like a mummy. I was terrified that you would die, but your mother assures me her spell will re-knit your muscle tissue and encourage your body systems to repair any damage done."

He tucked her hair behind her ear and sat back. She would have preferred that he come closer, and lay beside her. But he kept a careful, almost forced distance, and his tone was flat. Detached.

"I haven't learned anything new since you've been unconscious. Lady Falcestershire sent me some books about King Ernest Augustus of Hanover and the succession there, and I've put out word that I'm looking for details about his reign, but nothing has come to fruition yet."

Of course, that made perfect sense. In the vision, Dieter Seebach had had nothing but contempt for the Prince Regent, and she doubted he would have cared much for William IV, either, who'd been fairly progressive. But the Duke of Cumberland would have made a fine ally for Seebach, and many had feared—or hoped—that he would take the throne if something happened to Victoria before she could bear an heir. Her cousin Charlotte, after all, had died in childbirth.

Olivia managed to nod, and wished that she had the strength to summon another vision. It would be so much easier than spending hours bent over a table and reading through piles of books.

Immediately, she chastised herself. When had she started to rely so heavily on magic? She hated archaeologists who took shortcuts in research and excavation, and she'd managed to become what she hated.

Of course Savit should go and research. When she had rested and felt better, *then* they could try for another vision—with a specific event in mind.

"What I do have is a note from my grandfather. A lady of his acquaintance used to live in Hanover before it became part of the Prussian Empire, and she was friendly with the royals. He told her about my search, and she's requested that I come for tea this afternoon. Her name is Rebecca Waring, the Viscountess Dayning. She's a member of the Society, but is apparently house-bound these days."

Olivia knew that name. Viscountess Dayning was one of the few female full-members of the Society. She'd earned her place some years before by brashly challenging the elected leaders to a series of trials, including a grueling exam with questions ranging from pre-history to modern politics, a series of difficult translations from ancient tongues, and an essay, all prepared and judged blind by other high-ranking members. And she'd won.

Olivia struggled to sit up. She very much wanted to meet the viscountess, and damn whatever spell was keeping her in this bed.

"Rest, now," Savit said, and touched her face again, but so lightly she barely felt it. "And when you wake up, do try to speak to your mother. Neither of you has treated the other well, and though the bulk of the blame lies with her, I think you will never be able to have peace within yourself unless you confront her and listen to her response. But listen with your heart and mind open."

She wanted to snap at him for that last sentence, but he knew her better than she wanted to admit. She was more likely to yell at her mother—and tell her to go to the devil with her explanations—than to try to view the situation from her mother's side.

But what she wanted more was to get up and go with

279

him. "I…" she managed to say, and he leaned down to kiss her forehead.

"I know. I'll bring you to meet the viscountess once you're up and about."

How infuriating that he knew her well enough to comprehend the source of her frustration, but not so well that he failed to see that telling her all of this now, when she couldn't do anything about it, was the worst sort of dirty trick.

"I'll be back later today, and you should be able to get out of bed by then." He pressed another chaste kiss to her hair. She couldn't decide if she wanted to yank him down and kiss him properly or throttle him, but he retreated before she could attempt to reach up and grab either way. Not that she'd have succeeded, so perhaps it was for the best that he'd saved her the humiliation of trying.

"Promise me you'll talk to your mother." He stared at her with those fathomless dark eyes, and she finally managed an exasperated nod. "Good. Remember it's not for her benefit—it's for yours."

On his way out, he reached up and pressed the button to turn off the electric candelabra over her bed. The room plunged into gloom, with only the single shaft of sunlight between the curtains for illumination.

"Rest," he said again, and left.

She stared for a long time into the darkness, fuming. Her brain had finally muddled around to asking the question begged by his actions, so formal and distant—almost parental. Had he decided to break off their relationship? If they ever had one in the first place.

The darkness held no answers, and exhaustion claimed her.

～

AFTER LEAVING OLIVIA, WHICH WAS AN EXERCISE IN SELF-control, Savit's day got steadily worse.

The hour was too early to pay a social call to Lady Dayning, so he returned to Skye House to collect the volumes sent by the Queen's Sorceress. There were more hints, here, and questions he would be very interested to put to Lady Dayning.

He went to retrieve his grandfather, who insisted on taking out his new automobile. A uniformed chauffeur drove them at a sedate pace through the fashionable streets to the viscountess's lovely—if small—terrace house.

They arrived to find the place in an uproar. If his grandfather hadn't been with him, he doubted he'd even have been allowed over the threshold. But Brian Reilly was a known family friend, and the butler let them in. The servant looked haggard and harried, and told them that the lady seemed to have had an apoplexy during the noon-time meal.

Every hair in Savit's body stood on end.

Someone had known about all of his and Olivia's planned visits, back when their search was aimed at the late seventeenth century. Any useful evidence had been stolen or destroyed, except what reminded in the minds of the owners —which wasn't much. And without knowledge of Olivia's visions, their enemy couldn't have guessed that they would be able to discover anything from such meager breadcrumbs.

But a woman who had *known* the King of Hanover—she would need to be dealt with in a very different manner.

Savit had been careful today, keeping his awareness much more open than usual, checking for any presences that followed him or stayed in his vicinity too long. He'd sensed nothing out of the ordinary. But someone had known.

And that suggested that their enemy had eyes inside of the Society. The only other person he'd told about this visit, other than Olivia, was Archie. He'd wanted to let him know that he had at least one interview scheduled and to please keep looking for others. And of course, he'd mentioned the viscountess by name, as she was well-known to Archie.

Anyone with access to the administrative offices of the Society could have overheard their conversation, and now action had been taken to prevent him from speaking to Lady Dayning.

Unless it was coincidence, which he took leave to doubt.

Just in case, he asked the butler if he could be of some assistance, hinting at a medical knowledge he didn't have. But then, many doctors knew less about the human body than he did. He could, at least, study her aura and discover if she'd been attacked magically.

After a long moment when he thought he might be tossed out on his ear, Grandfather's presence or no, the butler nodded and showed them upstairs.

Lady Dayning lay on her back in bed, the covers pulled up to her chin. Her eyes were open, staring sightless at the ceiling. Her facial expression was just as blank, the muscles slack and her lips slightly parted. A maid sitting next to her had a handkerchief in hand and had just reached to wipe away a trail of drool when they entered.

The girl looked up, startled, and Savit recognized the stricken and saddened look on her face. She cared about her employer, and was devastated to see her like this. From Archie's comments, the woman had been an intellect to be reckoned with, even though her body had turned frail. This was a degradation of the highest order, and if magic had been used to do this to her, someone was going to pay dearly.

The butler murmured to the girl to let Savit approach. He did so, and asked the maid to retrieve Lady Dayning's hand from beneath the covers. Grandfather hung back, near the doorway. Savit pretended to check her pulse while he went into a light trance.

Yes, this was a deliberate attack. Someone had shattered her upper chakras to the point where he did not believe they could ever be reformed. He needed Chaitan's assistance before he would even make the attempt.

And if they could not restore her, it would be much kinder to release her from her gross body and allow her spirit to move on.

SAVIT WOULD HAVE CHOSEN TO AVOID OLIVIA AFTER THAT, because the moment she found out about Lady Dayning she was going to want to do something about it. He very much feared that their enemy would do the same thing to Olivia if they managed to capture her again, but she deserved to know what was happening.

He left his grandfather behind at Lady Dayning's, after explaining what had happened. The old man had gone paler than usual, and for once didn't bluster or pretend he didn't understand what Savit was talking about when he referenced magic. Instead, he took charge, proving that his success was not a fluke but the result of an ability to work well under pressure. He gave orders to the butler, who seemed relieved to have someone else to take responsibility of the household.

Savit arrived at Hazelby House to the news that Olivia was still asleep, and would be for another eight to ten hours. Rather than wake her, he decided to go speak to the duchess at Skye House.

Etta was just as enraged as he. "Can you prove that the tampering was magical? Is there something I or another practitioner of my way of doing magic would be able to see?"

"I don't know. Perhaps so, but perhaps not. I don't know what the mind looks like to you. To me, it is like a living crystal, one that can grow and change, liquefy and solidify, depending on a person's mood, personality, and thoughts. Hers was shattered."

"I'll talk to Cecily tonight. She's one of the most accomplished healers in England. If she can't fix it, I still have no doubt she'll be able to report on the injury's origin. And that is what we need in order to find out who did this and charge them with a crime."

"Will that be enough? Whoever this is has money and the highest of connections. The people on the Coalition in the past were brilliant mages of their eras. There's no reason to believe that they have stopped recruiting the best for their cause."

"No, but what is that cause, exactly? We don't know who is holding the spell now, and so we still don't know where to look to find people who would be ideologically inclined to support them. And money and power are motivators for a certain type of person no matter what, but is that who you would ask to join your secret coalition? Especially when the very first requirement for membership is a strong ability to do magic. That pool has gotten shallower and shallower in this country since the deep magic has been stripped away."

"Are you implying that they are looking outside of the country for help?"

"I would imagine, if the spell is still going somewhere into the German Empire, that there are a number of mages from that area involved, yes. But they do have ties here, and powerful ones, to have hushed things up so well during George's madness and then kept themselves hidden and active ever since."

"I am going to try scrying on the other plane tomorrow, after I've rested. I have seen this spell in action several times now in the visions, and it's possible I'll recognize something in the pools of power around the city."

"I wish you good luck, then. I'm going to go visit our

friend Lucien Blake and see what he can tell me about German mages in the country, or people with very strong ties to the German Empire or Austria."

"Why Austria?"

"Because that's where the man-who-would-be-king of Hanover lives."

"Ah. Well, then, I wish you luck as well." He folded his hands in front of him and bowed over them. "Namaste."

Etta inclined her head in return. He'd explained the gesture to her and its symbolism, and she'd been most interested in the underlying concept that bowing to another was to recognize and respect the divinity and necessity of the other person's existence.

She didn't use the hand gesture or the word, but he didn't doubt her sincerity or her respect. This duchess would never make anyone feel inferior because of their birth or class. She might, however, look down at someone who deliberately chose ignorance or cruelty.

If he continued to see her after this was over, he'd explain more about the concept of karma. He thought she would particularly like the existence of cosmic justice.

27

Olivia woke feeling tired and achy, but finally lucid and without paralysis. Her limbs moved when she told them to, and she didn't feel dizzy or disoriented when she sat up in bed, although her head did hurt. The first time this had happened, when Izarra trapped her in the vision, she'd felt much worse than she did now. But she didn't want to admit that to her mother. Or acknowledge to herself that she could have gotten this kind of magical assistance from Mother at any time.

A maid brought her chocolate and toast on a tray, but Olivia told her she would eat downstairs. She'd made a promise to Savit to talk to her mother, and she didn't want to put it off. Best to get the conversation over with and move on with her day.

Mother wasn't in the breakfast room. Father was, sitting with his paper and a plate full of toad in the hole.

"How are you feeling?" he asked when she'd filled her plate and sat down.

"Well, surprisingly."

"You've had a busy few days." Her father had a way with understatement.

"I have. Have you heard from Nan?"

"She's still in Brighton, although what she thinks to do there in the middle of winter I've no idea." He knew very well that she had fled there in order to avoid his wife and the rest of the Fays.

"I imagine she's visiting Great-Aunt Gloria," Olivia said, also avoiding any mention of the magic-ridden side of the family.

"Yes, well, I repeat my statement. Her sister is the most boring woman ever born."

"You only say that because she wouldn't let you run wild when you visited her house as a boy."

He grinned and they both giggled over their eggs. Life was so much more peaceful without magic.

The door opened, and Olivia's smile faltered. Mother entered, dressed in a gorgeous morning dress. Olivia once again wore trousers and a waistcoat, and this outfit had seen more than its share of wear.

"I'm glad to see you both here," Mother said, and bent to kiss the top of Father's head. Was that a new gesture, or had Olivia simply never been privy to these things before? She'd barely been out of the nursery when she was packed off to Switzerland, so anything was possible.

The knowledge of the interlude with Lady Falcestershire burned in Liv's belly like a live coal. Did Father know?

Despite her promise to Savit and her best intentions, she didn't have the strength for a confrontation this morning. Or to be more accurate, the strength not to give in to her own assumptions and past resentments. Discussions would have to wait until tomorrow.

She ate quickly, and excused herself from the table.

Mother watched her with disapproval—or was that worry?—but said nothing. Father smiled absently over his paper.

She went back upstairs, wondering if she was meant to be confined to the house or if she was free to return to Skye House. Probably the former. Mother wouldn't want her wandering off until she cast all manner of testing spells on her. Liv would just leave, but she wasn't sure if she would last the long walk to Kensington.

About half an hour later, a maid came up to tell her Savit had arrived. She went down to meet him in the front parlor, where Mother took formal callers. Why hadn't he just come up to her room, as he had last night?

He was dressed impeccably, as though he'd been out making calls of his own, or planned to be. She wanted to rip the clothes off of him, as though that would force him to reveal his true self as well as his skin.

"You look much better today," he said once she'd perched on the edge of an uncomfortable chair.

"I feel better. Not perfect, but I can move now."

"From what your mother explained yesterday, you still need more rest."

"I disagree. Now's the time to go for one final push and try to see where the spell went after being stashed in Hanover."

"Absolutely not."

She glared across the decorative table, her hands clutching the wooden arms of the chair for support. "What do you mean? We have to finish this."

"It's too dangerous. Yesterday, whoever had you kidnapped destroyed Lady Dayning's mind and memories. I was supposed to meet her to speak with her about the last two kings of Hanover, but now she'll never speak to another person again."

Olivia couldn't breathe. Up until this moment, there'd

been no real consequences to any of their actions. Yes, she'd been hurt, and drained, and Sorcha had gotten a minor injury. Some people had lost a few books. But nothing permanent.

"Great goddess," she murmured. "Is there no hope to heal her?" What a loss, not only for their cause, but for the cause of history and women researchers everywhere.

"I am going to ask your mother to take a look at her, and I plan to speak to my mentor again and ask for his assistance. But if they cannot, then no one can, and I am not optimistic about their chances. Our foes did their work well."

"What happened is terrible, Savit, but this just makes it even more important that we discover who is behind all of this and stop them, quickly."

"No!" He stood up and strode across the room, keeping his back to her. He spoke to an arrangement of crystals and geodes on the mantelpiece. "After I speak to my mentor, I'm going to do some scrying. Whoever our enemy is, they must have left traces that I can track. And I will."

"Let me help you."

"You haven't done enough astral practice yet. You would only slow me down."

She couldn't refute that, as much as she wanted to scream at him for being such a typical male. She'd been focusing on making the visions work, and not on what to do in her subtle body while simply present in the astral realm.

"I need to be able to help. Please don't shut me out." She tried to make the words light, so he wouldn't sense the very real vulnerability that inspired them. She'd lost everything else—her work, her writing, her self-respect. He couldn't take this away from her, too.

"I'm not." He finally stopped gazing at stones and came back to her. He settled into the chair next to hers. "But I've come to care for you too much, and it's clouding my judgment. When we're together, I let you lead me into rash actions, like seeing the vision at Windsor. I won't allow that to happen again."

"What exactly are you saying?" Was he breaking off their relationship, permanently?

"You aren't ready for the rigors of what you've been subjected to. I am going to seek out another to train you, since I have failed."

"So this is goodbye?"

He flinched, and she tried not to place too much hope in his discomfort at her suggestion. It could mean that he felt guilty and inadequate—not that he would miss her.

"For now, yes."

"When does 'now' end? When this crisis is over? When I've finished my training? When you stop being a total arse and treating me like a child?" She wanted to get up and pace, to stalk and fume, but she didn't trust her legs to keep her upright and she refused to let him see her fall. "You're teaching me, but you're not my master. You have no control over me except what I give you. So if I decide to keep trying for visions, or if I go out and paint a giant sign telling everyone how we're getting our information, I can do that."

"That's true, and it terrifies me. You're going to get yourself killed." His hand shifted in his lap, as though he wanted to reach for her, but he curled it into a fist and pressed it against his thigh.

Olivia groaned in frustration. "If you would just work with me, instead of against me, things wouldn't happen like at Windsor. The time before that was amazing. I know it would work if you'd just cross that stupid line in your head."

"You know why I can't do that. I've explained—"

"And your explanation is utter shite. I would respect your decision not to have sex with me if you'd made it from any reason other than fear."

"I'm not—"

"You *are*. You're terrified. And not of magical consequences, either. You're afraid of what will happen if you let me in. If you allow yourself to love someone, and to ask for that love in return."

He stared at her, silent. She didn't want to be on the wrong track, so she kept talking to fill the silence. "You say that you care too much about me, that I'm clouding your vision, but that's bollocks, Savit. When we're together, truly together, we see very, very clearly. You're the one who keeps constructing artificial barriers and then wondering why you can't see past the wall."

Tension rippled over his body, from the taut fists in his lap to the jumping muscle in his jaw. He stood, so abruptly the chair tipped over behind him. And just like he'd been doing from the beginning, he ran.

She shouted after him, "If you can't face what you've done, don't bother coming back!" He seemed to stumble over the threshold, but he didn't stop, and then he was gone.

Well, damn him and damn her for believing in him. For ripping herself open and hoping that this time, things would be different. That she'd found a partner. Someone who believed in her, and would support her.

But this was Talya all over again. Always having to have things her own way, never listening when Olivia spoke, never trusting her to know her own mind and heart.

And just like Talya, he hadn't stayed to watch the aftermath of his desertion. But unlike Talya, she refused to cry over him. Goddess, they'd never even fucked. He wasn't worth her tears.

The only thing she couldn't stop was her heart from cracking open inside. Because unlike everyone she'd fucked, including Talya, Savit was the only one she'd loved with every part of herself.

And every part of herself now ached with his loss.

She needed a distraction.

The door to the parlor opened, and one of the Hazelby House footmen announced, "Wilhelmina Jones."

Mina walked in, wearing a pretty pale blue morning dress very different from the somber uniforms she'd worn to work. She gave Olivia a very warm smile and moved to the seat Savit had vacated. It was still on its back, but she sat it upright and brought it even closer to Olivia—close enough to touch.

And, shockingly, she did. After they exchanged polite greetings, Mina bent forward and grasped Olivia's hand. "I was so worried about you."

Mina's thumb, encased in soft lace, brushed over Liv's palm, teasing the sensitive skin in the center. Olivia's whole body tingled with the contact, and she stared at their hands while heat built in her blood.

Then she remembered this was *Mina*, and turned her startled gaze to the other woman's face. Had she been wrong about her? Had she mistaken bone-deep suppression for disinterest?

Mina raised her free hand to Olivia's hair, tucking a loose strand behind her ear. "I'm so glad to see you looking well. I sent a message to you at Skye House and they said you were here, still recovering from your illness. But you look amazing."

Heat flushed Olivia's cheeks, and Mina cupped her hand over the warm skin, making it hotter still. "Er—my mother helped me. She's a healer."

"Is she? You're lucky, then." Mina's voice was huskier than usual. Had fear for Olivia's life caused her to overcome her reticence about going against society?

"I am. I'm sorry I didn't get in touch with you to let you know. We've been so busy, and I haven't felt well."

"No need to apologize. We're barely acquainted. You don't owe me anything." Her fingers twined with Olivia's and she squeezed. "But I bet you could do with some fresh air. The cold snap broke last night and the weather is tolerable outside. Will you walk with me?"

Olivia considered. She hadn't actually been told not to leave the house. And they wouldn't need to go far. They could stroll up Park Lane and back. The proximity to Hyde Park had been the only consolation when she'd been forced to come to London as a child, and she could take advantage of that again now—and maybe entice Mina into a secluded nook and see how far away from propriety she was willing to stray.

The spicy-sweet tang of Savit's magic rose up in her memory, bringing with it a sharp, tearing pain. She suppressed both. He didn't want her, so she was going to take what she could from someone who did.

"Yes. Let me get my coat."

CHAITAN LISTENED TO SAVIT'S EXPLANATION ABOUT Viscountess Dayning without visible reaction, even in his aura. Savit doubted he would ever have such complete control over himself, especially now. Being with Olivia had changed him, and he feared those changes were permanent. He'd tried, ever since he left her at Hazelby House, to find the serenity and emptiness that had come so easily to him only a few weeks ago.

But *she* was there, filling the void, expanding within him in ways both frightening and so *right* that he wanted to run back to her house, beg her forgiveness, and take her immediately to bed.

He couldn't do that—must not go back. Yet.

Chaitan said he would begin the journey to England tonight. It would take him two weeks or a little longer to arrive, but as long as Lady Dayning's body was kept alive in the interim, he would do what he could to repair her mind.

Now, he said, *tell me what you have decided about your Olivia.*

Savit started to protest, but it was pointless. The truth was written on his soul, and Chaitan was wise enough to read it. *If she'll have me, I would commit my life to hers.*

Until the words were thought and said, he hadn't understood his own intentions. But there they were, inevitable and resonant. She was his, and he was hers, and always had been. He'd been a fool to think his soul would not be irrevocably changed by hers. He loved her, and not in the abstract way he'd convinced himself was the only true way to love.

His love for her was both primal and necessary, engaging all of the disparate parts of him, from his flesh to the infinite reaches of his soul. It was active, and vital, and as soon as he'd completed the tasks he'd set for himself, he would go and tell her so.

But for now, a woman's mind was at stake, and he needed to make sure Olivia was safe before groveling at her feet and admitting that she was right. He was afraid, he was a coward, he wanted her more than breath and life, and he very much thought that when they came together, honestly and without barriers, the universe in all its mysteries would be revealed to them both.

So he would go back, once he'd discovered—and defeated —their enemy.

It is good that you have finally come to your senses. When we first began training, you and I, I knew that my path was not yours. But you were convinced it was what you wanted, and so I taught you. Have you never wondered why you did not achieve all of the things I could?

I thought I hadn't practiced enough. That I didn't understand enough.

That is true—you did not understand. The way of self-denial and mental focus is but one of many paths, Savit. It is not the only way, or the correct way. There is no correct way, except what brings you to enlightenment. Do not blind yourself by your respect and admiration for me. Discover your own path.

The warmth of Chaitan's words pulsed with a subtle magic between them. He did not require his mentor's blessing or his praise, but having both gave him confidence for what he must do next.

Thank you for taking in a fool all those years ago. If I hadn't tried so hard to follow you down your path, I would not be where I am now, with the woman who is the other part of my heart.

It has been my honor.

They both bowed over their hands, murmured, *Namaste*, and went their separate ways.

Now Savit had to decide how best to deal with the muddle he'd made this morning with Olivia, before she decided he wasn't worth the effort.

Olivia had just shrugged into her coat and taken her hat from the footman when her mother entered the foyer from the back of the house. She looked startled to see Olivia ready to go out, and even more surprised at Mina's presence.

When Olivia made the introductions, she expected Mother to relax, but she didn't. "I need to speak with you, Olivia. There are things you should know."

Liv's jaw clenched. She wasn't sure she owed Savit anything anymore, but if she tried to speak to her mother in this mood she would cause a permanent breach between them. And as much as she resented a lifetime of neglect and secrets, she didn't want to make her family choose sides between them. Even if she wanted to find him and punch him in the face, Savit was right that she owed it to herself to find peace and acceptance. Somehow.

But not right now.

"We can talk when I get back. We're just going to go for a walk around the park. The sun is finally out after weeks of freezing fog and icy rain, and we're going to take advantage of the warmth."

Mother's gaze flicked nervously back and forth between them. Olivia supposed she understood—someone out there meant her harm, and Mother had never met Mina before. But she could handle herself. Especially if Mina was in the mood for a little naughtiness.

"Very well. But please come back in a half hour." In a very uncharacteristic gesture, Mother placed her hand on Olivia's arm and squeezed. "Viola and Etta are coming to tea, and they will want to speak with you."

"Of course." Olivia's smile felt tight and forced, a mere stretching of lips. She tried to gently wiggle her arm away, but it ended up more of a wrench. Her mother's expression turned stricken, and then the so-familiar icy reserve returned.

"Be safe," she said, and walked away.

Olivia turned back to Mina, who was watching with open interest. "Let's go."

They headed down the street and across another row of huge houses to Park Lane. They chatted about nothing for a while, and the brisk air invigorated Olivia. She didn't need Savit, or her mother, or anyone.

She would head straight back to France once this mess was done, and demand to take back her dig. She'd find a way to discredit Henri—it wouldn't be hard, the man took more shortcuts than every character in folklore combined. She'd keep her promise to Izarra, and write the real story—not just the facts, but the Truth—about what had happened during the terrible witch hunts there.

See if any publication would turn her down after that!

In the park, Mina led her to a secluded spot formed by several evergreen shrubs that came together to create a little nook and then a private lane.

They'd been walking arm-in-arm, and now Olivia tugged Mina close. "Have you changed your mind about what we talked about in the archives? About taking a lover?"

Mina leaned in close, her smile seductive, and then Olivia looked up into her dark eyes, and trembled. There was nothing there of wanting, or charm. Only cold, and calculation. Her lips said she wanted a kiss. Her eyes said something very different.

The truth hit like a punch to the gut. Mina. She'd had access to everything, from the list of people they'd planned to visit and had been burgled, to Olivia's body on the night of the kidnapping attempt, to Savit's meeting with Sir Archibald to discuss his visit to Lady Dayning.

Mina was their elusive enemy.

Now Olivia had a choice. She could run, back to safety, back to Mother and Etta and the shield of Clan Fay.

Or she could stay, and play along, and try to discover everything Mina knew about the Aegis Spell.

Mina was only inches away. It took only the slightest of movements to bring their mouths together.

At first, Olivia thought Mina would recoil in horror. But she was committed to the game, it seemed, and after an initial stiffness, she pressed back against Olivia's lips. It was an awkward kiss, close-mouthed and dry, but Mina tugged Olivia's body to hers and their breasts rubbed together through their thick layers of clothing and Mina's corset.

Mina broke the kiss and said, "Come home with me."

That was exactly what she'd hoped for. Liv allowed Mina to draw her down the little lane and out again into a more open area of the park, headed north toward Oxford Street. There were other people strolling today, as well, grabbing the chance to be outdoors before the freezing damp set back in.

Near the corner of the park, it occurred to Olivia to

wonder where they were going. Unless Mina had lied about everything, her address was in Chelsea. That was south of the park, not north.

Then two large men dressed in shabby overcoats stepped onto the path on either side of them. She debated dropping the charade, but decided to keep going, and stopped. Mina took another step forward, but Olivia held her arm firmly and she had to stop, too.

"Can we help you gentlemen?" Olivia asked.

The one on the right frowned at her in puzzlement, as though she'd just spoken Mandarin or Ancient Greek. She faced the one on the left, who was watching Mina, presumably for instructions.

At her side, Mina grumbled under her breath. She reached into her reticule, and drew out a small metal needle with a tiny sharp end. Olivia stiffened and tried to pull away, but the man on her left held her tight. "Don' struggle, miss," he said in a rasping, soft voice.

Mina grabbed her bare hand, pushed her coat and shirt-sleeve up her forearm as far as they could go (which wasn't very far), and then jabbed the needle down into her flesh. The pain jerked through Olivia, sudden and sharp. Mina withdrew the needle and put it back into her handbag.

The world tunneled into dizzy darkness and Olivia fell back into burly arms clad in a very shabby coat.

BACK IN LONDON, SAVIT BEGAN THE TIME-CONSUMING BUT necessary task of adjusting his internal resonances with the city. He'd locked himself into the Casting Chamber at Skye House and the duchess had forbidden anyone to disturb him until he came out again, so he knew he had plenty of time.

In his lap were several items from the burgled houses, a

scrap from the dress Olivia had been wearing when she was kidnapped, and a handkerchief that had been in Lady Dayning's hands when she was attacked.

Something about these items was the same, and that something would resonate out in the city, at wherever their enemy plotted.

He had expected the search to be difficult, fearing that multiple mages had worked on the different spells and that he would need to dig more deeply to find the commonality there, but the pieces clicked together like cogs in a clockwork mechanism, turning and shifting, until their matching pieces were revealed.

Some of them clustered over the Society headquarters. That was not a surprise—someone there must have been watching them since the very beginning to have orchestrated the thefts and the toppling bust in the archives. But by adding the new information from those segments of resonance, he was able to create a more complete construct and expand the search again.

His consciousness drifted over the better parts of the West End, south from the Society, then tugged suddenly east, over the Park. There—a presence. A female mage, with a strong magical gift. She was moving fast, as though in a speeding hackney—or a motorcar. And…his blood froze, and everything inside him became ice and stone. Olivia was with her.

He almost lost the trance, but kept it, dogged, trying to reach for his lover across the miles. But there was something wrong. A haze separated them, keeping his subtle body at bay despite the strong connection that still existed between them. And then they stopped, and Olivia's presence vanished.

They'd come to a row of connected terrace houses, and he had to assume they'd taken her inside of one. But was it simply a very good ward, or had something else happened to the connection? It was possible Olivia had severed it herself. He'd left her angry, and Olivia in a temper was bound to act rashly. If she'd sensed him following her, she might have cut him off in a fit of pique.

Did she know she was with their enemy? He remembered, suddenly, the note she'd gotten at Skye House, from a woman named Mina. A woman she'd met at the Society, who'd been helping her with research.

The items in his lap vibrated when he thought the name. Yes, Mina was their enemy. And there was one more possibility for why he'd lost the connection with Olivia.

If Mina had found out that Olivia was the source of all their knowledge about the Aegis Spell, the most sensible option to protect the spell was to remove that source of information. Permanently.

LIV WOKE IN A DIMLY LIT BASEMENT ROOM. THE LIGHT CAME in from a tiny, barred window high in one wall. The room was cold, and her jacket was inadequate to the chill. She wished she'd worn her heavy greatcoat instead of this lighter version, but the temperature outside with the sun shining had been comfortable enough, and she hadn't guessed she would be ending her walk in a cellar.

Despite being cold and cramped after lying for some unknown amount of time on a hard stone floor, Olivia felt inexplicably light inside. She pushed up into a seated position and tucked her legs under her body the way Savit had shown her, placing her hands into the first position for meditation.

The proper mindset came far more rapidly than she'd feared. All of the practice and work they'd done was proving its worth now. Especially when she was able to determine exactly what was making her feel exhilarated: a massive sphere of stored magical energy, trapped and then sent into an infinite spin within the house.

She hadn't sensed this much magical energy in one place since she learned how to look for it. There wasn't another place in London this strong, and even the convergence at Windsor hadn't been this impressive, because that was unpredictable to work with and this magic had been stored for the express purpose of being used.

Almost the moment she connected to the power source, a vision wrapped around her. It was nothing like the visions she'd had since coming here. This felt like the ones in France —natural, and almost effervescent. She had no trouble controlling it, and needed very little additional power from the globe of energy.

Dieter Seebach proclaimed the consensus of the Coalition not to pass the spell on to William IV, citing His Majesty's continued use of his younger brother as viceroy in Hanover and his unpopular (to their group) action of championing said viceroy's efforts to create a liberal constitution for the tiny nation. Also held against William was his childless state. The next monarch would be a woman—but Victoria would not inherit Hanover. And to Seebach's mind, she was too young and weak to rule anything. Better to back the next in line, the Duke of Cumberland.

There was some dissent about that, and then a noise from the real world disturbed Olivia's concentration.

She came out of the vision, blinking, as the heavy wood door scraped open and Mina came in. Someone outside pushed the door shut. A clunk sounded as a latch or bar was put into place.

Olivia tried to will her body to move and stand up, but everything was stiff and sore from sitting on a rough stone floor, motionless, while her mind had been busy with the vision. Her legs had gone to sleep and now burned with pins and needles. In lieu of standing and making herself look more threatening, Olivia opted for insouciance. She looked at Mina expectantly. "Well, here I am. I suppose you have a reason for keeping me here?"

"You know exactly why you're here."

"Well, I thought we'd be fucking by now, to be honest, but cold dark underground places aren't much of an aphrodisiac for me, and drugging a potential lover is simply bad form. So I shall have to decline."

Mina's cheeks went crimson and she took two steps back until she brushed against the door. "I had no interest in your filthy perversions! I would never have done any of that, but my mother discovered your inclinations and thought I would make a suitable inducement. And she was correct."

"Ah. Your mother, the Reformist. She must think very highly of your ability to resist temptation."

"She knows I'm not a deviant like you."

"Oh, so it's less deviant to deliberately destroy a woman's mind just so she can't reveal your secrets?"

Mina flinched, and when she spoke, her accent thickened. "Zat vas necessary. I did not enjoy doing it."

The chill in Olivia's veins turned to ice. Until this moment, she'd been hoping that Mina was a pawn—that even if she knew what had happened, she'd been on the fringes of the act.

But no. She'd done the deed herself.

"Necessary." Olivia let out a long, controlled breath. "That's always what we say to ourselves to justify the terrible things we do."

"*Es war notwendig!*" Mina almost screamed the German words, then dragged in a breath and forced her voice back under control, although when she repeated herself in English her words still tumbled out rapidly. "It *was* necessary. You found out everything. Nothing I did stopped you! And my parents…you don't know what it's like, to have the weight of such expectations on you. Your family lets your run around dressed as a man and…sleeping with anyone who'll have you."

"You can say it. I like to fuck. It feels wonderful, and it harms no one. You should try it."

"Never! I must marry well, to offset the stain of my Welsh blood. And no good German boy will have me if I give myself to one of your English brutes first."

"Ah, yes, because your gods demand that all of their followers should come to marriage as untouched virgins. Oh, wait, no. Only people born with a vagina. Penises can do whatever they want."

Mina's face had gone nearly purple with shame and rage, and at that she screamed. "*Ja!* Zey can. But you don't have one, as much as you'd like to pretend you do. But you have *something*." She stalked toward Olivia. "How did you find out so much about the Aegis? You were able to give the Queen details that not even the highest-ranking members of our coalition knows. How?"

Olivia tried not to tremble, keeping her expression provokingly amused as she stared up at Mina. If only her limbs would cooperate! "I am very aware that I do not possess a cock, thank you. I don't want one. My quim has always served me well, although I do admit to not seeing myself as a woman if I have to define myself by Queen Vick's standards."

"Zat vasn't vhat I asked!" Olivia was perversely pleased whenever Mina's German pronunciation slipped out. But she managed to shift back into the nearly-upperclass British accent. "I know magic is involved, but how? How did a woman and a half-savage man discover in a few weeks what has remained secret for a hundred years?"

Liv stood, and Mina gasped and stepped back. All of the ice inside Olivia had turned directly to lava when Mina insulted Savit, and somehow that translated to her body leaping, literally, to his defense.

"The only savage I have met since returning to England is you."

Mina held up her hands, fingers flicking and moving rapidly. Olivia wouldn't have been able to tell what the spell was even if she could see it, but it didn't matter. Mina was afraid of her, and she didn't know the nature of Olivia's gift. Their secret hadn't been revealed. And Liv meant to keep it that way.

"Perhaps next time you can ask around a little. My mother's best friend is the Queen's Sorceress. She has secret records kept by the mages closest to the monarch going back to the foundations of the kingdom."

"If that is true, why hasn't the queen acted against us?"

"The queen doesn't believe something just because it's written down." And that statement was entirely true—in fact, Olivia had tried to keep all of her answers as close to the truth as possible. Fact has a ring to it that prevarication and lies can never attain, despite the skill of the charlatan.

"Nevertheless, those documents must be destroyed." Mina's hands still moved, and Olivia wished she could tell what spell she crafted. "The queen is old, and while her son is a worthless libertine, *his* son George is not."

Olivia knew very little about the younger generation of royals, but she trusted Mina to be well-informed. "I don't see how I can help you. The Sorceress is my mother's friend, not mine."

"Will she not do a favor for a friend's daughter?"

"That depends on the favor."

"I need to see those records. You will take me to her and ask to see them again."

"Won't it be suspicious that I'm bringing a friend? They're secret."

"Then why did she show you?"

"The nation's magic is being stolen. Why do you think she showed us?"

"So she couldn't get the queen to help her, and she asked you instead? Pathetic. Well, I'm assisting you with the research, am I not? Just tell her you're bringing me in to help her. I'm sure you'll convince her."

Mina's hands moved as she spoke, crafting the spell in front of her. Then she flicked her fingers, and Olivia felt the jolt as the spell hit her in the face. It spread its tendrils around her head and she resisted the urge to lift her hands and dig it off. Even if she could open her Sight or go into a trance now, that wouldn't help. She had no idea how to manipulate spells like this, or to break them. Savit hadn't even said that they could, with their way of casting.

"That little spell is one of my favorites. You'll follow all of my orders now." She made another little gesture and Olivia took two involuntary steps forward, then hopped from one foot to the other. She tried to speak, and could not.

"Oh, and aside from autonomic functions like breathing and blood flow, you not only must do everything I tell you, you cannot do anything *unless* I tell you. That's why I like it so much. No surprises."

So Olivia walked calmly and silently up the cellar steps to a waiting motor car. And when she saw Savit, Etta, and the rest of her family across the street, she could do nothing but calmly continue towards the car and sit down in the rear passenger seat.

She sat there, staring forward, while magic flew all around her. Stone and mortar from the building's wall exploded nearby and pelted her face with stinging bits of rubble. She couldn't even flinch as a rock sliced open her cheek and blood dripped down her chin.

Someone grabbed her around the waist as the driver of the car pressed the accelerator. The car moved forward, and Olivia was wrenched up and out, her back and hips banging painfully against the side as the automobile sped off down the street.

She lay in a heap on the pavement, staring straight forward, her view the unusually cloudless blue sky.

Then Savit's face moved into her line of sight, and his head descended to hers. He kissed her furiously and she wanted, more than life itself, to kiss him back. But she hadn't been ordered to do so, and so she lay, unresponsive, beneath him.

He collapsed on top of her, and didn't move again.

The blood dripping onto her chest and making a great sodden pool on her shirt wasn't from the cut on her cheek. He'd been wounded.

Savit was going to die on top of her and she couldn't even move her arms to embrace him or open her mouth to tell him that she loved him.

29

After his discovery of Olivia's second abduction, Savit had raised the same group of volunteers as before, but with two additions. Since Sorcha was an arm down for casting spells and Etta was restricted by pregnancy, they'd brought along a thirty-something army mage named Lucien Blake, who had been mentioned by the others before but Savit had yet to meet. And Cecily had refused to stay behind.

Savit climbed into the leading carriage with Etta, Mal, and Blake. Ronan, Evie, and Cecily took a separate chaise.

Blake had arrived alone, but as they drove to the place Olivia had disappeared, he told Etta he could have a squad of mage-officers at the ready the moment she asked.

"If it's like last time, we won't need them," she replied. "But I have a feeling Her Majesty read through the lines during our interview and may have spoken to someone of Olivia as the key to all of this."

"You think a member of Her Majesty's inner circle is a spy?"

"They may not think of themselves as a spy. We don't know who is running the Coalition now, but it's bound to include normal, upstanding members of British society. A bit of gossip about the Marquess of Hazelby's daughter having newfound magic may not sound like classified information."

Blake scowled at that.

"I know you treat everything as a state secret, but most people don't have your sense of duty or your uncompromising values."

"Or my blind loyalty?" His voice had an edge, but not a dangerous one.

"I didn't say it!" Had the situation been different, such an exchange might have resulted in laughter, but instead one side of Etta's mouth curled a fraction upward and she settled back against the seat of the carriage. Her husband pulled her into his arms.

There was a story behind their banter, but Savit didn't have the attention span to ask about it now. All of his thoughts were focused on that place where his love had vanished.

They didn't have far to go, and he would have walked here on his own and let the others catch up if Mal and Etta hadn't practically tied him to a chair at Skye House to await reinforcements.

Their destination was much more posh than the flophouse where Mina had stashed Olivia before. Except, when they all piled out of their conveyances, Evie's brow wrinkled and she bit her lip.

"She's not here. I can sense the spell that masked her from you, though—that was cast right over there." She pointed at a spot in the middle of the street. "But then they moved on again." She walked down Upper Belgrave Street a ways toward the southeast, and then nodded. "Yes. They went this way. I'll need to sit up with the driver." She jogged back to the chaise and climbed up to sit on the box with the driver. Everyone else got back into the interior of the carriages.

Etta sat beside him this time. "She's not dead."

"How can you possibly know that?"

"I can't, but you can. You would know if she were dead."

The words sunk into him like a boulder into a still pond, first with a splash, and then a quick, certain descent. He *would* know if she had died, because she would be freed from her gross body, and he would sense the departure of her soul.

So she was still alive, but shielded from him. The world tilted back into position, and he could take a deep breath all the way into his lungs for the first time in well over an hour. "Thank you, Duchess."

"Please. Etta. I think, if you can convince my sister-in-law to do something so conventional as wed you, we're going to be siblings by law at some point in the not-too-distance future."

He allowed her hope to buoy him over the fear, though that was still there, too, a jagged piece of metal beside her stone of wisdom.

He should never have left her today. He was the greatest fool in the history of fools for thinking she would be safer if he took on the danger alone. At least, if they were together, they could face it as one.

And they had already proven that they could be strong together, if he didn't undermine them with his insistence on adhering to a way of life that had never fit him properly.

He would not make that mistake again, if only he could have her back.

They drove and drove, making frequent turns, as though their quarry had hoped to confuse them by frequent changes of direction. There was a bad moment when Evie stopped them near the river and it took her a full fifteen minutes to find the trail again at the next bridge—they'd tried to eliminate the aetheric traces by crossing the running water of the Thames. Fortunately Evie and Ronan had guessed at their tactics and picked the correct bridge to check next, instead of continuing the goose-chase south of the river.

Finally, Evie alerted them to the end of the spell-trail in front of a modest building just off of the Strand. Savit had no doubts this was the place. Something had been done to the flow of magic around the building so that it formed a meander like in a river, and then the old flow had been reconnected, leaving behind a pool of magic like an oxbow lake. Eventually the magic, like the water, would disappear, but for a little while the people in the building would have a concentrated and strong source of power.

They drove the carriages to the end of the street and proceeded back on foot. They were only halfway down the road when Olivia's shining head emerged from the front door. Behind her was a woman with dark hair, pulled back in a tight and simple knot, wearing an equally simple sky-blue dress and spencer. Olivia wore her usual trousers and coat. He ran towards her, but she didn't look his way, even when he shouted. Instead, she got into a waiting motor car that must have pulled out from a side street after they'd passed the house. The engine was running, and a driver sat in the front seat, ready to go.

The woman—Mina—raised her hands at his shout and flung magic in his direction. Mal and Lucien were there, then, shielding him and flinging spells back. Three men came out of the house and added to the confusion. Someone's spell struck the building and stone and mortar shards flew everywhere. He couldn't see Olivia for the smoke, but he kept running towards the sound of the car engine.

He banged into the car, bruising his hip, and reached in to grab Olivia. She must be under some sort of compulsion not to have moved when that explosion hit. He managed to get his arms around her and then the car accelerated. He lifted with all of his strength and they toppled back onto the street. They landed side-by-side, and he crawled over to her.

She didn't move, only stared upward, and for an awful moment he thought she was dead from the way she hadn't even blinked. But then her eyelashes fluttered. Her mind still worked behind her immobilized flesh. She was still alive—but couldn't move.

He took her face in his hands and kissed her in sheer relief. She didn't respond, but that didn't matter. She was alive, and in his arms, and spells could be removed or broken.

The wave of giddy relief passed, and with it went his equilibrium. He collapsed onto her chest as numbness spread over his body. Had the spell transferred to him, too? But no, he could move; it was just very hard.

He shifted, and that's when he felt the pain in his upper chest, near the shoulder. He looked down at Olivia. The front of her grey coat and white shirt was brilliant scarlet with blood. Then she seemed very far away, as though he was being pulled backward through a dark tunnel, until everything went black.

IMAGES FLICKERED IN THE VOID.

His father, leaning down to pick him up, tossing him in the air and then settling him on his shoulders so he could see over the heads of the crowd to a procession of elephants.

His mother, sitting across from him at dinner, speaking in rapid Gujarati with a huge grin on her face, telling him to eat his Marghanu Shaak or he wouldn't be allowed to go out with his father to watch the stars that night.

He'd forgotten about the stargazing. His father had been

comparing stories about the stars in India with stories from elsewhere in Europe and Asia.

A new image: his grandfather, hurrying him up the gang-plank to the ship bound for Ireland, Rajani refusing to be left behind. Savit trying to turn back, to *go* back, not believing that his parents were gone forever...

Chaitan, asking an angry and frustrated Savit at a campus rally for the Irish Republicans if he wanted to learn how to harness the energy inside of him.

Then—and always—Olivia. The first time they met in the parlor at Skye House, her gorgeous hazel eyes glaring at him in haughty contempt. The first time they kissed, and the sweetness of her lips as she let him explore and didn't take control as she must have wanted to. The sheer, over-whelming glory when she'd taken his cock into her mouth. The wonder he'd felt when he could taste her pleasure on his tongue, and how it had roused him beyond bearing to bring her to ecstasy.

The expression on her face when they spoke of India, of the Indus River civilization and the work being done there—work that could satisfy them both. The future he'd glimpsed, and been afraid of. The future he desperately clung to now.

Olivia.

I'm here, Savit. I won't let you go.

Her presence was warmth and light in the darkness. She didn't look like herself. For the first time, she'd completely inhabited her subtle body, and lost the echo of the gross body beyond. A spurt of terror went through him—was she dead? Was this her soul, comforting him as she moved on towards her next life?

Shh. I'm not dead, and neither are you. Mother is using me as a conduit to heal you.

Awareness returned, of his flesh and bone, of Olivia's hand gripping his, of magic thick as honey covering him.

He couldn't open his eyes, but he didn't need to. Olivia was here, and she was safe, and he could let go.

~

"How long will he be unconscious?"

The worry in Etta's voice cut through the tableau of mother and daughter holding hands over Savit's still form, and Olivia blinked to focus on the physical world again.

"Not long," Mother said. "I'm adding extra power to the spell. He'll have a day, maybe two, of normal energy levels before he needs to sleep for several days and rest for longer. That's all I can give you."

Etta cursed. "Then we'll have to find these people in two days or less." She paced farther into the room. "Olivia, how are you feeling? Are you up for trying to find Mina, once Savit wakes?"

"I think so, yes. Did Evie fail, then?"

While Olivia and Cecily had rushed to Skye House with Savit, the others had tried to follow Mina and her associates. "It wasn't difficult to track them," Etta said. "Motor cars are becoming a more frequent occurrence now that the red flag laws have been repealed, but one driving down the London streets at speed is a spectacle few would forget. Unfortunately, they abandoned the car at a wharf and got on a boat." She growled with frustration. "Evie's no good over water. Ronan and Blake both tried, but they're just not as good at intuitive tracking as her, and they had nothing to use to focus a tracking spell."

"So you want Savit to do what he did earlier today." Mother had explained how Savit had used some kind of magical resonance to find Mina, based on the objects he'd collected from places their enemy was known to have been.

"Yes. As soon as he's awake."

Mother squeezed Olivia's hand. "That should do it. Stay with him. He'll wake in a few minutes. You can tell him what you need to do."

Etta left the room, and Mother moved to follow.

"Wait."

When their magic had touched to heal Savit, all of the truth of her mother's feelings had come along with the magic. She might not owe her forgiveness, but she was owed an explanation.

"Do you regret your choices?" She didn't have to specify which ones.

"Some." Mother turned her head away and leaned wearily against the doorframe. She looked so vulnerable, so human. Nothing like the untouchable ice queen of Olivia's childhood. "Most. I had my reasons, but we always do. I can't justify what I did to you and Percy, much less what I did to Mal and Viola."

"Mal and Viola?" Olivia couldn't keep the bitterness from her voice. But the time had come to let her pain show. "What did you do to them? They got all of your attention."

"They got too much of my attention." She rubbed at her neck, another unusual physical tell. "Talk to your sister about how well that turned out."

"So a surfeit is just as bad as scarcity?"

"In this instance, it was. And I am sorry for it."

Olivia swallowed, and lifted her chin in defiance. "I don't know that I can forget it."

"I don't expect you to. Of all my children, you are the most like me, and I don't forget grudges easily, either."

Olivia wanted to laugh. What a terrific irony, that she and her mother would be so alike—and that the similarity would drive them apart. "I may not be able to forget, but I will try to forgive. Savit reminded me that forgiveness isn't about giving credence to the wrong done, or pretending it didn't hurt—it's about making peace with the pain and not allowing it to rule your life."

"Your lover is very wise."

"He is."

"It may mean little, considering, but I am very proud of you, Olivia."

There was nothing to say to that, and in any case, Mother walked away and shut the door behind her.

"She loves you." Savit's voice was quiet, his tone gentle.

She whirled and threw herself down on the bed. The wound in his shoulder had closed up thanks to the magical healing, leaving behind a thin red scar where Mina had stabbed him.

Mina had leaned across as Olivia was dragged out of the car, but Olivia hadn't seen the knife or realized Savit was injured until he collapsed on top of her.

After Mina had gotten a certain distance away, the spell on Olivia had broken—or the connection had, in any case. Mother had gotten rid of all traces of it before she used Olivia as a conduit. But it had taken only a few minutes on the street for her to regain the use of her body and shout for help.

She did not want to relive the rush back here, but feeling him whole and alive against her brought back the keen edge of fear that he would die and the last thing she'd said to him was not to bother coming back to her.

"I know she loves me." She held herself above him so she could look into his eyes. "And that's thanks to you. I know that there was something missing in my life, and that's thanks to you, too. And I know that I love you, and if you ever try to run away from us again I am going to run after you and tie you down so you have to talk to me about what's wrong."

"I shouldn't have run. I realized, while I was in the darkness during the healing, that I was acting just like my grandfather. He ran from his pain, too. He doesn't talk to me about problems or what I feel. He just rolls right over any difficulties, because he's afraid if we talk about the bad things, they will hurt us more. And he's afraid if he acknowledges the things that I want that are different from what he wants, he'll lose me."

"Is that what you're afraid of with me?"

"No. I was very much afraid of how much I wanted exactly what you want. But it was still fear, and it had the same result. I won't run again."

"Good. Because we have to work together to find Mina and we're going to have to merge our gifts to do it."

"You don't just mean our gifts." He said it with a mock air of accusation, but the hard ridge of his arousal pressing up against her lower belly said he had finally accepted the inevitable.

"No. I don't." She kissed him, and pulled away. "Give me a second. I need to talk to Etta."

He gave her a bemused smile and sat still. She couldn't help admiring his body for a moment. He was stripped to the waist to allow them access to the now-healed wound, and he was gorgeous, all lean muscle, dark skin, and scattered black curls over his chest. His darker nipples peaked out of the curls and she had to turn her back and walk away lest she give in to the urge to go and lick them.

30

E tta waited in the room across the hall. Mal stood near the room's fireplace, chatting with Gillies the footman and MacGroarty, the butler. Mother and the others were ranged on various pieces of furniture. Olivia cleared her throat to get everyone's attention. "We're going to try to find Mina, but it's going to take, umm…intimacy." She didn't usually avoid using the proper terms for things, but her mother and brother were right there in the room, and she'd just determined to stop actively provoking her mother.

"What do you propose?" Etta asked.

"We'll need to go down to the casting chamber. If someone can wait outside the room, once we find her, we'll shout out the location, and you can go."

"Done." Etta told Gillies to help Savit down to the Casting Chamber. Gillies disappeared, and Mal stood and called his troops to order. They all filed out ahead of him, and he gave Olivia a quick, hard hug on his way out.

Etta took Olivia's hand. "I'm very glad that you and Savit are moving forward together."

"So am I."

"The wound healing spell Cecily did should hold under some strain, but be gentle with him anyway." Etta grinned, and despite everything, Olivia felt heat rush to her cheeks. She couldn't be embarrassed, could she?

"Um, only as much as he wants me to be." There. She could tease her new sister-in-law right back.

Etta took it in stride, without a hint of discomfiture. "Good luck with the search."

"Good luck catching her," Olivia said, and darted out into the hall.

Down in the Casting Chamber, Gillies had helped Savit over to the alcove dedicated to Sutra magic. They were piling up mats and pillows, Savit still stripped to the waist, and the flush that had receded from her cheeks returned. She wasn't normally a prude, but then she also didn't normally announce to the world that she was about to have sex.

Gillies elbowed her, and that made her laugh, and then everything was fine. He left, and she followed him to the door, locking it behind him.

She turned to find Savit tossing away his trousers from a nest of brightly-colored cushions and pillows. He was entirely naked, and very aroused. She forgot that anyone else in the world existed.

Olivia almost tripped over her feet getting to him, stripping off clothes as she went. Her trouser legs got stuck on her boots and she had to sit down, bare-arsed, on the floor to unlace them and throw them across the room.

Finally nude, she pounced on her deliciously bare lover. Savit caught her, and she pressed her mouth to his. He opened immediately, tangling his tongue against hers. Impossible to believe that he had no experience with kissing before her. He stroked a fire in her veins, a whirlwind in her soul.

His hands coasted over her body, from the globes of her

arse up her torso to her breasts, his thumbs dragging over the taut peaks and making her arch and moan. She broke the kiss to go after his nipples with her tongue, laving each hard nub in turn until he gasped and writhed beneath her. The movement made his cock slide through the wet folds her quim, its head rubbing the aroused bundle of nerves at the apex of her sex. Bliss seared through her.

She pulled away from his nipple with a soft pop, and groaned. "Inside me. I need you inside me." She took his cock in hand and lifted onto her knees, and he stilled. She stopped. "If you don't want—"

"No!" he practically screamed. "I do want it. Very much. But it's a very big step, and I need a moment."

She took her hand off his cock and laced her fingers through his instead. "I understand." She rested her body against his and the fingers of his free hand danced up and down her spine.

"I have never wanted any woman the way I want you. I will never want any other woman this way." He spoke the words against her earlobe, and they warmed her soul even as the press of his body against hers warmed her flesh.

"It would be a lie to tell you I'll never be attracted to someone else," she admitted. "But I will never want anyone, no matter what they've got between their legs, the same way I want you. Because I don't just want your body, as amazing as it is. I want all of you, with every last part of my body and soul."

He breathed against her ear, tickling the hairs there, and then licked her earlobe. "Let's do this together."

She sat up on her knees and took their entwined hands to his cock. Together, they gripped it, holding it into position. She licked her free palm and slicked it over the tip, making him moan. He grabbed her hip with his other hand, and when he was ready, pulled down.

THE SLIDE INTO OLIVIA'S BODY WAS LIKE NOTHING HE'D EVER experienced in his life. She was so hot, and wet, and tight, and if he did not have many years of practice at self-control, he would have climaxed the moment she surrounded him fully, his balls resting against the sensitive folds of her quim.

But this was more than a joining of flesh, and her magic surrounded him too, meshing with his, until they were one in body, heart, mind, soul, and power.

She moved, tentatively at first, gauging his reaction, lifting and sliding back down as he thrust up into her, until he clutched her hips in his hands, dug his fingers into her arse, and pulled her down, hard.

After that, they both lost control, and she rode him with a wild abandon as he plunged inside her again and again, each drive pushing them both higher and higher, until they glowed with every color of the aural spectrum and then everything went blinding white.

THEIR SUBTLE BODIES HAD BECOME ONE, A SINGLE AND VERY powerful entity hovering above the bed where their bodies shuddered and pulsed in a prolonged orgasm.

Speech was not necessary, nor was conscious thought.

With the power pulsing in their conjoined form, the resonance of one single mage was almost laughably easy to locate, southeast of the city and across the river in Rochester. The difficult part was remembering to go back and tell the others the address of the building.

They dropped down into their joined flesh just long enough to shout Mina's location to the rest of Clan Fay waiting outside the Casting Chamber, and then they were off again, leaving behind a flurry of activity from the brilliant spirit-forms of their family and friends.

Olivia/Savit returned to their quarry. She had a mass of spells around her, weavings of magical energy in a delicate architecture somewhere between a bird's nest and a spider's web.

One cluster of shining threads was bigger than all the rest. Power speared out of the three-dimensional shape like spokes or rays of the sun, spreading much farther than a single mage should have the ability to reach.

The Aegis Spell. Mina was a point in its design, a living conduit for draining magic away from England. The original spell had not been designed to do that—it must have been something added after their last vision.

Olivia/Savit pulled away from Mina, looking for the others who must be incorporated into this new spell matrix. There were many—at least a dozen—spread out across England like leeches, sucking the kingdom's lifeblood away.

The thought came through both of them—*This is how they've maintained it over water for so long. The original structure allowed power to be shared with Hanover, but not permanently linked to a monarch abroad. They need willing hosts to feed the spell, hosts born here or with blood ties to this island.*

The thought spurred a vision, but nothing like any of the visions they'd experienced before.

The Aegis Spell was of ancient design. They observed the original casting, by men and women wearing belted linen robes in a city between two rivers. Then another, years later, in a dry mountainous land. Again, with three different Mediterranean civilizations. Trajan's doomed attempt. Another by a Magister after the fall of the Roman Empire, that worked but was not transferred due to his sudden death by poisoning. The successful 1688 casting, and each transference to a new monarch, including the expansion under

George I. The failed attempt to reduce the spell under George III. An attempt by Napoleon, that failed.

And then—the moment. Several mages they'd seen before, and many they hadn't, standing around the Duke of Cumberland—now King Ernest I of Hanover—imbuing him with the spell. But because the loop could not be closed by an English monarch, the strain was transferred to thirteen mages: twelve in England, and one that would remain with His Majesty in Hanover. And a large portion of the spell—perhaps as much as a third—could no longer be removed from the simulacrum of George III.

There were more visions waiting, of other Aegis Spells cast or changed, but Olivia/Savit recognized the young Queen Victoria, and everything shifted. They were standing in a different room, where four people shouted at each other.

Everything had gone wrong. The queen was still alive. If she gave birth to a living heir, all would be lost. It was too dangerous to try again. The king must return to Hanover. Perhaps she would die in childbirth, and the babe with her.

A different scene, of two dozen mages casting wards and protection around the birthing chamber while Princess Victoria came into the world.

And another change to the Aegis Spell, in retribution for the birth of an heir, increasing the pull of magic from the very bedrock of England, into both Ernest and the statuette of the Mad King.

Then the vision went dark, as though a curtain had fallen between the spell and their seeking minds.

THEY WERE BACK IN THEIR BODIES AGAIN, SEPARATE EXCEPT FOR where Savit's cock was still lodged within Olivia's warm quim. He felt so good inside her, and aftershocks of pleasure pulsed through her body as she shifted her hips, even though she was sure that a long time had passed while they were in the vision.

"What happened?" she asked, lifting herself away reluctantly, but settling back down beside him, skin-to-skin.

"I don't know." He rolled onto his side to face her, and put an arm around her middle. She nestled into his warmth gratefully. "We were linked directly into the spell, I think, and the visions were being fed by its memories. Something must have happened to the link."

"Mina. Did she shield us?"

"I think it far more likely that she resisted capture, and is dead."

Olivia shuddered under his arm. "I thought she was my friend, and all that time she was trying to keep us from discovering the spell."

"You couldn't have known." His hand shifted to her hair, stroking through the beautiful short, choppy strands. "And I was too much of a fool, too wrapped up in my own fears, to comprehend how much you needed a friend to talk to."

"I was attracted to her, too, the bitch. And she used that against me. When you left, I was so hurt, and angry, and I wanted to hurt you, and she was there and flirted with me, and I thought I would drown my sorrows in her body." She clutched at him, and he held her close, and remorse burned behind her eyes with unshed tears. "I'm sorry."

"Don't be. I wouldn't have blamed you for doing it. In fact, I don't want you to be upset in the future when you are attracted to other people for whatever reason. What is between us is ours, but your nature is to be sensual and grounded in your flesh. To deny that part of you and chain you to my bed would be a degradation of all that you are."

Olivia nearly choked. "Did you just give me leave to take other lovers?"

He laughed. "Yes. I am not a jealous man. You are the only person who has ever attracted me strongly enough to reconsider celibacy, but I know very well that you are used to having many lovers."

"That truly doesn't bother you?"

"Why should it? Your heart and soul are mine, and always have been. I told you before that some souls are linked this way, through many lives. This flesh we wear now is temporary, and if it brings you pleasure to share it with others, then I am content."

"I don't think other lovers would fulfill me the way that you do."

"They do not need to. There are many ways to touch, and to feel. Not every passion or pleasure must be tied to our depth of emotion."

"Well, I will tell you if I ever get the urge to be with someone else, as unlikely as that seems to me right now." She snuggled close and nipped at his neck. "Maybe you'll want to join me."

He laughed again, and stroked his fingers down her neck, tracing her spine all the way to the cleft of her arse. "Perhaps. For now, I'd very much like to practice with just the two of us. It will take your family a long time to return from Rochester."

A moan tore out of Olivia's mouth as his fingers slipped around the curve and dipped into the sensitive, still-slick flesh between her thighs. She rolled onto her back, and he settled between her legs, his cock hard and insistent against her belly. It took a moment for him to figure out the proper position that gave him both entry and leverage to thrust, but while he experimented, he kept up a rhythmic teasing stroke against Olivia's clit that had her writhing and begging him, "Just fuck me, damn it!"

Finally, with a chuckle for her impatience, he slid home.

～

OLIVIA WRAPPED HER LEGS AROUND SAVIT AND THEY LAY, pressed as tightly together as possible. He stretched her in the most delectable way, and his hip bone rested against her clit so that the slightest movement set off another pulse of pleasure.

"I love you, Olivia Seward," he said, murmuring the words against her mouth.

"I love you, Savitendra Reilly."

Then he moved inside of her, transforming their love into motion, and their souls took flight together in an infinite dance.

Savit sat in his grandfather's shipping office and waited for the old man to finish his meeting. He'd been very unhappy when Savit disappeared for almost a week after his injury, but he'd used up so much magical energy after the healing spell and the subsequent search that he'd fallen asleep that afternoon and only woken to eat, drink, and use the watercloset for the next six days.

Shortly after he'd gotten out of bed, Chaitan had arrived on an express steamer from New York. He and Cecily had attempted to heal Lady Dayning, but with only minimal success. She could feed herself now, and perform limited other activities, but her brilliant mind and so-important-memories were lost forever.

Savit was up and about again, and with the knowledge of all that could have happened—and all he could have lost—it was time to tell his grandfather the truth. About everything.

"I was surprised to get your note," his grandfather said once they were seated in the inner office. "Is your—ah—business concluded?"

"It is. And I believe it's time yours was, as well." Savit

hadn't meant to introduce the topic this way, but the opening was there and he took it.

"What do you mean by that?" Grandfather looked surprised and a little offended.

Savit stood and moved around the desk, then knelt beside Grandfather's chair. "Bapuji, I miss them, too. Very much." He hadn't used that appellation for his grandfather since he was seven years old. Every word of Gujarati had been forbidden from the moment they stepped on board the boat to Ireland. It was time to reclaim that past, for both of them. "We have both tried too hard not to remember them and not to feel. We have made our work into our lives, and because my work is different from yours, we both feel estranged from each other."

He put his hand over the gnarled, spotty one that held onto the arm of the chair like a rope over a chasm. "It's time we considered something else."

"What…" Bapuji's voice trembled. He cleared his throat and tried again. "What do you propose?"

"I'd already taken a sabbatical from Trinity. I am going to make that leave permanent. In the spring, I am going back to India. I will be taking a woman with me. Her name is Olivia Seward. She's the Marquess of Hazelby's daughter and the Duchess of Fay's sister-in-law."

"You're what?" Bapuji's eyes went wide, and Savit remembered for the first time in years that his father Alex's eyes had been that same mix of blue and grey. "Are you planning to marry the chit?"

"Perhaps. She is not the marrying kind. But our relationship is of a permanent nature, and we're planning to live together while we work in the Indus Valley excavating the ancient Indus River civilization."

"If you're going to live together without marriage, it's better do it there rather than here. There are still the rare cases of Gandharva marriage there, where you wouldn't have to prove any ceremony took place or papers were signed."

"I'd forgotten about Gandharva marriage. I'll have to mention that to Olivia." He squeezed Bapuji's hand. "But I don't just want her with me. I want you there, too."

The chair scraped away from the desk and Bapuji stood up. "I don't know, Alex, it's been so long—"

"Savit."

"What?"

"I don't like to be called Alexander. That was my father's name. Mine is Savitendra." A flush crept over his grandfather's pale Irish cheeks.

"I'm sorry, Al-er, Savit. I didn't know you still felt this way."

"I have always felt this way. I was very angry with you when you took away my name."

The blue eyes widened in horror. "I never intended to do that. You were all I had left of my boy. I knew you'd be bullied enough for your darker skin, and I thought it would be easier for you if you had a normal European name."

"Perhaps it was easier. Who can say? But I have always felt that answering to my father's name stripped me of my mother, and everything that she would have wanted for me."

"I am truly sorry, Al—Savit. I am the last person to want to take your mother away from you. Kashvi was a wonderful woman, and died too soon. The memories of that time are still painful for me, moreso because they were so sweet at the time."

"I don't want to deny that pain, but I can't live as only half of myself anymore." Savit grabbed Bapuji's hands and squeezed tightly. "You loved India, too. I know you did. You can keep running your business from there as you did in the old days, or you can start handing over the reins to someone else. But I want you with us. It's time we both went back."

They stared at each other for a little while, until the storm of emotion inside his grandfather broke, and he wept. Savit held him, and allowed his own tears to fall.

The outpouring of emotion washed away any lingering bitterness Savit felt for his childhood. They would begin again. "Will you come with us?"

Bapuji smiled, a little hesitantly. "I don't know, Savit. It means very much to me that you asked. I need a little time to think."

"Then you'll have it. We're staying here for a while longer, anyway. Chaitan doesn't want to go to India and he's helping me train Olivia. So you have some time to decide."

OLIVIA BOUNCED A DROOLING TODDLER ON HER KNEE AND contemplated the possibility of ever having one herself. The idea appealed for all of about a minute, and then the child started crying and was promptly handed back to its mother. If she was the mother, she wouldn't have that luxury. Or she could, if she paid someone else to raise her children. But she'd lived that life, and she refused to do that to another babe.

So, no children then. She hoped Savit wouldn't mind. Although considering that until he met her he'd planned to spend the rest of his life a virgin, she somehow doubted children were something he desired.

He stood on the other side of the room with her brother and brother-in-law, and when she caught his eye his usually bland expression shifted to a smile, just for her. She enjoyed seeing the smile when they were in these larger groups, as they had frequently been in the days since their mutual extended recovery in the wake of her abduction and his injury.

For most of the first week, Savit had been useless to her. And to be fair, she'd spent the bulk of the time sleeping, too. After that, they'd been ordered to stay in bed for another two days. Fortunately, during that time he'd been *up* for certain activities that were best accomplished while confined to a mattress.

But now they were back to their regular lives again, and having to deal with the aftermath that they'd managed to avoid so far.

The reason for the abrupt severing of their connection to the Aegis Spell had, indeed, been Mina's death. She'd been destroying documents when the Fays arrived with an entire platoon of army mages, headed by Lucien Blake. She must have decided that even she couldn't fight so many sorcerers, and had cut her own throat when they reached her door. She'd still been spurting blood when Etta entered, but it had been too late to save her.

In the room's coal stove, Etta had recovered a few documents and a book that seemed to be capable of two-way communication with another book elsewhere. From its pages, she discovered that Mina had been sending messages and receiving orders from her mother in Potsdam. The book had been untouched by the flames—a magical precaution against destruction that Mina had either not known about or not had time to counter. It was a stroke of luck for them, as there were many secrets to be untangled from its pages, but Mina never used her mother's name or anyone else's, and they'd written each other partially in code.

Olivia and Savit had tried to scry out the other mages who helped channel the Aegis Spell, but had failed. The particular resonance they'd discovered through Mina was now gone, and they had only glimpsed the existence of the others.

Etta had been furious when she discovered she had no

evidence to present to the queen, and only guesswork as to who might currently hold the Aegis Spell. Their only clue was the statuette of the Mad King—something tangible that could be tracked.

Plans were in motion now to shift the hunt to the Continent, but Olivia and Savit would no longer be a part of it. Their expertise was the past, and they had traced the spell as close as the 1840s. Even without the ability to recover Lady Dayning's memories, Etta and the others knew that the former kings of Hanover must have been involved as recently as the 1860s—and perhaps still were.

Since Olivia and Savit had been released from their task as researchers, they'd begun a different sort of research, this time on ocean liners and the supplies required for a trip to India and an extended excavation there. Savit hoped that the greater quantity of magic available on the subcontinent would allow her to explore her visions and other gifts without risking her physical health and wellbeing. She would use her visions to pinpoint the best places to dig, and she looked forward to teaching him her excavation methods. He hadn't done much field work, and she wouldn't have to break him of any bad habits.

They planned to write a book together, and once it was done, perhaps come back to England. Where, surprisingly, Rajani had said she would be staying. She'd found a new cause for her life, and she'd wished Savit well in his return, but London was now her home.

Olivia's attention was drawn from contemplation of the future back to the present by her sister's voice. Viola sat beside her on the settee, the babe now toddling on the floor with a wet rag in its mouth. "She's teething. Mother says I was an excellent teether, and only drooled a bit when mine came in. Apparently Adaira takes after you and Mal, who were confined to the nursery from the moment the tooth started to move until it broke the surface and you stopped crying."

Olivia watched her sister watching her daughter. There was a fierceness there, as well as an almost aching tenderness. Viola would not be like their mother with her children. It humbled Olivia to recognize that whatever flaw Cecily had as a parent, she had it too—which was why she would choose not to procreate. But Viola was a patient, attentive mother. And a good example, too, since she didn't let motherhood stop her from also being her own person.

"I'm sorry, Vi."

Viola looked up, startled. "Sorry for what?"

"For blaming you for taking all of Mother's attention. It wasn't your fault any more than it was mine that she never wanted to see me."

"Oh. Well, you're forgiven if that's what you want me to say, but I rather felt the opposite."

"What?"

"I envied you because Mother left you alone. She had no expectations of you, and you were allowed to do whatever you wanted, including gallivanting off to digs all over Europe after boarding school. I had to stay here and debut, which meant learning the fashionable sorts of magic and pretending to be an empty-headed bit of fluff lest some Society matron give me a permanent moniker of shame."

"You slipped the bonds eventually. I hear you've even got Aunt Muireall sending one of her daughters down to help out at your school."

"Yes, but breaking free took years and some other things got in the way first." She glanced up at her husband, who was already looking at her. Sometimes their connection was unnerving—their magic was permanently fused. Having experienced a merge of magic a few times now with Savit, Olivia wouldn't have wanted it even on a daily basis, much less all of the time, forever. But it seemed to work for them.

"Then I suppose we'd better forgive each other, and maybe we can try to be friends."

"I would like that. Not that I'm going to see you much, with you moving to India." Viola poked her in the arm. "But we can write more than we have in the past. I'm very interested to hear all about your findings."

"I will bore you to tears with pages and pages of data, I promise." But her sister's smile said she would read those pages anyway.

"You should think about forgiving Mother, too," Viola said, testing the bounds of their new amity.

"I already have. But as I told her, that doesn't mean I can forget, or that our relationship will ever be close, or easy."

"Fair enough. But she's changed. Or changing. She and Lady Falcestershire held hands at a musicale last week. For a half hour! It's all I've heard when I go trawling for donations amongst society ladies lately."

"I'm both surprised and not. Mal told me Amelia's carriage has been at Hazelby House no less than three times in the last ten days. And not in the afternoon, either."

"Those shameless hussies! Oh, goddess, do you think Father's in on it?"

"I do *not* wish to speculate."

Both sisters shuddered, and then broke out into peals of laughter. It was the first step—of many, to be sure—to becoming friends as well as siblings.

LATER THAT NIGHT, IN THE BIGGER ROOM ETTA HAD GIVEN them at Skye House to share, Olivia lay in Savit's arms and recounted her gossip with her sister.

"It's good that you've reconciled with her. Family is important."

"Your grandfather agreed to come, then?"

"Well, first he told me he needed to think about it. Then I took him out for lunch and we went to see Rajani instead. He broke down, apologized for leaving her behind in London all those years ago, ate a good curry for the first time in over twenty years, and then said there was a manager at one of his warehouses who showed promise and initiative and would make a good superintendent for his London offices." She felt his snort of laughter against her back. "How did you guess?"

"You sounded a little too smug with that family comment. But I'm glad. For both of you."

"There's something else, though. Something still bothering you."

Olivia rolled over. She traced a line over the dark hair on Savit's chest while she wondered how to explain what worried her. "In my very first vision, I made a promise that I haven't kept."

"Yes, I remember. You told the woman Izarra that you would tell her story. That she would not be forgotten."

"But how can I do that now? There's no chance that Henri will let go of the dig. It's a big, important find, and will lead to more opportunities for him."

"Perhaps you do not need to write her story to fulfill your promise."

She lifted her head. His eyes were dark and contemplative.

"What do you mean?"

"I have been considering how your visions began so abruptly, long after the point at which most mages develop their gifts." He stroked a hand down the short cap of her hair and cupped the back of her neck. "Recall that there are three bodies, yes? This form here," he squeezed her skin gently, "the subtle body which is made up of our minds and the byproducts of the gross body's processes, and a third, called the causal body. This third is what your Western philosophies call the soul. It is the seat of karma, and is what passes on to form new subtle and gross bodies in each of our incarnations."

Olivia nodded. He'd explained that before, and she was pretty sure that was what she had experienced in that place *beyond*, where she had been everything and nothing at once.

"I believe that because Izarra was killed while still contained by the restraints, the magic of the cuffs and collar restrained her causal body as well. She has become what you might refer to as a ghost, and when you touched her remains, something of her spirit and magic passed into you, opening up a pathway for your dormant magic."

"But her body is back in France, and I'm still having visions."

Savit's hand moved back up to the top of her head, to her crown chakra. "Pathways, once open, do not automatically close. Under different circumstances, you might have learned to stop the visions. Or you might have lost your subtle body when the channel opened too wide. We are both lucky that we found each other."

She tilted her head up and captured his lips. The kiss distracted them for a while, but then she pulled away again. "So how do we help Izarra?"

"We release her from her bonds, and allow her causal body—her soul—to continue its journey."

"Show me how."

It was the farthest he'd ever allowed her to travel out of her physical form, and he'd insisted on merging their magic first, so that she would have the strength of his more experienced subtle body to rely on.

He took them high over the English channel, far away from the shifting magical currents of the sea, and back down to the coast of France.

I generally keep to the British Isles when I search for lost souls, but I occasionally wander the coasts of France, Belgium, and the Netherlands as well.

It's a good thing you do.

Labourd was a bustle of energy: humans, animals, fires, and even the winter-dormant plants all bright with magical potential. Savit showed her how to look beyond the distracting magic to the way she might see the streets with her human eyes, and that allowed her to find the building where the bodies from the dig were stored.

In this form, she could see Izarra immediately. The other bodies were quiet, lumps of matter with their magical energy long spent. Izarra's bones still writhed with light.

The part of their merged body that was Savit said, *Be careful. She is still very angry.*

I know.

They moved as one and approached the being that was once Izarra. *What was done to you was unjust.*

Her causal body didn't have distinguishable human features anymore, but there was something like a head, and arms, the brilliance of her light there was muted by dark smudges: the evidence of the cuffs and collar. She shifted toward them. She could no longer form words in any way a human mind could translate, but her emotions washed over them like a tsunami.

*You and everyone who died with you **will** be remembered. Knowledge of the atrocity of your deaths and the evil of those who ordered them will spread. You will not be forgotten.*

Pain, and sorrow, and longing.

It is time to move on, Izarra. Time to be born into the world again, to find your family. They are waiting for you.

Surprise. Hope.

Yes. Let us help you find them.

Together, Olivia and Savit reached out and touched the smudges of darkness on Izarra's causal body. With a surge of joy, the stains disappeared, and her soul glowed bright enough to match the sun.

Then she was gone. On the shelf, the melted and fused copper of the restraints had disappeared, leaving nothing behind, not even a streak of green.

"WELL DONE." SAVIT SQUEEZED OLIVIA AROUND THE RIBCAGE, their task complete. Then his hand wandered off to more interesting places. For a man who'd been a virgin barely a fortnight before, he had quickly become adept at lovemaking.

Tonight, they lay on their sides with him behind her, her leg draped over his hip. Their joining was shallower than usual in that position, but it allowed him to use his hand, and by the time he finally joined her in ecstasy, he'd made her climax three times.

"You have some very good ideas about positions," she noted as they lay spent and sweating after, her head resting on his chest. "The one the other day with me flat on my belly with my legs shut was one I would never have tried. I didn't think it could possibly work."

He laughed, and the motion made her head bounce. "I told you there are many paths to magic in my culture. One particular branch does so through physical stimulus, including food, various kinds of touching, and sex. There are several books, but the one famous in your culture is called the *Kama Sutra.* Chaitan made me read it before he would let me train with him as an ascetic. I decided to study with him, despite being intrigued by what I read. I should have known then that it was the wrong decision."

"It wasn't the wrong decision. If you hadn't trained with him, we wouldn't be here right now." She lifted her head and kissed him.

"That's true. I should say, then, that it was not my permanent path."

"That's better. But *you* are *my* permanent path."

"And I am yours."

EPILOGUE

Perceval Seward hated staying at Hazelby House, and when his older brother Mal had offered him a room at Skye House where he lived with his new bride, it had seemed the perfect solution to his general loathing of bunking with the parents. His stay in England was open-ended, which made renting his own lodgings problematic, especially since his major had hinted at new orders to come down soon. He was hoping for at least a few months rest before heading back out again.

Nine months previously, he'd graduated from *Preußische Kriegsakademie*—the Prussian Military Academy, or Staff School—in Berlin, and he'd been stationed with the court in Potsdam until seven weeks ago. He'd only been back in the country for two of those weeks and he'd barely gotten his brain back into the habit of thinking in English again.

His facility with languages was one of the only magical gifts he'd inherited from his mother, but if he was being sent abroad again, he wanted to go somewhere warm this time. Maybe Bermuda.

Unfortunately, the unsubtle hint had sounded like he'd be

going right back to the German Empire, for a mission that he would be briefed on in due course.

He'd arrived at Skye House to find the family on some sort of outing. The butler, MacGroarty, informed him that they'd gone to the theatre and would return later in the evening, but he was expected and a room was prepared. Since the trip down from his most recent abode at the barracks in North Yorkshire had been grueling, he took the opportunity to nap, and asked to have someone wake him up once everyone returned.

He'd expected to wake to a sharp rap on the door or perhaps something more mellifluous like a bell or call. He hadn't expected to be woken by someone climbing in through the window.

The room was dark, but he could make out the outline of the person as they turned to close the sash behind them. He slipped out of bed, grabbed the closest weapon to hand—a candlestick—and used one of the other tiny gifts from his family's magic. The gas jets around the room had been turned off, but there was a big paraffin lamp on the writing desk across the room. He ignited the wick with a thought.

A tiny slip of a woman stood framed by the window. She had almost unnaturally vivid red hair, and green eyes that were the exact color of new spring growth, vibrant and bright. She was only about five feet tall and weighed less than eight stone. She was also gut-wrenchingly beautiful; the kind of beauty that could make a man follow her to his doom. She looked like a siren, like a fairy queen.

And he stood facing her, nude, armed with a brass candlestick.

"Er…" she said, her gaze shifting about as though not sure where to land. He could suggest a few places—one in particular had gotten very interested in her appraisal. "I didn't know anyone was using this room." Her voice had the lilt of

Ireland in it, and something else that was a little more guttural and clipped. If he hadn't just finished several years in Prussia, he might not have recognized that tiny hint of German beneath the brogue.

"I wouldn't have supposed you did."

"I assure you there's a perfectly legitimate reason for my, er, manner of entry."

"I long to hear it."

"Perhaps you can acquire some clothing or a bedsheet before I explain?"

"Does my nudity impair your cognitive functions?"

YES. IT ABSO-FECKING-LUTELY DID, NOT THAT EVELYN FINN would ever in all of her life admit to that fact. Evie was an accomplished con artist, liar, and spy, but at this moment all she could think about was a broad expanse of tanned skin, covering a very well-defined musculature, and a cluster of dark curls from which jutted a very impressive erection.

He'd been asleep, and so she ought not attribute his tumescence to her presence, but the accelerated pace of her heart and the unfamiliar heat between her legs gave the lie to that attempt. She wanted his arousal to be because of her.

Finally, her survival instincts kicked in. She'd avoided men her entire life, and she wasn't about to get entangled with one now. She wove a quick glamour so he wouldn't see what she was doing with her hands and unlatched the window and slowly lifted the sash.

While she moved, she said, "Not at all. If it pleases you, I'm pleased to observe it."

A muscle leapt in his jaw. So he wasn't indifferent to her gaze, either. Damn. But it would ruin the game if she were caught, and she'd heard carriage wheels out on the street when she'd been climbing up. She'd have to pick another night to leave her present in Ronan's room—although his wedding anniversary was tomorrow and she didn't have much time left.

"Now that we've established that I am allowed to dress—or not dress—how I like in my own room, perhaps you can explain why you're in it?" She would never have imagined finding a bored, well-bred English tenor voice attractive, but the sound of him speaking wrapped around her brain, ensorcelling her. She almost swayed toward him.

She panicked.

"Of course I can."

Evie dove out the window.

His shout followed her, and she grasped for the upper lintel, hauling herself up and using it as a toehold to grasp for the next level above her. Moments later she was on the roof of Skye House and dashing across the tiles toward the back portico, where she could descend into the garden and make her way back around via the main entrance.

A quarter hour later, MacGroarty sent her up to the family parlor. Everyone was chattering about the play they'd just seen, but Etta hushed them when she came in. "Oh, good. You're here. I've just been informed that my brother-in-law is in residence, and that means we can move ahead with the next stage of our plans for the Aegis Spell."

That meant she was about to be sent to the German Empire, the realm of her grandfather, the Erlkoenig—or Elf King. She'd already volunteered to go, but a cold sweat broke out on her neck at the realization of who would be accompanying her—the brother-in-law, Percy.

The gorgeous naked man upstairs.

Great Danu, what had she gotten herself into now?

THANK YOU!

Thank you so much for reading *Memories of Magic*. I hope you enjoyed it.

- Want to know when my next book is coming out? Sign up for my newsletter at http://eepurl.com/bY89o1, like my Facebook page at https://www.facebook.com/caramckinnonauthor/, follow me on Twitter at https://twitter.com/cara_mckinnon, or sign up for release messages on BookBub at https://www.bookbub.com/profile/cara-mckinnon.
- Reviews help readers find books. Good or bad, I appreciate every one.
- *Memories of Magic* is the first book in the Fay of Skye series. Book one is *Essential Magic.* Book two is *A Theft of Magic. Secret Magic* and *Blood Magic* are forthcoming.

The secrets of her past are wild...

Evie Finn is a born trickster. Her faerie blood gives her an
affinity for glamours, and her childhood in a street gang
provided experience running confidence games and stealing
people blind. But the Duchess of Fay has just asked her to
pull off the most difficult heist of her career–without even
knowing who has the item she's meant to steal.

Enter consummate spy, Percy Seward. His magical gift for
languages and non- descript appearance make him an ideal
agent for the British Crown, and a perfect companion for
Evie in Austria and the German Empire. He and Evie will
locate proof of who is controlling the Aegis Spell draining
magic from England, steal it, and bring it back to Queen
Victoria. But six months into their assignment, Evie goes
rogue, refusing to enter Germany despite Percy's express
orders.

Evie doesn't want to defy Percy, but there's something more dangerous for her than any human spell waiting in Germany: Herla, the Elf King, leader of the Wild Hunt—her grandfather.

Soon, circumstances force her to face her fears—and her growing ardor for Perceval Seward. But there's no escaping her past, or her destiny.

~

Unedited Excerpt from Chapter One

Percy flung his suitcase onto the bed and started emptying the contents of his clothespress into it. Even if it hadn't been entirely clear that he was incensed, his decision to perform a chore normally left to his valet would have tipped Evie off.

If only he wasn't so magnificent when he was in a temper. She needed all of her wits about her, but she was fascinated. In the eight months since they'd first met, he'd never once allowed his emotions to stir the façade of unruffled calm he wore like a shroud. She'd taken to baiting him just to see how much he could take—and she'd learned he could take quite a lot.

But she'd finally found his breaking point, and rather than take shelter like any sensible person would, Evie wanted to dance closer—wanted to leap on him, take his mouth, and devour all of that pure, beautiful rage, transmuting it into passion.

He turned toward the wardrobe and saw her standing in the doorway.

"You have what you want. Get out."

"You know nothing about what I want." In truth, what she wanted was to go with him. No single person had ever drawn her the way he did. But she couldn't. And she couldn't tell him why. If she told him, he would say she was a danger to the mission and send her home to Britain. At least from Vienna she could still be of some use.

He flung open the wardrobe door and it banged against the nearby washstand. "I'm not staying here. Cumberland doesn't have the simulacrum. He has no power, magical or political. I don't know how you talked Blake into approving your plan to remain in Austria, but I want no part of it."

"I didn't ask you to stay." Evie meant the words to be challenging, flippant. But they came out soft and tinged with too much regret. She couldn't ask him to stay. He was right—Cumberland didn't have the Aegis Spell, and one of them had to continue their mission. It just couldn't be her.

"Then what are you doing here?"

What *was* she doing there? She didn't have a satisfactory answer to that question, not even for herself. She'd simply needed to see him, and so she'd come. He would never believe that, though, and if he did, it would make him pity her. His pity would destroy her.

She grasped for an explanation and found one. "We need to establish our method of communication from now on."

He reached into the wardrobe and pulled out several hangers-full of dark coats. He dumped them onto the bed.

She couldn't help herself. "You should really let Holz do that. You're going to ruin them."

He snarled at her. Actually snarled! His eyes had shifted from their normal grey-green-blue-brown into a green that nearly matched her own, and she sucked in a quick, hitching breath. If she threw herself onto him, would her body weight carry him down onto his bed and the pile of coats, or would he catch her, his hands all over her as she'd dreamed of nearly every night since they'd met?

She wanted to strip away the ill-fitting clothes he wore and trail her fingers over the sculpted body she'd seen beneath, that first night at Skye House in London. But she held herself motionless in the doorway.

"We'll use the same cipher as Blake's reports. You can add an extra ward if you want. Mine will be unwarded unless it's particularly sensitive, and then I'll get someone at the consulate to ward it."

Evie nodded at his curt words, not wanting to risk saying anything. She might blurt out something she couldn't take back, like why she had to stay in Austria, or how much she wanted him. She'd learned her lesson about men long ago. Never give them an advantage.

Instead of speaking, she backed away, and went to her room on the other side of the hall. They were posing as a married couple, and aside from the butler, her maid, and Percy's valet who were also British spies, none of the other servants lived in the flat to see that they never shared a bed. Plenty of married couples had their own bedrooms, and the girls who cleaned the rooms never came before ten, long after Evie was up and had dressed herself for the morning, making the bed in her room to obscure where she'd slept.

Now, they would pretend an argument—not that there was much pretense—and Percy would leave for Berlin, where he was well-known among those who thronged to the imperial court of Kaiser Wilhelm II.

Percy was here as himself. Pretending to be the wife of a marquess's son had given Evie instant cachet among the expatriates and exiled royalty who called Austria home. And Percy had been right to insist that she use only the tiniest of glamours on her hair and eyes. Just enough to make her look human—not so much as to mute their color or vibrancy. When she was working the Dublin streets, she'd never been the distraction—she was always the one with her hand in a pocket or skulking through a house looking for portable wealth. Later, in the cons and spying she'd done with Ronan, she'd been more active in the face-to-face part of deception, but always as a boy or a young man, with her face and hair fully obscured under dye, paint, dirt, and glamour.

Now, she was fooling everyone looking exactly like herself. But weren't the best cons the ones that cut closest to the truth?

And the truth was, a tiny part of her—tiny, but stubbornly resistant to her uprooting it—wanted to be Perceval Seward's wife. Or at least, to be his lover. To fall into the bed where he was probably still heaping his clothes and strip each other bare, until there was nothing left between them but skin and secrets.

She didn't let herself imagine much past that. Her two encounters with boys at the Fay School had been nothing special, and she didn't want those lackluster couplings to color her expectations for how it would be with Percy. He was nothing like them. They'd been good-natured and good-looking, but they hadn't made her blood nearly turn to steam with a single, heated glance.

He knew himself, knew what he was capable of and his place in the world. That steadiness was like a lodestone, pulling at her fractured, scattered soul as though she were made of iron filings. She'd never had a home, and even though she loved her adopted brother Ronan McCarrick with everything inside of her, he hadn't exactly provided stability.

She'd found both a home and stability, somehow, in the last six months working beside Percy. And now he was leaving, and she had to stay behind.

Damn you, Grandfather.

~

To find out more about *Secret Magic* and the Fay of Skye series, visit https://caramckinnon.com/the-fay-of-skye-series/.

Love at the Edge of Seventeen: A YA Romance Anthology
"Three Jagged Pieces"

COMING SOON

Born to Love Wild: A Paranormal Romance Anthology
"A Change of Heart"

ACKNOWLEDGMENTS

I always thank my editor, Anna LaVoie of Literally Yours Editing, but this time she went above and beyond. After we discovered the need for a major revision at a late stage in the project, she talked me down from my panic and made time for me to chat with her and come up with solutions to all of the problems. Thanks also goes out to my two amazing beta readers and fellow authors Alexa Grave and J.L. Gribble, who pointed out some of the flaws that led to the late-stage revisions!

Thanks also to the fantastic group of writers that holds my hand as I cry and try to make this micropublishing thing a success: A.E. Hayes, Sheri Queen, Carrie Gessner, A.J. Culey, Traci Douglass, M.T. DeSantis, Elsa Carruthers, Mary Rogers, L.J. Longo, Jennifer Loring, and all of the amazing alums and faculty at the Seton Hill University Writing Popular Fiction program. You are my tribe!

I once again got great feedback on my cover from Christina Robbins, Debbie Ranish, Denise Marie, and J.L. Gribble.

No acknowledgment would be complete without

thanking my husband, who always supports me—even when I don't come to bed until 3 am for several weeks in a row. And a special shout-out to my son and daughter, who are old enough now to respect Mommy's writing time!

And of course, my biggest thanks always goes to you, my readers. You make all of my efforts worthwhile. If you loved this book, I hope you'll take a moment to review it. Reviews are incredibly important, and I very much appreciate each one. Thank you!

ABOUT CARA MCKINNON

Cara McKinnon is the author of the Fay of Skye fantasy romance series. She is addicted to adding magic to other genres and creating fantasy hybrids. She earned her MFA in Writing Popular Fiction at Seton Hill University, where she found her writing tribe. She lives on the East Coast of the US with her husband, two kids, and an oversized lapdog named Jake.

PRAISE FOR CARA MCKINNON

PRAISE FOR ESSENTIAL MAGIC

- "McKinnon writes clear and often beautiful prose, utilizing apt analogies to give liveliness to the text. An American girl with native blood who lands in London society makes a good frame for this romance novel." —Publisher's Weekly Booklife Prize (semi-finalist)
- "Vivid backdrop...thorough research...very hot. An entertaining start to a new series." – Avonna from The Romance Reviews
- "Engrossing and dramatic.... Tantalizing details... enough passion and excitement to carry along even the most non-romance reader." –J.L. Gribble, author of *Steel Victory*
- "The writing is just lovely.... Characters you care about!" –Maria V. Snyder, author of *Poison Study*
- "The romance is sweet and hot at the same time,

and the historical setting and details are beautifully done. Highly recommended." – Amazon review
- "[A] great romance." – Goodreads review
- "Masterfully written." – Amazon review
- "Cara McKinnon does a masterful job of transporting her readers to magical 19th century Scotland. Her detailed descriptions of historically accurate attire and etiquette helped to fully immerse me in a story that I was unwilling to put down until the very end. Engaging characters, powerful emotions; all with a unique and captivating method used to describe the casting of spells." -Christina Robbins, author of *Seeking Solace*

PRAISE FOR A THEFT OF MAGIC

- "McKinnon hits it out of the park once again with this delightful blend of alternate history, historical fiction, action, and sensuality…an exciting magical romp from start to finish." – J.L. Gribble, author of *Steel Victory*
- "Politics, schemes, and betrayal…twists that I definitely didn't see coming. The sex started early and got steamier as it went." – Dawn from Up Til Dawn Book Reviews for The Romance Reviews
- "The characters are beautifully crafted, the historical details make the world come alive and seem so vividly possible, I almost want to search for the missing magic myself." -Amazon review
- "What a superb fantasy historical! A great read that I shall keep and reread again and again. Her way of blending fantasy and magic with history was great.

I was captivated and enchanted and enthralled by her writing and her stories. I cannot wait to see what else she does. You will absolutely not be disappointed in buying this book or the series." – Goodreads review

www.ingramcontent.com/pod-product-compliance
Lightning Source LLC
Chambersburg PA
CBHW030655120726
47905CB00001B/214